Love Songs and Lies

LIBBY PURVES

Love Songs
And Lies

HODDER &
STOUGHTON

First published in Great Britain in 2006 by Hodder and Stoughton
A division of Hodder Headline

A Hodder & Stoughton Book

1

A CIP catalogue record for this title is
available from the British Library

ISBN 0 340 83739 X

Typeset in Plantin Light by Palimpsest Book Production Limited,
Polmont, Stirlingshire

Printed and bound by
Mackays of Chatham Ltd, Chatham, Kent

Hodder Headline's policy is to use papers that are natural, renewable and
recyclable products and made from wood grown in sustainable forests. The
logging and manufacturing processes are expected to conform to the
environmental regulations of the country of origin.

Hodder and Stoughton Ltd
A division of Hodder Headline
338 Euston Road
London NW1 3BH

I shall never be friends again with roses;
I shall loathe sweet tunes, where a note grown strong
Relents and recoils, and climbs and closes
As a wave of the sea turned back by song.
There are sounds where the soul's delight takes fire,
Face to face with its own desire;
A delight that rebels, a desire that reposes;
I shall hate sweet music my whole life long.

The pulse of war and passion of wonder,
The heavens that murmur, the sounds that shine,
The stars that sing and the loves that thunder,
The music burning at heart like wine,
An armed archangel whose hands raise up
All senses mixed in the spirit's cup
Till flesh and spirit are molten in sunder –
These things are over, and no more mine.

A.C. Swinburne

PART ONE

Max

I

I can see her now, draped across the foot of my bed with her white-blond hair dishevelled around her face. It had, I always thought, the look of a Renaissance angel's halo, although to anyone who knew Marienka's habits this was quite staggeringly inappropriate. Max conveyed a more suitable picture – though still a supernatural one – when he referred to her as 'An aristocratic pixie'. That was Marienka: a county Titania, her small, pointed, beautiful features always alive with the promise of mayhem, yet without a trace of self-doubt or fear of reprisal. It was a very English, very unfakeable assurance: the crazy confidence of an ancient – albeit ruined – family.

Yes, I can see her: Marienka Tilton, named for God knows what middle-European ancestress picked up like a curio by some wandering Tilton boy on his grand tour. I can see her ragged blue velvet jacket with the embroidered pockets, and the jeans which she wore so tight my mother would have snorted, 'Indecent! You can see every crack of her!' If I close my eyes I can feel the warm careless weight of her arm on my feet, as she lounges like a Roman emperor across the grimy bedspread.

And, of course, I can hear her. I always have, because of what she said on that dreary February day in 1973 while the rain made grimy furrows down the windows of our damp little rented house by the Oxford canal. Her words of that day, assisted by certain lunatic romanticisms of my own, have more or less shaped the thirty years of life I have lived since.

They have been a credo and a burden. Now it is time for formal apostasy, and a tentative laying-down of that burden.

Not that Marienka should be blamed. She would be horrified to think that I even remember what she said at any given moment, because I doubt that she ever meant her counsel to be taken seriously. Indeed, she was capable at that age of giving opposite advice within the same conversation, even at times within the same vehement sentence. 'Oh, honestly, Kate! Ted isn't worth bothering about, just walk away, stuff him, he can't get away with being so ghastly to you, stand up for yourself, and if you really want him back tell him so, right out, just go for it, grab his trousers!'

Kate, who was our other female housemate, never listened to Marienka's advice at all. She was not one to be buffeted by random currents. She was a rock: pleasingly shaped, smoothly warm, sometimes glinting with unexpected gold ore, but definitely too solid to be moved. She allowed Marienka's advice to flow over her like water, like the transparent soothing nonsense that it was. Advice about Ted, anyway, was absurd: we all knew that she and Teddy Morton were in for the long haul, because they were so neatly suited. Both were thoughtful and ambitious and careful with money and – according to Marienka in a moment of unusual bitchiness – wonderfully well attuned to one another's feeble libidos. 'No fire in those bellies,' she said once, when Kate had gone to bed early and alone because she had a minor exam the next day, and Teddy had cycled back to college to write up his physics notes. 'They might as well be *married*.'

'I think it's nice,' I protested. 'Nice that they're so sure of each other they don't have to be always at it.'

Marienka rolled her eyes skywards and gave a complacent little wriggle of her hips.

'We're young,' she said. 'We ought to go at it. Time enough to be middle-aged.' Her awareness of youth was, I see now,

one of her rare qualities. I do not think that the rest of us were
ever so vibrantly conscious of being young. Weighed down by
worries about our studies, our exams, our loves, our friendships and our parlous finances, we generally failed to notice
how elastic were our bodies, how receptive our hearts to joy.
We were selfish all right, but the gaze we fixed exclusively on
ourselves was, in fact, blind. We saw nothing.

Marienka at least had the secret of enjoyment. She knew
how to ignore the past and scoff at the future, and never lived
anywhere other than in the shining Now. One result, of course,
was that all her money was gone by the third week of term;
another was that she was always in trouble with her tutors,
particularly since one of them was the college Principal. But
then – a week or so late – she would hand in a piece of work
so glittering, so original, so permeated with her own brand
of headlong intellectual joy that all would be forgiven; before
long she would be hauling on her indecently short black dress
for an invitation to sherry in the Principal's lodgings, where
she would be introduced as a star pupil.

Strangely, plodders like Kate and me did not mind this. We
did not want to walk along the edge of life, teetering and waving,
as Marienka did. We knew we were safer where we were, on
the firm ground, and felt obscurely honoured that a sparking,
smoking loose cannon like her was willing to be our friend and
housemate. We cherished her as one might an exotic pet or a
piece of impractical tapestry. Come to think of it, though, I
have no idea what it was she valued us for. She certainly did
not think much of our other friends. She did put high worth
on us and showed it: it was as if she had picked us out from
the rabble of ordinary studious girls-next-door in college, given
us a quick polish on her sleeve, and set us to glitter unexpectedly on her coffee-table, as *objets trouvés* which she was
inordinately proud of.

'Sally's totally brilliant,' she would say to her grand friends.

'Tremendous mind. Going to get a first. Marvellous with words. Kate is a geographer, isn't that thrilling? She's working on volcanoes.' We laughed at her for this, but she didn't mind; somehow, in the mysterious way that these things happened, we were friends.

Anyway, it was Marienka who brought Max into the house. He came from her universe, and shone as she did.

Perhaps I should begin by trying to relate how it was, back in the 1970s in our small rarefied university world. Today, looking at my children's generation, I shake my head in wonderment. They are legion, now, the students: half the young population, where we were less than a fifth. They are sophisticated and self contained, online and in control, equipped with dear little phones which enable them to make instant contact with one another. They check in with tutors by e-mail while they drink their lattes and cappuccinos like affluent Italian businessmen in brightly designed bars with computer terminals on the counter. They carry their burden of debt lightly, running as it does into thousands; nobody seems to mind. They do not get summoned, as Marienka often was, to be personally berated about their overdraft by strict bank managers wearing nylon shirts with their string vests showing through.

Marienka used to beg me or Kate – sometimes both – to go with her to these interviews. We hated it: we were embarrassed and belittled by the lofty and patronizing tone the managers took, though their victim rarely was. She merely crossed and re-crossed her long, black-stockinged legs in an artful attempt at distraction, and batted her beautiful eyelashes at her tormentor until he solemnly agreed to give her another month to scrape up the money or blag it off her parents. Today, the banks would react to such debt by pressing still more thousands on her by post, without even putting her to the trouble of meeting a manager's eyes or looking out a pair of unladdered black tights.

In our world it was difficult even to telephone home, and virtually impossible to ring one another; if we wanted to see somebody from another college or lodgings we walked or cycled round there. If they were out, and they generally were, we ended up talking to someone else instead. That, indeed, is how I met most of my friends. We drank quite as much coffee as students do today, but not often in cafés. The Cadena was expensive, the sort of place parents took you out to tea; in George's at the covered market it came out of a bottle and was disgusting. So most of our caffeine was borne to us via powdery stuff out of jars, and served in our college rooms accompanied by crumpets toasted by hanging them in front of the sputtering, headachey gas fire on a partially straightened paperclip. The burnt offerings would then be spread with slightly rancid, exaggeratedly yellow butter because although there were fridges in the communal kitchens, nobody used them for fear of butter bandits. The best buy of my first year was a pot made of porous clay with two wire hooks on it; you soaked it in cold water, put the butter in it and hung it out of your window. Only once did it fall down into the quadrangle below, and by great good luck it missed the Dean.

Thinking back now I can see, in every detail, the posters on my college wall. One depicted a monochrome stack of rhinoceri, standing on one another's backs; the other a hairy friendly monster from Where the Wild Things Are. Kate had one of Frank Zappa on the lavatory, from which I used to avert my eyes, because while you can take the daughter out of the vicarage it is always more difficult to take the vicarage out of the daughter. Marienka had wispy Indian hangings in her room, and a large, grubby oil painting of Loch Hourn which was too heavy for the picture hook and frequently crashed down, bringing lumps of plaster with it and incurring yet another surcharge on her college bill. She claimed the picture was worth ten thousand pounds and that she was keeping it safe to prevent her father from selling it; she did not, however, seem to mind very much when a teacake caught fire and sent sooty black streaks up across the oily waters of the loch.

Those tea-parties were as exotic as it ever got. Sometimes we ate Kunzle cakes, creamy joys robed in chocolate cases which we bought only if money was no object that week or if an essay was particularly trying. The modern-day student diet of panini, pizza, skinny cinnamon latte and double-choc muffins was something we could barely dream of. We filled up on stodgy pasta, hard peas and dry chicken in the college hall.

Of course, once Kate and Max and Marienka and I moved out of our colleges to the cheap house on the canal it was far too far to walk or cycle for dinner in hall. So, feeling very grown-up, we fed ourselves. For the first few weeks of term we cooked chickens and even the occasional steak; after the fourth week it was baked potatoes with stale, date-expired cheese from the shop by Folly Bridge, or a dish of mush-rooms and rice which Kate invented after a holiday in Italy. You stirred in powdery stale Parmesan at the last minute, and Marienka politely said it reminded her of being in a restaurant by the Grand Canal. In summer we could follow this treat with peaches stolen from the Warden's hothouse at one of the men's colleges. There was trouble about that; but then, there was trouble about a lot of things we did. Our generation had, after all, only just become legally adult at 18, rather than 21: even so College authorities thought of them-selves as *in loco parentis* and displayed a breezy authority unimaginable today. We were fined, scolded, threatened, and – in women's colleges like mine – coddled, like wayward but cherished daughters.

Ungrateful daughters, though. Kate and I were scholars and therefore offered the chance of continuing in spacious college rooms in our final year. But we turned them down and moved out. Marienka, who found the college's attitude to male night-visitors constraining, trawled the estate agencies for digs, rejected most of them as 'too ghastly' or too far east, and eventually found a tiny house on the canal towpath. It was damp, the paper was peeling from the walls, the stairs had rotten holes in them and the smallest bedroom – barely a boxroom – led off one of the others. The only hot water came from an ancient, rusty Rayburn boiler in the kitchen, which would need to be fed daily with coke, rattled and riddled and cleaned out. The upstairs landing window was stuck permanently in a quarter-open position. But Marienka burst into my dry, clean little college room in an exuberance of triumph.

'I've found it! It's wonderful! It's on the canal bank, right on the towpath! It'll be like living in Venice!'

Kate and I went down with her to see it, and managed to narrow our eyes and exclude all its faults. As Marienka enthused, we learnt to see through her eyes its beauties: the oily gunmetal gleam of the water alongside, the romantically stained Victorian brickwork ('probably from the steam trains in the cutting'), the dusty stained-glass panel in the door.

'We can't afford it between three,' said Kate flatly. 'Someone will have to sleep in the other downstairs room.'

'Yes,' I agreed. 'Who should we ask? Maureen's looking for somewhere, though I think she likes the Iffley Road because of the sports ground.'

'Not Maureen,' said Marienka. 'She's not – she'd not fit. She *rows boats*, dear, and you know what that involves. Early mornings and smelly T-shirts. I've got someone, anyway. He's a postgraduate, terribly clever, Arabist or something. He's keen. He's wanting something cheaper than the rooms he's in.'

We both turned to look at her accusingly, as she stood posed against the sagging gate which led onto the towpath. Hurriedly she added:

'Not a boyfriend. Scout's honour. Not my type. We did agree, no shacking up.'

'Well, it's out of the question anyway,' said Kate. 'College doesn't allow mixed digs.'

'Oh, pooh! What on earth has college got to do with it?'

'It's a rule.'

'We'll tell them –' she cast about for ideas, but it was me, ironically, who squared the circle.

'Why don't we tell them we need a man because of bringing in the coke. For the boiler. Big strong arms, good with hods.'

'Brilliant!'

It was brilliant, too. It worked. Without a murmur, the college greyheads accepted that three girls could not be expected to haul hods of coke in from the yard in the rain, let alone manage the riddling of ash. I think, in retrospect, that they probably saw the writing on the wall: we were grown-up voters now, no longer children. As Bob Dylan kept putting it, on the album that blasted out of every student room day after day, *your sons and daughters are beyond your command, for the times, they are a-changing.*

So Marienka organized for us to meet Max Bellinger; it was another of her theatrical coups, a *fait accompli*. Even if Kate or I had had other ideas the college permission was specific to Max, for he was a graduate. I do not know why the college thought graduate men less likely to assault or seduce us, but perhaps degrees were thought of more highly in those days.

It was the last day of the summer term, and none of us could afford even tea and toast in Brown's, so with her usual inventiveness our housemistress (as Kate now kept calling Marienka, to her disgust) begged some college champagne from a rich boyfriend at Christchurch, acquired four peaches from the Warden's garden at Max's college, and declared a picnic. We would meet by Folly Bridge, have the picnic on the towpath, then stroll along the canal to the house and peer through the windows. The agent, a terrible spoilsport, was refusing to release the key until September even though the little house stood empty. It was hot and overcast that day. Oxford, lying in its great damp hollow, sweltered in wet soupy air. Down by the river the flow of cool water brought a relieving breeze, and Kate and I sat fanning ourselves, waiting for the housemistress and the coal-heaver to join us and giggling a little at the absurdity of life.

Again, the image is diamond-clear. Kate, stocky and comely as a young cob, stretched out her solid calves beneath knee-length denim shorts. A vest top slipped off one brown shoulder, her chestnut hair fell straight, rich and heavy to her shoulders. She looked, as she always did, entirely easy. *Bien dans sa peau*, as the French say. Ted loved her, she loved Ted, their bodies and minds and hearts were attuned, they satisfied one another. They knew what bodies were for, and used them, and thought no more about it. Every line of good plain Kate displayed that unthinking, unassuming confidence.

As for me, I was – in the fashion of the day – robed from neck to ankle in grubby cheesecloth, with random ill-sewn Indian ruffles. Rather less fashionably, I was every inch the awkward virgin. Not at all *bien dans ma peau*. Maybe sport and exercise would have helped to balance me physically, but sport for young women was gravely out of fashion in those days, for we were still in thrall to the pigeon-chested, knock-kneed Biba fashion of the sixties. In theory, I was probably prettier than Kate would ever be. In practice, my gawky inexperience robbed me of allure. What did Blake say?

In a wife I would desire
What in whores is always found:
The lineaments of gratified desire.

Marienka, who also favoured the Indian-ruffle look in hot
weather, appeared at the far end of the towpath as a slender
red-and-gold tornado, and as she came closer a connoisseur
would have noted that she displayed a third sort of youthful
female physicality: the look of one who knows about gratified desire all right, but is far from serene, being always on
the look-out for further gratification. Kate moved with
smooth sexual confidence but without display; Marienka
slunk and shimmied, sharp hipbones always in motion, hair
adrift from its pins, always with an air of being freshly out
of bed and easily persuadable back into it. She did not, I
hasten to say, do this deliberately. She was no vamp, and
barely a flirt. It was simply that if animal adventures beckoned, her instinct was to run and meet them. Thirty years
later, among the boozy, lairy Friday-night girls in any city
centre or the rampant debs on the ski-slopes, she would
hardly have been remarkable for this. In 1972, she was.

Nor did I, at that moment, consciously make the compari-
son between the three of us, as young female bodies in different
states of erotic maturity. It is only now as I look back across
half a lifetime that I understand how we must have seemed
to the tall man who followed Marienka, carrying two bottles
of champagne and a plastic bag.

'This is Max,' said she, with the air of having conjured
him from thin air. 'Our officially approved stoker, catcher of
spiders and scarer-off of burglars and rapists. Observe the
hod-carrying muscles and the firm manly chin.'

She laughed up at him, her pale eyes dancing; but the look
in his eyes, I saw with a flutter of relief, was of mere amusement. Kate saw it too and we exchanged tiny glances; we

had each admitted a slight wariness about having a man mooning and sulking around the house, besotted with the fickle and unpredictable Marienka. Her discarded lovers already tended to hang around the stairways and corridors of college needing to be comforted with Nescafé and crumpets by more compassionate neighbours: I had had to listen to three or four of them during the year, and found that disappointed men were expensively heavy on one's patience and one's Kunzle cakes. Even more irritatingly, at the crook of their Belle Dame's little finger they abandoned my nurturing and undemanding friendship to go back to her, for just as long as she wanted them.

Having registered and approved the brotherly look on Max's face, we were able to examine him more closely. He was not actually particularly tall, only just on six foot; but he gave the air of height because in contrast to the slouching fashion of the day he held himself beautifully upright, shoulders back but not stiff, head poised with Apollonian grace on his long neck. He could not be described as classically handsome: a slightly lumpy, square brow and wide mouth gave him a distinctive but not particularly symmetrical appearance. His hair, mid-brown and dead straight, fell with unusual neatness just below his collar at the back, and flopped in a half-fringe across his eyebrows. It was brown, but a very beautiful brown, glossy and shiny as an autumn conker. He was looking at us gravely with deep green eyes as he said in a light pleasant voice: 'I have a feeling I have been dumped on you two. Marienka specializes in the *fait accompli*. I really won't be offended if you veto me, you know.'

He smiled, and his face was transformed. I found myself pulling my cheesecloth skirt tight over my knees and – there is no other word for it – simpering. Kate smiled back at him, unmoved but friendly, and said: 'Don't worry. We did need a fourth, and we couldn't agree at all on a girl. I daresay we'll get along fine. We can give it a go, anyway, can't we? For next term.'

'That's what I thought,' said Max. He sat down, folding his long legs with grasshopper grace, and began to twist the wire off the first champagne bottle. 'If it's awful I'll move out at Christmas. Thank you all, anyway. I didn't fancy trailing round the agencies all summer, once I found out that college wouldn't give out any more graduate rooms, and the place I'm in now is costing too much, on my own.'

'You're an Arabist, Marienka tells us.' My voice was artificially bright and social; I was shyer of this man than of most, for he seemed somehow more solid and less of a boy than the undergraduates I had got to know in the past two years. It suddenly came to me in a momentary qualm that I was now committed to sharing a bathroom with this adult male.

'Alas, she's wrong as usual,' said Max, pulling a sheaf of plastic cups out of the carrier bag and balancing them carefully on the grassy bank. He began pouring the champagne, waiting for the foam to subside, sharing it with scrupulous evenness between the flimsy cups. 'We met at the School of Oriental and African Studies all right, and it was an Arabic Art event. But I'm just another boring old art historian. European Renaissance. I went to the exhibition because my supervisor's got a thing about Byzantium, and I thought I might pick up some lines.' He handed me the first cup, a distinction at which I found myself unreasonably pleased; Kate had the second, Marienka the third.

'Well, I thought you were into Arabs,' said Marienka, gulping half hers down and wiping froth from her lips. 'You *looked* like an Arabist.'

'Must have been the shamagh and the camel.' He took her cup back and refilled it. The hand which passed it to her was long, white, slender and beautiful: hardly a man's hand at all. The nails looked manicured.

Kate's gaze followed mine. 'Are you sure you're up to the hod-carrying?' she asked, with not a little malice.

'Oh, we'll all take our *turn*,' said Marienka scornfully. 'It was only a *ruse* to get the old tabbies to let us do a mixed house-share.'

Max looked across at me with a charmingly conspiratorial air, and raised his cup. 'To equal rights and equal stoking,' he said. 'And our new house! Let's go and see it *soon*.'

'*Now!*' The red-and-gold whirlwind was upright again, hauling Kate to her feet and stretching out her other hand to me. 'Yes yes yes! It's all so exciting I could *spit!*'

'What about the other bottle?' asked Max, rising more slowly. 'And the peaches?'

'I have a plan about that,' said Marienka. 'Let's break in through the coalhouse window and have a secret picnic right inside the house.'

So we did. Max, protesting only slightly, gave each of us a leg-up through the unsecured window into the little house's pantry, and followed with some difficulty; the four of us sat round drinking and whispering on the frayed old carpet, discussing rooms and furnishing arrangements like children in a Wendy-house. It was one of the happiest afternoons I can remember. I was on the verge of a new kind of life, with the people I liked best in the world and who had unaccountably chosen me to be one of them. Yet there was still a long vacation to be lived through, and the delicious beginning of the new life could be savoured to the full during weeks of anticipation, free from the risk of disappointment.

And, of course, I was in love.

2

Students were not an industry thirty years ago, as they are now. There were fewer of us, and nobody had thought to make a profession out of organizing gap years, 'internships' or summer placements to further our careers. Nor were there cheap flights to tempt us far from home. So in the seemingly endless summer vacation the élite actors and comedians headed for Edinburgh, the rich for their parents' favoured European playgrounds, and the rest of us mouldered quietly at home, taking on any odd jobs that were offered in the neighbourhood until we could afford something that counted as a holiday. Kate and I had discussed a cycling trip in the Lake District, which would have enabled me to wander round Wordsworth's cottage and her to look at fossils as all good geographers must; but Ted got the offer of his uncle's cottage in Cornwall, and I could hardly hold Kate to my strenuous plans when such an alternative beckoned.

I had a hunch, anyway, that this time was important for her and Ted. So it was. It was during that summer that the two of them became engaged; Ted said later that he wanted to 'try out' keeping house together, away from the feverish atmosphere of Oxford in term time. The experiment clearly succeeded. When I heard this news, in an excited phone call from Kate in late August, I had a momentary qualm. Would she want to go back on our pact against resident boyfriends, and move Ted in now instead of Max? But calm, sensible Kate wanted no such thing. 'Time enough,' she said. 'We've got all our lives to share a breakfast-table. I don't think house-sharing works if you have special alliances. And we've both got finals.'

Marienka always vanished for the whole summer, staying with friends and cousins in various exotic places: St Tropez, New York, San Gimigiano, the Isle of Skye. She must have spent a week or two at the crumbling family seat in Yorkshire, because when term began she turned up with three more oil paintings, each larger and gloomier than the last. In the event we banned two of them from any public area of the house, so she slept all that year in her sliver of a boxroom with the Third Duke hovering insecurely over her head and A Storm Over The Sound of Jura propped on her dressing-table. My room was next to hers and she always used my mirror anyway, for the light.

But I am running ahead of myself. My own summer was, on the face of it, uneventful. I stayed home in the faded comfort of our house on the fringes of a small, unremarkable town on the borders of Norfolk and Suffolk. There were always tourists and hikers in the summer, for we were a gateway to the Broads; Eddie the landlord of the King's Arms would be glad enough to take me on as usual for some casual work. I worked in the pub kitchen mainly, hooking chicken portions and chips out of the deep-fryer and disposing them in wicker baskets according to the fashion of the time. Once, when I had burnt my hand quite badly on the steam-cleaner we used for the baskets, Eddie felt guilty enough to let me work behind the bar for a week, which I much preferred.

My father retired that year, relieving me of the social burden of being the local vicar's daughter. I had been looking forward to this release, particularly since it did not mean moving house. My mother, who was a deceptively stubborn creature for all her homely Women's Institute sweetness, had refused point-blank to move into the ruinous and sprawling vicarage when we first came to Dellingham twenty years before. She persuaded my father to let her use a small legacy to buy a cottage only five minutes away from his church. Over the years, as my brother Benedict and I grew up, they had grown the house haphazardly, putting a brick kitchen extension on the back with a square bedroom for Ben above, then later adding a conservatory at the side and turning a redundant woodshed into a proper study for my father. The front room was just about big enough for small gatherings of parishioners, although my mother always resented the intrusion; the Diocese sweetened the pill a little by offering a small extra allowance to the family once the old vicarage had been sold to a consultant surgeon and beautified beyond recognition. I still think the church got the best of the deal, and my mother agrees. My father refuses to speculate. But for us, the great benefit was that when Dad retired we kept our own bedrooms and our childhood territory. This mattered particularly to Ben after he joined the Navy and spent more than half the year away.

The parents were both intrigued by my new living arrangements when I told them about the house. Dad raised his eyes from the *Daily Telegraph* and said, 'Uh huh!' in a more than usually encouraging tone, and then added, 'Good to have your own front door, I would think. Less *conventual*.' I was always being surprised by Dad. Mum was a little dubious about the idea of Max being in the house with us three girls, but approached the subject in a typically oblique way.

'What does Trevor think about it all?' was her first question. I wriggled like a ten year old. In the family, a polite fiction persisted that Trevor Eades was my 'boyfriend'. Trevor himself tended to believe it. He was my age but for a few days, and worked as a trainee at the bank, having decided that university was a waste of time which could better be spent 'getting on in the world'. I tended to agree with him, where his own case was concerned. He had little interest in the world beyond the county, and no intellectual curiosity at all about things which did not directly concern the town, the bank, and his immediate environment. He was, on the other hand, an exceedingly good-looking lad and for a while in the sixth form I had been proud to be taken for walks with him along the muddy farmland tracks behind the town. He excited me on a purely physical level; his was the first hard male body I was ever pressed against, his the first hand to reach inside my bra. When it was dry enough we would lie in the long grass by the river and kiss for hours, letting our hands roam shyly over the strange territory of each other's bodies. We went no further. I was, after all, the vicar's daughter. Trevor put no pressure on me, and I do not think that in my absence he looked for any other partners. Certainly whenever I got home from Oxford his advances followed the same pattern: relatively decorous, respectful, but avid enough to flatter me that he had been thinking about me with hunger for weeks.

I carried on accommodating him out of mere habit, but with every holiday our grapples embarrassed me more. As for wider experience, in term time I kissed a few men but never went further. Perhaps – I blush to admit it – this was because I suspected that they would not be as easy to stop as my faithful and staid Suffolk swain.

'It's nothing to do with Trevor,' I said defensively when my mother brought his name up. 'Marienka's friend – Max or whatever his name is –' (ah, the duplicity!) '– isn't going out with any of us. It's quite normal for men and women to share digs, in Oxford.'

'Is it now?' said my mother, satirically. 'Well, I don't know.' She slid away at an angle, as was her habit. 'You'll get a proper rent agreement?'

'It's through an agency.' I was glad of her retreat.

Trevor came round later that afternoon and planted a

damp kiss on my cheek, taking possession of my hand and keeping it fast. He told me what had been going on at the bank, and that his probationary period was nearly over. He asked about my term, referring to my 'lessons' with a faintly patronizing air as if to underline the fact that I was still hardly better than a school kid, while he was a working man. We ate early in our house, and lightly because of my father's digestion, so my mother made him stay and join us for an omelette. Then, inevitably, as the warm evening closed in he said: 'Fancy a stroll?'

I glanced around, looking for excuses, but my mother was clattering efficiently in the kitchen and my father had retired to his study. Reluctantly, I followed Trevor outside and let him take my hand once more and lead me down the track to the river. The evening star shone, bright against the last of the sunset; soon a broad full moon was rising beyond a field of rye, and the spears of the grain stood ragged against it.

On such a night as this, I recited silently, *Troilus methinks mounted the Trojan walls and sighed his soul towards the Grecian tents where Cressid lay that night* . . . I wondered where Max was. Not that it was any of my business. But I sighed my soul there, all the same.

Trevor stopped, then, and I could see that we were close to our old place in the grass. He turned me towards him more roughly than usual, and kissed me. The kiss was familiar, and I responded with familiar dry ardour then with a damp parting of the lips; he pressed himself against me and suddenly, quite without affection and entirely without warning, I was overcome by lust. *Lust*, Marienka would often say, is only the German word for pleasure, after all. Trevor, at that moment, was pleasure. The hardness rising in his groin intoxicated me; I ran my hand down over his buttocks with a swell of appreciation that surprised me very much, and kissed him some more, pressing the whole length of my body against him. Then we were lying down and his hands were on me, pulling my shirt open. Eyes closed, I thought of nothing, certainly not of Trevor and his neat banker's shirt and tie. My body, rioting, rebelled against decorum as it never had before. Our teeth clashed, and I took my mouth from his and bit his neck; he pulled my bra right up and sank his face in my naked breasts. Over the top of his smooth hair I could see the hot moon rising, and felt my own body arching up towards him. My hand, shockingly, moved of its own volition towards his belt.

Then he spoke, and it was over.

'Are you sure?' he asked, throaty and breathless. And, of course, I wasn't. It had not been him I rose towards, not his hard body I wanted to explode against. I sat up, pushing him off, and began to do up my shirt.

'I'm sorry. I'm sorry. We can't do this,' I gabbled. 'It's not right.'

He looked at me, his face pale and transformed in the moonlight. 'It could be right,' he said hoarsely. 'We could make it right. I'd look after you. Sally, I want you to marry me. I didn't like to ask before, till I'd got through all the tests and that, but I'm not a trainee any more. We can get married, as soon as you like.'

There are no words to describe the moment. Pity, terror, embarrassment, remorse had me agape and aghast, panting with dread, unable to speak for a moment.

'No – no,' I said at last. 'I don't think you should talk like that. We couldn't possibly – I mean, there's my degree –'

'So you'd be away in term time,' said Trevor simply. 'I'd be OK with that. It's only eight weeks at a time, isn't it? But if you'd rather put it off till next July, the actual marriage I mean – that'd be fine. Honestly. Don't cry, love –' He brushed the corner of my eye. 'I'll look after you. We don't have to do it before we're married, if you don't want.'

I turned away, hunched, still struggling with my shirt and bra, which would not pull down.

'I mean I just can't – I mean I don't love you.'

He was silent for a moment, then asked roughly, 'What was all that about then? Just now?'

'I don't know.'

'I suppose all your student friends go in for that. Free love, all that. Fuck whoever you like, one-night stands, don't care.'

There was real anger in his voice and I had never heard him use that word before. An image of Marienka flitted through my mind, for of my friends she came closest to his description. I tried to match his anger with my own. 'No, they're not like that. And I didn't – I wasn't going to –'

'You been using me, girl.' His childhood Suffolk accent, so carefully ironed out for use at the bank, returned as his indignation grew. 'Snogging practice, was I?'

This time I had no answer. He was right. I got to my feet, gave him a flickering nervous smile and set off up the track in the moonlight. He did not follow at first but after a few minutes I heard panting and he was alongside me, slowing from a run.

'I'm sorry. I'm sorry, Sally. I love you, that's all. P'raps I shouldn't have rushed you. Let's take it slow. We don't have to be engaged with a ring and that –'

His apology was harder to bear than anything. I should have stopped, turned to him, told him again and gently. Perhaps I should even have admitted that another man had mesmerized me and colonized all my thoughts. But all my life I have lacked moral courage, and I was not brave or humane enough to turn this farce into an honest human encounter. Looking at his reddened face, I saw lips which suddenly seemed thick and wet, a lump beside his nose where a pimple had been, an Adam's apple which for the first time looked far too prominent. Revulsion swept over me: I had nearly – no, I couldn't have. Yes, I damn nearly had. With Trevor!

I turned my face away, ran home and took a long bath in the friendly, rusty claw-footed tub of my childhood. I ran my hands disbelievingly over my body, dipping my aching head in the water, letting my hair spread around me like a Burne-Jones Ophelia. The moon shone in through the un-curtained window, icy white, her rising ruddiness gone. I lay there until the hard Suffolk water was cold and scummy, and went shuddering to bed.

3

Humiliation drove me back to church. In the weeks after my encounter in the grass I signed on at the King's Arms, worked six shifts a week and spent the evenings going through the reading list for the next term. Trevor avoided me, markedly, and did not renew his suit. Odd whispers and glances confirmed to me that our corner of town knew something had happened; one evening when I was serving some lads at the bar I distinctly caught the words '. . . prick-tease' and 'vicar', before a dirty laugh obscured the rest of the sentence.

But on Sundays, to my father's quiet satisfaction, I went to church. I had grown up with it, of course. I had read C.S. Lewis with childish delight and adolescent interest, and marked the rolling years of all my early life with liturgical feasts: Christmas and Candlemas, Easter and Pentecost, palms and ashes, Lenten lunches of bread and cheese and the long beautiful solemn wait of Advent. My parents had, however, been canny enough not to raise any objection when in the sixth form I stopped joining them on Sunday morning except for the major feasts. I never actually announced, as some of my peers did, that I had 'lost my faith'. Rather I let it fade into the background. If somebody had held a knife to my throat I am sure I would have prayed. From time to time at Oxford I would argue with the smugger sort of atheist, protesting that there was no more scientific proof of their conviction than there was of my father's. But religion did not matter. It was not central. I could not imagine teaching it to any child of my own. I was, I suppose, a typical part of Arnold's 'melancholy, long withdrawing roar', of a Britain whose Christian tide was going out.

That summer, though, humiliated by the way I had treated poor Trevor I found myself sloping back into church, lounging in the back pews, taking childish comfort from the familiar hymns. *Dark is his flight on the wings of the storm . . . the shadows deepen, Lord with me abide . . .* We had a goodish congregation back then, in the 1970s. There was no Sunday shopping to compete and church was a social gathering. Young parents brought fidgeting children to the communion rail, and hale citizens in their forties and fifties diluted the elderliness of a rural congregation. Farmworkers still roared out the hymns as they might have done in Thomas Hardy's Wessex, flowers were competitively arranged by an overstuffed rota of ladies, and the Dellingham ironmonger and chemist served as sidesmen. It was comforting. My father, with exemplary self-control, made no comment on my return to the flock; Mum was less careful, twittered with pleasure and kept suggesting to the new vicar that I might read the lesson.

'Sally's got a lovely speaking voice, you know. She was Olivia, or was it Violet, in her school play, that Shakespeare one with the man in yellow stockings.' I had, in fact, been Maria. In the 1960s Twiggy was the ideal of female beauty and if you had a bust you always got the comedy parts. But I never did read the lesson: seeing my glowering face and my chosen niche in the back row, the new vicar wisely did nothing about the suggestion.

Something happened one week, though, just when I was at my lowest – missing Marienka and Kate, and trying (as I did every day) to tell myself that I did not know Max Bellinger and therefore could not be in love with him. Our vicar was called away to his mother's deathbed and my Dad volunteered to drive him north; for that Sunday's service the

Diocese sent us a very old man, a retired Bishop with a lean, ascetic countenance and a surprising mop of white hair. One lock of it, indeed, fell over his heavy brow in a way imme- diately reminiscent of Max's. Perhaps that was why I listened. But I think not: it was the sermon itself that was different. I, who had heard hundreds of the things ever since I first played under a pew with my dolls, was jolted into attention.

He said that when he first studied philosophy, the most important idea ever to be put in his head had been put there by Plato. He sounded more like a university lecturer than a preacher, and his gentle manner held me, as in a brief and courteously simple way he outlined the Platonic theory of archetypes and of the dark cave in which we see only im- poverished shadows of a great and permanent beauty outside and beyond it. He quoted *through a glass darkly*, and charmed my retrogressive childish heart even more by pointing out that it was precisely this truth which C.S. Lewis was illustrating in The Last Battle, when earth and Narnia and all the worlds were only Shadowlands, pale precursors of the eternal joys to come.

'We glimpse these verities, these beauties, at moments when we least expect to,' he said. 'And there is always a streak of pain in it, while we are here on earth. The pain is because we sense not only the transitoriness of earthly beauty, but the fact that it is never complete. It can never be quite the real thing which we know in our deepest hearts to exist. Have you never looked at a mountain or a bay or a beautiful face, eaten a fruit full of sunshine, hugged a child or heard a strain of music which enraptured you? And have you not at that moment felt both joy and an unreasonable sort of disappointment? If you have experienced this, be happy. You have seen a reflection of God Himself.'

I floated out of church that morning exalted. It seemed to me that the old preacher had explained everything, from my childhood wonder at the moon and stars to the way that I felt when Kate played her scratchy Mahler records. It told me why pleasure and grief seemed to mingle in me when, walking past the Holywell Music Room one winter night, a skein of music from some string quartet crept out into the medieval darkness. It made sense of a particular childhood memory of Scotland, when I had woken early in our bed-and-breakfast hotel and crept to the window to see that the sunrise had touched the summit of Ben Nevis. It looked as if the mountaintop was lit from within, and I wanted to cry without understanding why. It even eased my shame at the mistake my body had made, yearning for its own paradise and blundering into shadow and shame.

It made it easier to think about Max, too. I knew, now, what I had seen in his face. It was there in the fall of his hair, the gentleness of his green eyes, the quirky, tentative uniqueness of his smile and the heartbreaking harmonic of his voice. I had glimpsed it through him: the Ultimate Good, the archetype. Not God, exactly; to be honest I have always been rather embarrassed by the idea of God as a person, and squirm when Evangelicals speak of Jesus in matey terms as their 'friend'. But for a face and voice to conjure up an ultimate, archetypal joy now made sense to me. It was a vision I could look towards without guilt or shame. Max was the mountaintop, the symphony, the best fruit on the tree. To yearn for him was not wrong, not stupid callow calf-love. *We must needs love the highest when we see it.*

So I stopped reproaching myself and trying to laugh myself out of my preoccupation, and summoned medieval Platonism to bolster my calf-love. I quelled all cynical (or wise) instincts not to let myself dwell on a man I had met for one after-noon and never spent a minute alone with. The bishop had told us that all loves, all admirations, all yearnings partake of the divine. They lead us upward, however thick a forest of sorrow and disappointment we have to travel through. He had quoted Browning, too: *Ah, but a man's reach should exceed his grasp, or what's a heaven for?*

It was the message I most wanted to hear. Later, at home, I combed through my father's old copy of Browning's poems – I had never much liked the rambling intellectual passion of them before – and found the context. Andrea del Sarto, it seems, was a painter: he saw what he saw, and did what he did, 'unmoved by men's blame or their praise either'. I saw what I saw, and wanted it, and knew I was right.

That encounter with Browning – though God knows I read it with no subtlety – meant everything. I had always preferred headlong, passionate painters and poets and gardens to the tidy rationalist sort: better to try for the distant impossible vision and fail than just to organize the real world into pleasing pigeonholes. Between Plato and Browning and the preacher I felt changed. My mother remarked on it. In the pub I became mellow and affectionate towards even the grimmest customers; after work, instead of flopping on the sofa at home I took long walks alone, down the fields and along the river, rejoicing that the wild mallow and the golden reeds were part of the same vision which led me on my journey towards the best, the most beautiful, the perfect. To Max. Home again, every evening I bent to my books, and it was a Shakespeare term coming up, so I did not go short of corroborative evidence of my exalted point of view.

> Love is not love
> Which alters if it alteration finds
> Or bends with the remover to remove;
> O no, it is an ever-fixed mark
> That looks on tempests and is never shaken . . .

Faced with that, it would have been positively wrong to 'get over' my infatuation.

Moreover, it put Trevor in his place. He had shown no sign of being an ever-fixed mark, or of building a cabin at my gate to sing loyal cantons of contemned love in the dead of night, and hallow my name to the reverberate hills. He belonged to another world, the familiar world of offence and self-importance, of 'getting over it' and moving on. It was rising all around us, of course, that world: even though stolid Dellingham was Darby-and-Joan country and most couples seemed fixed in their ways, the new world shouted in at us from outside. It yelled from lurid divorce court battles reported in Dad's *Daily Telegraph*, from agony aunts who advised people to 'cut their losses', from pop stars and actors who bolted from one high-profile relationship to the next and gave interviews about how healthy it was and how right they were to do so.

I sometimes wonder now whether I was, quite simply, afraid. From a cynical middle-aged perspective I ask myself whether I was using this pure, incorporeal unrequited passion for Max Bellinger as a security blanket. Reading this nonsense you may well be suspecting the same thing; you may, indeed, have lost patience entirely with my younger self and feel a strong desire to slap her. Sometimes, given all that happened afterwards, I feel much the same way.

Yet at other times, near the mountains or the sea or walking by the reeds of my old home river at dusk, I give that daft young woman of twenty a little more respect. Certainly I was naïve, and certainly I had thrown up efficient barriers against reason and common sense; but common sense is not everything. I was irrational, I was infatuated, I was riding for a fall, but at least I was exalted. My eyes were on the stars and the mountaintops, or at least I thought they were. I had a dream and a passion which connected me for better or worse to centuries of human aspiration. I could understand medieval courtly love, breathe with Viola at Orsino's feet, abase myself with patient Griselda, forgive with Desdemona, sing silently alongside Violetta and Mimi and every operatic heroine who ever gasped her melodious last on her unreliable lover's breast. Kate might be more sensible, and Marienka had more fun. But I was, in my perverse way, very close to the heart of things. Or felt that I was.

In this frame of mind, when September came I packed and labelled my trunk and sent it off. Then I took my light overnight case, hugged my parents goodbye and set off for the station, the slow train through Essex and the fast one from Paddington. Marienka was not proposing to arrive until October, a few days before full term; Kate and I were to arrange furniture and get the stove lit, phone connected and spare keys cut. We did not know when Max would arrive. I had, at least, retained a sufficient sense of self-preservation to pretend to Kate that I didn't much care.

4

The house looked smaller, and considerably less Venetian. The garden was a tangled mess of long grass and overgrown shrubs; rank speckled weeds sprouted amid the small remaining store of coke in the shed. Kate had walked up to the house-agency to collect the keys, and I sat on my suitcase in the front garden, looking up at the grimy windows with excitement and trepidation. At that moment I was not even thinking about Max, but rather about the momentous and unnerving step we had taken in accepting responsibility for an actual house. Hitherto, arrivals in Oxford had all been the same: a bus up the Woodstock Road to college, a crowd of familiar faces amid the trunks in the Porter's lodge, the lugging of cases up narrow stairways, and the pleasant chaos of settling in to a room which was – if not necessarily our first choice – at least clean, warm, and with a made-up bed and a shared kitchenette which the invisible hands of 'scouts' would clean up daily, generally before most of us had woken up.

Now, suddenly, we bore all the responsibilities of householders. Our domestic duties were no longer confined to getting ourselves dressed and rinsing a couple of mugs. We had a compulsory and worrying relationship with a host of other material things: the crack in the coalhouse window, the electricity bill, the jungle garden, the cleaning. It occurred to me that none of us owned a broom, mop, dustpan and brush, or any of that stuff you wash up dishes with. I supposed there would be a Hoover, since the place was furnished, but wondered hazily

how much dusters cost and whether coke-fuelled ovens had
to be cleaned with dreadful caustic stuff the way my mother
cleaned the oven at home. I stood up, feeling a sudden need
to be active: a mouse scuttled past me in the undergrowth and
vanished, in an insouciantly accustomed manner, through a
crack in the air-brick beside the front door. I stood up to see
whether I could spot it running about inside the house, and as
I put my face to the window I came eye-to-eye with a very
large spider, working away on a cobweb.

'Oh God,' I said aloud. 'What have we done?'

'Know what you mean,' said a drawling male voice behind
me. I spun round, and saw that a taxi had drawn up un-
noticed on the road beyond the garden gate, and that Max
was standing, hands on hips, surveying the house.

'It does look a bit like Dracula's weekend cottage,' he went
on, thoughtfully. 'Can't you get in?'

'Kate went for the key.' I ducked my head; after the
summer's dreams I was terrified of looking at him in case
the gleam of divinity had vanished. When I did so, forced
by mere politeness, he certainly had a different air. In his
heavy cord jacket and scarf, his face a little thinner, almost
pinched, he looked shorter and more vulnerable than I
remembered. But the smile was the same, and had the same
effect.

'I don't think we'd better repeat the burglarious entry,' he
said. 'I've had nightmares about that. Marienka is a very bad
influence. Let's wait. We could stay here and think about
what to do with the garden.'

'Rather not,' I said. 'I sort of hoped we could just ignore it.'

'Don't you garden?'

'Not for pleasure.' I was growing bolder now. It was easy
to talk to him. He had a quality of polite, slightly absent-
minded detachment which made me far less shy than I had
expected to be. You could rattle on and not feel you were

boring him, because even if he did not respond to what you were saying he would deploy that melting smile. 'My mother adores gardens, and my father used to do a lot before his back went. She makes me weed a bit in our garden now, but I loathe it.'

'My mother likes gardens too,' said Max absently, then scuffed some dark brown earth with the toe of his polished brogue. 'I wonder if we could grow some herbs. They're quick. And they make things taste better. Actually, if we plant potatoes we'd get some in time for the summer term, wouldn't we? I love new potatoes. They're supposed to be terribly easy.'

'Grow vegetables? Us?'

'Why not? This is home now. For a year, anyway. I like the idea of it being our home.'

He smiled again: it was social, it was polite, it was not a special smile just for me. But in my deluded hunger I took it personally, smiled back into his green eyes and said with unnecessary warmth: 'Well, it will be. Our home.'

Perhaps I saw a flicker of wariness in his eye then; certainly there were enough rags of self-preservation in me to make me add hastily: 'There's a mouse in there, by the way. It's what I was trying to see when I was at the window.'

'I quite like mice,' said Max. 'We could tame it and teach it tricks.' He moved towards the window.

'Teach what?' said Kate, appearing from behind the largest bush by the gate. 'I got them.' She jingled the keys.

'Teach the mouse tricks,' I said. 'I saw one go in just now.'

'Mouse or rat?'

'Mouse, I think.'

'I'd feel differently about rats,' said Max thoughtfully. 'Which is unfair, really. There's no reason they shouldn't get the chance to learn tricks, too.'

Kate put the key in the lock, turned it with some difficulty,

and pushed on the peeling blue paint of the door. It creaked
open, and the three of us stepped in, crowding each other in
excitement, giggling. Max sprang suddenly sideways into the
little dining room which led through to the the kitchen, and
pointed.

'There it is!'

'Sally, you moron, it's definitely a *rat*!' This from Kate.

'I thought it was just a big mouse!'

'No, *rat!*'

The creature sat, washing its whiskers, under the battered
dining-room table. Max squeezed past us in the little hallway,
went into the other front room and emerged a moment later
with a poker.

'Max, no!'

'Leave it!'

Our squeaks were pointless: the rat was nowhere to be
seen. Max put down the poker and said, 'Thank God for
that. I hate these moments when one has to prove oneself a
real man. I'd rather have taught it to balance a ball on its
nose, if truth be told.'

'You can't *get* a rat with a poker, anyway,' said Kate scornfully. 'It's too narrow for a creature that moves fast. You'd
want something like a tennis racket, at least.'

Max wandered through the dining room and stood in the
doorway, one hand on the frame, looking into the shabby
kitchen. I looked at him, noting the breadth of his shoulders
and the way that his jacket, though old and rubbed, had been
beautifully cut to hang with elegance. He cannot have been
more than twenty-two, but he was a man and not by any stretch
of imagination a boy. I thought of Trevor and shivered.

Kate stooped to the doormat and picked up a handful of
damp letters. Most of it was junk mail or demands to buy
a television licence, but one bore Italian stamps and was
addressed, in Marienka's dashing hand, to 'Maximilian

Arthur Bellinger, and Harem'. She clucked, tore it open and we read it with our heads close together.

> *Dear Sally, Kate, and Max,*
>
> *Welcome to the Palazzo. Isn't it exciting? Is this the first real letter? I can't wait. So I will be back on the 1st of October, laden with drink and truffles. Marco is sending a whole dried ham and some salamis from his uncle's factory. We can live on it for weeks. Since I'm the last to arrive I deserve the little room at the back. No arguments. See you. Love love love (that's one each, share them fairly) M.*

'Who is Marco?' we said, together.

'My brother-in-law's business partner's brother,' said Max, coming back from his contemplation of the kitchen and glancing at the note. 'Marienka came to my sister's wedding in August. Sue's married a guy who's in some sort of finance business with the Italians. There's a spoilt little brother and that's Marco. Unspeakably rich. Marienka swept him off his feet, and the last I heard from Sue is that they were in Tuscany together. She's furious.'

'Who, your sister?'

'Yes, she'd got Marco earmarked for one of her friends. Told me I had no business inviting strange women to her wedding and messing everything up.'

'Marienka's not acquisitive, though,' said Kate. 'She'll give him back, once she's got all the salami and ham off him that she wants.'

'That is so *cynical!*' I was shocked. 'They might be really in love.'

'Oh, come on! You know what she always says –'

'Yes, but love can come over you – and if she fell for him that suddenly, at a wedding – I think an Italian would rather suit her –'

I wanted all the world to be in love. I also wanted Marienka well and truly spoken for, before she could fascinate Max in the daily propinquity of a shared house.

'She *always* pounces suddenly. Remember Robert? And Indarjit? And Sam Doulton-Byrd? And –'

'I'll have to get used to this, I suppose,' said Max. 'Do girls always keep tally on each other's boyfriends?'

'Don't men do the same thing with their friends' girlfriends?' countered Kate.

'No. Not interested. Honestly. Not a flicker. I don't even know who my own brother's hanging about with.'

'Oh. Well, you should,' said Kate. 'It's part of the – the narrative of life. If you care about your friends and family, you care about who they go out with.'

Max smiled at her. 'Sweet. OK, I look forward to a whole year of daily soap opera. Shall we have a bulletin board in the kitchen, like Daily Information in college?'

'A blackboard would be more practical,' said Kate. 'Given Marienka's turnover.'

'With just you and Ted painted on it, in indelible gloss paint at the top,' I said. Perhaps I was trying to remind Max that Kate too was out of bounds. But Kate had lost interest in the joke and was looking around her at the unappealing little house.

'Indeed,' she said vaguely. 'Do you think we ought to light that terrible stove thing?'

'It's not cold,' said Max, cautiously. The Rayburn seemed immense, forbidding, a great dreary industrial lump in chipped cream enamel.

'It's damp,' said Kate firmly. 'We have to get to grips with it, now. Before it does get cold, we ought to practise. Otherwise there's no hot water at all, the agent said.'

'Brrr!' said Max. 'Unthinkable. What does it run on?'

'Coke. There's not much coke, though. Should we order some, or something? How do you order coke?' Kate was bustling now, housewifely, an engaged girl getting in shape for married life. Max and I fell into step, and the afternoon passed pleasantly as the three of us played house. I ran to and from the corner shop for firelighters and cleaning things, and with a great deal of dusty rattling and many shrieks of alarm we got the flue open and the Rayburn stove alight. Max entered into the spirit of the occasion, joining the squeals and clutching at me and Kate in a wholly girlish way when the flames roared suddenly upward or outward, and coaxing them with words when they sputtered and died. We tamed them, closed the iron door with a satisfying clunk, then washed the windows.

When the new light filtering through them showed up how dirty the rest of the house was, we persuaded the horrible old vacuum-cleaner into life and I ran back to the shop for a new sponge mop-head. We toured the house and agreed that Max would sleep downstairs, Kate would have the large room above his and I would take the other front room, while Marienka lived in the back room – hardly more than a sliver of corridor – which led off a tiny awkward landing which was in turn effectively part of my room. There was some discussion about whether to accept her sacrifice, but Max held firm to his opinion that the little room was what she really wanted.

'Look,' he said. 'It's small, but she can have the big cupboard on the landing for her stuff. And I think I know why she chose it. She's not just being a martyr –'

He held up the rattan blind, whose cord was broken, and displayed the view. 'You can see the canal.' He was right; if you sat up in the landlord's narrow, creaking bed, you could look straight out at the narrow iron bridge over the canal and it was, in its sober industrial way, very beautiful. My room looked at the front garden, the road, and the council block opposite; Kate's view of the canal was obscured by a tree, and downstairs all Max would see was a dishevelled hedge.

'Clever girl!' he said. 'Still, I'd rather have bookshelves, and room to pace up and down in artistic torment. Are you sure you want me to be downstairs?'

'You can scare off burglars for us,' said Kate.

'I wouldn't know how to start,' protested Max mildly.

'Sit them down and start explaining the distinction between tenebrism and chiaroscuro in early Renaissance art.' Kate was more tart, more teasing with Max than I ever ventured to be. 'That'll see them off. Come on, let's finish, then we can go for a walk on the towpath.'

We became a family that afternoon and in the days which followed. We shared breakfast, set up a rota for stoking the boiler, and squabbled like siblings over bathwater. Sometimes we cooked an evening meal together and took a stroll afterwards, but quite often Max ate in his college and Kate spent the evening with Ted. When Kate and I were alone together we ate beans on toast; when Max joined us, we baked potatoes and made chilli con carne to put in them. 'After all, the heat's free when the stove's on,' Kate would say. Once, Max stayed home when Kate was away, and I roasted a chicken with crisp potatoes around it, and rubbed tarragon and rosemary into the skin because he had said he liked herbs.

'Wow!' he said as I took it out of the oven. 'What have I done to deserve this?'

'Oh, it's economical really,' I lied. 'The chicken was on special offer. And we can eat it cold for days.' I watched him eat my food with a joy so intense that I could hardly swallow my own portion. After supper he glanced out at the rising moon and said: 'Fancy a walk along the towpath?'

We walked together, watching the moon glimmering on the water, and he told me about his family. His sister Sue was older and, he said with a delicate shudder, 'rather on the bossy side. She's trained as a physiotherapist and likes big country-type dogs that bring pheasants to you. She makes it quite clear that I am a waste of space.' His father had died when he was fourteen, a year after divorcing his mother. I made sympathetic sounds, and he said frankly enough: 'Yes, it was a big disruption. Worst for my little brother, probably. He was devoted to our father. But it was probably the best thing. Dad wouldn't have remarried. Not sure he was ever cut out for it.'

I walked on, looking towards the dark water, digesting this piece of information. I could not quite make out what it implied, but it disturbed me. After a moment, and unusually for him, Max went on confiding. 'Mum married David pretty well straight after the divorce. He's been a good stepfather, specially to me and Sue. Bit of an exquisite, he is, not at all like my real father. Top Jewish taste. He took me to buy my first suit, at his own tailor on Jermyn Street. Actually, he still buys me clothes.'

Kate would have laughed at that; although she was not with us that evening we had all lived so closely the past fortnight that I felt her mocking spirit rise up in me. I almost said, 'That explains why you're such a dandy.' Indeed, Max's sports jackets and grey flannels fitted him with far more flair than most young Englishmen's, and his shirts were the wonder of the household: silk and linen and far too good for the rough old launderette the rest of us threw our jeans into. He entirely ignored the ornate, hippyish style of the day, and had never been seen in denim. But I was not Kate, and I did not tease him. Instead, I asked: 'What about your little brother?'

'He doesn't like David. Won't take anything from him.'

It is comfortable to walk and talk; gaps in the conversation are readily filled with the crunch of footsteps and the companionable breathing of the walkers. I was able to give myself time before asking, 'Why not?'

'Martin's a bit of a rebel,' said Max. 'He's very musical.

Was on a music scholarship, but he got expelled in the lower
Sixth. Now he sings in a group. Refused to try for university. Been bumming around for two years now. Actually –'
his step faltered, and he turned to look at me in the gloom
'– he's a bit odd. Sometimes he doesn't seem to quite get
things. I worry about him.'

'I think you always do worry about your brothers and
sisters. My brother Benedict is in the Navy.'

I told him about Benedict, and how surprised my parents
had been at his seafaring intentions, and how strange it was
not to see him at all for six months at a time and then to
have him home a great deal and calling in on me in college
when I least expected it, with time on his hands.

'He's so – outdoorsy. Energetic. Makes me feel like a pale
creeping clerk.'

Max really laughed now; I loved these moments when he
laughed at my jokes and ruffled my hair like a brother.
Impatient modern girls may wonder why for so long I toler-
ated, even nurtured, this quasi-sibling relationship with the
man I loved. They may marvel at my unwillingness or inability
to flirt, vamp him and generally push the whole thing further,
faster. They may be right. But to me it seemed natural that
we should get to know one another in this gentle way. I was
happy that we had got this far, and not impatient. For me
every moment with him shone with a light that never was on
land or sea.

'I know exactly,' he said now. 'It's odd when your siblings
are so different. Sue makes me feel like a silly little boy, and
Martin prowls around in his leathers and makes me feel like
a croaky old pedant.'

'Oh, you could never—'

I restrained myself. A dozen times a day, like this, I heard
the crack of adoration in my voice and controlled it. Max
clearly did not hear it this time. On the chilly towpath, beside

a venerable timber balance-bridge, its beam soaring up at an angle as if pointing to the Pole star, he shivered and drew my arm companionably into his. 'Cold. Let's turn for home,' he said. It was the closest I had been to him physically. I still cannot see that black-and-white lift bridge across the Oxford canal without feeling my treacherous heart turn over. I could have walked for ever, pressed against the smooth tweed of his jacket, breathing in the faint clean smell of the expensive after-shave lotion I had grown used to in the little house's bathroom. Too soon, we arrived at the gate; too soon, and without seeming to notice what a bleak yawning gap it left in the universe, he dropped my arm. The gate creaked open, and beyond the tangled bushes I could see that the lights were on. Kate must be back.

I was wrong. When Max opened the front door a pink-and-ochre whirlwind flung itself at him, then bounced up and down in front of me, flapping its hands.

'I'm here! I'm here! I couldn't wait, it's so exciting, and I had the meanest letter from Prof. Harding about my vac. work, Mummy read it down the phone to Marco's house, in a doomy voice. She always opens my bloody post. Cow. So I thought I'd better come back early.'

'How did you get in?' asked Max, removing one of Marienka's long pale hairs from his shoulder. 'Was Kate here?'

'No-oh! I got in through the coalhouse window, the taxi man gave me a leg-up.'

'We *have* to fix that window,' said Max. 'What the hell are those?'

Marienka's haul of oil paintings was stacked against the dining-room table, with two large suitcases. In addition there was an eight-foot-long copper hunting-horn, a stone sculpture of a naked boy with one hand missing, a case of wine and a hessian sack.

'The sack's best. Look!' She wrenched it open and pulled

out a large, beautiful air-dried ham, two salamis, a huge panettone in a cardboard box, and more cardboard, wrapped tightly round two tubes like a giant set of binoculars. Ripping at the packaging, she revealed two enormous bottles of single malt whisky, of a brand I had never seen before.

'For Max. Max only drinks top whisky,' she said, and planted a kiss on his lips. 'Marco bought it, said it's for his dear brother-in-law's dear friend's wife's brother. That comes out quite well in Italian. And he sends mille basia. That's a thousand kisses, in Latin.'

'It's a bit outside your excise limit, isn't it?' said Max, looking with fond awe at the labels.

'Thousand kisses? Nah, you're allowed five thousand at Customs.' Marienka was swirling round the room now, prodding things, exclaiming in excitement.

'I meant the booze. Case of wine and two litres of whisky?'

'God, you're a prig. Isn't he a prig, Sally? Has he been lining you all up for morning prayers?'

'I just wondered how you got it through,' said Max mildly.

'Marco doesn't do Customs. He got his cousin Ernesto to land me at Kidlington in his pr-rr-ivate jet.'

'No!'

'Seriously?'

Max and I were united again, this time in awe at Marienka's glamour. When he had borne off the bottles to the kitchen, I said to her, 'It is serious, then? You and Marco?'

'Christ, no!' She stared at me in amazement. 'Marco and I had a fabulous time. But he's got to marry some rich Contessa soon and go into the family firm in Torino. And I wouldn't want to live in Turin, not for anything. Ugh. No. We just had fun. Might have some more later on. What about you? How's the rustic childhood sweetheart?'

'Sour,' I said, grimacing, and Marienka clapped me on the

back saying, 'Good. You can do better.' Without waiting for a response she began hauling her things up the stairs.

When Kate came back, gently glowing from her evening with Ted, she found the three of us sprawled around the dining-room table, drinking Laphroaig out of Perspex toothmugs and ganging up on Marienka over her desire to obscure half the wall with a morose portrait of her ancestor the bishop.

'He had six mistresses, you know,' she said with hauteur. 'He wasn't just any old bish.'

'Then,' said Max sternly, 'he'll be happier with a woman to look at. Put in him in your room, he gives me the horrors.' She sparkled at him, and giggled, and reached again for the whisky bottle.

5

It grew cold, with a dank frost-hollow Midlands chill which we had never experienced during our warm sheltered lives in college. We kept the Rayburn roaring all day, and often crept down at three in the morning to make sure it would last the night. If someone else did it (usually Kate) the friendly clanking of the hod was a wonderful sound to hear as you burrowed under your blankets or lay watching your icy breath rise against the glimmer of the street lamp outside. I was writing about Keats during that term and *The Eve of St Agnes* ran through my head. *Ah, bitter chill it was! The owl, for all his feathers, was a-cold.* When I was half asleep at my desk, drowsy after one of our panfuls of rice and mushrooms, the poet's world seemed more real than my own. I saw the old monk's breath rising like incense, the sheep huddled in their woolly fold and the very statues freezing in their mail-coats. I was exalted at that time, drunk on a thousand years of words. I would murmur them to myself as I walked alone by the canal, looking up at the sky, always ready to read wonders there, *huge cloudy symbols of a high romance.*

Max and Kate found an army surplus store with a lot of old grey blankets for fifty pence each, and brought home a bundle; we shared them out and Max tacked up two of them over the windows in the dining room, so that the heat from the kitchen would not seep out through the rattling old sash windows. The rest of the house was freezing, for we dared not use up too much power on fan heaters and the decrepit radiators seemed not to function at all, despite all Max's manly assaults on them with an L-shaped key he found in the kitchen drawer. By night, Marienka did best because her room was right above the kitchen and the stove. Kate sometimes slept over at Ted's on really cold nights, although she came home tired from trying to cling on and not tumble out of his single bed. Max and I just piled on the army blankets by night and worked in libraries for most of the day. In the evening, in the dining room, the pinned-up blankets created a tent-like cosiness while he and I sat across the table from one another wrapped in more blankets, studying. Sometimes, on days when we were trying to do without the electric heater, I would look up and see our pale breaths entwining in the air between us under the plastic lampshade. Oh, I was happy then: happier, I thought, than I had ever been in my life. Marienka, coming in from some party in her bright pink maxi-coat, would laugh at us over her fur collar and cry, 'Peasants! Huddled round the samovar again, comrades? You'll never get to Moscow that way.'

Max rarely spoke of his home, but one weekend he was summoned home for 'a family meeting', and returned on Sunday evening pale and tired. The three of us girls were sprawled around the living-room table, experimenting with some nail varnish Marienka had bought at the market. The smell of varnish and acetone hung on the thick air: our nails were unwholesome dark-red talons. We shifted the paraphernalia to make room for him, but he stood by the door, silhouetted against the glimmer from the street lamp. He looked cross, as if we were somehow in the way.

'Had a jolly time?' asked Kate, dabbing at her thumbnail to see if it was dry. 'Bet it was warmer than here.'

'Not jolly,' he said stiffly. 'If you must know, Marty's been caught with some drugs. Hash and two tablets of LSD,' he said. 'My weekend job was to persuade him to wear a tie and behave in court tomorrow.'

'You aren't going to court with him?' asked Kate. 'Wouldn't that be best?'

'No. My mother wanted me to, but I'm sick of the whole business.' He sighed. 'It won't make any difference. He's pleading guilty and they won't shut him up. Christ!' I had never seen him so grim, his mouth set, his eyes hard. 'Marty's just bloody impossible. Might do him good if he did serve time.'

'Callous beast,' said Marienka, yawning and squinting at her hand. 'I think Marty's fab.'

'You look tired, Max. There's a drain of whisky left.' I was the only one who cared, clearly, and he smiled at me to acknowledge this. Then he shook his head and shrugged his shoulders as if to cast off all the worries of the weekend and his wayward little brother, and went into the hall, returning a moment later with a big soft bundle under his arm.

'Some good came of it, anyway. I borrowed these off my Ma,' he said. 'In winter she only ever drifts between a house heated like a Turkish bath and a taxi to Harvey Nicks. She won't miss them.' He unrolled a bundle of the finest, softest cashmere shawls, and flung them round our shoulders. Mine was pink, the size of half a sheet; Kate's baby-blue, Marienka's a stinging green. For himself, he shucked on a large, fluffy, patterned brown poncho which produced shouts of mirth as his serious face and elegantly cut hair emerged from the hole.

'David brought it back from a business trip to Argentina,' he said. 'He thought Marty might like it. Poor bastard, he does try.' The bleak look returned to his face, but he banished it with an obvious, conscious effort. 'Marty doesn't like anything to do with David, so he said I could have it.'

Marienka rushed upstairs and fetched a wide-brimmed black felt hat, which she crammed on his head.

'The picture is completed,' she said. 'Our hero the gaucho strides out to do battle with the sabre-toothed llama of the

– um – tundra.' She loved to wind up Kate for being a geographer. Max looked in the mirror which Marienka had hung on the chimney-breast, struck a few attitudes and seemed not displeased.

'I actually look rather fabulous,' he said. 'And so do all of you. Birds of Paradise. Shall we go to the pub?'

'I ought to work, but it *is* Monty Python night,' said Kate. We had resolved, in the dual interests of economy and Finals, that we would not have a television in the house, but some programmes drew us powerfully down to the Auger & Mallet on the corner, where beer was cheap and the heating efficient. We shuddered along the road, Marienka skipping a little to keep warm and flapping her green shawl wings, and Kate slipped into the phone box to invite Ted to join us. Once we were all inside, Max went to get the beers and Marienka spotted someone she knew and darted off to see him.

I found a small windowseat, just wide enough for two and with a view of the TV over the bar, and sat praying silently that Max would see the space and join me while the others milled around. He did. He flopped on the seat, pushed my beer across to me and smiled, and we watched *Monty Python's Flying Circus* feeling the comfortable warmth of one another's arms and thighs.

Such – and no more – were my joys during that autumn term. But if I could have stopped time for ever in that half-hour, with the beer bitter on my tongue, John Cleese on the screen and the shake of Max's laughter warm against my side, I would have done so.

I learned more about Max's brother Martin over the succeeding days: I daresay he needed someone to tell, and the other two girls had crowded emotional and social lives of their own. I, on the other hand, was an empty bucket, neglecting my dull old college compeers and yawning like a hungry baby bird for any scrap of information connected to Max. Martin, he told me, had his fine paid by his hated stepfather. He seemed – according to his elder brother – neither remorseful nor very interested in his own disgrace.

'I think he smokes quite a lot of hash,' said Max. 'I do sometimes wonder if that's what's doing it. Making him so – detached.'

'Lots of people smoke,' I said. 'Marienka does, a fair bit.'

'Well, we've all *tried* it,' he admitted. 'Socially. You have, haven't you?'

'Once.' I hesitated; generally, Max did not show much curiosity about me, and in my daft humility I expected no more; but on this occasion, something in my tone made him cock his head on one side and look at me with kindly curiosity. We were making supper; he was peeling mushrooms, something I could never see the point of but which kept him at my side while I sweated the rice and onions in the last of the butter.

'Only once? Didn't you like it, Salamander?' He was given to these whimsical nicknames: Kate was Katerina to him, as often as not. Marienka, obviously, needed no polysyllabic ornamentation.

'I got taken – too far.' I did not know how to explain it to him. Because I was not a smoker, I did not know how to inhale and the joints we passed from hand to hand as daring freshmen had no effect on me. But in our first summer term, after she saw the film *I love you Alice B Toklas*, Marienka had baked hash brownies and given me a couple, and for the first time I experienced the proper effect of marijuana.

I did not, however, become woozy and warm and pleased with life, the way the others did. I became intensely anxious, overactive, filled with a confused sense of dread: colours were too bright, noises too loud, people's faces full of unreadable menace. I went to bed and suffered nightmares, and screamed and woke the whole corridor. There was talk from my 'moral tutor' of referring me to the college's retained psychiatrist. For days afterwards I moved around in a cloud of unfocused shame. The shame had endured sufficiently to make me bury the incident and never even mention it to Marienka.

But I could not have secrets from Max. I tried to explain it to him, haltingly at first but then, under his kind prompting, more fluently. When I had finished he said: 'You're what they call a sensitive. Some people just are. It's one of the problems with drugs. You can have something which ninety-nine people just enjoy as a bit of a buzz, then the hundredth goes paranoid on it. My stepfather talks about it, I think he knew someone once.'

'I felt a fool,' I said. 'A complete idiot.'

'Well, you shouldn't. Just because Marienka's got the contitution of a particularly *in*sensitive buffalo . . .!'

At that moment, looking into that brotherly, irresistible smile, I knew with sudden clarity that I must save myself. Either Max must love me or I must stop loving Max. It was probably the first glimmer of sanity in the whole history of my relationship with this man.

I should have held that insight, hung onto the thought and turned my face resolutely away from him. Perhaps I should have moved back into college. But then – because I had stopped cooking as I faltered out my tale – he took the chopped mushrooms, tipped them into my pan, gave it a shake, and poured on the stock. And he turned back towards me, put both hands on my shoulders, and kissed me on the cheek, lightly and fondly.

'Salamander!' he said. 'Poor sweet. Freaking out like that. A hug's what you need.' I hugged him back with suitable briskness and moved away, flushed, to stir the steaming pan.

Never seek to tell thy love
Love that never told can be . . .

But it was Yeats not Blake, whom I took to bed with me
that night. Yeats, mourning for his hopeless love, for *that great*
nobleness of hers, the fire that stirs about her when she stirs . . .
O Heart! O Heart! If she'd but turn her head, you'd know the
folly of being comforted.

I would not be comforted. I would hope, till all the seas
gang dry. Love like mine, I knew from poetry and story, did
not go unrewarded. In earth or heaven I would receive reward.
Viola was on my side, and patient Griselda, and Marty South
in *The Woodlanders*, and Troilus in the moonlight sighing his
soul towards the Trojan walls.

As I bent to my work on those cold nights the poets fluttered like angels around me, reassuring and reinforcing the
glimpse of infinity I saw in the young man bent over his
books on the far side of the table. They were with me, on
my side, all of them: Shakespeare and Shelley, Lovelace and
Robbie Burns, every lovelorn maid or courtly swain from
Catullus to Auden. *Lay your sleeping head, my love . . .*

I cannot blame the poets: I conscripted them and made
them my allies, disregarding every warning they gave and
twisting every meaning. Madness; but how could I turn away
from such a madness?

It was almost Christmas. We had decided to stay on after
term, since the rent was paid anyway; money was tight, it
was still pretty cold, but a sort of family solidarity made us
reluctant to separate and scatter in early December as most
of our friends did. Marienka was, for the first time since I
had known her, working very seriously. 'I *really* had better
get a 2:1.' Kate divided her time between Ted's digs and the
house, and eventually left a week before the rest of us to stay
with her fiancé's family. So on December the 20th there were

just the three of us, tidying the house and saying goodbye beside the cold canal.

'You ought to take the shawls back, really,' said Marienka to Max, plucking reluctantly at the green fringe of hers. 'Your ma is going to be furious.'

'No. She won't notice. It'll be even colder next term. God, you really feel it when that stove goes out, don't you?' Max shivered, drawing his ridiculous poncho close around him. Marienka had been sent flowers by a besotted admirer at Magdalen, and had stuck a tulip in the band of Max's black hat. He looked exotic and boyish and beloved; I could hardly take my eyes off his smooth, serious, angular face.

'Is Annette going to be with you over Christmas?' asked Marienka casually.

'Yeah, that's the idea,' said Max. 'Oh, look, there's my lift.' A college friend with a car had promised to drive him home, but had no room for the other Londoner, Marienka. 'I'm sorry you're stuck with the train, girls –'

As the car pulled away I asked, as lightly as I knew how, 'Who's Annette?'

'His girlfriend. She's been in New York, on a picture-restoring course. She stays with his family in London, doesn't get on with hers too well. Oh goody, there's our taxi.'

I followed her, heart going like a trip-hammer, hardly able to control my voice when eventually I asked, still deadly casual: 'Are they a serious thing, then?'

'Oh, I think they'll get married. Family thinks so. Lot of hints being dropped at Sue's wedding. Really suitable, all that. She was going to be a dancer, very pretty. But he's a cold fish really.'

'He never talks about her.' I could not help a note of protest in my voice, but Marienka, rummaging in her bag, did not seem to notice.

'Nah,' she said vaguely. 'Out of sight, out of mind.'

'But he's faithful. I mean, there haven't been any girls—'

'Cold fish. Told you. Mister Fastidious. He can do without the temptations of the flesh. I used to think he was queer, but – oh shit!'

Marienka, preoccupied with turning out her expensive but much-abused leather bag to see if any pound notes had been lost in the lining, appeared not to notice the crumbling of my world. 'Can you lend me a fiver towards the train fare?'

I handed it to her, a willing payment for the service she had done me. Once again I knew in a moment of prosaic, chilly clarity what I must do with my rebel heart: quench it, crush it, tell it the score.

But we had all exchanged addresses, and on Christmas Eve a packet came, addressed in the beautiful flowing italics I knew all too well. There was a pink silk scarf, figured with scribbled ink drawings of Venice and edged in gold, and a card saying: *To Sally, the heart of the home. With love and thanks for many a fine supper – Max.*

So I dreamed again, through all the candle-fire and singing of the Midnight Mass, and all through the family rejoicing at brother Ben's engagement to a sensible Leading Wren from Gosport. Alone at midnight on a frosty New Year's Eve, wound into my new scarf, I wrote my name in my new diary and made all the wrong resolutions.

6

From schooldays onwards every teacher, pupil and parent knows that Easter terms are harder than Christmas terms. They should not be, surely; spring is coming and the year rising up instead of dying into ever darker evenings. But for some reason – winter weariness, festive letdown, February colds – Easter (or Hilary, at the older universities) is, and always will be, the worst of terms.

In the house by the canal we four felt it: still shivering, still struggling with the brutal chipped iron boiler, still fretting over our work. Marienka, inevitably, was the least affected by seasonal tristesse. She went to parties two or three times a week, as her social circle extended ever wider (and, I noticed, ever wealthier). She seemed to have given up on her spurt of conscientious studying and replaced it with a determination to use every remaining minute of her student life to the best advantage.

'I'll never get accepted for postgraduate unless it's a poxy teaching diploma, and anyway postgrads are poor sad old donkeys, mainly,' she announced one evening, earning herself a playful punch from Max. 'So my motto is eat, drink and get laid, for tomorrow we die.'

From time to time she dragged me along with her, because it had suddenly become a project of hers to get me paired off. In her simple narrative, I had broken with my childhood sweetheart Trevor and was in need of cheering up. In the chilly bedroom, with the fan-heater blowing hopelessly at our legs, she smoothed and trimmed my rogue hair and came at me with fistfuls of cosmetics. I had grown thinner since the summer, and she lent me various rainbow-coloured dresses and ridiculously short tunics; for one party she persuaded me into a pair of black velvet shorts – 'hot pants' in the idiom of the day – with a huge filigree green-and-gold butterfly sewn across the crotch. I thought them a touch obscene and said so, but once she had teamed them with some silver boots of Kate's, she dragged me downstairs to parade in front of Max.

'Male opinion, please!' she cried. 'Is this, or is this not, just the very look for Sally?'

'Lovely,' said Max. 'Suits you. Very gamine.' So, of course, I kept the outfit on and the butterfly rampant across my groin. I dressed for Max, even though he was not coming to the party. That night, once Marienka had dumped me among a crowd of noisy, healthy oarsmen and heirs to baronetcies, I did my best to flirt. I had moderate success. Marienka, stripped to her underwear and dancing like a dervish, had more. Over the deafeningly distorted sound of the Rolling Stones a big blond boy called Donald asked me where I lived, and offered to walk me home later. I inclined my head, hoping he would forget all about it, but half an hour later while I was looking for my coat he reappeared and gallantly insisted. It was frosty, and he took my arm on the slippery pavement of St Aldate's; we slithered along together, laughing a little at the difficulty, and then he drew me into an alley just before the police station and kissed me.

'Note,' he said, 'I am doing this in full view of the filth. You have only to scream and rescue will come. That's the sort of gentleman I am.'

I giggled. He kissed me again. But at that moment a terrible hollowness seemed to open inside me. The wrong kiss, the wrong man, could never fill the void. I had tried to believe Marienka's line that I just needed a bit of flirtatious fun to jolt me into normality: but this unfortunate youth was the litmus test that proved the theory futile.

'I'm sorry,' I said. 'There's someone – the fact is I'm not over someone else. You go back. Find a nice girl.' He was a kind boy, and held my arm as he protested gently that I was the nicest girl he had met for weeks; I tore away from him and ran down the road, slithering absurdly, making for the safety of the little house. He did not follow.

When I got in Max's light was on, a thin line glowing beneath his door. I spent a while in the dining room and kitchen, moving around and clattering mugs in the hope he would come out and share some cocoa with me as he often did. But there was no sound from his room, except once a kind of sigh, as if he were falling asleep with the light on; I went sadly alone to bed.

I must have caught a cold that night in my silly shorts. I became quite ill and spent two days in bed, missing a tutorial. Kate brought me up drinks and, when I could face it, beans on toast. Marienka drifted in and out. When neither of the girls were around, Max would bring me tea and toast and sit for a while. Miserably aware of my red nose and greasy hair I shrank from him at first. But on the third day, when I was round the house in my dressing-gown, he made me cocoa and stoked up the stove, and we sat together at the tiny kitchen table. It seemed there was something he wanted to unburden himself about. I listened, sniffing occasionally into the lavatory paper which was cheaper than tissues (exponentially cheaper, indeed, since Marienka generally stole a roll or two every time she went into college).

'I wanted to ask you something, now we're on our own,' he said, and my treacherous heart leapt. Then it dropped like a stone as he continued, 'It's about my brother.'

I settled to listen; at least I could be his counsellor in something that mattered to him.

'One of the conditions of his probation is that he under-takes some education or training over the next twelve months. He's rather surprisingly opted to do a photography course. David's done some research, and there's a good one at the Oxford Poly. It's a summer thing, three months from April. I know you three have got Finals at the end of May, but I was wondering – I mean . . . this house would be so good for him . . .'

He looked unusually shy, uncertain of his ground, and his deep green eyes were on me. There was a fleck of gold in the left one. I can see it now. He pushed aside his soft fore-lock and grinned, vulnerable as I had rarely seen him, and so entrancing to me that I could hardly speak.

'You want him to live here?' I said stupidly. 'But there's no more rooms.'

'He could have a camp bed in my room for a week or two, and then – well, Marienka did say she was going straight off after Finals, and hers finish really early . . . he could pay her share of the rent . . .'

'Why are you asking *me*?' I blew my nose, defiantly, at this man who would not see that I was not some kind of spare sister.

'Because you're so sensible and so good. You'll know straight away if it's something I shouldn't even be asking.'

'What you mean is that you want me to make the case to Kate and Marienka.' There was a flicker of pleasure in being, however briefly, a bit hard on him. I had so little power that this tiny taste was welcome. He looked duly embarrassed.

'Well, Kate did say – she wasn't a hundred per cent – but yes, I suppose I am asking that. Haven't raised it with Marienka at all.' He dropped his eyes for a moment, then looked me full in the face, destroying every defence.

'Look, Sal.' He sipped his cocoa, wiping the foam from his lip with fastidious care. 'This Marty thing is really causing a lot of grief in our family. My mother and David quarrel about him. Sue puts her oar in, but she's not much help and she's off in France with Peter's job. Marty just drifts around, high as a kite most of the time, sneering at everybody. I'm the only one who can help.' He looked at me and added, 'And you can help me . . .'

'Will you be able to work if he's around?' I asked, solicitous.

'Well . . . I don't fancy it any more than you do, but it's a sort of duty for me. I do know that it's not your duty, though. But the extra rent might help. David's willing to pay – over the odds actually – and it'd be a godsend for my mother to have Marty living away from home but someone keeping an eye on him. She gets really wound up by the way he snipes at David. I'd like to do them a favour, David's been so good to me.'

I sighed. He looked so beautiful, so earnest, this newly altruistic Max. I imagined him as mentor and counsellor to his troubled little brother, looking down gravely with a warm hand on the lad's shoulder. Perhaps I imagined myself at his side, a compassionate but humorously down-to-earth sister-in-law, part of the family.

'Perhaps,' I said carefully, 'it would be a good idea if he came down for a weekend. So we could all meet him.'

Max stared at me. 'That is *brilliant*,' he said. 'Of *course*.' I basked in this immoderate praise for a commonplace idea, and luxuriated in his smile. He had a way of smiling, Max, which made you feel as if you were the only person who could ever matter to him.

And then he frowned and said, 'Tell you what, he could come next weekend. Annette could drive him.'

I must have looked disconcerted, for he wrinkled his brow again and said, 'Oh. Didn't Marienka pass it on? She said it'd be all right. Annette – a friend of mine – is coming down to see someone at the Ashmolean about a job. I said she could stay.'

'Your girlfriend,' I said, as levelly as I could. 'Oh yes, I'd heard about her. Marienka knows her.'

'Well, girlfriend . . .' said Max with an air I could not quite define.

In the event Annette did not bring Martin Bellinger with her; I rather gathered from various remarks of Marienka's that this boy Marty disliked Annette almost as much as he disliked his stepfather, certainly enough to regard a car journey in her company as a penance. He would, Max told us at Friday supper, be coming on his own 'in a week or two'. I took heart from the fact that Max's brother did not like his girlfriend. I knew how much these things mattered in a close family: my own brother had been visibly anxious at Christmas that I should approve of Chloe the Leading Wren. It is ironic, the way the child of a happy family expects all families to function in the same way as her own.

On Saturday morning Annette herself came: an immaculate creature, tiny and graceful, with hair blue-black like a raven's wing and formed into a perfect ballerina's chignon behind her pearl-studded ears. She stood on tiptoe to kiss Max – I noticed that he hardly bothered to bend his head for this tribute – and offered the three of us girls a reserved smile. We were sitting round the table in an unusually tidy dining room, with the stove stoked up and the army blankets temporarily removed from the windows, since it was a bright and mild late February day and we had been starting to feel as if we lived in a cave.

'Coffee?' said Kate. 'Sally's made some amazing biscuits.' And indeed I had: my mother's recipe, soft chewy American cookies with raisins and powdered cocoa and cheap broken nuts from the market.

'I'd love a black coffee,' said Annette in a high, precise, well-bred voice tempered by a slight New York twang. She drank about half of the coffee Kate made but did not touch the biscuits. When we had made desultory conversation for a quarter of an hour she looked at her watch and said peremptorily to Max: 'We ought to go now. If we're to drop in on Eddie Aken before lunch.'

Kate and I goggled. Sir Edward Aken was legendary: former vice-chancellor, scholar and wit, a pinnacle of academic society. The sunshine of his regard was not widely available to ordinary students like ourselves.

'He's a kind of relative. Or God-something,' muttered Max, when he had helped Annette into her coat and come back for his own. 'She likes to check in when she's here.'

When they had gone, Kate merely shook her head in dour admiration and muttered, 'Sty-lish!' But Marienka pursed her lips, jutted out a hip and swept her untidy blond mane back into a bun in imitation of Annette.

'Eowww. Chilly bitch,' she said. 'She never changes. God, those two. Can't imagine them in bed, can you? Like two ice cubes clinking together.'

I could, though, and it was the worse for me. Annette stayed that night, presumably in Max's single bed; in the morning, still immaculate, she swept into the kitchen in her silk dressing-gown and leaned on the stove while Max made her coffee and I quietly ate toast in the corner. She was, I noticed, gazing around her with disfavour at the shabby kitchen, the worn lino and the peeling paint. Her pearl-pink silk mules crunched on some grains of coke from the hod, and she looked down, pained.

'It's nice being by the canal, instead of on some howling traffickey bit of Iffley Road,' said Max defensively, following her glance. 'We're comfortable here.'

'How can you be?' said Annette crushingly. 'It's freezing.'

'You've been in New York too long,' replied her lover. 'They turn the heating up way too high. It's unhealthy.'

Annette looked up at the ceiling, where a damp patch had

been gradually spreading throughout the term. The basin leaked a little upstairs. The landlord's agent knew about it, but did not care. Once we were out the whole place would undoubtedly be gutted and gentrified, using the money we had paid in rent. Meanwhile a few drips and stains were for us to put up with.

'Yes. I see. New York's obviously more unhealthy than this,' she said, and her dry attempt to amuse fizzled and expired. 'Anyway, I grant you it'll probably be quite pretty in summer, with those Babylonica willows across the canal.'

I can remember, bewilderingly, that I hated her even more for knowing the variety of our willows, something we had never given a thought to. Later Marienka told me that Annette's family had a large estate in Kent and her father Adrian Devereaux was a renowned plantsman. She left that night, after she and Max had come in from a dinner party and remained closeted in his room talking through most of the evening.

Looking back now with the experience of middle-age, I can see that she must have felt painfully excluded and threatened by Max's houseful of females, all of us so much at home in this ramshackle, bohemian little house in our motley shawls and woollies. I do not really know whether she loved him, or felt much passion for him. I preferred to think not, for to me in my heightened and hysterical state poor Annette loomed as the enemy of all joy and all fulfilment. I allowed myself to hate her and to interpret her reserve as hostility and snobbery. Marienka clearly disliked her for subtle reasons of her own; in terms of class and upbringing they were perhaps too similar to like one another. Kate was largely indifferent, remarking only that she thought there was 'a touch of inbreeding' there and that picture-restoring was becoming quite a vogue among Sloane Square girls, like china-mending.

After this visit I went into a decline. There is no other way to describe it. Somehow, for three-quarters of a year I had allowed this passion for Max to spread roots in every level of myself. Emotionally I had become utterly dependent on his approval. Nothing I achieved or said seemed to count unless he smiled on it. Physically I longed for him. Spiritually, I had confused him with every half-glimpsed, yearning arche-type that ever glimmered through a stained-glass window or echoed in a motet. Domestically I had grown accustomed to him, and loved every mannerism and phrase and idiosyn-crasy as, I supposed, a long-married wife might love her husband. We had dragged in the coke together for the boiler, enticed next door's cat in for a saucer of milk, cooked together, steadied one another's legs while standing on tiptoe on a chair draping blankets over the draughty windows. We were almost Darby and Joan: we had laughed over Marienka's antics and romances like a pair of fond exasperated parents and often sat together of an evening with our books, the lamp between us.

It was difficult to accept that he was nothing but a student flatmate, soon to be swept away on the tide of adult life. It was now even harder to accept that he belonged to another woman, a cool enigma in a shiny black chignon who shared his bed but seemed, in the morning, quite unmoved by the experience. After Annette's visit something broke inside me. My cold grew worse, I refused invitations, would not go to the pub and skipped another tutorial. I could barely eat and stayed in bed most of the day, frowsting with the fan heater on, not even caring about the electricity bill.

That was the point when Marienka came and sat on the end of my bed in her blue velvet jacket and pixie shimmer of pale hair, fixing me with her sharp blue eyes, digging her elbow into my legs as she lounged.

'Sally,' she began abruptly. 'What the fuck is the matter

with you?' The word was not as commonly used then as now, and it carried corresponding emphasis.

'I've got a cold, that's all.'

'No, it's not. Something's bugging you. Something or some-one. Spill. That great hulking rowing boy, Donald or whatever his name was, at the Christchurch party. He came back and said he really liked you but you were a hopeless case, mooning about someone in secret. S'true, isn't it?'

I had carried the worm in my heart for too long alone. I was hungry and weak and tearful and I crumbled before her brisk insistence.

'Well, OK. There's someone I'm keen on. He's not keen on me.'

Marienka sat up a little, looked at me with close critical attention, then slumped back onto her elbow, and took an interest in the candlewick patterns on the old bedspread.

'How d'you know?' she said after a moment. 'That he's not keen? I have a little bit of news for you, Sally. Most men are keen if you're keen. They're made that way. They follow the line of least resistance. *Keeping* them keen might be a struggle if you're that way inclined, which in general I am not. But not the first bit. Getting started is the easy thing: whisk them into bed. Then, when that's over with and they've had a pretty damn good time, you can take it from there.'

She broke off, looking at me now with exasperated fond-ness. A new idea had occurred to her. 'Are you playing hard to get, you old virgin, you? Hanging on for this man to give you a diamond ring?'

'No! He hasn't – he doesn't even know I—' The edge of tears was close, but the forbidden delight of confiding was too strong for me to pull away completely from her assault.

'Who is he?' demanded Marienka fiercely. Her eyes glit-tered, her hair seemed to lift on her scalp, a pale golden halo with a crackling energy of its own. 'Who is this bastard who refuses to lay siege to your increasingly moth-eaten virtue? Fool! You're a prize, a jackpot, a pot of gold, you are. Bright, beautiful, sweet as pie. Look good in shorts. You can cook. Dream girl. Who's this blind idiot?'

'I can't say who.' Max was downstairs; I could hear him in the kitchen crashing the coke-hod and laughing at something with Kate. My instinct for self-preservation was just strong enough to keep his name from Marienka.

'Well. Has he got a girl?'

'I think so. Not sure how serious.'

'Does he *really* not know he is the light of your life?'

'No.'

'Tell him, then. For God's sake. Life is not a rehearsal. Otherwise you'll both meet up again when you're sixty-four and you'll tell him you fancied him, and he will say, "O no, if I had only known, my life has been a wasted desert." See?'

'How on earth could I? Tell him?'

I was, in spite of myself, fascinated. Marienka, after all, had a dazzling track record of attracting men; if they never stayed around for long it was by her choice.

'Well. Come out with it. I suppose you're too shy to just bloody well proposition him.'

'Yes.'

'So do it with a gesture. Have a bubble bath, then wrap yourself up like a lovely big birthday present smelling wonderful and covered in silk. And be waiting in his bed when he gets there, saying "Ta-raa! Surprise" If he's in college –' she added practically '– you can always get the key off the scouts if you bat your eyelashes a bit. Or pick one up off the hook on their trolley while they do the room before, they nearly always leave it on the landing, and they've got masses of duplicates probably.'

I laughed at her for this piece of prosaic tradecraft, but then she uttered the words which chimed so fatally with my

own fancy. I had, remember, erected a great ornate structure of devotion: a dim cathedral of the mind designed to
keep out the light of common reason. In that deceptive space
Marienka unwittingly lit a candle.

'Love's supposed to be a gift, isn't it?' she mused. 'You
don't buy people presents then hang about waiting for them
to come and ask for them. If you want to give your all to
him, just hand it over. The worst he can do is turn it down.
Then you know where you are, don't you? Death or glory.
Tell! Go! Just do it! Give the gift!'

I stared at her, sitting upright now, suddenly aware of
my sweaty frowsty body and my faded old pyjamas. A gift!
Marienka, no doubt, thought of the manoeuvre in terms of
offering a present, shrugging off a refusal and promptly
bestowing it elsewhere with a smile. I saw it as far more momentous: a Galahad devotion, a nun's final vow. *Given not lent, and
not withdrawn, once sent*, like in the poem my father always
quoted in his Christmas Eve sermon. The point lay in the
giving, the refusal to conceal or withhold. *Not withdrawn, once
sent*. I would not let the worm destroy my dark secret heart. I
would be a troubadour, a Viola, a faithful Liu in *Turandot* willing
to endure humiliation and torture for a man even if he would
never love me. I would be brave. I would make my love known
and never withdraw it. That would have irresistible power.
Wouldn't it?

Heroic warmth flooded over me. At last I had a plan of
action. Perhaps the feverish cold helped a bit. Remember, I
was not yet twenty-one.

'Maybe I will,' I said to Marienka. 'Thanks.'

'Good! I'll tell the others you're cured of greensickness –'
She rose to go downstairs.

'Don't! Not yet! Please! Marienka, please – they'll
laugh—'

'Max won't laugh. He's like Heidi's grandfather where

you're concerned. He thinks you're sweet. He told Annette so, when she said—'

She paused, hand over her mouth, stifling a guilty giggle. 'Sorry.'

'Said what? I don't care, I don't like her either.'

'Well, she said you seemed a bit *young*. Max was up there defending you, at my expense I must say, with choice remarks about how good it was to have someone around who wasn't a world-weary old tramp —' She was laughing outright now. 'Cheeky bastard!'

I swung my legs out of bed and picked up my towel from the floor. 'Well, to hell with Annette. And that's very rude of Max. I don't think you're a weary old tramp.'

'Oh, I am, though! You know I don't do *ro-mance*.'

'But really, don't tell anybody what I said about being in love.' I was looking around for my wash-bag. 'Or I'll kill you. I'm coming down for supper, I feel better.'

'Good. Kate got some chicken bits from the market, and Max is making something Moroccan with dried fruit.'

She left me to wash and comb myself into presentability; as the fruity, spicy smells wafted up the cold stairway I found, for the first time in days, that I was hungry.

7

I carried my gift around with me for four days more, wanting to become strong again and as beautiful as I knew how. I took more care with my hair and clothes, borrowed Marienka's mascara, stood up straight and moved around on a cloud of proud hope. Max was affectionate, pleased that I was better. He proffered the occasional brotherly hug. Annette's name was never mentioned, nor did he seem to get any letters from her.

But another distracting cloud hung over our lives: Kate was out a great deal, working late hours in the library, and I got a whisper of a suggestion that all was not quite well between her and Ted. On the third evening she came back at five, slammed the door and went straight to her room on the other side of the landing from mine and Marienka's. This was unusual enough for me to go and tap timidly on her door.

'Are you OK? Do you fancy some coffee or anything?'

Kate looked up at me, her face pale, her usual healthy prettiness overlaid with something grim and dogged: she looked, I suddenly thought, as I had imagined her dour Yorkshire granny to look, back home in Bridlington.

'You may as well know,' she said gruffly. 'Ted and I have broken up. Finished.'

'You and *Ted?*' I was too scandalized and astonished for tact. 'But you're engaged. You're so good together – I thought if *anyone* could last the course—'

'Well, you were wrong. And so was I. It doesn't matter.'

She clearly wanted me to go away, so I did. An hour later, just as I was getting ready for bed, Marienka breezed into my room without knocking, as usual, and sat on the bed.

'Kate's engagement's off,' I said immediately. 'Did you know?'

'Not surprised,' said Marienka, very surprisingly indeed. 'He wasn't ever happy about her little fling. Surprised he took so long to flounce off. Stupid bastard, it probably never meant anything. I can't imagine why she told him, but that's gritty Yorkshire honesty for you.'

'What – fling?' I was both astonished and furious. I had thought that Kate talked to me as confidentially as she talked to the volatile Marienka, if not more.

'Oh – sorry.' My friend was disconcerted, and offered a type of engaging, girlish, 'oops-silly-me!' smile which I particularly detested in her. 'Of course, you've been ill. She only told me a week ago, probably didn't want to worry you with it.'

She was lying. I knew exactly why I had not been told: in matters of sexual adventure I was considered an outsider, a vicar's daughter with different standards. Kate had probably thought I would disapprove of her infidelity to Ted, whereas Marienka would understand. Hurt and embarrassed, I fidgeted with the bedcovers and wished she would go away.

'How's *your* campaign going?' she asked, changing the subject. 'Told him? The mystery man?'

'No. I haven't. Not yet. But tell me about Kate. What's been going on? This fling, who was he?'

'Oh, something and nothing,' said Marienka, a touch evasively I thought. 'Look, least said soonest mended. I promised I'd shut up about it. But look – if it was a stupid mistake, at least she went out and made it. You have to try things, don't you? If it wasn't a mistake, then good luck to her. And if she still wants Ted, he'll probably come round, if she tells him the other thing's over. Now, Sal – you're changing the subject again. I asked about your chap, what gives? It's time you flung that fling.'

'Me – changing the subject? You are!'

'No,' said Marienka. 'The point is, Kate followed an instinct and now she thinks it was a mistake. Probably. But at least she did it. What you're doing is just *stagnating*, keeping yourself folded up on the shelf for Sunday, and Sunday might never come . . .'

I sat upright then, and kicked at her through the bedclothes. 'Just piss off, will you? Stop trying to push everyone around till they're as promiscuous as you are – we're all different.'

'Suit yourself,' said Marienka, who by the look of her was not entirely displeased at having provoked a reaction.

She had provoked one, all right. I cried myself to sleep and woke the next day with a new determination. Finding Max and Kate half asleep over the breakfast table and Marienka nowhere in sight, I asked who was in for supper, since it was my turn to cook. My heart was in my mouth. I knew what answer I wanted.

'I am,' said Max, 'tonight, but not tomorrow, I've got supper with my supervisor. And on Saturday Marty's going to be here, so I'll cook then. If there was a baked potato or something this evening, that'd be good.'

'I've got a six o'clock tutorial,' said Kate. 'Then I want to go back to the Faculty library to collect some books. I'll get chips, don't bother with me.'

'But that play at eight?' asked Max, rather mystifyingly.

'Mm,' she said, gathering up her things for the day. 'That's the point. I'll go straight there from the library.'

'Save walking back here,' he agreed. 'See you at the door.'

'What play?' I asked, again with an obscure sense of hurt and exclusion.

'Marat-Sade. Guy I know's directing. Come, if you like.'

What else, I wondered, had been planned and discussed

while I lay upstairs nurturing my misery? Shame joined the sense of hurt, but Max smiled at me with an air of gentle comradeship and my heart turned over. At supper I would tell him everything. If it meant he never made it to Marat-Sade, never mind. A director and cast struggling to express an addiction to suffering would surely welcome a few empty seats with masochistic pleasure.

He stood up in turn, and followed Kate to the front door; I half heard a brief word exchanged between them but thought nothing of it. Upstairs there were sounds of Marienka stirring; I caught up my own book-bag to leave before she could intrude on my thoughts. Max wandered back into the kitchen and I said as brightly as I could: 'Supper, then? Sounds like just you and me.'

'Yes – great – about six-thirty?'

We often ate early, hungry after scrappy sandwich lunches.

'Six-thirty. I'm coming home at five, after the David Cecil lecture, so that's time for the potatoes.'

As I left, I saw Marienka through the window, leaning towards Max with a questioning look, her hand flat on his chest.

These memories are from long ago: bear with me. I am aware that to the clear-eyed sexual pragmatists of today much of this may seem ludicrous, as outdated as the courting rituals of the Edwardian aristocracy. My daughter's classmates seem to know their value in the dating market by the time they are fourteen, and some have not the slightest shame about experimentally 'having sex' with a number of partners before they turn seventeen. A generation of agony aunts trilling 'Dump the bastard!' has given them armour. Nobody mucks them about, or so they claim. Larger concepts of fidelity and betrayal have gone, together with the residual Judaeo-Christian sense that whenever a man and a woman lie together, something is set up between them that resonates for all eternity.

The Pill was new in the 1970s, and if shame was not dead yet, then neither was romance. Sometimes I wonder whether I would have been happier as a bed-hopping, boozy, lairy modern teenage girl with a capacity to 'move on' briskly from events which once would have been seen as shipwreck, catastrophe, lifetime heartbreak. Sometimes I wonder how happy those new girls actually are. Sometimes I even suspect that quite a lot of them secretly feel the way that I did, yearning and dreaming and clutching the dagger of unrequited passion to their breast, fools for love.

Mostly, I just do not know. Youth is a foreign country.

But anyway I floated through that day sick with nerves, bought chicken and tinned asparagus I could ill afford, and had supper waiting: not in the bleak dining room where the four of us would usually sit, but at the small table in the kitchen near the stove. Max trudged in at half past six. I could barely eat; he noticed, and smiled across at me.

'Not hungry? It's delicious.'

'Max,' I began, and then stopped and stared at my plate. To this day I dislike tinned asparagus. 'Max, I have to tell you something. About me. You might not want to hear it, but it's true, as true as the sun rising in the morning. And you have to know.'

'Tell.' He speared a chunk of chicken and began to chew it, nodding encouragingly. 'Spill it out, Salamander. We've known each other long enough.' He clearly had no inkling of what I was going to say, and looking back with the wisdom of maturity I now know that I should have stepped back sharply at this point. If a man has never thought of a girl as an object of love he is not going to be persuaded by this kind of hungry, needy declaration. Marienka's system of briskly invading his bed might have had better luck. Young and desperate and silly, I ploughed on: 'Max, I love you. I have done for months now. I'm telling you because it's a – a gift. I love you. Blake says never seek to tell thy love, but Shakespeare says build a willow cabin and cry it aloud, and Shakespeare outranks Blake. I think.' I faltered, as he looked at me unfathomably for a moment. 'So that's it, really.'

Even to me it sounded terrible; yet at the moment of uttering the words I felt a great numbing blanket of peace fall over me. It was out, for good or ill. I had not realized how heavy a burden it had been.

'Oh, Sally!' he began, and his warm hand slid over my cold one on the shabby little table. 'I'm honoured, and flattered, and you're the loveliest person – and the courage of you, the honesty, it takes my breath away –'

I knew I had lost, then.

I did not know the worst, though, until he carried on.

'The thing is, you ought to know – I'm involved.'

'Annette? I know, but I thought—'

'Not Annette. I think that's been over, really, for quite a while. Sally, forgive me – it's a complicated thing – but Kate and I –'

He dropped his eyes and spoke to the congealing remnants of the meal I had made him (so many meals, so many gestures of care and support and true love, so much devotion he had had from me over these months, while Kate was out, or working, or tucked up in bed with Ted!).

'We – it sort of happened – the night you were at the party – we've always really got on, well, the four of us have. But she and I—'

'You slept together? You were the fling? That's why she's split with Ted?' My voice was high and unnatural.

'It's not just about sex. It sort of was, that night, and Kate did pull back, but we've understood now that it's probably serious.' His eyes softened and he looked right through me, seeing something marvellous. 'It's the real thing. Perhaps, anyway. I don't think I ever understood—'

I could take no more of this. The scrape of my chair on the tiled kitchen floor screamed as if from a long distance, and I fled the room, the house, the canal-bank, the whole structure of deceit and betrayal that my life had suddenly become.

8

I ran up the road in the gathering dusk, coatless. After a few minutes I got to the town centre and realized I was shivering cold; instinct drove me into the fuggy warmth of a Wimpy Bar and I found a few coins in my jeans' pocket, enough for a coffee at least. I do not know how long I sat there nauseous in the smell of mince and onion, the bright flow of shoppers beyond the window blurring through my veil of tears. It cannot have been very long, given what happened the same evening, but I felt as if hours passed in that sanctuary.

For it was a kind of sanctuary: a bright, bland plastic universe where things like shock and outrage and shame and twisting pain were too incongruous to survive. Lunatic emotions would surely die like bacteria on the sterile Formica surfaces. You cannot plumb the depths of tragedy in a Wimpy Bar. I had never been into the place before, and none of my student friends used it; sitting in the corner nobody would intrude on me. I was safe.

Little by little, though, the numbness faded. Max knew that I loved him. My reticent disguise and my dignity were gone. He, on the other hand, did not love me except with a vague brotherly liking; even that, I realized with a stab of sickness in my stomach, did not go very far. If it had done he would surely have confided in me about his lightning rapprochement with Kate. Come to that, Kate might have told me as a friend. She did not know, after all, how I felt about Max.

But maybe – the sickness rose again – maybe she did. Maybe he did, too. Maybe the two of them – three, with Marienka – had puzzled over how to break it to me kindly, and wondered how to deal with a poor lovelorn babyish fool. I rubbed my eyes, tried to straighten the tangle. No: at least Marienka did not know I loved Max. She had been openly and clearly convinced that it was somebody else, in a college away from that house. She was not one to keep secrets.

But Kate? She might know. She might have been 'protecting' me. Hence the murmurings between her and Max, half noticed over the past days, hence the studied casualness of their conversations when I was in the room. She had been discussing me with Max, plotting with kindly patronage how best to let me down. 'She's a bit moony about you, we'd better be tactful.' Despite the humiliation of this thought, I found that I welcomed the rage I felt against them all. It dulled the far greater pain of lost and hopeless love.

My untouched coffee was cold; I had no money with me to buy more. Rain had begun to fall in the darkness outside and the wheels of the buses made a damp swishing noise as they rolled by, warm comforting boxes of light. For a moment I entertained a fancy that I might jump on one of those buses, marked CUMNOR or WITHAM or BANBURY, and simply ride away from it all. This absurdity led on to contemplating other more rational forms of flight. College might, just possibly, find me a room. I was a scholar, after all, and I knew that there were a couple of student bedrooms free, being used for casual visitors, because two girls had been sent down. Maybe I should immediately move out of the house and turn my back on the whole treacherous set: on Kate and Max in their sickening happiness, on crazy Marienka whose light-hearted advice had done me so few favours, on this druggy brother who would soon be turning up to create still more distracting difficulties.

It would be warm in college, and studious, and there were other acquaintances who would know nothing about my humiliation. Max could move his little brother in, the step-father could cover my rent, and everyone would be happy. It would be as if I had never lived in the little house by the canal; the waters would close over my struggles and become smooth again.

As I stood up, a wave of dizziness came over me, a physi-cal manifestation of distress. Resting my palms on the red Formica tabletop, I shook my head, pressed my lips together and regained control. Like an automaton I walked out through the heavy swing doors onto the wet pavement, uncertain where to go. A church bell was ringing somewhere over to my right, and I turned my head; as I did so a half-familiar voice said: 'Ullo ullo ullo! Well met – er – Sally.'

I jumped: looking round I saw the hulking, cheerful figure of the boy Donald, who had tried to walk me home from the party and kissed me so politely by the police station. I tried a stiff smile; unaware of my difficulty he went on: 'Thought I might see you again. How's tricks?'

'Oh – fine. I'd better –'

'You heading my way? I'm late, better scamper, but we could scamper together. Got a brolly, see?'

So he had. It was a vast colourful golf umbrella. Hardly aware of what I was doing I fell into step alongside him; he was heading for broad St Aldate's, which was on the way to the house, and I slowed my steps once I realized it. I still did not know whether I could ever show my face in my Oxford home again. Automatically I found myself asking Donald: 'Where *are* you headed?'

'Christ Church. Got to sing, see? Evensong. Choral scholar. Bass-baritone. Even when I was a little brat, apparently I growled like a teddybear, never could have been a tenor. Bit of a bore, between you and me, booming away under the

main tune, but there you go. Break my mum's heart if I gave
it up.' An idea occurred to him: he had the kind of face on
which it was possible to track every thought as it presented
itself.

'Why don't you come and listen in? We are most bloody
good, you know. People come miles. And it's a big one tonight,
which is why it's late. Foreigners coming or something.'

It was, though he could not know it, a lucky shot. While the
aseptic brightness of the Wimpy Bar had served to numb my
first grief, I realized immediately that what I needed now was
a cathedral, and music. I nodded and expressed inarticulate
enthusiasm, and Donald hurried me on, frowning again as
another thought struck him.

'Bloody cold in there, though. Tell you what, you have my
jumper –' it was an Arran sweater, immaculately white –
''Cos I have to wear a robe thing anyway, and I never get
cold.' He peeled it off, still walking, so that I had to help him
through some comic moments involving the sleeve and the
handle of the umbrella; I pulled it on and it was warm from
his great body.

In the bone-chilling cold of the Cathedral I was even more
glad of the strange boy's kindness. Wrapped in his big sweater,
hidden safe in the shadows of the flickering candlelight, I felt
the sharp springs of my misery slacken a little. Around me,
other churchgoers breathed quietly; cool timeless peace crept
slowly in and curled itself around me. After a few moments
the choir filed in; Donald flicked an eyebrow at me as he
passed in his demure white surplice, and a couple of the small
boys from the choir school scuffled almost imperceptibly and
were quelled by the stern eye of the Organist.

I do not remember everything that they sang: Gibbons,
Tallis perhaps. I remember the candlelight and the harmony,
and the softening it wrought in my own taut misery. It hinted
at a more general concord, a music of the spheres in which

no honest love could ever be wasted, but might take its place in the deep harmony of eternal things. I did not think of God or religion that evening, but I saw the possibility of ultimate harmony and clung to it. My grief of today was part of a pattern, invisible as yet, but if I acted rightly it could be an honest thread. Suffering was part of the picture, just as the deep bass line was necessary to the high soaring melody.

I do know what the final piece was, because by chance my father was a devotee (one of the few, at the time) of the neo-Gregorian anthems of a French organist, Maurice Duruflé. He had taken me to Ely Cathedral a couple of years earlier to hear them in concert, and here again was the greatest of them.

Ubi caritas et amor, Deus ibi est, sang the boys. Wherever is charity and love, there is God. *Amor* . . . Then the deeper voices took up the theme, harmonious and sure: deeper still, down to the impossible depths where Donald sang; then again the words soared with the boys, sending shivers through my arms and legs. *Caritas et amor.* Wherever. Whenever. Whoever. Love, charity. Kindness. I thought of Max's moments of kindness: of his wrapping us in his mother's shawls, of his anxiety for his wayward brother. I thought of Kate, too, and the night at the end of last term when we were all broke and she got a birthday cheque from her uncle and spent it all on a joint of beef, a huge expensive chocolate cake and four bottles of red wine so we could carouse together. *Ubi caritas.*

We had been a family, the four of us in that house. We had loved each other in our different ways, and something good had been among us. Not, perhaps, God. God was very far away, if anywhere. But something good and real had been there, and still could be among us. *Exsultemus et in ipso jucundemur.* Rejoice and delight. I could hardly bear the last moments, the long, long notes stretching out *Amor*, and the long Amen.

I was young, I was hungry and tired and shocked and I believed in invisible things. Rising from the pew as the service ended I waited a few minutes for Donald to re-appear and claim his sweater and then made a hurried farewell.

'You don't fancy a coffee, do you? Room's just across the quad –' he began, but I smiled and rubbed his shoulder companionably and told him I had to rush.

'You sang wonderfully,' I said, to make up for leaving. 'I loved it. It was – actually, it was life-changing.'

'Come again,' he said, with a sudden seriousness which sat oddly on his jolly red face. 'Oh, and it's still raining. Keep this. I pinched it off my dad anyway.' He pushed the umbrella into my hand and would not take a refusal. I was glad of it: the rain was pelting down, making streams of the gutters, heading down the broad hill to cause trouble on the Thames flood plain below.

I walked home slowly in spite of it, almost dry beneath the vast garish umbrella, and when I opened the door on a stricken, white-faced Kate I managed to smile.

'Hi,' I said. 'I thought you'd gone to some play.'

'I – we – Max – we were a bit worried about where you'd got to. Plus, it's raining.'

'Oh, I went to choral evensong at the Cathedral. You should go. They're really good.' The effort of lightening my voice was immense, but I did it.

I could see the shadow of Max, moving around in the kitchen.

'I think I'll go to bed now. I'm a bit cold-y, still. Look at my fantastic brolly, one of Marienka's gorgeous hunky rowing boys gave it me.'

Upstairs, in the cracked bathroom mirror, I saw how un-convincing this lightness must have been. My nose was red, my mascara smudged, my eyes bloodshot. It should, perhaps, have occurred to me to be impressed and grateful that the bass and bonny Donald still seemed to like me in this state. But it did not.

I lay awake listening to the evening sounds of the house that night: Marienka's return, peals of laughter suddenly stilled, murmured colloquies, running water, flushing lavatories, footsteps making their way to bedrooms. Kate's door opened across the landing, and closed again; twenty minutes later, when everything was quietening down, it opened softly once more and her footsteps creaked down the stairs towards the cramped hallway and Max's room beneath.

I turned over then and wept. But once I was asleep, the vision of *caritas et amor* and suffering redeemed came back, vague and beautiful, and when I woke in the night I found myself whispering over and over again like a mantra: *honest love is never wasted.*

It would be idle to pretend that after that night things were easy between the four of us in that house. The old familial ease was damaged, all the more because none of us discussed what had happened. Kate's nocturnal move into Max's room was discreet, and she avoided being alone with me whenever possible; Marienka acted as if nothing much was happening, and Max himself was scrupulously kind and friendly. Sometimes, it seemed to me, his eyes followed me round the room, trying to detect turbulence or misery. I resolved that they should see nothing. I continued to nourish the *caritas et amor*, to do him favours, take his turn getting the coal in if he was in one of his smart shirts, make his tea, ask politely after his research. I continued to love him. He remained as entrancing to me as he ever was. He and Kate avoided public displays of affection. They owed me that much, and they knew it.

All these changes and behaviours began straight away, on

the morning after the revelations. They were made a lot easier by Marty's first weekend visit to Oxford. So, in a sense, the first thing Max's brother ever did for me was a considerable favour.

9

Marty came as a surprise. I had expected a younger, thinner, sulkier version of Max, but this brother of his bore no obvious sign of their relationship. He was taller, broader and darker, with startling blue eyes under an untidy mop of coarse black hair. His face, narrow and saturnine, seemed set in a permanent ironic sneer. He looked Spanish, Marienka said admiringly.

'Or perhaps there's a touch of the tarbrush. I wonder where old Helena was putting it about in the naughty fifties?'

'Surely not –' I began, automatically. Marienka and I were out in the almost empty coke-shed, filling up the hod with loud rattlings which I hoped drowned our voices.

'Oh yes,' she said, straightening up the hod and taking the shovel off me to reach the last few nuts in the corner. She was surprisingly practical, for an aristocratic pixie. 'Sue, the sister, now *she* looks exactly like Max. Floppy brown hair, brown eyes, Frankenstein forehead, jaw like a shovel. What looks good on Max looks pretty rubbish on a girl, I'm telling you. Now Marty – whooa! He's out of another box entirely.' She hefted the hod, I took the other handle, and we turned from the cold garden to carry it through the kitchen door. 'Indian cricket-box, I shouldn't wonder.'

'Really!' I was scandalized. My numbness and my crazily pious resolution to spread love and harmony were still with me, and it was still a torment to see Max and Kate exchanging glances; but Marienka had and still has an extraordinary power to distract one from the miseries of life with explosive nuggets of gossip or wicked speculation. At that moment I was shocked enough by her easy assumption to forget it all in my surprise at her imputation over Max's mother. 'That's a terrible thing to suggest! I know what it'll be – you get these genetic throwbacks, it's quite common – some dark ancestor –'

'Yeah, yeah,' she jeered gently. 'I do believe you,' and then the door was open and we were back among the company. It was Saturday lunchtime. Kate was making a salad with deft, economical movements and Max was sitting at the little kitchen table opposite his towering, scowling brother. Marty's untidy plastic holdall blocked our way to the stove. Marienka kicked it out of the way without ceremony, remarking airily, 'What a ghastly bag.'

'Who?' asked Kate, absently, scraping a gnarled carrot with her tiny sharp knife. 'Who's a ghastly bag?' I blushed, remembering what Marienka had been saying about the young men's mother.

'She's criticizing Marty's luggage,' said Max. 'It is disgusting, Mart. Looks like something a tramp would leave prison with. Haven't you got a case or a rucksack?'

'Jesus,' said his brother. 'Mum's right. You *are* turning into a pompous prick.'

It was almost the first time I had heard him speak. As Marienka clattered the coke into the stove and banged the lid back on the hole, I leaned on the wall alongside and looked at this rude changeling with more care. He returned my gaze with brief stony insolence, and then quite unexpectedly smiled. I saw, then, that he was indeed related to Max. The features were utterly different, but the smile was the same. Perhaps it came from their mother. If so, I could quite see how she might have been a temptress: it was a smile worlds could well be lost for. I had to answer it somehow, so I managed a smirk and said loyally: 'I don't think Max is pompous.'

'You probably don't have him going on at you about your habits and your hairstyle and your career all day,' said Marty. 'Or criticizing your bloody *luggage*.'

His attention seemed to switch off as suddenly as it had begun, and the long dark face became blank again. Max, more ill at ease than I had ever seen him, began to witter about the photography course and what a good chance it was; Marty raised his eyebrows a little and looked vaguely over his brother's left shoulder. I was fascinated, not least at the sight of someone so robustly unimpressed by Max. It made me realize that in our little ersatz family all of us girls had come to revolve around him like a small solar system. Even Marienka, who mocked him, paid him attention. Max had become a sort of sultan among us, his harem. This odd young man had the ability to ignore him entirely. It was as if the room had tipped into another plane: disconcerting, uncomfortable.

We moved through to eat the salad Kate had made, an uneasy little party round the dining table. Marty ate lightly, looking around him at the room with the air of an astronaut of fastidious tastes who had just descended on a new and unimpressive planet. Then Max with rather strained heartiness proposed a walk along the towpath. Kate, standing behind his chair with her hands on his shoulders in a sickeningly proprietorial pose, said: 'Oh, you go. I really do have to get on with some work. But you ought to show Marty our canal, if he's going to be staying here.'

She was altogether too sweet, unlike her bluff old Yorkshire self; I felt that she was being false and began at that moment to hate her.

Marienka in turn demurred. 'I ought to finish my essay too. We'll see you later.'

Max turned to me then, his face oddly anxious.

'Sally, you'll come? Won't you?'

I did not refuse Max's requests, ever. So I went. There was just space on the path for the three of us to walk abreast, and I was slightly crowded between the two men. Max's nearness was, as ever, a delicious torment; but this time it was made even stranger by the striding, silent presence on my left side.

'What do you think of our canal?' asked Max after a few minutes, still with that odd note of forced enthusiasm in his voice.

'It's a canal,' said Marty. 'Definitely a canal. Brown. And wet. That's the way you can tell.'

We walked on. Max seemed so untypically unsure of himself that my heart turned over in pity for him. This was an awkward brother and an awkward moment; he had set much store on the idea of Marty staying in the house, even though it meant things would be harder for him and Kate to carry on their affair this summer until a separate room came free with Marienka's finals. I honoured him for his fraternal devotion, and wanted to make things easy between us all, because I loved him so.

'We're really looking forward to having you stay next term, Martin,' I said. 'It'll be fun.'

He stopped in his tracks then, and stared at me. I stopped too, wondering what he meant, and Max had to come to an awkward halt a pace ahead of us.

'Fun?' Marty said questioningly. Then the smile again, directly at me and only for me. 'Yeah. Sally. It'll be fun. For once, old Max has had a *goood* idea.' And, astonishing both me and his brother, he decisively took my hand.

'Race you,' he said to Max. 'Me and Sally, we can go like the *wind!*'

I have never been much of a runner, but with Martin's hand in mine and his colt legs racing alongside, I gave it all I had.

There was a dizzy, perverse joy in fleeing from Max along that narrow towpath, brushing past bushes and branches, only a footfall away from the canal's edge with the strong hand in mine. Max, behind us, was growing out of breath and shouting irritable reproaches at his brother.

'Marty! Don't be daft, you'll have her in the canal! You'll both go in! Marty, are you pissed? Or high? Aahh!'

The last exclamation was distressed enough to make me flag and turn my head back as Marty dragged me onwards. I tugged furiously to free my hand from his grip. 'Marty – don't – he's fallen over!'

Marty laughed and tried to run on; I tugged my hand out of his firm bony grip and ran back towards Max, who had fallen awkwardly and was rubbing his ankle. Overcome by devotion I threw myself down on my knees beside him, an arm round his shoulder.

'Are you OK? Oh, Max. Now look what you've done!' I spat at his brother, who now stood grinning above us.

'You ran too,' said Marty. 'You ran like the wind, just like I said you would. Come on up. Max's fine. He always made a big thing of it when we were kids and he fell over. Ruined a whole ski trip pretending to sprain his stupid knee, and Mum pulled me out of ski-school in case I did mine in. And he wasn't even hurt, just chicken.'

'Martin, shut *up*,' said Max, hobbling to his feet and glaring like a schoolmaster. 'You poisonous lying little toad – I don't know why I – owww!'

I stood aghast between them, as an ancient unsuspected feud reignited in the green eyes and the blue. Then Max recovered himself, and turning to me with all the lightness he could muster said: 'Sorry, Sal. Brothers, you know.'

Martin's face had become impassive again, faintly sneering; we walked back to the house carefully, none of us speaking until Kate came out to greet Max with a kiss on the cheek,

like a wife. When he was out of earshot the younger brother
bent to me and said softly: 'It won't last, you know. He's
play-acting, as usual.'

'What do you mean?'

'Max and that Kate girl. Jeez, what a lump.'

I felt I should defend her, though his words made my heart
sing. 'She's not a lump – Kate's lovely—'

'Ah, shut up. You know she is. Boring lump. Yorkshire
pudding. Why doesn't he go for you, or even that slutty
Marienka? Though you'd be a better bet.' And the imperti-
nent, impossible brother of the man I loved leaned over and
planted a most unbrotherly kiss on my shocked, parted lips
before I could protest.

'You – no – stop it – really—!'

Kate was there, watching, wide-eyed. Max had limped into
the house, but she stood holding the door. As I went in,
following the insouciant Marty, she murmured to me: 'Quick
worker, you are! He's a good-looking boy, isn't he?'

I had had enough. I snarled at Kate, 'Shut the fuck up!'
She pressed her lips together and walked away.

For the rest of the day and the evening she and I avoided
each other, neither Max nor Martin said much to one another
or to me, and at the end of the day I went to bed sore and
angry, with a sense of having been unfairly made a fool of.

Marty was a terrible house-guest, in many ways. He smoked
pot openly, leaving his stubs and papers and crumbly stash
of marijuana lying around in full view of the windows, as even
Marienka never did. He lay in late, then wandered round the
house in his underpants making sardonic remarks about all
of us, many of them dangerously near the bone. He amused
himself on the Saturday evening by raiding Marienka's room
and painting his face with her rouge and lipstick, lengthening
his already lush eyelashes with her best waterproof mascara

and then pouring a jug of water over his head 'to test it'. He produced a mouth-organ from his scruffy plastic bag and played long Dylan riffs, deafeningly, all through a long wet Sunday afternoon when Kate was trying to write an essay on glacial landscape formations. When he started chatting again he told embarrassing, and I firmly believed unfounded, anecdotes about Max's boyhood. And he made it ever clearer that he had taken some sort of perverse fancy to me.

'Sallee – Sallee! Pride of our alleee!' he sang. 'Shall we have another run? We run like twin stags, we do.' Or more painfully, 'Max, when you've got a pick-your-own harem like this, why choose that great Yorkshire pudding when you could be feasting on gamey stuff like Marienka or rare and delicate viands like this little Sallykin?' He was odd, odder the more I watched him: he alternated bouts of unwelcome eloquence with long periods of silent brooding, over which he seemed quite unembarrassed.

'He smokes too much weed,' said Marienka, while he and Max were in their room getting his things together to head for the station on Sunday evening. 'And I bet you never thought *I'd* say that about any human being.'

'Well, you do a fair bit,' I said.

'No, I don't. Whole days and nights pass without a Rizla touching my lips. Marty is high all the time. And I tried some of his stuff, it's Dutch. Twice the poke of what we get round here.'

'Is it dangerous?'

'Not usually. But admit it, he's bloody odd.'

Marty was a year younger than me, and despite his height and breadth I had come to feel oddly maternal towards him. My heart bled for Max, saddled with the responsibility for this troublesome cuckoo, and forced to put up with not only his vagaries but a number of downright and pointed personal insults. With *caritas et amor* still beating in my wounded breast, I wanted to help. When Max came through, looking pale and tired and leaving Marty in the downstairs bedroom for a moment, I drew near to him and said in a low voice: 'I think you're doing a great job with your brother. I reckon he'll be really grateful to you one day for all the help.'

Max looked a little startled, furtive even; but then, ever since our brief disastrous exchange over the chicken-and-asparagus supper on Thursday he had been wary of me. My steady effort to be normal and pleasant around him appeared so far to have made him more nervous, not less. It occurred to me, in a painful moment of humility, that Marty's extravagant pretence of fancying me might be part of an elaborate tease to make his elder brother feel even worse; perhaps he knew everything including my infatuation. Anyway, Max's reply was: 'Thanks. But I don't think gratitude is one of the things he does best.' Then after a couple of heartbeats he added, 'I do worry about what the drugs are doing. He's even stranger than he used to be.'

'I like him,' I said. 'I think he's not a bad boy at all.'

Suddenly Marty was standing in the doorway.

'I'se a *good* lickle boy,' he said mockingly. 'Bread and milk and early bed, that's all I need to make me nice and rosy and lovable again.'

It was clearly one of his sociable moments. Max flinched, and started to urge him to finish his packing and come to the station lest they miss the train. Marty gave a wide wicked smile and said: 'I'm not going unless Aunty Sally takes me. I can't be a good boy if Nanny's not there, can I?'

After some awkwardness I agreed to walk down the towpath to the station with him. Max looked both relieved and furious, and my heart yearned towards him. When we were clear of the house, I found enough firmness in myself to take Marty on, head to head.

'Why are you so *filthy* to your poor brother? He's only trying to help you.'

'Why are you in love with the boring little turd? Mooning at him with cow eyes—'

'How dare you—!'

'Deny it, then. You treat him like God Almighty. All three of you, even tarty-tits Tilton. But you, you look at him with soppy spaniel eyes – ugh – I saw you give him the last chocolate biscuit!'

I was silent for a moment, falling reluctantly into step with his long legs as he walked on, his eyes fixed on the path ahead. It was always hard to tell when Marty was joking, but there was sometimes an edge to his outbursts which compelled a serious response.

'Why should you care?' I said finally.

'So you admit it?'

'I'm very fond of him. But Kate is my friend too, and she's his girl and I accept that. Friendship is a form of love, too. We've all four got on really well this year. Nothing's going to be allowed to break that up.' I added, after a moment's pause, 'Especially not a spoilt brat like you.'

Martin slowed, and looked at me, with that sudden disconcerting smile. 'That's right, that's good, tell me off! Hey, did you like it when I kissed you after lunch yesterday?'

'I thought it was a bloody nerve.'

'You're right there. Will you come and see me in the holidays?'

Perhaps it was his mention of 'the holidays', or the suddenly less than bantering tone in his voice, but suddenly he seemed to me more normal than he had all weekend: just a shy cussed schoolboy not quite certain of his ground.

'Why do you want me to?'

'I like you. You're real. Not a posey ponce like my dear brother, or a lump of suet like that girl of his, or a posh

cold-hearted tart like Marienka. You're like a nice fresh
currant bun, you are. And you use words well. I like the
way you talk. I sing words, so I like that.'

'Oh, thanks!' I was amused despite myself, and a little flattered, and not as cross as I felt I should be at his insults to
my friends.

'Come to one of my gigs. I'm in a band. We're good.'

'OK,' I said. 'But you'll have to give me warning, 'cos I
live in Suffolk when I'm not here.'

Martin smiled.

'Come to London. Stay the night at my mum's house. It's
in –' he shuddered a little, '*Knightsbridge*. Now you know
why Max has his little white nose permanently in the air. He
plays at slumming it down here in Chateau Crumbling, but
he and my ma and I are kept in tee-riffic style by a greasy
dago, did you know?'

'I don't think you should be rude about your stepfather,'
I said primly. We were almost at the station, on the very
steps, beneath the scalloped planks of the fascia.

'Oh, I can be as rude as I fucking well like,' he retorted.
'I'm not the one who gets paid lots of lovely bunce for making
me behave.'

But before I could ask what on earth he meant, train doors
were banging open and a hollow announcement summoned
him to the London platform. With a fey little pirouette and
a wink, Martin Bellinger was gone.

10

I forgot about that conversation for a while, because my normal misery returned so sharply after the distraction of having this oddball brother in the house. I wept alone by night, struggled to be cheerful and friendly by day, and resisted all the efforts of time and work and daily life to deflect me from my hopeless fealty to Max Bellinger. Even in my lighter moments I sought song and poetry to answer my state of mind: I hummed *Did you not hear my lady?* with its dying fall of, '*Though she may never look at me, I love her till I die.*' I copied out Yeats' poem about Love without Hope, and immersed myself beyond the needs of my course in the honeyed toxicities of medieval courtly love.

I worked hard in the library that term, revising my last two and a half years' work with a vague idea of proving my quality to the scholarly Max. I would lay a First at his feet in the summer, and perhaps the scales would drop from his eyes and he would realize that I, a sensitive Humanities graduate, was a fitter mate for him than Kate the down-to-earth geographer.

Marienka, of course, had found out my secret. I suppose Max had told Kate the night I ran out into the rain, and Kate had told Marienka. She bearded me in the kitchen a few days after Martin's visit and was as forthright as usual.

'You idiot! Max is the *last man in the world* you should be thinking about. He's absolutely not your type. If I'd had the slightest idea you were thinking about him I would have *shrieked* warnings! To think I egged you on – I thought it was someone from the party!'

'What do you mean, he's not my type? You mean he's too good for me? Out of my league?' I was startled by the assault, and lashed out. 'Is that what you mean?'

'No-oh! Rather the opposite, if truth be told. He's a puddle in the sunset, as my old nanny used to say. Golden and glorious but not worth getting excited about. You don't love him!'

'What the hell do you know about love?' I was angry, caught off my guard. 'You just sleep with anyone you fancy and leave them flat.'

'Perhaps I leave them flat because I've got the brains to know that it's not going to last and it isn't meant to. You haven't got the brains you were born with. You just need a bloody good screw, that's what you need. Honestly, duck, this is just virgin fantasy. Max is a—'

She stopped abruptly and did not finish the sentence. I stared.

'He's your friend! You brought him here. What do you mean, "he's a . . ."? What are you saying?'

Marienka sat down, plonking herself on the wobbly kitchen chair with some force, and sighed loudly. Her bright eyes and long white hands worked excitably as she tried to express what she meant.

'He's too *weak* for you. Of course I'm fond of him, but I know him, and believe me, he's a cup of weak sweet tea. Unsatisfying. He'll hurt anybody who loves him, and then stand there looking martyred and holy as if it was him who'd been shafted.'

'You think he'll hurt Kate?'

'Well,' said Marienka. 'That little flingette, I admit, is bloody weird. I suppose it's Nature's way of evening out the gene pool a bit. Like when you breed hunters. You wait till one side of the bloodline is hopelessly inbred, with spindly racehorse legs and a head like a deer and shying at everything. Then you bring in a sturdy cobby mare to solidify things a bit. But they don't make the poor bloody mare and the thoroughbred *live* together, in the same *stable*.'

She had a way, Marienka, of making you temporarily see things her way; not for long, just while you were laughing at the way she put it. The idea of Kate as a solid carthorse pleased some small, mean part of me.

'So which horse am I?' I asked, prolonging the moment.

'Fucking stupid donkey, right now,' said Marienka. 'Seriously, forget about it. If you carry on mooning, he'll eventually take you up on it once he's broken with Kate, and then you'll *really* get hurt. Girls like you take sex horribly seriously and end up burnt to a frazzle. Keep away. Honestly. I'm really sorry I ever introduced you.'

'I can't take it back,' I said. 'It's like you said. Love is a gift. *Given, not lent, and not withdrawn once sent.*'

'Oh, sweet Almighty!' cried Marienka, who was a good enough student and near enough to Finals to recognize a quotation when it flitted past her. 'Now you think you're Jesus, do you? Sent down to save Max from vanishing as he undoubtedly will, right up his own arse—'

Max's footfall in the dining room ended the conversation. Flashing angry warning eyes at me, Marienka slammed out through the garden door. It was warm enough, now, for us all to be outdoors without coats; the blossom was on the canal hedge and the willows were putting out pale green ragged leaves. Max came in to the kitchen, filled the kettle and smiled at me.

'All right?'

I smiled back, without prudence or restraint. 'Never better.'

Term wore on; in eighth week, although I had intended to stay on for some of the Easter vacation, I felt a powerful longing

for the wide cool skies of East Anglia and the calm dullness of
home. Marienka was off to Italy to see Marco, whose flame
appeared more durable than anybody had expected ('Or else
she just wants more of that ham,' said Kate). Kate herself went
to Yorkshire, though from murmured snatches of conversation
I gathered that she and Max had plans to be together in London
for a while, after the first week of the break. I stayed on for
an extra day to tidy up the house and allow the agent to make
his six-monthly check for damage; such tasks generally tended
to fall to me. Morose, tired and depressed I went through the
motions, weeping a little as I Hoovered Max's bedroom. But
on the last lonely morning I was surprised to get a postcard
from Martin Bellinger.

Remember the promise, it said. *Gig is on 8 April. Hammersmith,
place called The Dive. Ticket on door in your name. Meet you
after at the Stag, opposite. You can stay at my mum's. Virtue quite
safe. You did promise.*

I turned it over, mystified and a little flattered. I had assumed
that Max's difficult, druggy, eccentric brother would have
forgotten me within minutes of getting on the train. I had put
him from my mind, except as a possible temporary housemate during part of the summer term. I see now what I did
not see then: that my whole idea of my own value and attrac-
tiveness was hopelessly skewed by the long attrition of wanting
only Max to love me, and knowing that he did not.

It may interest – or appal – the 21st-century generation to
know that in the early 1970s the notion of 'low self-esteem' as
an affliction had not yet developed. We were bred up, remember,
in the dour 1950s, in a Britain whose adults still remembered
the dutiful austerities and the routine griefs of war. It was not
an era when self-esteem was considered an important acces-
sory. If I fussed about my clothes as a child my mother certainly
used to say, without much thought, 'Nobody's going to be
looking at you, dear.' At school it was a dire criticism to say

that somebody liked to 'make herself important'. Hanging around in front of mirrors or preening in shop windows was not something you wanted to be caught doing. The post-war aristocrats and the working-classes took up the idea of fun again much faster than those of us in the centre: we middle-class girls drank in diffidence with our mothers' milk. Subsequent academic successes did not quite eradicate it.

I do not think it was quite as bad for boys; but then they had other disadvantages. They were expected to be manly, and not cry. They were expected to stand up for themselves with fists. It was only years later that I understood how that unthinking expectation of macho behaviour had helped to skew and poison the relationship between the Bellinger brothers. Marty knew how to use his fists; Max never did.

But again, I run ahead of myself. Standing in the grubby hallway of the house by the canal I turned the slip of cardboard over in my fingers and decided that I would go. I could not answer the note, because I did not even know the home address of the brothers, or indeed their stepfather's surname to look up in the phone book. Nor had I, to my memory, really promised anything at all. But I would go to the concert and meet Marty at this pub, and then decide whether to go to his house. I suppose I wanted to meet Max. I knew, though, that it would be risky to meet Max and Kate together there: they would surely look more like a permanent couple than ever in that family setting.

If I decided not to go to the house, I could stay with an old Suffolk schoolfriend in Hammersmith. Jess had married young, and loved to show off her new husband and her collection of tall glass pasta-jars and wrist-breakingly heavy Le Creuset saucepans. So I was safe. I would go. It would be a distraction.

My parents were touchingly pleased at the plan. I realized that they had been thinking me a bit odd as I mooned around at home in the vacations instead of trying to see my 'exciting new college friends'. I chose my clothes with care – for yes, I might see Max – and settled on a red needlecord skirt with a slight flare at the hem, and a tight black skinny-rib jumper made out of itchy wool-and-acrylic mixture. I can feel the tickle of it still.

I took the coach because it cost half as much as the train, and rode the Underground to Hammersmith. Here I hit a snag: The Dive did not signal its presence lavishly on Underground station maps, as if it were the Palais. I had to look it up in a torn phone book in a smelly booth, then find the road name in the *A to Z*, then negotiate a maze of concrete flyovers and roundabouts to get to the right side. Eventually, out of breath and almost late, I found a gap in a stained concrete wall with the word DIVE painted in flaking, curly psychedelic script, and a cardboard sign tacked to it saying TICKETS: BASTARD & SONS 2 NITE. To my surprise I was handed a ticket immediately I said my name, and the pimply youth at the desk said with some respect, 'Issa special one. Downafront. Betterhurry.'

Inside, tiers of wooden benches made an angular shape around a stage bristling with drums and amplifiers; to my horror my ticket directed me to the very front row. I have never been good at listening to loud music, and I shrank from the threatened proximity of the drums and amps. I noticed that only the front row seats were numbered, and in a moment of sharp decision darted back and eased myself onto the end of a bench near the back wall. Looking around at the clothes of the fans I felt an utter fool in my tidy skirt and sweater, and wished that I had at least had the wit to bring a bandanna for my head or a pair of felt Yeti boots. I looked like a nice sensible primary-school teacher, not a rock fan. But within minutes my self-consciousness faded as I eavesdropped on the conversations around me. The audience were young, some of them of school age, and knowingly hip.

'You seen them before? I have. They're fab, man.' The boy was wearing a military jacket with gold froggings and had curly hair over his shoulders. His friend, less ornate, wore a World War II bomber pilot's jacket and a pink chiffon scarf.

'I saw them when they were called Madbastards, at Watchfield. Before the pigs busted it.'

'Madbastards broke up. One of the guys went off his head, heroin, kind of thing. Marty Bell and the drummer started up as Bastard & Sons.'

'The drummer's cool.'

'I like Marty,' said a pale thin girl in tight jeans and a vest with flowers on it.

'Dinne change his name? It was some posh thing,' said the boy loftily.

'He changed it,' said the girl, who I divined from her air of unflirtatious contempt must be his sister. 'From Bellinger. It was in NME. Says he's a rock tart. Like, prostitute. He's cool. I'm gonna go round after –'

I smiled. What, I wondered, would these children think if I told them that I knew him, and was his guest? Would they worship me as an icon of cool myself, or look in horror at my needlecord skirt and turn from their idol in cruel disappointment?

''E wun't look at you, ugly,' said the boy crushingly. Yes, I thought. Definitely a brother.

Screaming began. The band trooped on stage, five of them in black leather trousers and shiny gold silk-rayon shirts, already with discernible damp patches under the arms. My own ribbed sweater was far too hot. It occurs to me, writing this, that whenever I look back at the 1970s the memories are all bound up with hideous artificial fabrics.

I could not at first see which was Marty, since three of

them were dark and all were wearing sunglasses despite the cavernous gloom of the room. Then, as the first deafening wall of twanging and thumping rolled up to where I sat, I saw the boy I knew step forward, broader-shouldered than the rest, and recognized the sneering mouth. I sat back – or would have done, had the bench had a back to it – to enjoy myself.

There is always something magical about seeing an acquaintance from everyday life step into his métier and perform an unfamiliar and showy role. Ben, a Captain now, took me aboard his ship a few years ago and I had the same frisson of excitement watching him give commands on the bridge. Marty's mastery of his art was different, but equally inspiring and surprising to me. In the racket and the screaming and the group's stamping, preening, hip-thrusting, teasing show I managed to forget most of my own troubles. I even giggled once, thinking with a flash of disloyalty of the reverent Mahler evenings we had in Oxford and reflecting how much the fastidious Max must hate his little brother's performances. I could not see, at that moment, how the pair of them could possibly come of the same blood.

Were Bastard & Sons any good, really? I am not the one to rule on that. Look them up, if you like, in the rock chronicles of the period, or in the memoirs of John Peel or some other contemporaneous seeker of talent. Or else go to a cultish record shop and see if you can find some of their rare vinyl, in a faded and thumbed old sleeve with the five of them glowering fashionably above leather collars and shiny shirts. All I know is that on that night I absorbed and enjoyed the energy of the performance in Hammersmith, but was glad when it was over and my battered ears could become attuned to ordinary sounds again.

I climbed the concrete stairway to the street, which was dark now, and looked around uncertainly for a pub called the Stag. It was just across the road, and outside it stood a couple of muscular men in vests, already repelling groupies.

'Piss off, kiddo,' one was saying to my erstwhile neighbour in the flowery vest. 'No groupies. Not tonight. They don't wanna see you, right? Go home.'

'I want 'n *autograph*,' said the flowery girl, with commendable firmness. 'I'm not a groupie, so *you* piss off or I'll tell my Dad you groped me.'

I hung back. This was not my world, not at all; I should run away now. A flustered sense of courtesy held me there, though, hesitating: Marty had after all given me a free ticket, and he had sung and stamped well, and I should tell him so before fleeing the scene. I stepped forward.

'I've got an – er – invitation,' I said, my voice sounding squeaky and embarrassingly posh to my ears. 'From Mr Bellinger – er, Bell –'

'Yeah,' said the man, glancing down at a list. 'You Sally? Get on in.'

To loud protests from the flowery girl and her brother, I slid past him through the swing doors of the pub and found myself face-to-face with Marty. He had taken his sweaty shirt off and thrown a leather jacket on, open over his bare damp chest.

'I thought you weren't there!' he said accusingly. 'You didn't use your seat.'

'I was late,' I lied. 'And anyway, I think you hear the whole – er – balance of the music better from the back. Away from the amps.'

'Yeah,' said Marty. 'But it's that bit harder to throw your knickers at the lead singer, innit?'

'I shall remember to bring a high-velocity long-distance knicker launcher with me in future,' I said. 'Anyway, I must go, I just popped in to say thanks for the ticket, and I really enjoyed it, and you're ever so good. The audience loved it.

All round me, people were raving.' I sounded a bit like a vicar's wife, even to myself, but at least I knew what to say to performers; enough of my Oxford friends had been in the Drama Society and done plays on college lawns.

Marty gripped my arm. 'You're not going anywhere,' he said. 'You're having a drink.'

The other four members of the group ignored me, each being equipped with a shiny-haired and swinging girlfriend (interchangeable long-legged blondes). Marty attempted no introductions, except to the stout barmaid, to whom he said briefly, 'Whisky for Sally. She's my boring brother's flatmate.'

'That's nice,' said the woman in a motherly tone. 'Is your brother here too?'

'God, no!' said Marty. 'I told you, he's a pillock. I'm saving Sally from him.' He took out a packet of Rizla papers and groped in his jeans pocket.

'None of that,' said the barmaid, slapping down two whiskies and scraping the water-jug along the tiled bar towards us. 'Put your frigging Rizlas away in here.'

'Only tobacco,' said Marty protestingly.

'Bollocks. It's just as bad for you, anyway.' The woman appeared to be on easy terms with him. 'And tell Fatty over there the same.'

Marty moved across to the stout drummer, and in a moment he too had meekly pocketed his stash of cannabis and his papers. I was impressed by the barmaid's control and caught her eye. She winked at me.

'They're only kids really,' she said.

11

The whiskies kept coming. A warm, fuzzy golden feeling filled the dark sad gap inside me. Through the haze I was aware of Marty, never far from my side, and of the other band members gradually acknowledging me with nods and grunts. The girlfriends, I noticed, had gravitated to the bench at the other end of the bar, and sat together sipping Bacardi-and-cokes and chattering with their glossy heads close together. From time to time I thought I caught a venomous glance at me from beneath one of the long fringes, but very soon I was past caring. Since I had not gone to the girls' bench, and Marty showed no sign of relegating me to it, the other boys talked to me a little. They were gruff, boyish, surprisingly shy. One, I remember, insisted that his name was Friggy Tarka.

'Froggy?' I said vaguely.

'Nah. Friggy. An' Tarka, like the otter.'

I peered at Friggy with the earnest myopic intentness of the conversational drunk.

'You read *Tarka the Otter*?'

'Yeah. When I was at school, like.'

'Thass nice. Oh, very nice. I love that book.'

'Mart!' said Friggy almost indignantly. 'You found yourself a bird that can read!'

'She's at Oxford,' said Marty with dignity. 'She's gonna write me some lyrics. She knows a lot of words. Clean ones, an' all.'

'I didn't say I'd write you lyrics!' Through my happy golden haze shone a ray of sober indignation.

'Thass because I never asked you yet,' said Marty, whose style of speech modified itself and slid towards East London when he was in company with his band. 'But I bet you will.'

'Why?'

'Because you've got stuff to say, about the stuff that's in songs.'

'What stuff?'

'Love stuff. You know. *Baby baby baby . . .*' he crooned a line from one of the songs they had sung that night. '*Lady Lady Lady . . .*'

'Haven't you got your own stuff to say about love?' I felt I should challenge him, although suddenly I had felt a dart of pure pleasure at the idea of exorcising my demons in racket, of writing wild sad songs of devotion and having these leathered longhairs howl them across a stadium. Still I demurred. 'You don't need me. I bet you could write your own.'

'Nah,' said Marty bleakly. 'I don't do love.'

We spilled out of the Stag at closing time, on to a pavement spattered with greasy rain. A silent red-headed boy was loading the band's amplifiers and instruments into a Citroën 2CV van with their name crudely stencilled on the side. I had not been so drunk since a family Christmas when I was fourteen and Ben brought home a bottle of cherry brandy. On student money, this sort of thin, sharp drunkenness on pure spirits was a luxury rarely to be afforded, and I had never liked beer enough to drink it heavily. I found that I was glad of Marty's arm, and fell into a taxi with him without any further attempt to abandon him and go off to Jessica's. I had my overnight things in the embroidered Peruvian shoulderbag which served me as a handbag, and when I flopped back in the cab, head spinning, and found myself jammed between two band members I was willing to be taken anywhere. Looking into the van Marty scowled, then grabbed Friggy by the arm and manhandled him into the back with the amplifiers. He climbed in himself and sat beside me, his chest still bare beneath the leather jacket, shivering slightly in the night air. 'Y'awright, babe?'

The cab took a detour into Islington, where the other two boys got out, or in Friggy's case fell out; then we made our way westward and drew up at a tall house near the Park. It was quite the grandest even in that road, a plaster wedding-cake in a millionaires' alley of Knightsbridge mansions. Marty fumbled for his key while I gawped openly at the magnificence of his home and asked stupidly: 'Does your family live in *all* of it?'

'Yeah.'

'Even the basement?'

He looked at me and smirked. 'Basement. Thass what you need.'

'What is it then? A dungeon?' I was too light-headed to care; momentarily I had even forgotten that this was Max's home as well.

'Come and see.'

Inside the wide hallway, we crossed deep carpet past marbled walls (the faux marbling, ahead of its time, spread down ludicrously over the radiators). Unsteadily I followed him down a flight of steps where carpet gave way to smooth parquet. Marty flicked a switch and stepped through an archway, and I found myself in a tiled cavern with a long narrow swimming pool glimmering to my left and a pine door ahead, into which was set a glass panel which appeared to be covered in condensation.

'Good,' he said. 'It's been left on. Sauna! Sweat out the booze now and you won't have a hangover.'

Five minutes later, giggling tipsily, I was sitting stark naked on a slatted bench, gasping in the unaccustomed heat, my clothes in a heap on the floor outside.

'You have to be naked. It's not rude in Finland,' said Marty with authority. Being with him like this hardly troubled me any more than if I had met Benedict on my way to the bathroom at home. He threw a panful of water on the artificial coals, and steam rose around me. I was modest by nature even after a few drinks, but found that with this man I had no sense of wariness or self-preservation. He was friendly, even complimentary, but too matter-of-fact to seem like a sexual threat. After a moment he sat naked opposite me, rolling a spliff one-handed and pushing back his unruly hair.

'I need a smoke,' he said. 'Bloody Bertha at the Stag.' He lit it, took a deep breath and exhaled into the steamy air. 'You?' He pushed the cigarette towards me.

'I don't,' I said. 'I don't – ah – *dishaprove*, but cannabis made me ill once.'

'Tough luck,' he said, and took another dizzying suck of the spliff. 'Aaaaaahhh!' His long body relaxed, and he threw his head back, stretching his legs towards me. They were covered in wiry, dark hair; I averted my eyes from the place where the hair grew thickest, and shifted on my bare bottom. The heat was starting to dissipate my drunkenness, and mistily, gradually, the oddity of my situation bore in on me.

It bore in even more powerfully when through the steamy door panel I saw a dark shape and heard a familiar voice.

'Marty?' said Max. 'You back? I heard a racket, David told me to check that the sauna was off. Are you in there?'

With brotherly lack of ceremony, he pulled the door open and came upon me, his housemate and worshipper, stark naked, drunk and lounging with his equally naked brother in a cloud of steam and hashish. Neither of us distinguished ourselves oratorically. Max said, 'Oh!' and I said, 'Issnot whattit looks like.'

Marty did rather better with, 'Piss off, Max, it's past your bedtime.'

Then I stood up, looking around for a towel to cover myself, but overcome by drink and steam pitched forward in a dead faint at his feet.

Waking the next morning in clean sheets, with spring sunlight at the window and a sweet-faced Asian maidservant clinking a tea-tray gingerly onto the bedside table, I found that my first preoccupation was how to get out of the house which had seen my disgrace. My second was a sense of wonderment at the rich style in which Max and Marty lived at home. I remembered Max eating baked potatoes and cheap risotto night after night in the house by the canal, taking his turn with the coke-hod and pinning blankets over the windows to save heat. Was he pretending? Or slumming for the thrill of it? Or had he, perhaps, a yen to reject the stifling luxury of his home for a genuinely austere life of scholarship and humble economy? Loving him, I assumed the third and immediately became overwhelmed by a longing to see him, even if Kate were here, so that I could affirm the innocence of my preceding night so persuasively that he would have to believe me. I took a deep, shuddering breath and sat up to face the day, and the family. My clothes, immaculately folded, lay on a chair.

It was curiously easy, as it happened. Twenty minutes after delivering the tea the kindly maid – I had never met a real maid before – returned to show me the way to breakfast. I had found a small golden bathroom tucked elegantly into a rounded corner of the bedroom behind a curved door. The luxury of the house still dazzled me: to this day, whenever I come across a particularly grand hotel on holiday I compare it in my mind with that Knightsbridge house. It rarely matches up. Smoothing down my ribbed sweater and adjusting my dowdy skirt, I followed the maid down a wide staircase (flinching a little at the thought that I must have been carried or at least helped up it by Marty, or Max, or both, with barely a towel on me,) and was shown into a long, light, pretty room with pale blue panelling to shoulder height and a golden ormolu cabinet at the end. The shining table was laid, and one of the most beautiful middle-aged women I had ever seen sat there eating toast and squinting at the *Daily Express*. I recognized the pose: my mother too had reached the age for reading glasses but detested wearing them.

She turned as I came in, and jumped to her feet. She was a greying blonde with beautiful, bird-fine bones and a figure as neat as a dancer's; when she smiled I knew who she must be.

'I'm Helena Jacobowitz,' she said in a clear, light happy voice. 'I'm so glad to meet you. Marty told me you were coming.' Her eye swept me from head to toe, assessing me, but it was not an unkind perusal. Her manner made it clear that the pleasure of seeing me was real, if small: she had the air of a woman to whom any distraction from the inner life was always welcome. But it went beyond that: she was so transparent that I could have laughed aloud. She was any mother, naively glad that her most difficult child had found a 'nice friend'. I remembered when my brother Ben had been unhappy at school and said that all the boys were rough bullies; then one day he brought home for tea a studiously polite child called Nicholas. My mother treated that eleven-year-old like royalty, and now Helena treated me much the same way.

'Tea? Or coffee? You must have a terrible, terrible head if Marty made you listen to his band. I tried once and I took a week to recover my hearing afterwards. He's not down yet, but Fina's going to roust him out, it does him good to behave like a host from time to time. Now – do you like scrambled egg? Fina makes it so beautifully – and with brown toast there's nothing like it – but perhaps you're a cornflakes person?'

It did not seem as if news of my apparent sauna orgy and ignominious collapse had reached Helena Jacobowitz; or perhaps such moments were so common in her family life that she took them in her stride and was merely grateful that I did not have a skirt up to my crotch and a needle hanging out of my arm. I accepted cornflakes and answered a few questions about my life; she seemed oddly surprised to know I was at Oxford. 'Oh,' she said, 'I've got another son who's there. I wonder if you know him?'

Before I could recover from the implications of this question, the door swung open to admit a tall, grey-haired, imposing man with the face of a clever eagle. David, I thought. The stepfather. He was dressed in a beautifully cut pearl-grey suit and a pale pink heavy cotton shirt of the same expensive Jermyn Street type that I had often washed by hand for Max. His tie bore the diagonal stripes of some impressive school, or club perhaps; his eyes rested on me with the same sort of careful but not hostile judgement I had seen in his wife's.

'Hello,' he said. 'I am David Jakobowitz. I take it you're Marty's friend who risked her hearing by going to his performance. If so, you will know me better as the wicked stepfather who can never do anything right.' There was a twist to his mouth as he said this, belying the flippancy of his words.

'Dah-ling!' said his wife with kittenish reproach, moving round the table to put her beautifully manicured little hands on his shoulders and kiss him on the cheek. 'That's not what poor little Sally wants to hear! Marty doesn't mean it! He's a big baby, that's all it is!'

It wasn't all it was. Hungover, nervous and socially inept as I was, I could still read the slant of an eye and the chiselling of a jaw. I could see why Marty looked nothing like Max. If there was one person in the world he did look like, it was David Jakobowitz. His stepfather: the man his mother married – according to Max – some time after her divorce from the late Samuel Bellinger. I gawped.

Then Max himself came in, apologizing smoothly to his mother and stepfather for having overslept and greeting me with friendly reserve. Fina the maid smiled and brought him coffee. It is a measure of my shock and sense of discovery that during the rest of breakfast I hardly looked at Max: instead I stared at his stepfather who, oblivious of any crosscurrents of feeling, was eating buttered toast and reaching for the *Financial Times*.

12

Family resemblances are a strange business. A face can wander through an extended tribe like a ghost, so that one day a young child turns on its mother with the imperious stare of a long-forgotten tyrant, or a widowed great-grandfather is ambushed by grief at a little girl's smile. Women look into cots in the bewildering early days of motherhood and see relatives, half forgotten, flitting through the unformed baby features. 'Cousin Tim! Oh, Ben – heavens, it's your grand-father . . . oh no, now he's the image of my mother-in-law with her dentures out . . .'

Within days that haunting vanishes and the infant becomes only itself. Within families it is often those nearest and most intimate who cannot see resemblances at all. It is always the visitor who throws the cat among the pigeons by accosting some scowling teenage girl with, 'Ah, she's the image of her mother!' while the victim bridles and refuses to accept any parallels between herself and the dowdy tyrant in the brown cardigan. Yet the mark of kinship is there, and the outsider sees it clearly.

I supposed it possible, therefore, that none of the Bellinger-Jakobowitz household had ever actually noticed that Marty had the same face as his stepfather: his loathed stepfather. I suppose – though it is hard for me to believe now, and was almost impossible then – that in the well-bred affluent chill prevailing at their level of society, it is conceivable that no outsider had pointed it out to them. Maybe nobody wanted

to believe it when they did see it. Certainly in that moment
of shocked understanding I valiantly tried to rationalize away
what I had seen. Finally I conceded to the evidence of my
eyes, but even then I clutched at straws, reflecting that there
was no reason to think that this Jakobowitz had sired Marty
twelve years before his mother's divorce. Maybe beautiful
Helena had a casual lover – as Marienka assumed – and
showed definite and consistent enough tastes to choose the
same physical type as the man she eventually married, years
later.

No: even that would not do. These two were close kin.
The line of David's jaw, the twist in his mouth, the eagle
eye, the sudden blank absence as he withdrew his attention
from the company and sank into his newspaper – these things
rooted a deep conviction in me and not a little pity and
horror. Marty hated this man. It was one of the few things
I knew about him. Did he not see him daily in the mirror?
Did Max not see it either?

Breakfast ended quickly; David, with a polite general murmur
of farewell, vanished to the City and Helena drifted into the
kitchen to confer with her Serafina about lunch, or polishing,
or some such châtelaine duty. I was left alone with the two
brothers. Marty was still chewing absently on his roll, and Max
was looking uneasy, as if he wanted to get up and leave as fast
as possible. I felt I had to speak to him, to break the odd spell
of our meeting unexpectedly as near-strangers over his family
table. I came out with the only line I could manage.

'Where's Kate? I thought she was going to be in
London . . .'

It was not the question I really wanted to ask, which was,
obviously, a melodramatic cry of: 'Why the hell does your
mother not even know that I am your other housemate, and
your friend? Why does she assume I only know Marty? Max,
why are you disowning me?'

But my feeble social question would have to do. Max replied to it, evasively. 'Oh, Kate – she's in Yorkshire, I think.'

'Best place for her,' said Marty scornfully, his mouth full of toast. 'What a lump.'

I expected Max to defend Kate and was surprised at his silence. So I persisted. 'Is she coming down later, before term?'

Max flinched, and turned on me with sudden venom. I had never seen him like this. 'Look, I'm sorry, Sally, but it's nobody else's business when Kate does and doesn't come to London.'

'Told you it wouldn't last,' said his insufferable little brother. 'God, and then you have the gall to lecture *me* about not settling down to anything—!'

'Will you shut UP!' roared Max, angrily. 'It's our business.'

'I'll ring her,' I said sharply. 'She is my friend, after all.'

Max gave me a look which pierced my heart: I thought in that instant that he really hated and despised me. I began to bluster towards an apology, a reconciliation, anything; but he rose from the table and left the room, slamming the beautiful duck-egg blue panelling as if it were one of the scruffy peeling doors in the Oxford house. I stared at it, helpless.

'Oh, let him sulk,' said Marty. He yawned. 'Jesus, my mother always makes Fina wake me up early, it's her idea of torture.'

'She woke you up because you had a guest.' It was a relief to me to scold him a little. It eased the pain of being in Max's disfavour. 'Me. I'm a guest.'

'Yeah. Shall we go to Islington and write some songs, round at Friggy's?' He stood up, and I followed.

'I want to ring Kate. Is that OK? If I do it from here? I'll keep it short, on your phone bill.'

'Wouldn't, if I were you. Things didn't go too well here.' He gave his twisted, half-sneering smile. 'She won't want messages from this house any more.'

I was aghast. 'You mean she's been here already, and something happened?'

'Oh yes.' He stood there, grinning, as if witholding information was a prime pleasure in his life. 'Something did!'

I sat down again, put my two hands palm-down flat on the table, and glared at him. For some reason I always felt, with Marty, that I could handle him: when he behaved like a child my normal hesitancy and awkward self-abnegation vanished and I became transformed into a strict nanny or a confident teacher. Perhaps it is because I never depended on him for approval. With Max I always felt small and anxious and eager to please, and therefore obscurely disgraced. On this occasion, alone with the infuriating Marty, I called on sources of power which I never realized that I possessed. Between gritted teeth I said: 'Marty. I will come and write lyrics with you at Froggy's or whatever he's called. But first of all you have to tell me everything you know about what happened with Kate. Now. Spill!'

Marty smiled again, far less sneeringly, and sat down.

'OK,' he said. 'It wasn't much, but it was enough for her, poor cow. She came here. She stayed. My mother gave her the once-over and didn't rate her, but she's polite and she knows how fast Max gets through the women, so she didn't give Kate any grief. But then Ma decided there had to be a family dinner, with everyone there. David got back from the City, and they had drinks, and I got forced to join in, which is how I know.'

'Know what?'

'What happened. They were chatting away, and Ma asked Kate about her family, and she said they were in Hartlepool or somewhere –'

'Bridlington.'

'Somewhere north, yeah. And it came out that her dad is some kind of commie.'

'He's a Labour councillor.'

'And so the politics started up. Ba-ad idea. And it got on to the miners and the Vietnam war and Cambodia and the Americans being shite —'

I winced. I knew how passionate Kate could get about her causes.

Marty went on with his story. 'And then it sort of got on to a rant about international working-class solidarity. Not a good idea, round my dear stepfather.'

'Oh God.' My jealousy evaporated, and I felt a wave of pure anxious sympathy for Kate. 'Did Mr Jakobowitz give her a hard time?'

'No. He wasn't rude or anything. But he took the piss out of her. Ran rings round her with figures and names and political things that he knows first-hand. He talked about Stalin and Useful Idiots – you know, all the usual clever Tory stuff they do. Made her sound like a squeaky schoolgirl Trot. He's very convincing,' added Marty reflectively. 'I give him that, the arsehole.'

I dreaded the answer, but had to ask. 'What did Max do?'

'What do you think?' The sneer was back now.

'I think he'd have stood up for her. Or changed the subject.' I really hoped that it was so. For all my earlier burning jealousy of Kate, I flung my whole being into that hope.

Marty gave his devilish little smile and shook his head with ill-assumed sadness. 'Nope. Rather the opposite. Ma was so sorry for Kate that she tried to be a bit lefty herself. *Not* an easy pose for a Harvey Nichols junkie who's never done a day's work in her life. So it was boys against girls. Bloodier than Vietnam, in its way. David ignored Ma and napalmed Commie Kate, and Max stood by and held the cylinder, agreeing with him.'

'But he's not all that right-wing!' I wailed. 'I mean – at the house he seems to agree with a lot of Kate's stuff. He did over the firemen's strike, anyway.'

'Oh, that came up too. Nasty! Seemed that David knew exactly how firemen's shifts and pay grades work and Kate didn't. Max said that yes, it obviously was important to look at the figures and the recruitment facts, and David said he had his head screwed on.'

'But Max thinks—'

'Max,' said Marty inexorably, 'thinks it's a bloody good idea to suck up to Mr Moneybags. Who pays his maintenance, and buys his poncey clothes, and incidentally is chucking him another very healthy wad of shekels to be my keeper when I do this photo course in Oxford. *If* I agree to do it at all, which is why my big brother's terrified of annoying me right now.' He assumed a stagey West Indian accent, rolling his eyes irritatingly. 'If I no come, Max he no get de money. Oh, Max knows which side his bread is buttered. Preferably both.'

I paid little heed to this last revelation, but sat silent amid the débris of the breakfast table. I could imagine Kate, red faced and upset, arguing ever less effectively as she grew flustered under the cold, clever eagle eye of David Jakobowitz. I could see her darting pleading looks at Max, to find only a brittle enemy. I could, reluctantly, imagine Max siding with the powerful patron at the head of the table: he had once or twice displayed a pompous side to his nature, particularly over Marienka's drugs.

Marty watched me while I sat in silence, thinking about these things. At last I asked: 'So was that why Kate went away the next day?'

'Nope.' He was enjoying the withholding of information again, and I threw him a terrifying teacherly glare. Hurriedly he went on: 'Because she went away *that night*. Got up from the table, asked Max if she could have a word outside, then had the word – I wouldn't imagine it was a nice one at all – and there was a lot of slamming of doors and running on stairs, and she was gone. Eleven o'clock at night. We eat late, because of David ringing American bankers.'

'She went to Yorkshire late at night? On her own?'

'Can't have done. No trains, are there?'

'Did Max take her?'

Marty looked at me, almost with pity. 'Max,' he said, 'came back to the table and apologized to David for Kate's behaviour. And finished his pudding.'

I was angry, but not angry enough. I am ashamed of myself now for not grasping the enormity of Max's behaviour, but I was not ready, then, to despise him. I cast about for a scapegoat. 'What about you?' I said harshly. 'I bet you helped foment all this – all this horribleness. Did you think of helping her at all? It must have been awkward for Max, with their relationship; he must have been upset too, p'raps he thought she was doing it to get at him.'

'As it happens,' said Marty, looking a little hurt for once, 'I got up when I heard the slamming, and unlike Max I didn't stay for pudding. I went to the front door and looked up and down the road to see if she was OK.'

'Was she?'

'She'd vanished. Thin air. It was raining.'

'I have to ring her!' I said. Warring emotions jarred me: a female and vaguely left-wing partisanship with Kate, worry about her, fury at David, relief that Marty was not as cynical as he seemed, and bafflement about Max.

Yes, you may well sigh and beat your head on the table at the very thought that I was trying to excuse Max, and that I went no further than bafflement; but that is the way it was. I knew him in my deepest heart to be good and sweet and wholesome, the highest Platonic ideal of a man. In a very few seconds I efficiently discounted all I could of Marty's story, and airbrushed the rest. It was a relief to turn away from this effortful whitewashing exercise to something I could do immediately.

'Please can I ring her? Please? I won't say where I am. She'll think I'm at home.'

Marty led the way to a dark oak-panelled study, where everything was rather too shiny and new for its faux-clubbish style, and motioned to a streamlined phone on a desk which must be David's. 'Sit here. I'll shut the door.'

So I rang Kate, and mercifully she was in. I did not say where I was. She seemed nervous, quite glad to speak to me but thin-voiced, apathetic, unlike her normal robust self. I put it down to the break-up with Max, but she did not mention him so I did not ask.

The other thing she did not mention, and that I did not know for a long time afterwards, is what happened when she walked out that night in her short evening dress, carrying her small case and heading towards Kings Cross station where she planned to sleep on a bench till the early train.

She took a short cut, so she thought, across the Park. Here, in the heavy shadow of a stand of trees, she was seized and raped by two young men. They ran off laughing as she gathered torn rags of shiny satin round her bruised body. They luckily omitted to steal her case, so she changed into jeans and went on alone. She did not report the attack, for sheer shame, and it was years before she spoke of it to anybody.

Max could not be blamed. Or at least not by me. Not then.

PART TWO

Marty

13

The songs I wrote with Marty that summer were slushy with longing and radiant with misplaced faith. Thus they met unexpected success in the pop world and still do. You will hear a few of them to this day, 'covered' by pretty boy bands and cruise-ship chanteuses; before I was twenty-five my words and Marty's tunes had been recorded by Paul Jones, Leonard Cohen, Eartha, Streisand. From time to time they turn up on karaoke machines and burble in hotel lifts. This implies no particular genius on our part, for sixties and early seventies pop has, in general, extraordinary longevity; there was something in the air back then, some blend of roots and generational conflict and reckless liberation that continues to strike straight to the heart. It applies even to the cheesiest songs: go into a back-alley bar in Venice now and the odds are that the radio is playing 'The Mighty Quinn'; walk down an Irish street at closing time and somebody will be singing 'Hi Ho Silver Lining'. My songs – our songs – share that weird immortality.

I have no idea why Marty decided in the first place, on such minor acquaintance, that I should be a pop lyricist. Clearly he had an eye for facile talent and the undisciplined emotion that best drives it. In Islington with Friggy, then during the rest of the vacation and the tense hot Finals term in the little Oxford house, he and I strummed and hummed and fitted self-indulgent feeling to easy tunes. I found it addictive, a clandestine release for the terrible despairing love that still racked me. In the months afterwards we tasted our first success, and that too had an addictive element to it.

It is not what an Oxford English degree course is designed for, but I suppose that I was already more than half trained for the task. My own feelings were strong and anything but incoherent. I had a fairly good mastery of the language of yearning, all the way from the age of courtly love to the clipped emotion of Yeats and Auden. Christina Rossetti's 'When I am dead, my dearest' gave me the germ of 'If you wanna forget'. The opening of Book II of Chaucer's *Troilus and Criseyde* provided just the right springboard for 'Your love is the wind', with its haunting refrain about black sea-waves of sorrow. Catullus provided 'Hi, goodbye!'. Shelley was a tremendous help, notably with bad-boy songs like the one beginning: 'Baby, I don' *do* no ordinary love, but I'm the night and you, you're my tomorrow'. Poor old John Donne whirled in his grave as I stole his most famous conceit for 'Round an'round goes my old heart/ An' you just stand and smile'. The dashing cavalier Lovelace gave us the erotic rustling of 'Silken Julia', which was temporarily banned from Radio One and consequently shot to the top of the charts for six weeks in early 1974.

It was Marty's only Number One hit, that one; just before the Bastards broke up and everything changed. Through all the griefs that followed I was glad I did that for him. As for work, my tutor never found out about my sideline and by the time I had my Finals results, so much else had happened that it didn't seem to matter that Marty's influence had steered me well south of the First which the college had expected.

Anyway, the irony is that if I had not had Marty's erratic, infuriating, childlike company during that summer term I might in fact have done worse. I might have walked out, abandoned my degree, collapsed entirely under the weight of unrequited and unhealthy longings. Marty was troublesome and often stoned and abominably untidy and squalid around the house; but he was funny, and bore no grudges, and made music. Moreover, at that stage of our working relationship I could curb his worst excesses merely by threatening to withhold the latest batch of lyrics. I once got him to wash up all the supper things, including the burnt rice-pan, merely by making it a condition of my finishing the refrain of 'I'm gonna build a hut at your front gate/ An' sing your name all night', a shameless imitation of Viola's willow-cabin speech. He added a Dylanesque, neo-country-and-western middle-8 on the harmonica, and it made me cry even before I had finished it.

On top of all that, his comic sparring with Marienka provided daily distraction from our other domestic troubles, which could have been considerable. For Kate never came back to the house by the canal. As far as I know she never spoke to Max again. After Easter she organized herself a college room, and then in the third week of term we heard through friends that it was 'all on again' with Ted. They married in the summer of that year, and although I was invited and travelled north on the train to stand around on the fringes of a no-nonsense wedding party full of red-faced uncles, I hardly spoke to her that day. She was a pretty bride but a thin, pale and subdued one: more of a lily than the bright Yorkshire rose she had been before Max. It was a very long time before I heard the missing part of her tale and learned of her ordeal in the Park. I wanted very much to express my feelings about what David Jakobowitz had done to humiliate her, but there seemed no way to do it without making matters worse.

Back in Oxford Marty moved into her room, his rent paid by David, and sporadically attended his photography course. He made it clear more than once, though, that his stay: 'wasn't to help Max get his bung from old Shylock. It's just so I can have my tame lyricist on tap, right?'

Max was exactly the same towards me as he ever had been, despite that odd strained morning in Knightsbridge. He greeted me fondly at the start of term, hugged me, carried the coke in, lit the stove, and continued to treat me as a well-regarded little sister. From time to time he listened to Marty playing our new songs on his Spanish guitar – for in one of those moments of firmness which surprised me, I had banned Marty from introducing the acid shriek of electric guitars and amplifiers into the house. Max listened to the try-outs, and even reservedly praised the lyrics. Those with experience of lovesickness may imagine the emotions that ran jagged through my heart when Marty sat cross-legged on the worn old carpet of our home, his hair hanging over his face, and sang to his brother about the love that I bore him.

Outta these black waves, only your love can sail me
Black waves of loneliness, O Baby don't fail me . . .

Yes, it looks terrible on the page. Pop lyrics usually do. But it worked for me, and for Marty, who may have put various muddled inchoate longings of his own into setting and singing it. And it has obviously worked for the millions who bought the record when other groups made the song greater. Even Joan Baez recorded it once, on one of her minor albums, and to this day the smoky voice intoning my girlhood longings makes me snivel. We were unbeatable in the world of lyrical *lurrrve*, Marty and me. Nobody could resist us.

Except Max, obviously. There were a few days, in the third week of term, when it seemed to me that he was at last looking at me with different and more loving eyes. If my devotion had begun to fade, that short time rekindled it. He sought me out, sat with me alone, walked along the towpath with me and confided his anxieties about continuing and funding his post-graduate research, and his ambition to get a junior fellowship of some kind in America. 'It's the only place the money is halfway reasonable for my kind of research.' For this, a period at the Courtauld Institute in London was necessary; but David, it seemed, was doubtful about the value of an academic career. According to Max the stepfather was – with steady, polite, ruthless pressure – trying to steer him towards a straight job, preferably in the Bank.

I listened, offered tentative advice, and sycophantically reinforced his vision of himself as an important art historian who must not be lost to the world of scholarship. I told him to convert David by citing such affluent and successful examples as Sir Kenneth Clark, and to tell him that as the country grew richer a knowledge of the arts would become profitable. As it happens, I was right, but at the time I was just saying the first thing I could think of to comfort my fretful beloved.

Marty, meanwhile, grumbled at my wasting time 'arsing about' on the towpath with his 'tight-arse brother' (most of his expressions had 'arse' in them; his most common expression of disgust was his own coinage, 'arseful'. You can see why he needed a lyricist with a larger vocabulary).

Marienka carried on her party life, more irresistible than ever in thin summer cottons, looked on at the three of us, and one night said to me: 'You and Max, then. Is something starting up now Kate's off the scene, or am I wrong?'

I was flattered and excited that she, with her legendary expertise in these matters, should think so. But Max, it seemed, wanted only a little sister and an acolyte. I was still cooking his supper and ironing his Thomas Pink shirts, after all. And as Marty and I became ever more entangled in our lyrical work, with me suddenly thinking of lines over supper and Marty grabbing the guitar and picking out a tune while I fussed about syllables, I suspect that Max increasingly saw us as one unit: his lively siblings, under his quasi-paternal care. Marienka rolled her eyes and told me I was 'hopeless', and that if I really wanted Max I should seduce him forthwith,

'with vigour and if necessary by force'. Not my style, I said, and she with some accuracy replied 'All the worse for you, then.' I stayed within my style: humble, devoted, and inactive. I did not know how to flirt or seduce. I had been raised in a Suffolk vicarage, and only knew how to be devoted and faithful.

One night stays in my memory, encapsulating the atmosphere of that term. The weather had turned hot, a blanket of stuffy air filling the Oxford hollow just as the freezing damp had filled it before. *Oxford*, wrote the 17th-century anecdotalist John Aubrey, *is no good aire*. He was right. Only a few rare winds freshen the heart of the old stone city; why else would generations of donnish families have migrated to its Northern and Western edges? Down by the canal we were grateful for the water and the willow-trees, but the little house exuded ever-stronger smells of rot and defective plumbing. A few days of heavy rain and high river once brought our foundations to a state where we could pull up the loose floorboard in the dining room and see water glimmering, inches deep, below us. One day Marienka bought a clockwork speedboat, wound it up and sent it exploring beneath the floor, bumping joists and brickwork and buzzing suddenly in far corners a long way from its point of entry. Inevitably, we couldn't get it back, and while its clockwork soon ran out, from time to time there would be a buzz and a bump under the floor as some change of temperature reanimated the spring.

On this night we were sitting round the table, eating Marienka's beef stew ('no, it's boeuf en daube, it's got wine in, don't be such a *peasant*, Sally'). Max was irritable, eating silently and sighing when Marty provoked him. Marty, in return, made sure to provoke him every few minutes. The subject turned to independence, as Marienka had passed her twenty-first birthday and come into a small inheritance. She was as debonair and unembarrassed about discussing money as she was about discussing sex.

'The *relief*,' she said, 'of not being doled out an allowance. I can't tell you. Of course I can't live on it in London, but it'll top up whatever pittance I manage to earn. Without even having to *speak* to my parents, oh, the joy!'

'Sally and I are going to be millionaires,' said Marty, with a sly eye on his brother. '*We* won't be asking for handouts from any parents. Or *step*-parents.' Max glowered, but stayed silent. Marty gave a little sneer of the lip – his stepfather's sneer – and went on, still watching Max: 'I talked to Andrew at Maximusic yesterday and he's done a deal with some Americans to buy two songs for a new guy called Eldon Munro. Never did I think I would be feeding the country-and-western monster, but hey, it's a thousand bucks upfront . . . and they want us both to go out there next year, do some deals.'

'You sound like a *Texan*,' said Marienka scornfully, mopping up her gravy with a lump of my heavy home-made bread.

'You've never met a Texan, you arseing upper-class twit,' countered Marty. 'You're not a world-trading citizen like me and Sally. You and Max are basically hicks. Small island people. We are the future!'

'I don't think you can categorize Britain as a small island,' said Max stiffly. 'Still less can you so cavalierly write off mainland European culture.'

'That's right!' I said enthusiastically, smiling on Max. 'Really, if you think about it, Mart, the pop music world is a much narrower, more hick sort of world than the art world.'

Max rewarded me with his beautiful smile, but – 'Aw, shit, Sal!' said Marty lazily. 'You've got more creative power in your little finger than brother Max in all his *purple folders*.' Marty had seen Max's emerging thesis, bound in a series of tidy grape-coloured card folders, on his bedroom shelf and been unaccountably and consistently rude about it. 'You and I are makers. Creative artists. He's just a critic. Critics are shit. Parasites on the artist.'

'You know nothing about –' began Max, then broke off, understanding that he was rising to a bait. Marienka looked at me, as I fumbled for more words to make Max happy, and then she looked at Marty and then at me again.

'Sally,' she said, mockingly but with an undertone of real concern in her voice. 'Wrong horse. Backing the wrong horse, you know. It'll end in tears.'

'What is that supposed to mean?' said Max, and suddenly the atmosphere changed from bearable domestic bickering to an electric storm of hostility and emotion. 'What are you talking about, Marienka?'

'I'm talking about Sally,' said Marienka, with the air of one who has made a decision to confront an unpleasant blockage in a sink. I had a crazy momentary illusion that she was actually rolling up her sleeves. 'Sally here, my friend Sally –' she flashed me a curious look, almost apologetic. 'And the way you string her along, Max. It's got to stop. No, shut up. You know how things were last term, and how well Sally behaved when you were mucking up Kate's life in your usual way. You're a tease, and you're a bloody dog in the manger, that's all. I think you should leave Sally alone. Marty suits her much better, if she'd only see it. And she won't see it while you keep on hauling her back and throwing her to her knees before your altar.'

Max sat stunned, looking at her. I was on the edge of tears, incoherent with fury and embarrassment. Marienka had never been this open, not in public; none of us was given to soul-baring analyses of our chain of house relationships. Especially not since the business of Max and Kate.

I blustered: 'Marienka, this is none of your bloody *business*, and anyway you're wrong, Max is perfectly well behaved, unlike you.'

'No, he's not,' said Marienka rudely. 'He's an arsehole, as Marty would put it. One minute he's taking you for walks and confiding his soul to you and giving you gentle-Jesus smiles, to keep you ironing his shirts. The next moment he's off screwing someone else or ignoring you. Wake up, girl! Can't you see when you're being strung along?'

I got up from the table, clumsily, and blundered out of the door in tears. As I closed the door behind me I paused for a moment, my legs trembling too much to climb the stairs.

I heard Marty say: 'Bullseye, girl. But you do push your luck, don't you? Maxy isn't as feeble as he looks. He could kill you with one blow of his purple folders.' There was an angry scrape of a chair, as if someone was getting up and leaving. I knew it was Max.

Upstairs I lay face down on the bed, sickness rising in my chest with a foul aftertaste of stew. After a few minutes I heard footsteps on the stairs, not Marienka's light pattering tread but heavier male steps. I held my breath: perhaps this catharsis had made Max understand how it was between us. The door opened quietly, and I rolled over and pushed myself up on my elbow, blinking away tears.

It was Marty, of course. He sat on the bed, put his arm around me and pulled me up until we were sitting side by side. I looked at the grubby window, not at his face. After a moment he put his cheek to mine, with a gentleness I had never known in him, and murmured, 'It had to be said, you know. We all know how it is. It's in all the songs.'

I wanted to pull away, but there was unexpected animal comfort in the warmth of his arm and his lean body. Nobody had hugged me for a long time, except Max in brief casual brotherly contacts I would cherish and re-live for days. Marty held me firmly to him, and I let my head fall on his shoulder. I was still crying.

'Women do fancy Max,' he said, 'the same way they fancy my bastard stepfather. That's why they get on so well. They belong to the International Society of Irresistible Arseholes.'

He frowned; I could feel the change in his face rather than seeing it. 'Er – I-S-I-A – Issia. We could have t-shirts printed for them.'

I pulled myself together. 'And you, of course, wouldn't join that club at all? You and your groupies?'

'I only ever had two groupies,' said Marty with an attempt at dignity. 'They tasted of really cheap lipstick made of lard. The second time I couldn't get it up because I had to go and be sick. I'd rather have you, any day. You smell *nice.*'

'Fat chance.' I wriggled away, but he was making me feel better. Miraculously, unexpectedly, he was healing the scars of humiliation.

'Max doesn't love you and he never will do,' said Marty. 'He doesn't love anybody. He never has.'

'He loved Kate. And Annette.'

'Bollocks. He confuses women with mirrors, really flattering mirrors. Sometimes he has to entice them to play the part of mirror, and get them into bed, but you do it all the time naturally, without him having to bother seducing you. So he won't get round to the seducing. He's a cold bugger, actually. Nasty chilly little worm it is, that he keeps curled inside his smart trousers. Ugh! Besides . . .'

'Besides, what?'

Marty hesitated, something he very rarely did before speaking. I see now that he was afraid I would be angry with him and stop producing song lyrics. After a moment, and more prompting from me, he shook his head like a shaggy dog getting rid of a fly and went on, with an uncharacteristic air of desperation: 'OK, I'll say it and then you can hit me with a shovel and throw me dead in the canal. Sal – you're not his type. He likes them smooth and elegant, enhancing his image. And you're more on the sweet lovable side.'

'Kate wasn't smooth and elegant. She was like me.' I

realized it only as I said the words; it was true, Kate and I were alike, separated only by her experience of love with Ted. It was Marienka who was from the planet Elegance. 'And he . . . he . . . went with Kate.'

'Yes' said Marty. 'But Kate belonged to someone else, didn't she? My brother wouldn't have liked living in a house with a woman who thought the sun shone out of another man's bum, would he? He'd want to do something about that.'

'He's never been like that about Marienka.'

'Oh, Marienka!' he said scornfully. 'Old history. They slept together last year, but they didn't like it much, either of them. She says he was a terrible lay.'

It was too much to take in at once. I shook my head, and Marty got up, dropped a brotherly kiss on the top of my head, and left. At the door he turned and said, with his lopsided smile: 'If you need a spliff or some acid, I'm over the landing. I guess we all need chemical assistance tonight. Marienka's smoking like a demon in the kitchen, and Max has gone for a walk.'

Then he uttered a sentence I never heard from him before or since. 'I'll wash the dishes.'

14

Amid all the prosy arguments and warnings about soft drugs, not enough is made of the way they stop the process of thought, stop it dead. Stoned people – and I have known a great many – are amiable, non-violent, sometimes visionary in a glaucous, misty rainbow way. But they don't readily come to conclusions or act on them; nor are they afflicted by a proper sense of shame or embarrassment at their own behaviour. After a few years of constant smoking of the stronger varieties, these characteristics spill over into their non-stoned, or normal, behaviour.

'Chill, man,' they say, and if you won't chill they whine, 'Get off my case.' Never mind that the case against them is watertight: the evidence lies all around. They ate your food when they had the munchies, half wrecked your room looking for the guitar they left on the bus, or forgot to bring the baby home from the park. Their world is fuzzy and beautiful, and they cannot accept the hard-edged concepts of conscience, atonement and restorative action. Perhaps there could be a campaign. Forget 'Drugs Kill'. No sensible child ever believes that anyway, not of cannabis. Maybe the authorities should try: 'Drugs Make You Really Annoying'.

On the morning after Marienka's outburst she woke late, and was not visibly sorry – though she did bring me coffee and a flapjack as I sat grimly studying in my room. Nor was Marty in any way discomfited by the emotional scenes of the night before. He slept until two o'clock, woke up, used Max's razor and borrowed one of his precious shirts, then wandered off to the Polytechnic to put in one of his rare appearances at photography lectures. After he had gone Marienka came back and plumped herself uninvited on the end of my bed, addressing my back where I sat at the desk.

'Sweetie,' she began emolliently, 'I may have been a bit out of order last night, but it clears the air, right? You know, you could do worse than old Marty. Heart of gold, he's got. I was all wound up last night, Max was bloody rude to me after you bolted, and I didn't have any gear left so Mart gave me some of this wonderful Dutch skunk he got in London. He's a lovely guy. Like I say, you could do worse. You'd be good for him.'

I twisted round to look at her. The magic, the fey golden quality which had captivated me in our first light-hearted friendship of a year ago, had fled. She was no aristocratic pixie now, no oracular speaker of truths about the gift of love. She was just a thin, blonde sharp-nosed student, under-dressed as usual, with tired, puffy eyes and an air of flippant dissipation. In a flash I saw how she might look fifteen or twenty years on: skinny, a bit too darkly tanned, elegantly weary in strappy high heels, a classic society divorcée on the prowl.

'Marienka,' I said, with real regret for what had passed away, 'I don't have to listen to your advice on love. I don't have to listen to any of it. I *know* about love.'

'Yeah,' she said. 'You might know about love, but not about men, huh?'

I let the silence lie between us, turning back to my books. Then she said: 'Would it jolt you out of this crush of yours if I told you I've slept with Max? Last year, twice, because there was once in the Christmas holidays when I stayed over in Knightsbridge?'

I was able to keep my voice steady. I had had the hours of night, after all, to think about this. Through all my anger and unhappiness I recorded a brief prayer of gratitude that this was not the first I was hearing of this awful fact.

'I knew that. Marty told me.'

'Max is not worth it. Trust me,' said Marienka. 'Cold, cold, cold and boring. Just like I always said.'

'So why did you sleep with him?'

'I dunno. Curiosity, I suppose. Except in Knightsbridge, that was because I was drunk and more or less ordered him to. He thought I might make a racket and wake up his parents.'

Against my better judgement I was drawn into an argument with her.

'It's not surprising it was bad. You don't love him, he doesn't love you. I'm not a baby, I know people do it just for the sake of a quick thrill. But I doubt that there's really much point in the sex, when they do.' I sounded like my mother in one of her advising moods.

Marienka was disconcerted. 'So knowing he screwed me doesn't make you think any differently about Max?'

'No.' There was a cold, painful pride in saying so. 'No. I don't sway about that easily. An ever-fixed mark, I am.'

'You're a fool. He takes advantage, you're humiliating yourself.'

'Not,' I replied coldly, 'without a lot of help from you. *Sweetie.*'

And that, for the moment, was the end of our friendship. Marienka, still clouded and disinhibited by Marty's Dutch skunk, felt that I had snubbed her just when she was honestly trying to help me. I was angry, bruised, and stubborn. It seemed as if the only clean decent thing I had to hold on to was Max; more precisely, my feelings for Max. *Honest love is never wasted.* Whatever morally and emotionally shallow worlds she and Marty chose to live in (and Max to dabble in – well, we all have faults), I was safe in the imprisoning walls of my moral dream castle. Love without hope was surely better than their casual couplings and stoned gropings. Love without hope would keep me clean and safe. And on clean shores like mine, surely, the sun of love itself would one day dawn.

When Marienka had slammed out of the house I went downstairs, collected Max's clean shirts from the pillowcase I had brought home from the launderette the day before (how I loved to let my t-shirts swirl with his!) and ironed them. Then Marty came home, wearing one of the unironed shirts crumpled and hanging open across his hairy chest, for he was broader than Max. At his insistence I left study and ironing alike and sat down with him to write a plaintive love song ripped off from one of Wordsworth's Lucy poems ('You got no praise, Lucy girl, you never got no love/ But now you've gone away/ O well, I think about you, girl, each an' every day'). When I told Marty a bit about the Lake poets and where they lived, he went to get a book of folk-tunes which he kept in his room for inspiration, and wound a sweet Cumbrian pipe tune around my words. I went to bed that night not entirely unhappy, thinking of Lucy in the poem and of how, unpraised and unloved, she got her man's appreciation in the end. Never mind that it was a posthumous devotion she could never enjoy. Perhaps I would have to die before Max realized he loved me. Well, so be it. Faith, like love, is always beautiful even in death. Isn't it?

This part of the story has not been easy to tell, not thirty years on, in this prosaic twenty-first century. I know that confessional memoirs are all the rage, with celebrity magazines and newspapers always full of admissions that would once have been called 'damaging'. The former perpetrators of bad deeds airily say things like, 'Well, hey, I was in a really hurting place back then, I did some bad things, but the experience made me grow.' If I were relating a bygone heroin habit, a prison sentence, multiple adulteries or a terrorist affiliation I am sure I would be met with nods of tolerant understanding and even admiration for my personal growth. Owning up to a prolonged, unrequited, virginal devotion is quite another matter. It is, frankly, embarrassing.

But the events of that last student year and the decade afterwards shaped my life, and other lives too; and those events were driven by one predominant emotion. So I admit to it. I was a fool for love, but in my own eyes a holy fool. And Max Bellinger never loved me back: never. Not for a minute. Not even when, in the last week of term, we slept together.

Rub your eyes, shake your head in astonishment: yes, indeed, he took me to bed. Marty had gone to London to practise the new songs with the other members of the group and Marienka was out all night at a party. Finals were over and I was restless, roaming around the house looking for something to do and rather wishing I had agreed to go to the party. Marienka and I were on cool terms, but she had asked me. In cold pride I had refused.

That early evening saw one of the rare moments when I found the hold of my faithful love weakening, under the influence of normal youthful high spirits and physical energy. I wanted to dance, and flirt, and drink. I had not forgotten Max but he had blurred momentarily into the background, as religions tend to do when the blood is young. I had music playing, and was bopping and twirling mindlessly round the kitchen wondering whether to make something to eat. Max, I believed, was eating in college. But unexpectedly he came in by the back door, and stood in it for a moment until I whirled round and saw him.

Perhaps (though I do not like to think this) he observed that I was full of spark and energy and almost, just conceivably, ready to drift away from my subservient allegiance to him.

However it was, he stepped forward and put out a hand; I gave him mine and we jived. We were not bad at it, because Marienka had had a retro passion for 50s rock 'n' roll in the Christmas term, and taught us all the steps. Then, when the song ended and the record on the old gramophone squawked and shashed into silence, he drew me into his arms and we danced closer to unheard rhythms, the beat of our own two hearts.

'Sally,' he said. 'Dear little Sally.' And he kissed me, and I suppose it must have felt good to him because he went on, and drew me towards his bedroom, where I lay helpless with desire and astonishment and relief and headlong reanimated love.

I wish I could say that it was jolting, disappointing, difficult and disillusioning. It was not. I had loved him for a whole year at close quarters, and now he had finally made me his for ever. Afterwards we lay quiet, not speaking. In my silence lay every message of love and allegiance ever thought or spoken. In his silence – but ah, who knows what lies in another man's silence? I would rather not speculate.

I thought he would want me to spend the night beside him, but after half an hour he said, quite gently: 'Difficult, in a single bed, isn't it? Perhaps we'd better . . .' and I left, trailing my fingers lovingly over his smooth, bare well-beloved shoulder. Next morning, waking at eight, I crept into his room with a tray of breakfast, his favourite crisp bacon and Scotch pancakes with the last of the golden syrup (we were eating rather better since Marty and I had got the money for the first song).

But he was gone. His bed was turned back, the curtains hung partly open and motes of dust danced in the empty sunlight. There was something odd about the room too, that I did not immediately understand. I took the tray back and met Marienka, who looked at me with open horror, seeing everything in a moment.

'Shit!' she said. She was still in her party dress, mascara streaked, lipstick smudged, one shoe caked in mud and missing a heel; this was nothing unusual after all-night outdoor parties at that time of the university year.

I hastily changed the subject, or so I thought. 'Good party? You only just got in?'

'Slept an hour at Joey's. Met Max on the way in. He's gone to London.'

Later I went into his room, always tidy, and opened the wardrobe. All his clothes were gone, and the folders with his thesis. That was the oddity I had half noticed earlier. No purple folders. Only the bookshelves were untouched, which is why I had not understood straight away.

I went home two days later, despairing of Max's return. Our lease was almost up and Marienka, who was avoiding my eye as if I were the victim of some terrible crash, volunteered to clean the house and hand it over to the agent. Max, she said, had asked her to box up his books for collection by a carrier he had arranged. The cardboard boxes, folded flat, were already in the hall. Her voice quivered as she told me this, and for a moment I wanted to be properly her friend again, but pride stood in the way. Marty was still in London, and Marienka said that his few scruffy possessions could go up with Max's in a couple of spare boxes if he didn't return to get them. His guitar was with him, so there wasn't much to pack.

She had become suddenly efficient, dismantling our communal home just as, a year ago, she had brought it into being. There was nothing left for me to do but go home to Suffolk, to my parents, and decide what to do with the rest of my life.

15

My wedding day was drizzly and cold, the worst sort of October day that Suffolk could throw up. The little church was half full and only half festive; guests were scarce because of my mother's fear about gossip, for beneath my nylon chain-store wedding dress there was a bump which even she had noticed. I do not know how many guests spotted it: I was very thin otherwise, and the dress was a hideous crinoline. My brother, faithful Ben, was in the front pew with his own new wife, having sweetly bartered three weeks' leave for one so that he could be there. My father took the service. The reception for forty was at the King's Arms and included chicken in a basket. Kate was not there – though I had struggled up north to her damn wedding, and resented her absence a great deal – and Marienka was not invited. I regret that. It was mean of me. Two college friends did come, for which I was grateful. My aunt Jenny sniffed loudly all the way through.

It was, frankly, one of the dreariest weddings I have ever been at. Its only distinction was lent by the Mayfair elegance of David and Helena Jakobowitz, and the tall, well-tailored good looks of the groom's brother. His sister was away somewhere with her new husband, for which I was grateful. We had never met, and I did not want the eyes of smart strangers on me that day. I could see my parents' Suffolk friends craning their necks to look at the London family even as I walked back down the aisle, bouquet clutched over stomach, to the squawky sound of Miss Aitchison the organist making gallant assaults on Handel's *Music for the Royal Fireworks*. The Jakobowitz group were swans among the grey provincial geese, and Helena at least betrayed in her sweet smug pussycat face that she was aware of the attention.

The most cheerful person there was Marty. He held my hand for the photographs – I had not wanted any, but Ben booked the photographer as a surprise – and despite the chilly turmoil of my feelings there was surprising comfort in his lean warm body and his dry, firm hand. He chattered beguilingly to the aunts and neighbours, and did not pick fights with his stepfather. He was a bit stoned, of course, which explained much of his good behaviour, but his mellow kindness helped me through that awful afternoon and I am grateful. I could not look at Max, not even when he debonairly joined the family photo group, and I still cannot look at those photographs without a surge of half-forgotten rage and regret. Max looks, to be honest, every bit as smug as his mother.

During the reception I slipped away to the Ladies' in the King's Arms, a room I had mopped and wiped often enough in my teenage holiday jobs at the pub. I stared into the mirror at my embarrassing bridal reflection, dabbing my hot eyes with a piece of lavatory paper and wondering how I had come to this pass: wrong groom, wrong wedding, and the hovering doom of childbirth.

It was mainly my fault, of course. After a week of the summer had passed at home in Suffolk I gathered up all the courage I had and went up to London uninvited. I found Max alone in the Knightsbridge house indulging a bout of self-pity. Helena and David were off on somebody's big yacht in the Mediterranean, he said. In the kitchen I found remnants of a depressing little lonely meal. He seemed pleased to see me, despite having made no effort to contact me since Oxford or explain why he had disappeared after sleeping with me. I did not hold that against him, though I cannot from the security of middle-age at all understand why; I suspect that my daughter's generation, casual as they are about sex, would not be nearly so forgiving of plain bad manners.

Anyway, I cooked for him and successfully reanimated our pathetic 'affair'. He was still concerned about his postgraduate funding, and was having some sort of battle with David about it; his morale was low. I was available and more than willing. He was a man, after all, and I was laid out on a plate for him. I was also so devoted, and no longer virginal, that sleeping with me must have been the line of least resistance. I cannot really blame him even now.

Anyway, I made love with him three times more, body and soul, and took no precautions whatsoever. My gift was still wholehearted. On the third occasion I failed to keep our customary silence as we lay in the tangled sheets, and poured out my heart and my long devotion luxuriously and without restraint.

There was no fourth time. Marienka would have said, in her brutal way, that he 'took fright'. I found out much later from Marty that Helena, ringing home and learning that he had a houseguest, was the one who really took fright. She persuaded David to fund him for a trip to Assisi to look at some frescos 'before the poor boy gets too entangled with that strange little girl of Martin's'.

He left. I mourned and hoped, and in early September began to nurse a horrid suspicion. Pregnancy tests, in those days, did not come in handy sticks with blue stripes, but in the form of a rather messy kit involving a test-tube, a wobbly folding cardboard stand, and a mirror to place under the tube. In this mirror you might or might not see the reflection of a brown ring. I saw five, enough for the Olympics, as kit after kit from a Norwich chemist delivered its grim unvarying message in the chilly Suffolk bathroom. I was scared even to buy the test: it took three long separate bus trips to the anonymous city, three different chemists even there, and two brands of testing kit, before I convinced myself of the disaster.

Today, unmarried motherhood is commonplace and even potentially quite chic and liberated; even so, girls often admit to sharp horrified shock at the first intimation that they have fallen. In the early 70s we were theoretically liberated by the Summer of Love, yet in places like my home town we still lived very close to the age of Disgrace and Ruin. Well, not quite disgrace but at least its direct descendant: vast embarrassment. I was not, like some 1930s girl, at risk of being locked up as a 'moral imbecile', and there were newborn charities starting to coin the phrase 'single mother' and to strip the contumely from it. But all the same I was frankly terrified. I did not know how to tell my parents. I could not contemplate abortion or adoption yet had no idea how to manage motherhood. I froze, and did nothing for a week; then I wrote to Max at his London address, with 'Please Forward' in shaky blue ink on the top left-hand side of the envelope. I found a draft of the letter in a bundle of old essays and notes the other day, and as a belated penance for my stupid young self I reproduce it here:

Dearest Max,

I hope Italy is going well and the work is proving worth it. I am writing to you because something has happened which I didn't expect and you didn't either, but it is my fault, I know, and I'm not trying to put any pressure on you to come back or anything like that. It's that I'm expecting a baby. It is due at the beginning of next April, probably. Or the end of March. You're the only man. But like I say, it's

my fault and it's my decision, so as Marty would say, chill!
I hope to see you though.
 All my love,
 your salamander

It took me two days to write, the most difficult sentence being the last one before the sign-off. 'Hope to see you soon . . .' – no, too presumptuous. 'Hope to see you again . . .' – no, that admitted the possibility that we might never meet again. 'Hope to see you' – again, that accepted a possibility that I might not. 'Hope to see you though'. Yes, that was right. Meaningless but faintly optimistic.

It did not occur to me to hope that he might be pleased at the thought of paternity. I was not that unperceptive or ignorant of his ambitions and his nature. Besides, in those decades before all the modern excitement about genetic codes and biological fatherhood, pregnancy and babies were regarded as very much a woman's affair. More so, indeed, than before the Greer generation of feminists had banged on about women's human right to the contraceptive pill and abortion-on-demand. The cry, 'My body, my choice!' was, I fear, taken very literally by a lot of young men.

'OK, girls – your body, your choice, your baby. See you around sometime.' We were stuck between cultures: not protected by men but not able to demand much of them either. Reproduction was a women's problem, like period pains or bra-sizing or eyeshadow.

The letter went off, marked 'Please Forward'. Nothing happened. I imagined it bouncing along dusty white Italian roads from one poste restante to the next while Max strode ahead, coming into his noble heritage of ageless and sacred art. I bought a book about Italian frescos in the hope of understanding his world better. No reply came.

Then one day Marty turned up at my parents' house,

unannounced, with news that two more of our songs had been taken up on very favourable terms indeed by an American company nursing a new balladeer. He was always scrupulous about my share, though we had never signed any contract, and handed me a cheque for three thousand pounds: a fortune, three years' worth of lowly subsistence in some bedsitter for me and for the baby.

The comfort of it was immeasurable. At least now I was a little bit independent. When Marty handed it to me, with a flourish and a crooked grin, I began to cry in long, tearing, unbecoming sobs. He took me comfortably in his arms and went, 'Hey, hey, it's not that much, we'll do better, baby, wait till "Silken Julia" hits number one.' I jerked and sobbed some more and told him that I was really, really glad of the money but that the crying was because I was pregnant. He pushed me away to arms' length then and said roughly:

'Fucking Max?'

'Yes.'

'The arseing fucker! I'll chop his prick off!'

'It was me who wanted it.'

'Oh, for God's sake! Even with the groupies, guys use a French letter. Even when the girls say they're on the Pill.' He shook me, not gently. 'Did Max think you were on the Pill?'

'We didn't discuss it.' I felt sick. The shaking had brought back my morning nausea. 'Marty, let me go. I shouldn't've told you. Thanks to you I've got the money now, so I'm fine.'

He let me go. He was alert that day, unlike his usual half-stoned, amiably dopey self. 'Do your parents know?'

'No. I don't want to tell them yet.'

'They'll give you a bad time, won't they? Freak you out?'

'Yes.' I began to cry again. 'Marty, you're making it worse.'

He paced up and down the room – we were in my parents' living room, and by the mercy of God they were out to tea.

'Had an idea,' he said after a few moments. 'Solve everything. Shut your parents up, keep you writing good songs.
Marry me.'

'You?' I was sitting on the floor by now, with my back
against the end of the sofa, and was suddenly glad that there
was no futher to fall.

'Yeah. You can always divorce me after a couple of years,
but meanwhile you've got a wedding ring, the baby's got a
legal dad and your parents are happy.'

'But you don't love me!' Even as I said it, a faint chink of
treacherous hope opened up, surprising me greatly. I was
fond of this man, very fond, and he was demonstrating
strength and decisiveness. Pregnant women, the psycho-
biologists now tell us, are programmed to fall in love with
the nearest strong-seeming male; that is why they moon over
their gynaecologists. If Marty had declared himself at that
generous moment, my hormones might have sent me surging
towards him.

Being Marty, however, he did not take the opportunity to
say the dramatically correct thing. 'Well yeah, no, I s'pose
not . . . but neither does Max.' Hastily he added, 'And I'm
not an arsehole like he is, and I do really dig you. And I
don't fancy anyone else. Most girls I ever meet are really
stupid bitches.'

'But marrying! It's serious!'

'It's not 1873, baby. Marriage isn't prison. I think we could
have a good time and do more songs and – yeah, it'd be cool.'
He considered for a moment, then slyly glanced towards me
beneath his long dark lashes. 'You don't have to screw me, if
that's the problem.'

'Well, that's kind!' I said, recovering a little, and getting to
my feet. But then I saw his face and said more softly: 'Actually,
that *is* kind. You're really sweet. But, oh God, Marty – we
can't, it's a travesty, it's disgusting.'

'It's traditional,' he said with a crooked smile. 'It's in all those books. Marriage of convenience. I'd make an honest woman of you.' He ran his hand through his tangled hair. 'Max won't, you know. No point hanging on for him to do the decent thing, the kid'll be forty before he gets round to it.'

'Wouldn't you mind about being called the baby's father when you aren't?'

His eyes hooded. After a moment's silence he said: 'I knew a man once, who was a good father to the child of a complete bastard who made his wife pregnant.'

'Did he – the father – know?' I sensed that we were on dangerous ground, remembering my instinct about David Jakobowitz.

'Yeah. Think he did.'

'And did the kid know?' My own trouble faded for a moment in the intensity of his look: he was gazing past me into some sorrowful distance where I could not follow him.

'The kid worked it out in the end,' he said shortly. 'He preferred the proper dad to the biological one, trust me.'

I knew what he was talking about; he did not know that I knew. I stared at the familiar threadbare pink Persian rug on the splintery floorboards of my parents' living room. Battling weariness and fright and humiliation, I laboured to work out just what this flare of emotion might mean for my own child's future. It seemed that Marty had loved his mother's husband, Max's real father, and detested the usurper who begot him and later married his mother. I suddenly thought of Hamlet: God, maybe Claudius and Gertrude – but no, even the most tormented Shakespeare scholar never suggested that the usurper-King was Hamlet's real father. The phantom on the battlements was the real thing all right. And there was no question of Helena being Gertrude: Marty did not seem to despise the mother who had put him in this position.

So perhaps my own child would not despise me, even if it discovered that 'Uncle' Max was its father.

A wave of nausea came over me again as I blundered through these complexities in my mind. I felt deep horror that I had done this thing to us all, and a premonition that it could bring grief one day to the baby within me.

I muttered, 'Sorry,' and ran to the lavatory; there, in the chipped old bowl I had known all my life, I threw up for long minutes, retching and gasping. Then I stood up, trembling, rinsed my mouth and stared at my pale wild reflection in the little Chinese fake bar mirror with a naked lady (another family landmark. Ben had brought it back from his first tour at sea and my mother had prudishly banished it to the downstairs cloakroom). The naked lady in the mirror had a companion now, for I had not closed the door in my haste: Marty was standing behind me in the doorway, his long dark hair framing a hawk-sharp face, now soft with concern. He looked nothing like Max. He was no substitute for Max. But he was my friend and he wanted to help me. I turned to him, but he spoke first.

'It wouldn't be that bad,' he said coaxingly. 'I don't want to be properly married, not ever, I've seen what a rip-off it is. So might as well use my eligible status to help you out. For a bit.'

'Well – I did want to be really married, one day . . .'

'You still can be. When we divorce. But right now you're struck on my craphead brother, who is going to run a mile when you tell him you're up the duff. So we might as well make the best of it, huh? And write more songs? Go to the States, perhaps, have some fun?'

He was smiling, but after a moment the open anxious smile changed into a sly grin. The bitter seriousness which had gripped him during that odd moment in the living room had vanished, wiped away in an instant as Marty's emotions always were.

'And there's another reason it'd be a gas,' he said, watching me. 'Guess!'

'You want to poke Max in the eye,' I said stiffly. 'Give him a shock. Wrongfoot him.'

'Yeah. I do.'

'Well, I don't. I think that's a despicable reason to marry someone, just to piss off your brother.'

'Aw, c'mon,' said Marty. 'It's not the main reason, is it? We can do this, Sal. We really can. Queen Victoria's dead and gone. Let's do the thing that makes life happy, huh?'

So we did. I did give it some thought: I walked by the river for an hour alone while he went and slept in his battered van down the lane (he had, as usual, been up most of the night). Then I came back and sheepishly said yes, half convinced that he would have slept on it and withdrawn the offer. But he did not: he seemed pleased in a sleepy sort of way, and gave me an absent-minded hug. So on the fifteenth of October, 1973, at the parish church of St Mary and St Jude, I became Mrs Martin Bellinger. Or, to Friggy and the other members of Bastard & Sons, 'Marty's bird'.

The wedding, as I have said, was one to forget as quickly as possible, but the marriage was at first surprisingly enjoyable. I had not wanted to 'poke Max in the eye' as Marty put it, and took care not to catch his eye while I was wearing my horrid wedding dress from the Bridal Beauty Boutique at Tuttles of Lowestoft. The best word to describe my feelings at that stage is 'numb'. The baby did not seem like his: it was my problem, a biological catastrophe afflicting my body, a disease to be gone through until it was over. Everything had happened too fast for understanding or sane consideration; I craved only safety, shelter from parental disapproval and small-town Suffolk embarrassment and a haven from loneliness. I wanted a hole to hide in until it was all over.

But once Marty and I were set up in a rented flat off the King's Road, living on the proceeds of our songs and working on the Bastards' first album, there were unsought compensations. There was a faint treacherous comfort in knowing that Max was still living stiffly at home in Knightsbridge, studying at the Courtauld, without a girlfriend in sight and childishly dependent on an allowance from his stepfather. My life was at least progressing, though I had no idea in what direction it would go. Max would see this, and admire me as a free spirit. One day, we might yet be together.

The difficulty of my being married to his brother did not occur to me when I entertained this fantasy. That is how numb I was.

16

I was four months pregnant on my wedding day, and Marty and I did not sleep together. It seemed natural not to: there was a modest queasiness on my part, and a mixture of delicacy and sexual indifference on his. We shared a bed, chaste as Morecambe and Wise, simply because there was a big double in the furnished flat with plenty of room for us to lie apart. Marty smoked so much strong dope and kept such late hours that his sex drive seemed to be in abeyance most of the time, and certainly it was not directed towards me. We were comrades, colleagues, at our closest almost brother and sister. The shape of our daily lives in any case was hardly romantic. When the band was practising or doing a gig I would stay home in the evening, watch a bit of television or read, then turn in sleepily at ten o'clock to half wake in the small hours as a heavy figure slumped on to the other side of the bed. I would sometimes tousle his hair in a gesture of greeting, but almost immediately fall asleep again till pregnant restlessness woke me three hours later.

Marty would sleep on until after noon, then get up, eat two bananas (it was my job to keep us stocked up) and smoke a spliff (supply of hash, mercifully, was not my job). Then he would pick up his acoustic guitar and start to play, usually still wearing only his underpants. When I was home and the mood was on us, we would write more songs. Those from this period have not lasted as well as the Oxford ones, although from time to time you may hear a crooner on the radio giving

his all to 'Burden of Love', the first song I wrote about pregnancy. My lyric at first began: 'I'm carryin' your load, the happy
weight of loving . . .', but being an all-male band the Bastards
had to change it to 'You're carryin' my load, baby, I've weighed
ya down with lovin'', which for some reason always made Marty
giggle and make jokes about fork-lift trucks.

The pure love songs, however, had lost their edge. I did a
bit of work on Shakespearean songs to see if I could pirate
some sentiments and phrases from them, but the only one
which endured was 'Foolish rain' ('When I was a little boy,
love was nothin' but a toy'). And when I moved back to Byron
for inspiration I threw aside my Biro in despair: I was simply
too heavy to care about romance. When I told Marty this he
laughed, and said I would be fine in a month or so when it
was over. He was, in his insouciant way, very comforting.

Then we would eat a mid-afternoon lunch, more like a
nursery high tea from my childhood with eggs and bacon and
fruit and toasted crumpets, which Marty adored. Then it was
evening again, and he was off out. I did try going to his gigs,
but I fell asleep so easily that it became an embarrassment:
even in the less febrile celebrity culture of the 1970s there was
always a chance that a photographer would snap the lead
singer's pregnant wife sleeping, with her mouth open.

I do not think that anybody but us had the faintest idea that
we were in what the French call a *mariage blanc*. Marty showed
a laddish affection for me, gave me the odd bear-hug and
commented jokingly on my bump, but I assumed he had no
more idea of embracing me as a wife than if I was Friggy, or
Sam, or any of the others from the group. I had resolved that
if he wanted to sleep with me I would grit my teeth and put
up with it, in return for his undemanding good-fellowship and
the way he had saved me from embarrassment and loneliness.
But he showed no interest, and I was glad. I saw few of my
old friends, so nobody asked about the marriage. The new

friends I made in London that winter were of a different sort, and not at all likely to be inquisitive about my ménage.

For I did make new friends, in spite of everything. It began by accident: I had read somewhere that 'expectant mothers' should listen to great music and look at beautiful pictures, in the interests of their foetus' future intellectual ability. I felt guilty enough about this baby, having foisted life on it in such shaming circumstances and having no particular affection for it as yet. Although aborting the child had been too revolting an idea for me to countenance, I couldn't yet bring myself to feel love for it. So I tried to be dutiful instead. Now that the nausea of the first trimester had worn off, I resolved to embark on its pre-natal education by going to concerts and to the National Gallery.

My visits to the Wigmore Hall lunchtime piano recitals were not a great success, since my bladder seemed unable to make it through even the shortest concerto, so on one mild February day I took the Underground to Trafalgar Square to see if great pictures would be easier to take in. It may have been in my mind that this was Max's child, hence destined for the life aesthetic. Anyway, I spent an hour wandering round the galleries, avoiding the stern gaze of long-dead prelates and pausing wonderingly before calm-eyed Madonnas with pudgy infants held aloft. As I emerged into the sunshine of the Square a flock of pigeons rose suddenly in a cloud of glittering dust, alarmed perhaps by a car backfiring. As they spiralled upwards into the dazzle, over the lions and round the column, I felt an unwonted easing in myself, as if a small stiff knot had loosened. The knot had not resolved or untied itself, merely given up its hard impenetrable quality to show gleams of light between the tangled loops. I could not bring myself to go straight back into the dark tunnels of the Underground after this epiphanic moment, and wondered vaguely whether it was

possible to walk home to the King's Road: my London geo-
graphy was hazy. I set out in what seemed to be the right
direction, but before I had gone many paces my attention
was arrested by a sign down a side street.

ALMOST FREE THEATRE, it said. PAY WHAT YOU CAN. I had
heard about this; at that time it was impossible for anybody
who read a London evening paper not to know about the
hippyish, innovative projects of the counter-culture movement, particularly Ed Berman's 'InterAction'. I had been
vaguely intrigued to read about this reckless synthesis of
social action and theatre, playgroups and rock, politics and
clowning and squatting and ramshackle city-farms with cows
being milked alongside the Elephant and Castle. And here
was a bit of it right in front of me: a little dive of a theatre
with the Almost Free banner. I walked towards it, and was
about to pass by with a sly embarrassed sidelong glance when
a man in patched jeans, with a lot of bare chest showing
under his floral shirt, accosted me with no sign at all of
embarrassment or British restraint.

'Hi! You coming to the show? It's really good. It's Ubu Roi,'
he said. He smiled at me, his red lips startling against a straggly
black beard. His voice was oddly classless, unplaceable: not
quite American, not quite English. I paused, confused.

'Jarry. Ubu Roi. Like I said, it's good. Only forty-five minutes,
you can get back to work by two – feed your mind –'

'I don't go to work, it's OK.' I had not talked to anybody
but Marty and the corner-shop lady for weeks, and my voice
sounded strange and high.

'Cool! Unwaged, you get in free,' he said. 'So go on in.
You'll love it.'

I smirked, almost ran away and then despised myself for
the impulse and went in. In the darkness I sat down on a
wobbly chair. The play was indifferent, really: too much
shouting. I knew a bit about Jarry from college drama society

play-readings, and I have never been a natural aficionado of absurdist political comedy. Yet as it went on I felt a sense of liberation in just being there, in this dark scruffy little room, with the sparse audience around me breathing and fidgeting and guffawing at scatological jokes. At moments when the lighting increased – it was a hit-and-miss affair technically – and cast a dull gleam over the audience, I glanced around and studied them: an odd mixture of office workers, tramps, students and straggle-haired hippies.

Warmth crept into me. It was not happiness, a state still far off and improbable; yet the oddness of the event had comfort in it. Ubu raged onstage, the winos laughed at the wrong moment, young voices giggled, a man in a neat city suit snorted with reluctant amusement, the lighting-rig wobbled and sent a bulb crashing to the concrete floor. I smiled in the darkness: life was odd, people were odd, I was in an odd situation in my life. So what?

When the bare bulbs overhead that served for house-lights cast us back into squalid reality I heaved myself up from the chair – I was gravid by now to the point of clumsiness – and followed the audience as it straggled to the door. Again I emerged blinking into sunlight and noticed that a few of the students were putting money into the box. I fumbled in my bag, and the black-bearded boy on the door said, 'I told you. Unwaged, you don't have to pay anything.' He looked at me and grinned again, with that disconcertingly unEnglish lack of embarrassment. 'Unwaged and pregnant, definitely nothing.'

'I'm not unwaged,' I said with a sudden communicativeness that would have been impossible before the Ubu hour I had just spent. 'I said I'm not working because I don't go out to work. I'm a songwriter. I got some good money last year so I'm OK. I'd like to pay.' I put a pound note into the box, with a little flourish. But the boy was looking at me with new interest.

'Songwriter? Like, words?'

'Yes.'

'Damien!' He turned to a figure behind me in the dark doorway, and I recognized the actor who had played Ubu. He was scrubbing casually at the remains of his make-up with what looked like an old dishrag, and over his arm hung the tatty regal robe he had worn. 'Damien! We got a songwriter!'

The actor peered at me, then threw his robe and rag backwards into the auditorium with the air of a man moving on to the next challenge in a complex and unpredictable, but generally enjoyable, life.

'Cool!' he said. 'You can help us.'

I stared. Blackbeard patted me on the shoulder, in an astonishingly familiar way for a brand-new and tenuous acquaintance, and said, 'Yeah. We need words by tonight for the demo. The Wages for Housework Campaign sweep-in. Five hundred women are going to sweep Parliament Square, right? To make the enslavement of women to domestic chores visible. Only we've got to practise the song, and put it out on the duplicator, and we haven't got words.'

'Don't you know any words yourself?' My voice was less high now, more confident.

'Yeah, but none of them rhyme.'

I think I prevaricated for a little longer, but one way or another it came about that within minutes I was back inside the auditorium, sitting on a chair being passed a sheaf of paper (the reverse of an Ubu script, in fact) and a series of Biros. The fourth of these proved capable of writing, and Blackbeard – who had announced his name to be Jake – said, 'OK. We thought it'd be cool to use the seven dwarfs' song from *Snow White* as a tune.'

'It's copyright!' I had been involved enough in the music business to be scandalized. 'Disney could sue!'

'So let them sue five hundred women who don't get paid

anything,' said Damien happily. 'That's the beauty of demos. Nothing to lose.'

'Well, don't tell anyone I helped.'

'Can't. Don't know your name, do we?'

'True.'

Twenty minutes later the scrawls and crossings-out on the back of the Ubu script had taken form.

> Hi ho, hi hay,
> We work all night and day,
> And all we want – and all we want –
> Is pay! Just pay!
> Hey hey! Hi Ho! Hi hoo,
> You know just what to do.
> Just show you care and play it fair
> And pay! And pay and pay and pay . . .

It is possibly the worst lyric I have ever written, but as Damien and Jake reassured me, the main thing is that a chant should be easy to remember 'even if you're a bit stoned' and intelligible to any listening microphones and reporters.

I went home, told Marty about my day and made him scrambled egg and crumpets. The next day, tired out, I slept as long as he did and spent an idle afternoon. But at six o'clock we switched on the news programme and saw a reporter standing in Parliament Square framed by hundreds of women waving mops and brooms. A ringleader wearing a huge badge saying WAGES DUE LESBIANS was interviewed, together with a Labour MP's wife who had – presumably to her husband's chagrin – joined the Wages for Housework Campaign. Then in the background a chant swelled:

'Hi ho, Hi hay, we work all night and day . . .'

I screamed with horrified delight, and pointed at the

screen: Marty lifted his head from the guitar he was tuning and watched for a moment.

'You never wrote that crap!' he said, with a tang of admiration in his voice. 'Did you?'

'Well, there were two other guys,' I said.

'It's a really stupid campaign,' Marty ruled. 'Imagine if someone paid my mother for putting flowers in vases and bossing the help. But hey, it's another footprint in history for you, huh?'

'Yes.' I could not tear my eyes from it. 'It does make me feel – kind of contemporary.'

'Luther King, step aside,' said Marty, not unkindly, and went back to his tuning.

When I think of that time in our scruffy little flat, the sound which rings in my ears is always of guitars being tuned; a quiet, homely ting-ing sound with an occasional low discordant growl.

After that, I took to visiting the Almost Free Theatre two or three times a week. Sometimes Jake or Damien would be there, on the door or performing, and sometimes others of their set. They welcomed me with a matter-of-fact but distinctly absent-minded pleasure, as if I were a cat that wandered through their lives from time to time and needed stroking and plying with leftovers. They introduced me to the others as: 'Sal, who helped with the sweep-in'. I sat through the performances: Italian socialist revolutionary playlets, fragments of South American surrealism, dreary rants about the Vietnam War, and occasional finely judged, rather poignant slices of life from playwrights who I felt, with a thrill of early discovery, were going to endure for decades or centuries. But the people themselves were the real reason I kept going.

I liked Jake a lot: he was, he told me, Canadian but 'on the run from moose hunts and mother-love'. Damien was harder to like, more pretentious and at times politically shrill. His girlfriend Anna was a silent restful hippie; her friend Natalia a militant lesbian who wrote angry polemics for the underground press and had twice been arrested for indecency in various louche demonstrations. 'It's my vagina, it's my statement.' Her idea of political action invariably involved exposure below the belt. Then, my favourite of them all, there was a smiling young giant called Gordon who alternated between labouring on the latest phase of the Barbican Centre and playing blues harmonica in pubs. Gordy was a joy to know, like a bigger soberer version of Marty: he would always greet me with bear-hugs and displays of unaccountable but agreeable joy, like a big kind dog.

One day Anna asked if I would like to come to supper. I hesitated: late nights were still difficult for me and I was heavy and torpid, eight months gone. Marty, however, urged me to take her up on it – 'You need some new friends' – and I went several times to the squat near Southwark Cathedral where she lived with Damien, Natalia, Natalia's girlfriend Sukey and two InterAction workers. Getting in was interestingly commando: we had to cut across the Cathedral precinct, climb a low wall and squeeze down a narrow alleyway to a flaking and filthy back door by some dustbins. I think it had once been a shop; the front was boarded up. Inside, however, it was not unpleasant. The girls (without, I noticed, demanding wages for their housework) had draped Indonesian print cotton swatches and sarongs over the damp and peeling plaster, and thrown other more or less exotic, if shabby, textiles on the floor. The place smelt of dry rot and incense, and tinkled with ethnic bells hung on straps from various non-functioning electric sockets. We sat around on cushions by candlelight and ate a meal of rice and vegetables which Anna said was macrobiotically balanced, followed by some Turkish baklava which made us exceedingly sticky (there was no cutlery except spoons for the rice). Pinging, twanging sitar music played from a rather stretched cassette tape, and joss-stick clouds hung heavy on the air.

It was like being a student again: the heady talk of change and revolution, the rudimentary food, the circulating spliffs, the assertions that Harold Wilson was no less of a Tory than Ted Heath. But there was something else there which I honoured. For all their hippyish home lives these people were busy. They were setting up plays and demonstrations and children's drumming groups and community 'projects' which drew in the frequently baffled, but generally game, women of working-class South London. They were louche, they were forthright, they were (especially Damien and Natalia) a bit pretentious, and several of them claimed to be anarchists. But they were in general trying to make things better, in their own wonky image: there was an earnestness about them. As a child of the Vicarage I felt unexpectedly at home.

Above all, none of them ever behaved as if there was anything strange about my being pregnant and without an obvious attendant male. I walked taller when I had been with them. Their causes were not mine, their lives would drive me crazy within days – I had self-knowledge enough to see that – but they accepted me, knowing nothing about my degree or my background or even that Marty and I were married. Their friendliness came without a price-tag or any assumption that I was enrolled in their tribe. Once I had haltingly explained my physical reluctance to use drugs, they stopped offering them and seemed not to think any the less of me. All they ever asked of me, for assistance in their projects and campaigns, were a few rhymes, taglines or lyrics. I could always provide these. Gordy Wise would hug me ecstatically when I delivered them and say, 'You're the words-girl, you gottem. Cool!' Sometimes I wondered what Max would say if he could see me lolling on grimy mirrored Indian cushions with this lot. But not often. I was trying not to think of Max. With my counter-culture friends I came nearer to forgetting him than at any other time.

I met another friend too, in comic contrast to Jake's set. Coming back from the theatre early one afternoon I was almost knocked over by a broad-shouldered, long-legged striding young man in a pinstriped City suit, heading eastward at a tremendous rate. He caught me before I could fall and began blushingly to apologize: 'So sorry – God, what a clumsy oaf I am – not looking where I was going – are you all right? Oh, your ankle – did I? Terribly sorry—'

I cut him short. 'Hello, Donald.'

He looked so blank that for a moment I was afraid I had got it wrong; but then a great smile split his face and I knew for certain that this was the same young man who had taken me into Evensong and lent me his sweater, long ago in that other world.

'Sally!' he spluttered. 'This is – astonishing. Amazing. Epic. Enchanting. How *are* you?'

'Pregnant,' I said. He knew this, obviously; my state had been the reason for his acute discomfiture at knocking into me. But there was so much surprise and chagrin behind his smile that I felt I must confront the facts and explain myself as fast as possible. There was a quality in Donald that compelled you to be straight with him.

'I got married in the autumn. But it's not straightforward, exactly –' I hesitated. 'Marriage of convenience, you might say. The baby is not – um, – associated with the marriage, really.'

I lost my way and blushed, suddenly aware that I was draped in a batik tent dress and a silly sequinned scarf, hugely pregnant, babbling out my embarrassing life story to a neatly suited City banker type who was even, I now noticed, carrying the traditional rolled umbrella. I seized on its presence, grateful for another topic.

'And you,' I continued with all the brightness I could muster, 'have not lost the habit of always having an umbrella.'

He blushed, now. 'Oh, you remember!'

'I'll never forget,' I said seriously. 'That Evensong was beautiful. And –' I lied, 'I've still got the coloured umbrella.'

He looked down at me, and all the hurry and embarrassment was gone from his face.

'I still sing.'

'Oh, where?'

'Round the corner – there – the actors' church, on the edge of Covent Garden market. It's got a really good choir. A lot of Bach. We have lunchtime practices, which is why I was rushing back to work by way of the sandwich bar.'

'I might come and listen. Music's good for the baby, apparently.'

'Oh, do. Wednesdays and Fridays. One o'clock.'

So I went one day, and sat in the splendid Georgian music-room that is St Paul's church listening to Donald and a dozen others soaring and swooping around a section of the *Missa Solemnis*. There were tears in my eyes when it ended: it carried me back to an earlier time, less than a year ago, when everything seemed possible if you only loved enough and gave enough and never faltered in the loving and the giving. I slipped away before Donald could disengage himself from the conductor's final briefing, and went home in a chastened, depressed mood.

Marty did not notice. He was exultant, crowing with delight. Bastard & Sons had got a short but significant US tour. They were leaving in four weeks' time. He wished I could come along, but I would not be allowed to fly in my condition. It would take nearly a month, would I be OK?

I told him of course I would, made cheese on toast for us both, and went to bed early.

17

Marty flew to New York at the beginning of March, excited and apprehensive and stone-cold sober. He smoked no weed at all in the week before, but fussed like a real professional over guitars and amplifiers, repertoire and wardrobe. I rewrote some lines for him where we judged that they would be difficult for American audiences to follow, and Friggy and he spent long hours closeted together, planning the shape of their sets and agonizing over whether certain bits of the act were too raw for the Mid-West.

'If we crack it over there,' he kept saying, 'we're made. Remember how it was for the Beatles. They love Brits. If we can sell in America, baby, we're set up for life. And the industry over here really respects you if you've cracked the States. You win both ways.'

I was languid, heavy, and amused in spite of myself.

'Mart, you sound like a young executive. Not a wild man of rock. Perhaps you shouldn't *be* trying so hard to please them. Just be yourselves.'

'It's important, honey.' He was even using American endearments, practising for the new words we had sneaked into our British songs. 'I want to get bread. For you and the baby. Move somewhere with a garden for the pram. God, do you think we should change our name? Apparently the Yanks are a bit weird about the word *bastard*. We'll never crack the Bible belt – that, like, matters, when you've got a family – there's millions of them believe in morality and stuff.'

He whirled round, twanging the guitar exultantly, then shimmied over and patted my bump. He was acting more and more like a husband, and seemed to have completely forgotten that we were getting divorced once the baby had arrived and the dust settled. He rubbed my vast stomach gently once more as he left for the airport, and then gingerly took me in his arms and kissed me on the mouth for the first time.

'Stay safe. I'll be back before it's due. You two look after yourselves.'

When he had gone – Friggy picked him up in the van, and he banned me from going to the airport because it entailed too much standing – I rubbed my lips incredulously, remembering the kiss and the kindness. Then I went through to the empty bedroom and cast myself down, ungainly and unhappy, on the bed. For one thing, I felt abandoned: I had not realized how much I valued the protection of having Marty wandering round the flat in his underpants tuning his guitar. But worse, the kiss had reminded me of Max, who should be with me now protecting and expecting his baby. I had not heard a word from him since the wedding. All my distractions and new friendships could not camouflage that stark central fact. I told myself that he was being chivalrous, giving my marriage to his brother a chance, renouncing his child out of nobility; but still it felt more as if nobody loved me, or my baby. I wept, but it was for the loss of Max; to my shame I almost forgot about Marty until he rang next day from New York to say he had arrived safely.

Two days later, there was a paragraph in the *Daily Express* about the latest British group to hit New York, with a spiteful little aside about their indifferent success in the UK, 'apart from the fluke sensation No 1 *Silken Julia*, formerly banned by the BBC, which perhaps owed more to scandal than to merit'. There was a picture of the Bastards snarling prettily at the camera. Helena and her husband must have been *Express* readers, because on that same day I had a telephone call.

'Is that Mrs Sally Bellinger?' said a plummy voice, unmistakable as a senior secretary. I said that I supposed I was.

'I have Mr Jakobowitz on the line for you,' said the voice with efficient reverence, and after a pause I heard the confident tones of Marty's stepfather.

Or, possibly, father.

'Sally. I'm sorry we haven't seen more of each other. I was wondering whether you'd care to come to lunch with me, as you're on your own.'

He hadn't seen much of us – anything, indeed, since the wedding – for the simple and well-known reason that Marty could not bear the sight of him. His tone, however, was that of a man suavely executing a family duty towards a favourite daughter-in-law while the son was away. It was well done. It made the feud itself seem silly. It made my resentment of his alleged treatment of Kate seem juvenile. I could hardly say no.

'That's very kind. I'd – ah – like to.' Perhaps, I thought, I could help to mend the rift with Marty. At any rate the outing would get me out of the lonely flat. I felt too heavy now, and generally too sad, to get over the back wall and spend time with my friends at the squat.

'Good. Wonderful. If I could just put you back to Brenda, she has the diary –'

His secretary returned to the line and smoothly made a date two days away ('He's got a window, that *is* lucky,' she said, in tones designed to impress on me how fortunate I was to be booking a slice of the precious Jakobowitz time). The restaurant she named took my breath away: it was so legendary, so expensive, so achingly fashionable at the very top end of smart London, that I was filled with terror at the thought of crossing its threshold in my batik tent. I went out on to the King's Road and lumbered from shop to shop in search of something more dignified – I can remember thinking the word 'dignified', and realizing that I had never before sought such a look. Clearly Mr Jakobowitz' aura of suave middle-aged importance was having its effect on me already. At last I found a brown wool-mixture maternity dress with an embroidered yoke and a white cotton collar, which made me look like a camp Friar Tuck. I found some tights in a paler brown, and bought two pairs so I could cut them up and use one leg of each. None of the shops in our shabby-chic part of London sold uncool things like maternity tights, and I was too tired to lumber up to Peter Jones.

Inevitably they laddered, so that I felt awful yawning holes with their edges biting into my fat thighs; I hesitated miserably outside the restaurant on the appointed day, feeling ugly and forlorn and entirely uncertain about whether to go in. Moments later, a long black car pulled up and a lithe figure jumped from the back seat and hurried over to me. David Jakobowitz was disarmingly boyish in his apology.

'I'm so sorry – you've been waiting in the cold – I meant to be early but the traffic –' Taking my arm with old-fashioned chivalry, he guided me in, nodded to the bowing figure by the tall desk without giving his name, and steered me to a table which even my inexperienced eye could see was one of the best: a roomy alcove. The chairs, I saw with a sinking of the heart, had arms to them. I was going to be uncomfortable with my eight months' bulge spreading sideways when I sat. Jakobowitz' eye followed mine, his head inclined very slightly, and a dark eyebrow shot up at the hovering maître d'hôtel. Seconds later, not one but both the chairs were replaced with armless ones.

When we had settled, studied the menu and ordered – his flow of reassuring small-talk continuing throughout, as courteous as I would have expected – he raised his glass to me and said: 'Here's to you and Martin and the child. *Mazel tov*.' He sipped his wine abstemiously, and put the glass down. 'I hope that all is well?'

'Yes, thank you.' I sipped in turn, grateful for the warm fruity bite of the claret. 'We're all fine.'

'And your flat? Is it comfortable?'

'Well – it's fine. For the moment.' I had not expected the question, and it threw me off balance. 'Landlord's furniture, you know.'

He smiled, and again I saw Marty's face in his.

'When I first came to London,' he said, 'to study account-ancy, I lived in half a room in Brixton, with a bathroom on the landing and a curtain down the middle.'

I was intrigued, as he had meant me to be, at the discovery that he had started life poor.

'Who was on the other side of the curtain?' I asked lightly.

'My father,' he said. 'He wasn't well.'

I drank more wine and contemplated this unexpected vision of a young Jakobowitz – looking just like Marty – caring for some sick or demented old father in a bedsitter and studying his books every evening to escape whatever post-war ghetto they had come from.

'It was not comfortable. So I very much wanted Martin and his lovely bride –' he raised his glass to me, but did not drink '– to be comfortable in their first home. Martin may not have told you, but I had hoped he would accept the small security of a flat from his mother and me.'

I inclined my head. I did know this: Marty had said, with a sneer, 'My mother's fancy-man tried to buy us for the price of some stinking flat in Maida Vale.'

'He refused. Martin is a proud young man. I suppose that's a good thing. I have been proud myself, in my time.' Jakobowitz looked so woebegone that I began to feel sorry for him.

'He wants to do things on his own,' I agreed. 'I'm sure it's not personal.'

His dark brows snapped together, and I saw the clever, shrewd banker return in an instant.

'Oh, but it is,' he said sharply. 'You must be aware of the distaste my – ah – Martin has for me. Surely?'

Wrongfooted, I babbled a little. 'Yes, yes . . . but he's head-strong . . . I mean, I believe in family, people getting on with relatives . . . I'm sure it'll wear off . . .'

'He dislikes me,' said David Jakobowitz heavily, 'because he has a profound loyalty to the late Samuel Bellinger, my wife's first husband.'

I looked him in the eye. 'His father?'

For once he did not return my gaze, but fingered his knife on the shining tablecloth. 'He resents my presence in the household. It is not unusual. Max – my elder stepson – takes a different and more mature –' Was it my imagination, or did he flinch? '– and more rational approach. You know Max a little, I believe?'

Now it was my turn to gather myself for some plain speaking. 'Look,' I said, 'I don't know what Max has said to you and Mrs Jakobowitz, but as a matter of fact we were housemates at Oxford, and ironically I knew him much, much better than I knew Marty, until we started writing the songs.'

'Is that right?' He looked genuinely astonished, and once again I had a sense that he was flinching a little, re-arranging his view of the two brothers. 'Well, Max is a more – ah – complaisant character. Easier, more accepting of his mother's choice of second husband. I have always found him charming.'

'Marty doesn't do the charming thing,' I said lightly, because I did not want to have to talk about Max.

David Jakobowitz smiled with real relief. 'No. He is very honest about his feelings. That may be your good luck, in the long run. But Sally –' there was a pause while the waiter fussed round with two plates of prawns and aïoli '– Sally, may I ask you, with an old man's impertinence, one or two things about my— about Martin?'

'Do.' I speared a prawn and waited. He fixed me with his clever dark eyes, but the question when it came was unexpected.

'It is about how you operate when you write your songs together – and by the way, I like them very much indeed, particularly "Your love is the wind" and "Building a hut".'

I gaped, amazed that he knew them.

He went on: 'Am I right in thinking that the words are all yours, and the tunes his?'

'Yes. I'm the lyricist.'

'Does Marty ever suggest or re-order the words? Many composers do.'

'N– no' It had never occurred to me to think about it, but the stepfather was right: Marty was not good with rhyme or metre, and stumbled over his choice of words. 'He's just amazingly good at the music, at getting the emotion into it, which matters a lot with pop songs . . .' I petered out, because I was thinking hard new thoughts. Marty was growing less articulate, most days. It was true.

'Has this pattern changed, over the months you have worked together?'

I put down my fork and stared at him. A small voice, mine, said: 'Yes.'

'Got worse?'

'I wouldn't say worse. It's how we work. He used to suggest lines more, that's true. Like he used to chat more. Perhaps it's just that I've got faster at writing, and he doesn't need to.'

'Of course. And you work very well. And I respect his musical abilities, more than he knows. But I was hoping that you would say that the two of you were more – verbally collaborative, and that things had not changed in recent months.'

My hand was unsteady on my glass: I was easily upset in those late days of pregnancy. Although I did not wholly understand him, a sense of vague dread was upon me.

'The day he left,' I said, 'he was talking much more than usual.'

'Had he, perhaps, been smoking less hashish?'

I ducked my head. 'He does smoke, yeah. And he did lay off it because he was so busy getting ready for the States.'

'So to recapitulate,' said Jakobowitz, pushing away the rest of his prawns. 'He uses a lot of the drug as a rule, and when he uses less of it his mind works better. The effect, then, is capable of reversing itself.'

'Well,' I said defiantly, 'when you're not stoned, you're sharper. That's obvious.'

He gave me a hard, unfathomable look. 'You believe then that there is no long-term mental damage?'

I stared. I had never thought about it. Nor had any of the potheads and acid-freaks I knew at university. We knew that heroin and cocaine were dangerously addictive, but they were distant monsters, far from our lives and ludicrously beyond our budgets. The idea that smoking the occasional joint could harm you was miles off the radar. I sometimes wished that Marty smoked less, just because of the mess and the smell and the erratic domestic behaviour – pillows in the bath, mucky cheese sculptures melting on top of the fridge, murals done with my lipstick all over the bathroom mirror, that sort of thing. But the idea that it was changing or harming him permanently had never occurred to me. After a moment I answered his stepfather as honestly as I could.

'Well, I've never seen anyone suffering much from it. I know your generation disapproves, and I don't use it myself because it freaks me out. But I've known a lot of people who smoke a lot and they're all absolutely fine.' I thought of Jake and Gordy and the girls at the squat.

'People are not all the same,' he said, matter of factly, and then there was another pause while the waiter brought our Dover soles. He repeated it, with precisely the same emphasis.

'People are not all the same. Some have sensitivities and are additionally vulnerable to being damaged or pushed into danger by psycho-active drugs. I have noticed that Marty's conversation has changed in recent years, growing ever more disjointed. Obviously, he rarely speaks to me directly, because of the hostile feelings we are both aware of. But when he is with his mother or his brother I have noticed a gradual change. Perhaps as a third party, an outsider, it is easier to see this. One listens critically, as if to music or a radio play, when one is not expected to respond.'

Suddenly, I felt desperately sorry for him. There was no tremor in his voice and no demand for pity, but his situation seemed to me almost insupportable. I had seen the way my father looked at Ben, the son who made him proud and fond. This man too was a father, albeit an unacknowledged one. I had noticed the 'my son' which had almost slipped out earlier, and his next words confirmed what I had known ever since that uneasy breakfast in Knightsbridge.

'Perhaps,' he was continuing, his attention apparently on his plate, 'I am particularly aware of this because my father was a musician and also an addict. I looked after him in the year before his death.'

'When you lived in Brixton?'

'Yes.'

'What was he addicted to?' It seemed kindest to ask straight questions, as he clearly wanted to tell me all this.

'Alcohol, at first. We came from Russia, and things had been hard for him. England, I think, felt like exile. He was a violinist, rather a fine one, but his hand was injured when he was . . . questioned by the Soviet police. So he drank. Then once over here, various substances became available and he found them more stimulating. In the end it was heroin. But what I remember best is the way that his speech patterns changed, the way that his grasp of language seemed to fade before anything else.' I was about to speak but he forestalled me, raising his hand apologetically. 'You will say that it is not always so. You are right. I know that some remarkable art and literature has come out of drug-takers, from De Quincey to Timothy Leary –'

I must have looked surprised, for he gave a crooked, unmistakably Marty grin and said, 'Even bankers read, you know.'

'I'm sorry.'

'No need. Anyway. I am aware that the pot-smoking habit of your generation is mainly harmless. There are times when I would rather relish the escape myself. But I believe that there are people who are peculiarly sensitive, and peculiarly in danger.'

'Well, I know this,' I said. 'It freaked *me* out when I tried. I felt really stupid.'

'Which is unreasonable of you. Human biology is variable and we know little enough about the brain. But as I say, I believe that some people are vulnerable. They need it too much, too quickly, and at the same time it confuses them more severely. So they cannot perceive the damage. I believe this to be as definite a characteristic as red hair, or musical talent. And I also believe –' he fixed me with his dark sorrowful eyes so that I could not look away '– that it is hereditary.'

There was a heartbeat's silence, as I took in the fact that he was admitting the truth to me without disguise. Finally, shifting heavily in my seat, I just said: 'I know. I mean, I know why you said that. I saw it straight away.'

He was twirling his empty glass now, with a hand that shook slightly. He seemed to be concentrating on it, but then his eyes met mine again and he said, 'Good. You are perceptive.'

I felt myself flush, and muttered before I could straighten my thoughts, 'The thing is, I think . . . I think Marty knows.'

'I think so too.'

We had run into the sand. Neither of us could continue the conversation; we ate in silence for a few moments. Finally, with a great effort, he looked up again and said: 'I do not want to frighten you. But I worry about my son, and I was very happy that he had found himself a good, clever woman and had a baby on the way. The luck seemed unbelievable. I very much still hope that you and the child will be the saving of him. My father had only me, and I was young and impatient, with my way to make in the world. I paid him too little attention. He had lost his music, he had no friends in England, my mother was dead. Marty is more fortunate, and so he may be far safer.'

'What do you think I should do?' The question was wrenched from me, unwillingly.

'Keep him happy, keep him away from drugs.'

'Oh, come on!' I was almost angry now. 'You can't keep a rock musician away from drugs. Nobody can.'

David Jakobowitz looked at me steadily.

'I am sorry,' he said quietly, 'if that is really so.'

Marty's father sent me home with his car and chauffeur, and I paced around the flat for half an hour, unable to get comfortable in any chair after sitting for so long in the restaurant. Indeed, that day marked the beginning of the final lap of my pregnant discomfort. For days afterwards, every time I lay down the baby began to kick with more than usual violence; this brought on nausea, so I would get up again and do some light housework, anything to keep moving. For some reason I could not read a book: my concentration slid away after half a page and I was left staring into space, despising myself for having let my brain go to mush. I thought a great deal about what David Jakobowitz had said, and thought too about the old widower, the violinist without music, trapped in a stinking bedsit in Brixton with an impatient ambitious son, consoling himself with heroin.

On the third day – without Marty to mess up the flat – I had nothing left to do but spend half an hour cleaning the windows with fistfuls of damp newspaper. By an association of ideas this made me pick up my bag and keys and head out into the street in search of a newsvendor. On the corner near the Quant shop I bought the *London Evening News*, and took it back up the narrow stairs. The front was full of angry news about the latest GLC argument, so I flicked the page over and found myself staring at my husband's pale, contorted face.

LONDON GROUP 'TRASH' SAY ANGRY YANKS BASTARDS HEAD FOR HOME

Heart sinking, I read on.

'Ever since John, Paul, George and Ringo infected the USA with Beatlemania, the dream of every British group is to crack the Big Apple. For a few days in hip New York it looked as if the melodious bad boys from London, Bastard & Sons, were going to achieve at least an echo of that success. Venturing further afield, though, proved sticky for the controversial group, whose single 'Silken Julia' was at one stage banned by the BBC. The City of Boston, once famous for throwing our tea into its harbour, came close to doing the same for Marty Bell's crudely named band.

Heckled by Evangelical Christian protesters at the Showbowl, the group – in the words of bassist Friggy Tarka – 'freaked' and the subsequent fracas . . .'

Fracas, it seemed, was a polite way of putting it. What might have been an easily contained demonstration against the song's 'obscenity' and the group's accompanying gestures (oh, Friggy!) was aggravated when Tony, the drummer, jumped from the stage and laid about the protesters with his sticks. The Boston police presence took a dim view of this, and moved in; whereupon the other three leaped down clutching microphone-stands as weapons. Matters escalated from there. The group spent a night in the cells, aggravating their offence, according to the *News*, with torrents of obscenity; they were found to be in possession of copious quantities of cannabis resin and illegal amphetamines. They were being deported, and lucky not to be charged in the US.

I read it through twice, then stood up, feeling that I should be doing something. Phoning David Jakobowitz perhaps, or finding out what plane Bastard & Sons were getting home on. But no sooner had I hauled myself from the chair than an agonizing pain shot through my back, taking my breath away and fading only slowly into a dull ache. Then came another, and five minutes later another; panting and panicking, I picked up the phone, knowing that my hour had come.

18

Charlotte Helena Bellinger was born at ten past three in the morning, on the far side of a painful, sweaty interlude of loneliness and terror. David Jakobowitz had shyly offered during our lunch date to pay for a private hospital, but I turned him down, out of respect for Marty's pride and with a dash of political leftishness that was all my own. There were moments during that night when I regretted this: the public ward was full of groaning frightened women, the nurses were hard and brisk and the indignity of being strapped immobile in stirrups was entirely hateful. When at last the baby had been extracted – no other word for it, some terrible rubber plunger device was involved – she was laid on my chest in wrappings so impenetrable that I could not feel her warm skin. Then she was whisked away to 'the nursery' before I could feed her.

'Better you get some sleep,' said the nurse sharply. 'This time of night. Baby's a good weight, she won't need to feed until the six o'clock round.'

I lay awake, listening to the heavy breathing of the women asleep along the open ward and to the distant mewings and 'rlah! rlah!' wailings from the room where the babies were imprisoned. I thought, through the pain and stiffness and hunger that afflicted me, that I could hear my own baby. Falling briefly asleep, I woke in terror from a dream of ragged torn-off foetus legs, an image from some horror pamphlet handed out by anti-abortionists at college. I could not even remember whether they had said 'boy' or 'girl', and sobbed into my pillow, fearful of waking the others or attracting the nurse's attention.

She came over, though, holding out a pill and a glass.

'Sleeping pill,' she said brusquely.

'I can't. I've got to feed my baby at six, it's five o'clock now.'

'Baby can have Formula.'

'I don't want her – him – it – the baby to have formula milk.'

'Trying to feed Baby won't do any good if you're tired and confused. Why, Mummy, you can't even remember if you've got a little boy or a little girl. You won't be any use to Baby till you've had a rest.'

I could not rest. I would not take the pill, or eat the sodden bran flakes they brought me for breakfast at six-thirty. I climbed out of bed and walked around in my bare feet, attracting further scoldings from the nurse, and only at eight o'clock did I manage to make her bring me my baby.

Looking at her, I saw nothing that I recognized. Nuzzling her neck I smelt only generic baby smells, overlaid with the harsh scent of hospital soap and the glutinous formula milk they had fed her on the dot of six. I wept. Charlotte bawled. I had named her instantly, in a desperate attempt to know her, though heaven knows I never have liked that name and have no idea where it came from. I suspect it was the first name which came into my head when I realized that I could not opt for Maxine. It became permanent very quickly, however, because the registrar of births came round on her ward visit while Charlotte was still howling and I was fumbling inexpertly with dry nipples and a desperate questing little mouth. I spoke the name quickly to get rid of the woman, throwing in the 'Helena' because she had her pen poised for a middle name, and I thought that Marty and

David would like it, and that it would be good if they liked the baby because then it might not die from having a bad mother like me. I had thought from time to time about leaving the space for 'father' blank, but when she asked me, rather impatiently, 'Your husband's Christian name?' I said 'Martin' before I could stop myself, and she wrote it down.

I suppose it saved a bit of trouble. As for my own feelings, at that moment I was finding it hard to entertain love, or triumph, or tenderness, or any of the maternal feelings I had read about. My main driving emotion was protective panic. I did not see how I would ever manage this tiny but positive personage on my own. I wanted her to have protectors and patrons. Helena, Marty, David – what did it matter? Poor child, she must have people of her own!

'Helena's a pretty name,' said the register, writing the name on the official form with a silver fountain pen. 'Now, the surname – is it B-e-double 1, or B-a-double 1? Is it a Huguenot name?'

Eventually, the child began to feed and I felt a dizzy rush of oxytocin like a stiff drink spreading through my veins. I had read about this hormonal effect but it still came as a surprise. I looked down and realized that I did, after all, recognize this sucking baby with her closed eyes and rhythmically moving cheeks. She was mine, child of my violent and faithful devotion to Max. Mine, and his. He might never admit the fact, but it was true.

I did not quite love the child yet, but I marvelled at her solidity. She was a fact. Nothing could rub her out. She was physical and inalienable proof of her own existence: hence she confirmed mine and Max's. It was as if I had been a ghost before, drifting through life insubstantial, making little difference to anybody I met. Had not my friends drifted away, my lover shown no care for me? I forgot Marty, of course. But anyway, from now on I was solid, anchored by this soft unsmiling little lump of humanity. When they took her away again to the baby-gulag they called the nursery I wept for loneliness.

But I slept, and woke, and fed her again and ate a little and then slept once more; and when I woke up this time Marty was at my bedside, beaming and saying, 'Man!'

I stared at him, groggy and confused. He had a black eye, his arm was in a sling and his trouser leg rolled up over a huge bandage. When he saw that I was awake he leaned forward and put his other arm across me, pulling me to him in a rudimentary hug.

'You all right, babe?'

'I'm all right. I've only had a baby. You look as if you've been in a fight with Muhammad Ali.'

'Two fights, and a tumble down the gangway of the plane. Cut my leg on the Tarmac. Was my fault, I was doing a power salute to the fans, only they turned out to be police.' He cackled.

'Is the arm broken?'

'Nope. Dislocated shoulder. It'll be OK in a week. But how are you? Where's the baby? Gimme!'

'They keep taking her off and putting her in a nursery room. They don't like you keeping them on the ward all the time. I really miss her.' My eyes filled with tears. 'I don't get her back now till – oh, four o'clock.'

'Bollocks,' said Marty. 'I'll go find it for you'. He limped off despite my protestations, and through the glass window I saw him glowering and gesticulating at Sister with his good arm. Astonishingly, it worked. Byronic looks and a complete disregard of snubs have their advantages in hospitals. Moments later my least favourite nurse appeared wheeling a plastic crib containing Charlotte, fast asleep.

'Since Daddy's here,' she said primly, 'Sister's made a special exception. Not for long, mind. We don't like daddies disturbing the rest of the nursery and bringing germs.' She glared meaningfully at Marty's wild hair, but he grinned at her and a faint blush was visible on her retreating neck.

Marty sat on the bed, which would have earned another glare, but she had retired to the nursing station desk and began banging around, opening and shutting drawers with an air of thwarted importance and taking care not to look in our direction. Clearly another grin could have unmanned her completely.

'Well!' said Marty. 'Look at that!' He peered at the sleeping baby with interest, then glanced back at me. 'Who'd've believed that was inside you? It must have been, like, all curled up.'

I reached into the cot and stroked Charlotte's tiny cheek with the back of a finger. 'Do you like her?'

'She's – something else,' said Marty, echoing my own feelings of wonderment at the solid actuality of the baby. 'Someone else. A new person. Just turned up at the party, can't send her back now.'

'Well, yes.'

'No, but I mean it's weird, isn't it? One minute it's a bump under your dress, the next it's – um – somebody. Marilyn, or Hitler, or John Lennon or whatever.'

'Mm.' It was comfortable to have Marty there; for once I could barely even feel the usual undercurrent of guilt when he talked about the baby. Charlotte was not his daughter. She was his niece. In fact she was only his half-niece, if such a thing existed. But for the moment, even the sorrowful tangle of Bellinger relationships and of my own faded into insignificance next to the marvellous solid reality of the new life. Suddenly there was movement in the cot: a humping wriggle, and the tiny mouth open in a pink yawn.

'It's waking up!' Marty was transfixed. 'Cool! Everything, like, *works!*' Charlotte's 'aha – aha – mlwaaah!', like an engine coughing into life, galvanized us into action. I picked her up and put her clumsily to my breast, pulling open the night-dress with total disregard for modesty. Marty leaned foward with his good hand on his knee going, 'Whoa – whoa – hey, babe – it's OK.' Head weaving, mouth open wide, she fastened on me with almost frightening expertise and began to suck.

'What a little goer!' said Marty in heartfelt approval. We looked at one another with triumphant pride, and it was a full minute before I realized that this was the first time he had ever seen my naked breast.

They kept me in hospital for three days more, as was the leisurely custom of the time. At first I wanted very much to go home, but the nurses, with their swift pitiless routines of bathing and pinning nappies, sapped my confidence in my own ability to cope, and as the days went by I became more and more afraid of the moment when the baby would depend on me alone. Matters were made worse when Helena and David Jakobowitz appeared unexpectedly for a visit. It was not visiting hour, and the first I knew of them was when I woke from a doze to hear Helena's voice raised in piercingly posh soprano complaint at the nursing station, with a deeper obbligato of remonstrance from David. I was wearing a nastily sprigged stiff hospital nightdress, my own being dirty; my hair was lank. Propping myself up in bed and trying to push the litter of nipple-shields and tissues into the drawer of the locker, I felt like a charity case as Helena swept towards me, immaculate in her Bond Street suit and followed by David in City pinstripes.

'We had to come and see the little *granddaughter*,' she said, peering into the cot with a tinkling laugh. Charlotte had been delivered to my side while I slept, ready for the noon feed. 'Goodness, though, how *ageing* to be a grandmother. Serves me right for being such a young bride.' She giggled, and for the first time I noticed the faint crowsfeet round her big blue eyes. 'And for having a son start a family so early! He told me about the middle name, I'm tremendously flattered, it's sweet of him, isn't it? Goodness, though. It doesn't look a bit like Marty, does it? I mean she, not it? That square forehead is really much more like Max. How funny.'

I cringed inwardly. David looked down at the baby in silence, then gently put out a finger; she gripped it and stared up at him.

'She's lovely. Well done,' he said. A note of painful loss in his voice made me glance up in surprise; but his face was impassive. He was very sharp, was David. Perhaps he had seen what Helena unthinkingly saw, remembered my emotional insistence at lunch that I knew Max well, and made immediate sense of it. This was, after all, no grandchild of his. If he had hoped for a mystical calling of blood to blood and a fresh start, he was disappointed.

I was close to tears now, what with the humiliation of the nightdress and the hair and Helena's unfortunate witterings. Seeing this, David recovered himself immediately, leaned forward and surprised me with an avuncular kiss on the top of my head.

'Really lovely. You must be proud.' But I knew, as he drew back and looked me in the eye, that he knew my secret. Oh, we had special antennae, we concealers of genetic truth. We recognized one another.

I was glad when Sister bustled up and announced that the Jakobowitz' exceptional permission to visit out of hours had run out. 'My ladies will be seeing Doctor soon and I must have the ward clear'.

Marty came later, at the proper visiting time, but I did not tell him I had seen his parents. He talked about the group mainly, but angrily and a little incoherently: I could tell he had been smoking again. There were problems with the British record company after the New York débâcle. Friggy, who had started the fight, was now acting up and blaming him. There was even talk of a split. Charlotte picked up the mood and grizzled through much of his visit. Then Sister came by and informed me brusquely that I was discharged as from nine o'clock the next day.

'Daddy had better bring in some clean clothes, but remember, Daddy, nothing tight. Mummy's going to have a bit of a tummy for a while.'

I was afraid to leave. I cried my heart out that night, alone in the crowded, murmurous, sighing ward of women.

19

The flat was cheerless. The baby's presence made that fact suddenly apparent. I had never noticed before quite how depressing were the landlord's brown furniture and the stained old green carpet. I put Charlotte to sleep at first in a drawer, pulled out of the chest in the bedroom and lined with old sweaters covered with a folded sheet. I had bought nothing for her; she came home in a hospital gown and an Aztec knitted poncho instead of a shawl. I knew it was far too hairy, and felt intense guilt whenever I pulled loose fibres from her little hands. The first days passed in a sleepless confusion of wailing wakefulness, sore breasts and sour smells. I did not know how to bath her unless by climbing in with her myself, and often there was not enough hot water to be had from the spitting, fuming bathroom geyser. I fumbled with terry-towelling nappies, and when I washed them they grew stiff and horrible and chafed her soft skin so that I wept to see it.

Marty saw this, and at first stood helpless, confused as a child himself by my blundering incompetence.

'We could get a nurse-type person in,' he said. 'You're tired, right?'

'You think I'm hopeless! You think I should have had her adopted! You hate me!' I screamed unreasonably. Marty pursed his lips, shook his head, and left the flat. Two hours later, when Charlotte and I had cried ourselves to sleep, he reappeared with three huge carrier bags, which he manoeuvred with some difficulty through the door, the lightest of them hanging from his wrist in its grubby sling. One held a baby's folding cot, with mattress; another a supply of disposable nappies, quite a novelty at the time, and a padded changing mat; the third held three books on babycare and a bewildering array of creams and talcum powders. 'The girl in the chemist told me what we need.' Together, giggling a little, we assembled the cot and stood back in awed admiration at its pastel padded neatness, its utter suitability for the purpose. The cot's professionalism soothed us: it confirmed what we had hardly believed until that moment, the fact that other people had babies and managed them fine. Marty tidied the vodka bottles and empty cans off the sideboard, wiped it down with a damp cloth and laid out all the ointments and creams.

'Ready when you are, babe,' he said to the sleeping infant in the drawer. 'Come and get it.' I moved uncertainly towards him, driven by gratitude, and was seized by his free arm and hauled towards his warmth. I could feel his lean body shaking with laughter and his long wild hair tickling my neck. 'It'll be OK,' he said. 'It's only a baby. Chill. Those shops, man, they're so full of stuff and women and babies – there's hundreds of the little bastards.' He gave me a brotherly little shake. 'It's fine. Be cool.'

A small demon made me say, into his t-shirt, 'But it's not fair. It's not your baby, you shouldn't have to—'

He stilled me with a tighter hug. 'Who gives a shit whose baby it is? It's sweet. I like it. I like you. Stop going on about it.'

So things went better, and better still after the first week was over and Charlotte – remarkably early, I now see – decided on a pattern of feeds and sleeps. Marty celebrated her first six-hour uninterrupted sleep by going out to the junk shop on the corner and bringing back a tattered but cheerful kilim rug for the floor of the living room. I knotted together two towels and improvised a papoose to carry her round on my chest; but I never went out, being too disorganized and half dressed to essay the stairway, the hall, and the roaring Chelsea street. Apart from forays to the supermarket Marty was in the flat a lot too, tuning his guitar and making phone calls to other members of the band, to which I did not pay much attention. In the third week he came home with a push-chair, square and hideous but with a conveniently reclining back, again from the second-hand shop.

'I'm sorry it's not new,' he said, 'but they were more than fifty quid in that poncey shop on the King's Road, and I got this for three pounds fifty.'

'It's perfect,' I said. 'Are we getting a bit broke, then? We can't be.' I had thrown my share of the song money into a joint account with his when we moved in, and rarely gave finances a thought.

Marty shuffled. 'Thing is, we've been using it up a bit. Things . . .' he said airily. 'And I put some into the studio fees, Friggy's really broke.'

'Yeah, but we had masses from the American sales.'

'Mm.' A look came over his face which frightened me, and he saw the fright and looked away. 'But there were the fares to the US and some stuff out there, and it looked like really paying off.' He was over by the window now, fiddling annoyingly with the sash-cord.

'But the record company paid for America!'

'Not – completely.' He shut the window with a bang, and turned towards me, his thin face unreadable and sullen.

The cold premonition grew inside me. I felt sick. 'Marty, how much? How much money have we got left?'

'Next month's rent is OK,' he said flatly. 'And nearly a hundred quid on top of that. I was going to discuss it with you.'

I sank onto a chair, dropping the bundle of baby-suits I had been preparing to put away. When I made my original calculation that the baby and I could live on a thousand a year, reasonably comfortably and in a London bedsit, I had assumed that with my three thousand it would be three years before I needed to think about work. I had never reckoned with the effect of tossing my stake in with Marty's. He never seemed to buy clothes, living in ripped jeans, and I did not see how his hash and my housekeeping could have melted away six thousand pounds in six months. With his reckless feckless generosity, I realized, he must have been paying the expenses of all the others in America.

I wanted to be furious, and ironically enough if he had been a real and properly loved husband, I could have been. But the curious nature of our relationship forbade any such outbursts: how could I rail like a fishwife at this man who had chivalrously saved my good name? A mean voice inside me pointed out, even in that slack-jawed moment of shock, that by marrying me he had also in effect seized control of money I had honestly earned with my lyrics, and that this at least was not the action of a Sir Galahad. But as I say, I couldn't be angry. Not only was he perfect with the baby and never cross with me, but something in me was still chronically humble, and I could not bear to see Marty looking desolate and humble too.

While I was staring at him the baby woke, and I picked her up and sat down in the faded chair to feed her. The nurses had told me to change her first, but she was always so ravenous on waking that I ignored this instruction and took my own line. Marty moved closer: he could never resist the sight of her absorbed little face as she suckled, her ears twitching and tiny fists opening and closing with the effort. After a moment I looked up and asked him quite gently: 'Is any of the money that's gone – for America and all that – is any of it a loan? I mean, might the guys give us some of it back, some time?'

He was silent. I carried on. 'Yeah, OK. I see. Only this does mean we've got to earn some money quite soon, doesn't it?'

'There'll be royalties on Silken Julia,' he said. 'And the country and western stuff. But not much before next January, apparently. That's how they do it. Or else I got stitched up.' He winced.

'And the album?'

'Ah.' He sat in the chair opposite, eyes still fixed on the baby, and gave me a fuller picture of the finances and current status of Bastard & Sons and their relationship with the record company which had planned their first album.

It was not – I later learned – at all an unusual story for pop groups of the time. There had been hubris and innocence, ignorance and illusion, self-indulgence and far, far too much optimism. There had been major financial decisions made while they were all very stoned indeed. Their small success had benefited their agent and record company rather more than the boys themselves. Marty, as songwriter, had done far better than the others because of the cover versions of our songs made by US country singers, and so he had felt honour-bound to pay more than his share of the travelling costs when the professionals neatly swept these sideways into the group's lap. A tax bill had surfaced rather suddenly while they were in the US, and been paid by the agent without consulting the boys, who could have deferred it for a while.

They had, in short, been culpably silly. As I say, it was not uncommon. Marty was mortified that he had used my money as well as his own, particularly as he realized I too would shortly get a tax return to fill in; but he had been genuinely convinced that the US tour would make their name.

'The songs are good, really good,' he said. 'And we're pretty good. We've got nearly everything the Beatles ever had, and the Stones, and a bloody sight more than Freddie and the Dreamers or Peter and Gordon. I'm not Buddy Holly, but put us all together and we're *good.*'

'Are the others broke too?'

'Yep, obviously. Only they don't have babies, do they? And Friggy and Pete both live with their parents.'

I hesitated, but with the baby heavy on my lap I found the strength to say: 'Well. You've got parents. David and Helena would probably love to help.'

His head went forward; for a moment I thought he had fallen asleep. When he raised it again it was with a countenance more haggard than I had ever seen: it frightened me.

'I said I'd take nothing from Jakobowitz,' he said. 'But you're right. This is where I eat humble pie. I deserve it. I'm really, really sorry, Sally.'

'You'll ask him for a loan?'

'Yes. He won't agree to a loan. He'll give me a handout.'

I looked down at the baby, hesitated again and then heard my voice say: 'Don't. Not that. It's not worth making yourself miserable. I quite like your stepfather but we've got to stand together, haven't we?'

'Sal—!'

I went on, as steadily as I could: 'We can work it out without asking them for anything. It'll only be till the royalties start coming in. We'll sell more songs. The bank will give us an overdraft, you've had a number-one hit, they'll be really impressed. They're not to know that you've accidentally run out of bread.' I did not usually say 'bread' for money, but my friends down at the Southwark squat did; the expression sprang to my lips and reminded me of them and their shoestring existence, and suddenly I felt better. That alternative arty crowd had no money at all most of the time and it didn't bother them a bit.

Marty came over and knelt beside us, his arm round me, his other hand stroking the baby's little towelling feet. 'Do you mean that? You'd put up with the worry, and being broke all summer? It's not fair on you.'

'Yes. I will if you – if you'd . . .' A thought had come to me, a memory from my lunch with David Jakobowitz. '. . . if you'd do something for me.'

'What? Anything. You're a saint, Sal, you really are. I really don't want to ask Jakobowitz for anything. I'd feel like bloody Max the Human Sponge.'

I winced, but carried on with my condition. 'What I want you to do is stay off the hash. No weed. Nothing else, either. It's bad for you.'

He knelt back and looked up at me. 'Hard bargain!'

'It's not a bargain. It's a request.' Suddenly I was filled with a wholly new feeling, an unshakeable matriarchal authority conveyed to me by the baby on my lap and the penitent man at my feet. I felt, to be honest, like Agnes in *David Copperfield*, pointing upwards with serene tranquillity, playing the good angel of a weak man's life. Blame it on the hormones, if you will.

Anyway, I said:

'I'm not your keeper, I know everyone does it, but I honestly think it fuzzes up your brain too much. Look how lively you've been this last fortnight at home, without it.'

'That's 'cos of Charlotte.'

'Not entirely. So will you do it?'

'It's hard to play without something in your system, Sal.'

'Try.' It was all I could do not to point upwards with a saintly Pre-Raphaelite smile.

He exhaled noisily.

'OK. For a bit.'

The baby stopped sucking, and gave a little gurgle of contentment as the bright milk dribbled abundant down her chin. Marty got up, fetched one of the muslin rags he had bought, and wiped her mouth.

'I'll change her.'

'Thanks.' My eyes followed him as carefully, gently, he tended the baby. His hair still hung wild around his gaunt face, the stubble was thick on his chin. But we had tamed him, the baby and I. Without a shot fired, without even caring as deeply as we should, we had conquered a citadel.

20

The first months of Charlotte's life, I often tell her, were both the poorest and the happiest I ever spent. I was not really aware of this at the time, being too busy; but once or twice, looking into the cot, I was conscious that I had become different. The mental climate had changed: some grimy old black cloud had rolled away to leave the sky clear – if not quite shining – overhead.

I have heard from other women that babies have this effect: providing a powerful yet volatile focus for your life, they enforce absolute concentration so that smaller irritations and difficulties fade away. If she was smiling and chirruping contentedly, Marty and I were content. If she was howling, both of us were on panic stations, labouring to placate her. Marty was at home a great deal in the daytime, and doted extravagantly on the child. He was hardly smoking at all. Certainly I never caught him at it, and it seemed to me that his mind was clear for more of the time than before.

As for the outside irritations, once we had accepted that we were broke, rather to our surprise we found we were able to treat penury as a game. Marty informed the group that paid gigs were more important for the moment than chasing after unlikely record deals, and began energetically canvassing the humbler London pubs and clubs which Bastard & Sons had thought to put behind them forever. The drummer left, and he recruited a new one with quite uncharacteristic dispatch. 'He's not Tony, but he's OK.' He reckoned that two nights a week would cover our rent, and a third one help towards the food.

Meanwhile I looked in the local shop windows and found a job cleaning an estate agent's offices between seven and eight-thirty in the morning, four days a week: Charlotte always woke early for a feed at six and then slept again till mid-morning, and Marty was home and sober in case she did wake.

He was horrified at first when I announced that I was taking this menial job, but I was adamant that I should work, at least for a few hours. I had landed him with a quasi-wife and a baby, and ruthlessly used my influence to moderate his hash habit. The least I could do was cover the cost of washing-powder and baby clothes. In the event, it was a serendipitous blessing that I chose to deploy my indifferent cleaning skills at Brignells' Agency. It brought me the most unexpected promotion of my life.

One morning in the third week I arrived to find the office in chaos, with files spilling all over the floor and thrown open on the desks. I thought it must be a break-in, and moved to ring the police, but then I realized that I had just let myself in with my keys, that no doors or windows were damaged and that the safe was untouched. I decided that it must have been some unaccountable outbreak of fury by the staff themselves, or some estate agents' wild saturnalia of an office party. So I picked up the files, re-ordering and replacing all the scattered house details and paperwork as best I could, merely so that I could sweep. Soon after eight o'clock, however, Mr Brignell senior himself came in and looked in bemusement at me.

'What are you doing?'

'I'm Mrs Bellinger, the cleaner,' I said primly. 'Remember, you took me on and gave me the keys? I'm usually gone before people get in.'

'What have you done?' He was a short, pasty, heavily wrinkled man with startling dark eyebrows; there was something
quirky and comically plaintive about his look, which I warmed
to. In another life he might have been a clown, a Fernandel.
He looked, at this moment, as if he were about to cry with
sheer bewilderment.

'I found a lot of mess on the floor, so I've just tidied it up
a bit,' I said gently. 'I put the papers back in the files.'

'Ah. Yes. Very kind. But unless I'm remembering things
wrongly, and I may be –' he mopped his brow '– it was
chaos, when we left last night. I should tell you that my son
and I have had a serious professional disagreement. He is
no longer part of this agency. How did this –' he fingered
a file and glanced through its contents '– all get put together
again?'

'Well, I did it. I told you. It seemed logical.' I showed him.
'See? Houses here, flats here, under-offer file, conversions –'

'It's wonderful. Are you a trained filing clerk? Or have you
worked in estate agency?'

'No,' I said with dignity. 'I have got a degree, though. It's
not rocket science, now, is it? It's obvious from the labels that
you file the houses by street and area, and the commercial
stuff like shops was in the blue box-files, and—'

'Why are you charring,' said Mr Brignell abruptly, 'if
you've got a degree?'

'Got a baby. The hours fit.' My glare defied him to criti-
cize my choice in life any further. To be honest, one of my
greatest dreads at that time was that an old university
acquaintance would somehow spot me through the window
with my overall and mop. But Mr Brignell was not interested in scoring points over my wasted education. He looked
at me with something like hunger.

'Would nine to four fit as well? We're desperate for
someone brighter than these dollybirds my son hired. One

of them's gone with him, anyway.' He exhaled, a gusty sigh. 'Trollop! I beg your pardon, but there is no other word.'

'No,' I said it regretfully. 'Nine to four is hopeless. The baby wakes up again at ten or eleven, or even before, and my husband needs his sleep, because he's a musician. It wouldn't be fair to use him as a nanny when he's out gigging till one or two in the morning.'

'Nice baby, is it?' said Mr Brignell. 'Quiet sort of baby? My son –' he added bitterly, '– was a noisy little bastard if I remember rightly. Wife said she never had a minute's peace all day.'

'Charlotte isn't bad. If she keeps getting fed and has things to look at in her basket.'

'Suppose you brought the baby in with you, put it in the back room, popped in and out . . . ?'

This suggestion was revolutionary, especially at that harsh time before the concept of a workplace crèche had taken root. I gawped at Mr Brignell stupidly. He would, I thought, want to recant the offer made in a moment of stress. There were other people he could employ in the front office. But he did not withdraw. He went on, wheedlingly: 'Just for a bit? Just so I know there's someone in this office who isn't a moron, when I have to go out to see clients and measure up?'

'But suppose the baby needed a lot of attention? Suppose I was distracted?'

'You're *clever*.' He said it urgently, the great black eyebrows working. 'Believe me, cleverness is the only thing. You'd work something out. Or tell you what!' His ugly clown face lit up. 'If she cries, the moron girl could take her for a walk round the block in her pram, how's that?'

'I don't have a pram. Only a push-chair and that's another thing, she can't be in that all day, it's bad for her back. And I could hardly bring a cot in. Anyway, if this girl's a moron—'

'Oh, she's a *woman!* She'd be fine with a baby, dim women always are, it's just *work* they don't like. I'll buy you a pram. Yes, that's it. I'll buy you a pram. Big black pram. Think of it as your company car. And I'll pay you a proper wage. How about that?' He frowned, his lips moved silently, and a moment later he named the wage.

The money was irresistible, and the little man himself hardly less so: once he saw he had me on his hook he began swaying delightedly from one foot to the other, rubbing his hands.

Marty was enchanted, and told all the rest of the band how clever I was. I no longer had to get dressed after the six o'clock feed, and came back to bed for two blissful hours. Mr Brignell was as good as his word and paid for a large Silver Cross pram, in which Charlotte spent happy days in the little back room behind my desk, gurgling, kicking off her covers and watching a mobile of cymbals and guitars that Marty brought home one night. My work was pleasant enough: minding the office, taking the calls and pulling house and flat details out of the files for customers who wandered in off the street. Some were young shopworkers looking for rooms to rent, but some were of a more affluent caste, visibly excited by their daring in hunting for a home at the wrong end of the King's Road, far from their natural habitat in Sloane Square. When the baby needed me I could melt into the back room for twenty minutes even if Mr Brignell was out – as he often was, having been abandoned by his son and partner – and leave Sylvie, the typist, on her own.

I thought at first I might have a bit of trouble with Sylvie, who was only seventeen with a great blond beehive of fluffy hair and sharp red talons. She was inclined to sniff at the fact that I had been put 'over' her and had replaced her bosom friend Dawn.

'Only she went off with Paul Brignell, *his* son,' she said.

'They've gone to New Zealand. She reckoned she was pregnant, so she gave him an ultomato. She was reely reelly nice.'
I tried to be conciliatory, and took some of her typing load
off her with the heavy old Remington which stood severely
shrouded on the vanished Dawn's desk. I could touch-type,
having taught myself on my mother's old machine in boring
Suffolk holidays. I was also a lot better at deciphering Mr
Brignell's handwritten notes on the properties. I let Sylvie
know, explicitly, that I was not trying to usurp her tenure of
the office's only electric typewriter. Somehow, since the baby
was born I found it easier to be clear and direct with other
adults.

I came to understand her a little: she was not, in fact, a
moron. Her only problem was that she did not like her job,
did not see any non-financial point in having a job anyway,
and was consciously (and very conscientiously) preparing
herself and her fingernails for the happy day when she would
catch a man with prospects, marry and leave office life
forever. This made her a little distrait over filing and spelling,
particularly when she got too deep into a magazine article
on modern home-making; but hers was a point of view, a
clear life-plan and not an uncommon one at the time. Having
myself drifted and bumped and tumbled from one thing to
the next with no plan at all, I respected her for that. Sylvie,
I suspected, would never allow herself to get 'knocked up'
by a man who had no intention of even coming back from
a study trip to Italy for the birth, let alone making an honest
woman of her. But the thing which clinched our working
relationship was the arrival of Marty in the office one day,
resplendent in his leather jacket and studded jeans, to collect
Charlotte for an afternoon walk.

'Your husband is *gorgeous!*' she breathed when he had left.
'Is he really in a rock group?'

'Mm–hm.' I was preoccupied, stooping over the bottom

drawer of the filing cabinet collecting copies of details for a very demanding client in Burmah Oil who wanted a London pied-à-terre near the river but away from street noise and at absolutely no risk of flooding. He had turned down one in Flood Street entirely because of the name. 'He's in Bastard & Sons. They were in America—'

'Ooh! They had a fight, didn't they – it was in Rolling Stone magazine!'

'Indeed they did. He came home with his arm in a sling.'

'You are lucky,' she said wistfully. 'He's like something in the movies. Fancy him being married to *you*.'

I let the imputation pass, and after that she regarded me and Charlotte as an office asset, and spent an unconscionable amount of time hanging over the pram trying to find traces of Marty's lean dark face in the baby's round pink one.

I told Marty he had a fan, and he grimaced and said, 'Lucky there's one.' The gigs, disastrously, were drying up. There were too many new groups willing to play bars and clubs for nothing just to get themselves known. The American adventure had damaged the Bastards more than I had thought possible: other groups managed to behave atrociously and thrive on it, but for them it was the start of a miserable decline. Almost the worst of it was the fact that our songs were doing well for other groups. We wrote two more during that time, and one of them, invented in a giggly moment at the end of my office day, has lasted and been satisfyingly profitable. You may know it: it begins 'I bought you a pretty liddle house, ba-ad baby, but I didn' have a lease on you'. Marty put in some lovely riffs and key-changes, and we had at least the satisfaction – and later the profit – of hearing the Shamaans take it to number one six months later. Marty himself sang it in a couple of clubs, but never got to record it. By then, it was all too clear that the group was finished for the time being. By December, although we scuttled for the post every day in the hope of royalty cheques, there were no gigs at all and my Brignells' pay was all that kept us going.

And Charlotte, it sometimes seemed, was all that kept Marty going. As the work dried up and his relationships with the rest of the group fractured he spent more and more time at home, until I hardly had to bring the baby in to work at all. She weaned herself at five months, developing a passion for strained apple and cheesy stuff out of jars; when I put her to the breast before getting out her solid food she would stare at me in comic disgust, as if to say 'do we have to go through this charade?' Marty thought this hilarious, and took over managing her mealtimes; sometimes I thought uneasily that his devotion had itself something addictive about it.

One evening, suddenly, he said: 'If I didn't have Charlotte and you at home, Sal, I'd bloody top myself.'

I stared. 'It's not that bad, is it?'

'It is. All I've ever been able to do is the music. Now it's falling to bits. I'm going to have to get a job in a burger bar, aren't I? Or go back to fucking college and be an accountant?'

'Well –' I began, thinking of lecturing him on the benefits of being flexible in life. Then I saw his face and changed my line. 'No. I don't think you should give up. You should go solo, sing the songs you and I write. They're good. Everyone else seems to do OK with them.'

'Yeah, but I don't,' said Marty sadly. 'I'm not that good a singer, am I?'

I had no answer. He wasn't, not really. His voice had neither the balladeer's syrupy sweetness nor the grainy individuality of a Bob Dylan. He sang in tune, he had energy, he was a far better than average guitarist and a composer, I truly believed, of some note. But as a performer in a crowded genre he was not in the front rank. 'I'm not Eric Clapton,' he said baldly, and it was impossible to soothe him with lies.

Suddenly that day I felt an overwhelming affection and

pity for him. This was my friend, my creative partner, my flatmate and carer for my baby, yet at that moment I saw him with new and more maternal eyes. He was just a troubled boy who had lost his father too young and fallen out with his mother over her new husband; a boy who nursed unspeakable angry suspicions about his paternity, who had won an identity of his own by fluky success in a capricious trade and now was losing even that. Marty was adrift: instinct made me get up from my chair, cross the room and bend to put my arms around him where he sat sprawled on the sofa.

'It'll be all right. Mart, it'll be all right.'

His arms tightened round me then, and he pulled me down into a hug. I felt a brief convulsive movement of his body, and after a moment the slippery wetness of tears where his cheek touched mine.

'Marty. Mart. Don't cry, baby. Don't cry.'

21

If my life were a romance, the happy narrative would end there and then. It would make a pretty picture indeed: me and Marty in each other's arms, the baby we both loved snuffling in her cot, Marty's eyes filled with tears of happiness, me nestling on his chest overwhelmed by the realization that here, in this faithful friend, was the true love I had been pining for. In that moment, forever and with relief, I would have reclaimed and reallocated the love I had wasted for so long on the worthless chimera of Max.

Unfortunately, life rarely displays such symmetry. We certainly were overwhelmed, both of us, but our emotions did not quite interlock. I think Marty did love me – well, I know he did, rather to his own surprise – and certainly at that low moment he needed me very much. Equally certainly he loved Charlotte, who drew out something new and rarely seen in his nature. He also wanted me physically. I became aware of that on the shabby sofa as soon as his tears abated: there was a tension, a tightening of his muscles, which took my breath away.

As for myself, I was filled with powerful but vague and dangerously unexamined feelings. I felt sad for his faltering dreams, his alienation from Friggy and the other boys, his loneliness and sense of failure. I loved him for loving my baby and for being a faithful friend to me over the past bewildering year, and for setting my yearnings to music as if they were of some value. When he kissed me I did not resist;

when his hands slid down over my body my arms went round his neck and my breath quickened. When he took me by the hand and led me towards the bedroom, I went in a trance of willingness.

So there, on the big scruffy bed where we had slept together in amicable chastity for over a year, wordlessly we made love. Later, when Marty lay asleep with his arm over my naked stomach, I lay and stared up into the darkness.

It is a bitter irony that instead of cementing a new and better union, the act of making love with poor Marty should have revived my obsession with his brother. Perhaps it was inevitable; perhaps this was why I had remained celibate all these months. The last man to make love to me – the only man ever – was Max. I had tried very hard to forget him and nearly succeeded. During the pregnancy I had mooned and yearned for him, but since Charlotte's arrival his image had definitely faded. The baby, the job, Marty's difficulties and the constant preoccupation with financial survival filled my life and rendered it almost contented.

Max was supposedly studying in Florence, but Marty never mentioned him and I had not seen David Jakobowitz for months. Helena called round from time to time to admire her grandchild, bringing gifts of ethereally delicate little smocked dresses which I promptly ruined in the filthy laun- derette on the corner; but she spoke of little beyond herself and the prettiness of her grandchild. Marty and I spent most of her visits trying to remember not to give away the facts that I was working and that Charlotte spent a good many of her weekdays and Saturday mornings in a pram in the corner of a Chelsea estate agent's office. The subject of Max was never likely to come up.

So I had thought that the wound was healing, scarring over, almost vanishing. Now this complacency was overturned and I was wrecked all over again: the fact of being naked and passionate with a man had brought it all back, and the darkness of the bedroom pressed on me, suffocating and terrifying. I was truly married now, married to the wrong man, defeated and alone. *O heart, O heart . . . Love is not love which alters when it alteration finds* . . . Dangerous old words returned to mock me.

When I was sure of not disturbing Marty I gently moved his arm and crept out to the sitting room to huddle on the sofa, dozing and shivering and suffering. Charlotte woke in the small hours with a thin cry which echoed my own desolation. I fed her, and soothed by her baby gentleness I fell asleep myself on the sofa. I was half aware of Marty moving around a while later; I suppose he must have missed me, wondered where I was, padded in to the sitting room and seen all too clearly how the land lay. I had never slept apart from him in the flat before. I daresay that he, too, went back to bed cold and dismayed to doze and suffer until morning.

He was coolly composed, though, when I woke. Shifting my stiff neck on the lumpy cushion, I opened my eyes to see him standing beside the sofa with a mug of tea for me in one hand and the baby on his other arm.

'You'd better get up for work,' he said shortly. 'She's had her breakfast.' He put the baby down in the cot and started to turn away, but as I gathered the shawls around me he added over his shoulder, in a cold bitter tone I had never heard before, 'Sorry about last night. Won't happen again.'

I tried to answer, but infected by our unhappiness Charlotte began to whimper and then emit a full-blown bawl. He reached down into the cot and picked her up again; I fled to the bedroom, dressed hastily and went to work without another word.

Marty kept the baby with him that day, so I had nothing to distract me from grey misery except Sylvie's witterings.

Another treacherous line ran through my head: *Nothing now can come to any good.*

'Where's the bay-bee? I reely miss her,' Sylvie was saying. 'You are lucky, having Marty and little Charlotte, I went out with Albie Knights again last night and he went on and on about his horrible motorbike club. He says he doesn't want kids, ever. But he will, won't he?'

'Dunno,' I said shortly. 'Not everyone does, that's for sure. They're hard work.' I tapped out a few lines on the stiff old typewriter, describing a riverside flat as having a 'spacious living roof', swore, and reached for the Tipp-Ex. Usually I was better than Sylvie at this: she was a faster typist than me but could not spell very well, could not read Mr Brignell's writing and had little interest in guessing the right word. Thus her property descriptions included novel promises of 'occluded gardens' and houses in 'exscelint deccative ordure'. This meant I had to do some painstaking work with the viscous white fluid and brush before photocopying them. Mr Brignell had taken to giving me rapid verbal notes on properties, and trusted me to write the description and even sometimes the advertisements we put in the press. He had also put my money up, on condition I did not tell Sylvie.

She was restless now, kicking the leg of the desk with her long slim pretty leg in its clock-patterned navy Quant stocking.

'Oh, but do you think I ought to marry him anyway and just have one, one first baby, and he'd get to like it? He'll expect me to like his motorbike, won't he? So? That's fair?'

'No,' I said. 'A motorbike doesn't need feeding at three in the morning or taking to school for years. I don't think anybody should ever get married or have children unless they really mean it and understand each other. It just leads to unhappiness all round.'

'No, but—' began Sylvie, but at that moment the door

swung open. In deference to Mr Brignell's number one house rule, we suspended our conversation to present the customer with as encouraging and interested an expression as we could summon. It was a woman with short, elegantly cut blond hair, pale peaky features, huge expressive eyes and a suit so redolent of Parisian chic that we both immediately felt as if we had been transformed into clumsy-footed hippopotami.

'Kin I help yew?' said Sylvie in her most carefully posh voice. I said nothing, because I was looking – for the first time in almost eighteen months – at Marienka Tilton.

She stared at me, ignoring Sylvie.

'It is you – isn't it? It is? Sally?' I was surprised at her confusion: she looked startlingly different, with her smooth neatly groomed head and her business suit and silk blouse. I, on the other hand, knew that I had hardly changed at all; my hair was longer and tied back more tidily, and I had always preferred skirts to jeans. In fact, the printed corduroy skirt I was wearing had come from Oxford market two years ago.

'I heard you were living in London,' Marienka went on hurriedly, 'but it's wonderful to see you. This is the last place –'

I realized to my surprise that she was shy of me. I thought back and tried to remember why. We had not parted on very good terms. She had not been asked to my wedding. I knew these things intellectually, but did not really feel them: it all seemed to be a long time ago, like childhood quarrels in the sandpit. Perhaps that is what having a baby does for you: it detaches you permanently, with one neat snip, from the sillier sensitivities of adolescence. I felt no animosity towards her, only stunned unreasonable bafflement that she still existed at all.

'Are you living here now?' I asked mechanically. 'Working here, I mean?'

'Well, partly –' she hesitated. Sylvie was glaring at her. 'Look, I've just got to pick up some house details for someone, it's a maisonette he rang in about, but he wants to see the photos. Could you come for a drink after work? It says out there that you close at lunchtime, that's why I came in early, for my friend, I mean . . .' Her voice tailed away and my amazement intensified. She was nervous of me.

I thought. It was Saturday, and I was free at one o'clock. Mr Brignell had asked me to lock up. Marty would be all right with the baby. I did not want to go home, anyway.

'Yes,' I said. 'That'd be nice. Meet you here?'

'Thanks,' said Marienka, with real gratitude.

She left. So surprised was I by this encounter that it was ten minutes before I realized that she had not taken any property details with her.

22

We sat in a wine bar just down the road from the office: a new, smart place with shiny foil on the walls and aggressively simple Danish tables and chairs. I had never been there; Marty and I rarely went out except to walk in the park or beside the river with Charlotte in her push-chair. I looked around at the casually, fashionably dressed young drinkers with a troubled sense that I had lived for a time on another planet, or at least in another age group. I had not really been aware of my clothes lately, but suddenly the faded corduroy skirt and skinny ribbed sweater felt shabby and frumpy.

On the other hand, Marienka herself also stood out sharply against the hippyish jeans and smocks and peacock-bright jackets of the other customers. Her wool suit was dark, collarless ('Chanel,' said a surprisingly well-informed voice in my head) and her blouse the most beautiful pale pink silk, with tiny pleats. She looked soignée, restrained, quite unlike her student self and strangely out of step with the current fashion of the streets. The bartender clearly thought so too, because he left his post and came over to the table she had selected, in a corner away from the window, to ask what we would like. Other customers, I noticed as time went on, had to go to the bar to order.

'Sally? What are you drinking?' She still looked anxious whenever her eyes were on me, and I could not fathom the reason why.

I chose white wine, and Marienka murmured the name of

a drink I had never heard of. My drink arrived, and for her a pale cloudy liquid in a small glass, which she ignored. She was gazing at me with a degree of attention that made me uneasy. At last she spoke.

'I can't tell you how glad I am to have found you. I didn't want property details at all, actually. I was shopping and I saw you through the window of that place. I panicked. I lied about the maisonette.'

'Ah. There you are, then.' I sipped my drink; she continued to ignore hers.

'I've been wanting to get back in touch for ages, and I had *absolutely* no idea how.' She sounded a little more like her old self now, with that exaggerated '*absolutely*'.

I relaxed a little and almost smiled as I challenged her. 'You could have asked the Jakobowitzes. They knew where I was all right.'

Marienka blushed, a phenomenon I had rarely seen. 'Ah. Yes. Well, they aren't terribly keen on me, if truth be told.'

'Why not?'

She avoided my eye, but then gave a mischievous glance up at me to gauge my reaction, just as she used to do when she was confessing to some disgraceful escapade in our student days. A surge of love surprised me, and made my hand tremble as I tried to drink. Dear Marienka. Dear, wild, generous, sunny pragmatic Marienka.

'Well,' she began, 'you remember Max's sister?'

This was the last reference I had expected. 'Never met her, but heard of her. Susan?' I kept my voice level, even though hearing Max's name spoken had shaken me a bit, on this morning of all mornings.

'Yes, Sue. Remember, I went to her wedding and met Marco, and she didn't think much of that, because he's really rich and she'd got him earmarked for a friend of hers.'

'And?'

'Well – I was with Marco for quite a while actually, we were living in Milan, then Paris, and I started to work for his company. It's shipping, the money side not the actual ships. It's more interesting than it sounds, actually. You wouldn't believe it but I took a course and I rather like it.'

So that explained the suit and the Parisian chic. As to the rest, I was still mystified. 'Why would that annoy the Jakobowitzes? Marco wasn't Sue's property, was he? He could do what he liked?'

Marienka looked so embarrassed now that I felt more at ease, drank up my wine, and signalled to the bartender for more. She had not touched her drink yet, and shook her head when I motioned towards it. As my own drink warmed me I let the other warmth creep back: I had loved this girl, this wayward friend, laughed with her and been proud to defend her vagaries for three youthful years. Nobody had replaced her, and I was happy to have her back.

'Oh God, Sally!' she was saying. 'I'm not sure I can tell you, you'll walk out on me!' The old comic air was just beneath the chic surface, and I instinctively reached out a hand to touch hers.

'Come on. Spill the beans. What've you done *now*? Can't be murder, can it?' It was an old catch-phrase from our student days.

'Well, not murder but pretty evil. Marco and I were drifting apart, quite amicable, you know, he never really wanted a dippy English bird, not for good. Italian men need to marry their mothers, in the end, and that's all to the good, frankly.' She took a sip of her drink and put it down with a hand that shook slightly. 'So anyway, as the mother-yearning thing kicked in with old Marco I was sensing a certain lack of attention. And he said he still wanted me in the company, they like to have native English speakers, it helps with the American side, but if I was working for him the affair wasn't *convenable*. Blokes

do come out with the weirdest excuses, don't they? So I said
OK, cool, and we gave it up.' She took another minute sip of
her cloudy drink, and grimaced before going on.

'So . . . anyway . . . this guy Peter came out, who works in
an English sister company – you wouldn't believe how thick
they all are now, what with all this Common Market stuff –'
She broke off again, and I had the curious impression that she
was going to start talking about shipping insurance, that
she would find that more comfortable than revealing her own
romantic tangles. I saw that she had indeed changed. Back in
Oxford she had never recounted her affairs with anything but
relish. Now it took a deep breath for her to go on:

'Anyway, Peter. I knew I'd met him somewhere before, but
I forgot where. And we just clicked. It was such a *relief* to
be with an English guy again, we laughed at the same jokes.
I had no idea he was even married, till way way too late . . .'

An awful suspicion was growing. I stared at her. 'Sue's
husband was called Peter! I remember Max saying!'

Marienka now picked up her drink with an air of final decisiveness, and knocked it back in one gulp, wincing as she did
so. I wondered why on earth she ordered the stuff, so little
pleasure did it seem to give her.

'Cor-rect. So you can sort of see why I didn't like to ring
up the Jakobowitz household to ask where you were. Sue's
suing for divorce, citing me, and it's all quite nasty. Peter
says it was a ghastly mistake marrying her, that she was just
as cold and mercenary as her bloody mother, but all the
same!'

'Someone's new husband! Yeah, and when you were at
the wedding . . .' I said it sympathetically, she looked so
woebegone.

'Yeah! Hell, even I felt guilty. As well I might, only in my
defence I really had no idea at first.' She shook her glossy
head, amazed. 'I certainly didn't know it was the Jacko

family. Do you know they actually hauled Max back from Italy to confront us in Paris?'

The fascination of this saga almost cancelled out the pain of hearing Max's name and being made to realize that his life had been taking its own course this past year without the slightest reference to mine and Charlotte's.

'Blimey!' I said, graceless in shock. 'What on earth was that like?'

'Oh, Max came to the apartment and wittered on a bit about trust and betrayal of friendship.' She scowled. 'And he told Peter I was a slut and a one-night wonder and that he'd regret it, just as he regretted it himself when he was stupid enough to sleep with me. Rude bugger. And then Peter threw him out.'

'Physically?'

'Oh yes. That sort of made things worse, actually, Sal, because our steps are a bit steep and Max lost his balance and banged his nose.'

The waiter, unasked, now brought us both another drink. Obviously the intensity of the story was attracting him, too.

Marienka went on: 'And you know how it is with nose-bleeds. So there I am sitting on the step behind Max, forcing his head back, and there's Peter trying to get some ice out of the fridge to put down his neck, and dropping it all over the floor, and Max is making a terrible fuss. Then the concierge comes out and calls us *sales Anglais* and *peu convenables* and shrieks about the blood . . .'

'So Max went away and told his parents it was no go?'

'He did.' She drank her second drink, again in one gulp. 'And as of even date, as we say in the insurance trade, Peter and I are still together. Six months on.' She looked directly at me. 'Which is one of the reasons I was a bit nervous of what you'd say. I assumed you knew, and you'd be just as anti-me as the rest of them. I sort of couldn't bear that, which is why I was thrilled to find you in that shop window. It was like an omen. But you must have known, didn't Marty tell you?'

I shook my head, as much to clear away my own confusion as to reply to her question. 'No. Or at least he never mentioned it, and he would have done, wouldn't he? I mean, he used to know you quite well in that summer term? God, what a strange family they are, aren't they?'

'That's what Peter keeps saying. He's thrilled to have cut loose from all of them. But really, are you saying Marty didn't mention it?'

'I don't think,' I said slowly, 'that he even knew that his only sister's husband had done a runner. We've had quite a pre-occupied time, really, what with the baby growing bigger and trouble with his group. The family don't register much. He doesn't seem to care about any of them. Except Helena, a bit.'

'Do you see Helena?'

'Yes, sometimes, but she never breathed a word. Actually –' I frowned in sudden understanding '– of course, Max was so odd about not explaining to them about our household in Oxford that maybe she doesn't really know that I know you so well. Or perhaps she didn't want to upset me.'

'No,' said Marienka. 'That wouldn't be it. Helena has no conception of other people's feelings. Even I spotted that, ages ago.'

'Well, she knows I don't know Sue and Peter, because they were in Hong Kong and weren't there at our wedding. So perhaps she thought I wouldn't be interested, or it wasn't my business.'

'Or perhaps,' said Marienka drily, 'she's just chronically self-obsessed. But she'd have told Marty?'

'Maybe she just said Sue and Peter were divorcing. She doesn't know that he knows you. And Marty knows I don't know Sue.'

We both sat for a while in silent contemplation of the

uncommunicative Jakobowitz-Bellinger clan. Then Marienka looked at her watch and said, 'Shall we go and eat? There's a place over the road that looked all right.'

'I'm broke,' I said flatly. 'Things aren't easy just now.'

'My treat. I'm a city shark now, remember. I'm a Common Market shipping money profiteer person. Please. Please!'

She had become once more what she always was at Oxford: irresistible.

The restaurant was in the opposite idiom to the wine bar: small, dark and friendly, with candles stuck in Chianti bottles and check tablecloths. Confessions over, our intimacy blossomed; after the first bottle of wine and plateful of sardines it was as if the friendship had never fractured. Eventually, after an hour of reminiscence about the house by the canal and friends we had in common, Marienka asked about Marty and how I was enjoying married life.

'It surprised everyone a lot. And the baby. But a nice surprise, it was. I always said you two were much better together than you would have been with that frigid old fusspot of a brother.'

The drink, my first alcohol in months, loosened my tongue. For eighteen months I had had no female friends to talk to, apart from the earnest squatter girls in Southwark, who I had not seen much anyway, and the meringue-brained Sylvie at work. I became rapidly and recklessly confidential. 'It's not Marty's baby, you know. He only married me to be kind, and we'll probably divorce quietly in a bit. We're not – lovers.'

Marienka stared in real horror now. I realized that she had filed me as happily married, settled, a less complex and better-conducted person than herself.

'God almighty! What a mess! Whose is it, then?'

'Max.' I took a final bite of my chicken Kiev and almost choked.

When I had been patted on the back by a concerned waiter,

Marienka said quietly: 'You got him, then? You got what you wanted and didn't like it?'

'No. I did like it. I went on loving him. I still do. I'm not – changeable – like some people. He just didn't want me, that's all.'

'But his baby! Does he know?'

'I wrote to him. He came to the wedding. He knows, all right.'

'And he let Marty take it on? That creep! When I think of how pompous he was with me and Peter! Oh, I could spit! You wait till I get hold of him, it won't be just a nosebleed!'

There was something comic about the rage of this Chanel-suited, sleekly groomed businesswoman, ruffling her pale hair and grinding her teeth. The old Marienka was bursting out of the smooth silken cocoon of her adult self, and I liked her for it.

'It wasn't his fault,' I said quite calmly, taking another large glug of wine. 'I should have been on the Pill. He probably thought I was. Even if Marty hadn't come along, it would have been wrong to foist the baby on Max.'

'Oh, bollocks. He ought to take some responsibility, at least pay for her. How old is she now?'

'Nearly nine months. She's adorable. Oh God!' I looked at my watch. 'I ought to be home soon. Marty's looking after her and it's not fair.'

'Can I come and see her?'

I hesitated. I had pushed to the back of my mind the reason why I dreaded going home that afternoon, but the opportunity of bringing a calming stranger into the flat was heaven-sent. Marty and I would have to talk, but not yet.

'OK. Yes,' I said, perhaps slurring a little. 'That'd be nice. But it's half-past three, we ought to get on our way soon.'

As we left, Marienka laid a hand on my shoulder, light and warm. I was glad of it.

★   ★   ★

It was an early December dusk. As we walked up the main road and turned into the urban lane where our block of flats stood in gloomy redbrick squalor, I found that I was rather looking forward to showing off my home and child to Marienka. She might be a glamorous adulteress with a flat in Paris and a mysterious job in a smart European office, but I had a bright and beautiful baby. I also had a dutiful devoted Marty looking after her. The flat was looking better, too, since even during our months of penury we had bought a few posters and some cheap Indian cottons to throw over the dreary furniture. Marty had become quite tidy in his sober weeks. She would see that however unsatisfactory my love-life, my domestic interior was enviable. I was still quite drunk.

We climbed the dismal stairs together, her smart high heels clicking on the bare concrete and me fumbling for my keys and chattering nervously about how the landlord was likely to repaint the lobby, really quite soon, and how terrific Marty was with the baby. As we reached the landing below ours I paused, disoriented. There was a battering and banging in the air, deep and insistent, and I realized that it was rock music, playing beyond the flimsy door, inside our flat. There was something else, too, which a mother's ear immediately distinguished from the racket: the high distressed wail of a baby. My baby.

I ran on upward, forgetting Marienka, stabbed the key into the lock with trembling fingers, wrenched the door open and ran towards Charlotte, who was lying in her cot red in the face, fists flailing, her mouth a round red furious O. I grabbed her and looked around, desperate to cut the noise, and moved towards the battered stereo which Marty had cherished since his fifteenth birthday. In my panic I could not remember how to silence it, so I bent to the wall and yanked out the plug, still holding the screaming child in my other arm.

In the silence, ears still ringing, I straightened up and looked about me. The bright cotton throws were pulled off the sofa and askew on the chairs; the little table where we ate our meals was on its side, and a chair with a broken leg lay against it. Marty lay white and still on the floor, his head pillowed on Charlotte's teddy bear, his hair spreading black around his pale face. My first thought was that we had been burgled, and he had been attacked; but what kind of burglar or murderer leaves the stereo turned up and takes nothing? It was Marienka who pointed silently at the two vodka bottles, and stamped on the still-smouldering remains of the joint on the floor, smoking thinly and seeming to my terrified eye to writhe malevolently like a tiny Tolkien monster. Another few minutes and it could have set the carpet alight. To this day, when I am tired and low, my nightmares feature that stained little white demon, that killing fire which never happened.

I had the sobbing baby in my arms: it was Marienka who knelt down next to Marty, checked his breathing and turned his head to one side.

'I think he's just pissed,' she said. 'He must have lit up after he finished the drink, and forgotten about it.'

'I told him to give up the weed,' I said stupidly. 'I didn't say not to drink.'

Marty groaned, and moved his head. With this proof that he was not actually dead came a wave of fury at what he had done to Charlotte. Still encumbered with the gasping, quietening child, I wanted to kick him hard and scream my fright and anger; it took all my self-control not to. After a moment, a bleary sense of social shame replaced the rage and I said to Marienka – who was kneeling beside him like a nurse, holding his wrist, 'He's normally fantastic with the baby and the flat and everything. I wouldn't risk leaving her otherwise. I don't understand. It's not my fault, I have to go to work—' and shamefully, tipsily, just as the baby stopped I began to cry myself.

23

Marienka was unexpectedly calm and reassuring. She laid Marty in what years later I saw described in first-aid books as the 'recovery position', replaced the teddybear under his head with a cushion covered in a teacloth from the kitchen, 'in case he's sick', and wrapped him loosely in a blanket from the bedroom – which as I saw through the doorway was also in considerable disarray. Then she came over to me, gingerly took Charlotte from my arms and made me sit down on the sofa with another teacloth, this time a rather less clean one, to cry into. This I did for several noisy minutes. Marienka jigged the unfamiliar infant in her arms, inexpert but deter-mined. Looking down at the child's feathery gold hair with a sort of half-comic surprise she said nothing while I composed myself.

'What does it eat?' she asked, practically, as my sobs subsided and the baby began to whimper again. 'Is there anything I can feed it?'

'Little pots. In the kitchen. She likes them,' I gasped. 'Apple, cheesy stuff. Or a banana. I'll do the milk after – uhuh! – when I . . .' I began to sob.

'OK. Are you all right to have her for a minute?' She lowered the child onto my lap with care and stood upright for a moment, hands on hips, contemplating us. Thus un-burdened she went through, banged around with cupboard doors for a minute and came back with a jar of puréed apple, a plastic spoon still in its wrapper which had come free with a box of cereal, and a banana on a plate with a fork. 'We could sort of mash it? Maybe?'

She sat on the sofa so that Charlotte was propped between us, took the grimy teatowel off me to spread it awkwardly on the baby's front, and prised the lid off the apple sauce. My daughter's small face was screwed up with anticipation and greed, and her little hands whirled like propellers as the spoon came towards her.

'Oh, how sweet!' said Marienka. 'Do you know, I've never done this. Do I push the spoon right in, or does she sort of suck?'

'Just the tip,' I said. 'Look, I'll do it –'

'Oh, go on. Let me!' The baby's mouth was now open so wide that the whole bowl of the little spoon went in, whereon it clamped shut and Charlotte put her powerful suction into action. Marienka exclaimed in delight. 'Oh, fab baby.'

I picked up the plate from the floor and began to mash the banana. Charlotte, who loved banana more than life itself, swivelled her head towards it, so that Marienka almost pushed the apple-spoon into her little ear.

'Oi!' said her newfound nursemaid. 'You! Concentrate!' Between us, giggling a little in reaction after the crisis, we fed the eager baby while her foster-father lay unconscious, breathing heavily, on the floor six feet away. When the meal was ended I got up and took her to the bathroom to change her nappy: it was filthy, sodden and soiled as I had never seen it. Marty could not have changed her all day and it was clear he hadn't fed her for hours, in that cold lonely flat where the music shook the furniture and the smoke curled from his spliffs. A spurt of rage made my hands shake as I dabbed at the rough reddened skin of her bottom. Bastard! How could he do that to her? He must have heard her crying and made himself deaf. Angrily I pushed aside a guilty voice which told me that I had stayed out for lunch, and that in any case it

was my noctural surrender and subsequent desertion which
had driven Marty to the edge. Rejecting self-blame, I clung
to the hard legalistic facts: this was his fault, and he might
have burned the building down and my child inside it. No
mere emotional upheaval could possibly excuse such a horror,
or even the risk of it. The safety of the weakest came before
the dramas of love and frustration. Even as I thought this, a
curl of reproach came back towards me like smoke. Had I
lived by this principle, or had I only that minute learned it?

Back in the living room Marienka was kneeling beside
Marty again, her hand on his forehead.

'He's ever so cold,' she said. 'I hope it *was* just vodka. Does
he do any other drugs?'

'I told you,' I said. 'He doesn't do any drugs, I made him
stop, otherwise obviously I wouldn't have left the baby with
him, I'm not irresponsible –'

'Oh, for God's sake,' said Marienka, who seemed now to
have reverted completely to her old student self, even down
to the way that her hair was ruffled in pale spikes and her
suit jacket hanging open. 'Stop going on about that. I can
see you might want to keep saying it's not your fault, but
nobody's saying it is. Marty's had some sort of binge, that's
all. No harm done to the baby. Look at her, she's fine. But
we ought to know what he's taken. I hope he's OK.'

Marty groaned and half opened his eyes. 'Charlotte –' he
said. 'Baby. Ohgod. Baby, is she OK?'

'Yes,' said Marienka. 'Are you?' She jumped aside, too late,
as a stream of vomit sprayed her skirt.

'Shorry,' said Marty. 'Dranktoomuch. And stuff Friggy gave
me. Horse tranx, 'parently. Things onna mind. Didn' take the
horse things though – not both of them anyway –' He focused
on her for the first time. 'Whatthehell you doing here, Blondie,
you don't live here?'

'Have you taken anything else?' She separated the words

carefully. 'Have – you – taken – anything – else? Bloody tell us!'

'No,' said Marty, and groaned again. 'I had a smoke – and the horse thing but I dropped the other one – had another joint.'

'And left a burning stub on the carpet to burn the bloody place down!' I broke in furiously. 'You could have killed yourself, and the baby, Marty, how *could* you—'

'Oh, leave the poor bastard alone,' said Marienka. 'He knows he's been an asshole. You –' to Marty '– you'd better go to bed. We'll clean up.'

She hauled him to his feet and supported him as far as the bedroom, where a groan and a creak told me he had collapsed onto our bed. I went to the kitchen to fetch the baby's bottle, ran it briefly under the hot tap – she had got used to barely warm milk by now – and settled down to hold it to her eager little mouth. Coming back, Marienka shut the door and said briskly: 'Right. Now, what needs doing? We ought to find the pill he says he dropped, before the baby does. Can it crawl yet?'

'You are amazing,' I said. 'Where did you learn to sort people out like that?'

'Misspent youth,' she said. 'Englishmen. They all drink like that, useless buggers. That's probably why I got on with Marco. Italian men just *don't*. They'd crease their suits, for one thing.'

'And Peter?'

'Oh, he did it once, the night Sue found out where he was and rang up and screamed at him. He told me it was all my fault and I was a witch and he stormed out and the concierge found him dead drunk on the stairs at half-past one. Sweet boy, I do love him, you know . . .'

Through all my fear and confusion, the thought drifted through my mind that the concierge at Marienka's Paris apartment had had a lot to put up with, what with drunkenness and nosebleeds and emotional scenes on the stairs. No wonder she found them *peu convenable* as tenants. I smiled, and Marienka noticed this and said encouragingly as she plumped herself on the sofa next to me and the baby: 'That's the spirit. When he wakes up you can discuss whatever brought this on. He's a good guy, Sal. You oughtn't to look a gift horse in the mouth. Talking of horses –' she pounced on the floor near where Marty had been lying, and picked up a capsule. 'Temazepam. He really shouldn't mess with this.'

'He doesn't. I've never seen any.'

'Guy I knew was into it. Injected the stuff you get out of the middle of the capsules. Flush it.' She slipped the pill into her bag and turned to me, pushing her dishevelled hair out of her eyes. 'Sal, what's wrong with him? You said it was all OK?'

So, sitting there with the infant between us, I told her about the night before, and why Marty might have been upset.

'And it's still no go, for you?'

'No go,' I said sadly. 'And what with today, it's made me see that I really am going to have to sort this out and live on my own. It's not fair on him.'

'Bloody bloody Max,' said Marienka, staring at the wall and shaking her head. 'Leaves his mess all over the place, swans off to Italy, then has the gall to call *me* a one-night wonder . . . !'

I was silent. What, I mused, would Max have done if his unseen, unknown baby had indeed died because of his brother's negligence? Would it have hurt him? Swift and treacherous as a cobra, a fantasy unwound in my head in which he heard the news and rushed home, realizing how precious was this child, and by association how precious was her mother. Marty and I could divorce, Max could be a real father to his baby.

Marienka brought me back to earth. 'There's something

else you ought to know about Max,' she said flatly. 'He's engaged.'

A beat of silence, a dying dream. I held the baby close; she wriggled, bored with confinement, wanting to lie and kick on the mat. I unrolled her blanket in silence, put her down on her tummy and began to tidy the room. Marienka joined me, carrying dirty mugs through to the kitchen and running the taps. At last I said: 'Who to?'

'Annette. Remember Annette? Ballet-dancer type, boring?'

'Yes. I thought they broke up?'

'They un-broke again. I don't know what happened, but she's pregnant, and her family were pretty keen he should marry her. The Devereaux. They are –' she added, '– bloody rich, and on bloody good terms with Helena and David. I think her dad works in a big bank or something. I doubt Max was given much choice.'

'But she was pregnant by Max?'

'So it seems. Fertile bugger, isn't he, for a prude?'

Marienka spent an hour cleaning the flat, checked Marty again and pronounced him safe. 'Sleeping it off. He's breathing OK now.' Then she left.

'Don't lose touch,' she said rather plaintively. 'I mean it!'

'You live in Paris,' I said dully. But we exchanged phone numbers, and as she left she leaned forward and planted a swift unaccustomed kiss on my cheek. All I could think of, as I bathed Charlotte and put her to bed that evening to the sound of Marty's stertorous breathing, was that my parents were not bloody rich, and not Knightsbridge-and-City friends of the Jakobowitzes. A Suffolk vicar and his wife could never have made Max marry me, could they?

I am ashamed, now, of how bitter this reflection made me.

24

Marty woke twice that night, moaning for a glass of water; I was worried enough to sleep next to him on the big bed, not touching him but passing a chipped mug of cold water across and once helping him to the lavatory. He was heavy-stepping, confused and twitchy; afterwards he snatched his pillow and lay on the floor, mumbling that the bed was stopping him breathing. Charlotte woke whimpering and I took her into the bed with me, but she kicked so much that I put her back in her cot before dawn. Carrying her sleepily across the room I tripped over my unconscious husband and – clutching the child for her safety – landed heavily and painfully on my knees. Afterwards, lying in the dawn gloom as the church bells rang, I resolved that for the baby's sake at least, Marty and I must separate.

When he woke in the middle of the morning, though, it took him less than fifteen minutes to persuade me otherwise.

'Sal, I'm sorry. I got pissed off. There was a call from the music publishers yesterday afternoon, a lot of hassle, Friggy's claiming he wrote some of the songs and he's got the rights, which is balls, and then Charlotte threw up her lunch on me and I got lonely and had a drink – I didn't start till two o'clock, honestly, she'd had her lunch—'

'You could have killed her. You could have made her deaf, with the music that loud. You didn't change her, she was filthy. You could have set the *flat* on fire –'

'I know. I'm sorry. I wanted to take the horse pills and die anyway, I mean, I knew you'd be back, Sal – for the baby – but I dropped one – and I was so freaked I had another drink.' Marty was crying now, and I could not resist his sorrow. I put my arms round him, awkward and unwilling. There was a silence, broken by his sniffs, while I stared past him at the posters on the wall.

'It didn't happen. It's OK.' I said it mechanically; my knees were swollen and hurting from the fall and my shoulders ached. He was drooping on me, leaning helplessly as I stood by the kitchen worktop. I knew it wasn't OK, not OK at all, and a horrid premonition was with me that this was not an aberration but a beginning. Still some primordial, quasi-maternal reflex forced me to soothe and reassure. There is something horribly powerful about other people's need, particularly when you are adrift yourself, sore and hopeless and sad at not being needed by the one you really want. Max was to marry, so that dream was over for good. Marty was here, and weepingly begging me to understand, and stay, and protect him. He went on expressing his misery and remorse so inarticulately and for so long during that Sunday morning, that in the end I was forced to change the subject. We were sitting on the sofa by now, with Charlotte doing spirited sea-lion impersonations on the rug in front of us. She, at least, was completely recovered.

'Marty,' I said, 'something else. I saw Marienka. She was here yesterday.'

'I sort of remember. Blonde bint, used to be in Oxford. Did she take me to the bedroom?'

'Yup. But the thing is, did you *know* she was living in Paris with your sister's husband?'

So strange had the last twenty-four hours been, so weird my perception of the Jakobowitz clan, that I almost expected him to say, 'Yes, sure, what of it?'

Marty, however, stared in astonishment. 'What? Your old Marienka, with Sue's wimpy Peter?'

'Yes. They met up at work in Paris, and they're living together. Your mother sent Max to tell them off.'

Marty gaped. It had, at least, taken his mind off his own troubles and theatrical remorse. 'Chee-eeese!' he said – a curious recent expression he had taken up, after deciding he should swear less in front of the baby. 'Jeezus cheesus!' Then, 'Why didn't Ma tell us?'

'Search me. Are you sure she didn't?'

'Well, she did mutter something about Sue and Peter not getting on too well – I didn't listen, frankly, Ma going on about Sue is not my favourite thing.'

'Perhaps she's forgotten that you know Marienka. Or perhaps she didn't know it was her that Peter was living with. Or she thought it would all blow over. I dunno.' I paused. 'Anyway, there it is. And she also told me that Max is engaged.'

I darted a hard glance at him: in the light of day, it was seeming to me unforgivable that hot news from Marty's half of the family should reach me only by way of a chance meeting with Marienka. Especially news about Max. Marty raised his shoulders in a brief shudder; his eyes were fixed on the puffing baby, who was hauling herself determinedly towards her squashy felt ball. His silence told me all I needed to know.

'You knew that, didn't you? Mart, you knew about the engagement?'

He turned to me, a pale thin face in a wild dark frizz of hair. 'Yep. I didn't want to . . . stir you up. Sorry. I know how you feel about bloody old Max.' He put a tentative hand up to my cheek, and touched it before hurriedly pulling it back as if I might bite him. 'Sorry. But she's a silly little cow anyway, that Annette. I can't think why he's doing it. To be honest, I'd lay bets they won't actually marry.'

'She's pregnant,' I said flatly. 'Marienka says her family will make them get married.'

Marty leaned back, sighed heavily, and said, 'Oh. Yes. That explains why Ma was so shifty about it all. She told me while you were getting the push-chair up the stairs, that time we took Charlotte to the park. I thought it was weird. P'raps I should have told you.' He yawned. 'God, I'm tired. Feel sick.'

Our moment of connection was broken; he threw up in the bathroom and went back to bed. After a few minutes of glum reflection I gathered up the baby and thumped down the stairs with the push-chair, to walk her across to Battersea Park in the thin winter sunshine. She chuckled and cooed in her pink woollen hood, appreciating the ducks and the Salvation Army band, welcoming the world as if it would forever be glad confident morning. My footsteps on the path as I pushed her were heavy, dutiful and slow. I was twenty-two years old, and there was not much left in life for me, not now.

When we got back, Marty was awake and penitent all over again. He had even been down to the shop, and was chopping up carrots and onions to make his one *pièce de résistance*, a beef stew liberally laced with Guinness.

'Your mother rang,' he said. 'About Christmas. Are we going to them or to my family? She wanted to know.'

'What did you say?'

'Suffolk. Is that OK with you? I thought you might like to go home, and I really love your folks. I wish I'd grown up in a vicarage.'

'You can't get pissed there,' I said. 'Or smoke. Or do any drugs, what-so-ever.' We had only made one visit since the wedding, to introduce them to the baby. It was not in my view a great success, because I was tense, Charlotte tetchy, and Marty had spent a lot of time in the woodshed, sitting on a roll of old carpet smoking weed while pretending to chop logs for the fire. The shed reeked of it: my father had commented afterwards on the 'particularly aromatic quality' of his latest batch of pine-logs from Tuddy Feaveryear in the village.

'I won't,' he said. 'I'll be an angel. And we can do what you want, you're the gaffer, Sal. But I didn't think you'd want to go to Knightsbridge.'

'Certainly not,' I said, and suddenly giggled, catching his eye. There were times when we thought exactly alike, Marty and I: I swear that I had in that moment the same picture as he did. There would be David Jakobowitz looking longingly at Marty and receiving silent scowls in return, Helena in some thousand-pound suit exchanging beautifully wrapped cashmere nonsenses with an equally elegant Annette, Max in a new shirt nervily discussing frescos with his long fingers waving, and a tearful Sue, husbandless and shrewish, hating the lot of us.

'Suffolk it is, then,' I said. 'At least my parents go in for a quiet life.'

Christmas 1974 was a mild and muggy one, with none of the crisp snow on the gorse and prickling of the nose which I remembered from childhood. It was peaceful, though, and my parents were simply and unaffectedly glad to see us and pet the baby. With great ceremony they moved out of their sagging old double bed for us, and laid the best Welsh quilt on it. I would far rather have gone to a single bed in my childhood bedroom and let Marty take the guest-room; but we kept up our pretence and on Christmas Eve, rolling together in the middle of the musty old bed, we made love again, gently and resignedly and half asleep. When I woke in the morning to the baby's thin cry and found my cheek jammed companionably against his warm shoulder, I said to myself that I was indeed married, and had better make the best of it.

Marty seemed to realize this change in the emotional weather, and on Christmas Day was almost his old self again, joking about music with my father, drying up the dishes, coming meekly to church and singing my praises as a mother and tyro estate agent.

'It seems such a pity you girls having to work these days –' began my mother, but Dad threw her a warning glance and deflected the conversation.

He seemed to have understood by some process of clerical intuition that Marty's musical career was in trouble. Later, when Marty and my mother had taken the baby upstairs for a nap and we were alone, he confirmed this by hesitantly asking me: 'Are you OK? Is everything OK with money, and work, and all that?'

'Yes, Dad. Honestly. My job can keep us, and we'll have some song royalties coming in again soon. Whatever Mum says, it's normal for women to work now when they've got babies, and she's really well looked after.'

'But Martin's career? Not going too well? In the – ah – pop world?' He snuffled, like any hesitant vicar in a sitcom, but his eyes were sharp and bright. It was a relief to tell him the truth.

'I think he's probably finished. The band broke up. He's taking it hard.'

'No – ah – openings in other fields, then?'

'I don't think he's thought about that.'

My father smiled, lopsided and apologetic. He had grown a lot older over the past year, I thought, but there was comfort in his mild elderly goodwill, just as there was comfort in the rickety familiar bookshelves behind him and the rattling black-painted Suffolk latches on the plank doors.

'Strange world,' he said, tamping his pipe. 'When these young musicians can become so rich and famous in a trice, but then look around them and find they aren't really trained for much else. Footballers too, they tell me. And hairdressers, sometimes.'

I could only agree.

★   ★   ★

I really believed, that Christmas week, that Marty and I could find some sort of normal happiness. The dull benign normality of home made me think so. Charlotte, nine months old, learning fast and chortling with happiness through most of her day, was a powerful focus of optimism. I surrendered to her point of view: squib though she was, she had a palpably strong personality and clearly believed that the world was wonderful and Marty and I were gods. So most of the time, I found myself trying to go along with her optimism. As for Max, his engagement had the salutary effect of silencing a certain thin treacherous voice in my head which habitually ruined my attempts to forget him by whining, 'But he *nee-ee-ee-eds* you.' He didn't need me. He had Annette, and would soon have her baby. QED.

Marty, on the other hand, obviously did need me. My duty was clear. Slowly, gradually, a new moral imperative was taking over from the old headlong devotion. The moth was learning to ignore the distant star and think about its mate and its pupae. In church on Christmas morning, ignoring the unseasonal warmth, we sang 'In the Bleak Midwinter' and although it was nothing like evensong in Christ Church Cathedral, my heart lifted a little with the music as if it might learn to fly again. *What shall I give him? Give my heart.*

On the day after Boxing Day we went back to London to our grimy makeshift home, and found on the doormat a large, preternaturally stiff and lavishly embossed invitation to the wedding – only a month away – of Annette Cecilie Devereaux and Maximilian David Bellinger. The wedding list, we were given to understand, could be viewed on request at Peter Jones. Marty used a rude word and said we weren't going. I, in my new mood of family virtue, said that we must. I walked the baby up to Peter Jones and spent £15 I could ill afford on a tablecloth from Annette's list; I bought in the Oxfam shop a flared red wool dress with folksy embroidered flowers round the hem, dressed Charlotte in a pink smock sent by Helena and not yet ruined by me, and persuaded Marty into a smartish leather jacket and clean jeans.

The reception was in a hotel, gilded and soulless. Max looked handsome and distant, Annette fragile and pale in a necessary crinoline, not blooming at all. David Jakobowitz made a point of talking to me and admiring the baby, who mercifully was angelic all day, smiling and cooing quietly and reaching out to the white flower arrangements. Helena, doting ostentatiously on her new and far smarter daughter-in-law, pointed out very loudly to all onlookers that Charlotte's pink smock was a gift from her, not my taste at all.

If the baby was angelic, Marty was quite otherwise. Some toxic old family fumes got him by the throat and transformed his mellow Christmas self into a demon. He got very drunk indeed, told David loudly that he was an arsehole, insulted the bride's father, informed a group of total strangers from Annette's circle that his stepfather was a 'fucking Mafioso', then fell into a petulant rage when I wouldn't leave before the speeches. He stalked out alone.

I did not see him for three days, and convinced myself he had died in the Moorgate Underground crash. I wept, shaken by loss and confusion and a terrible guilty streak of relief.

I was shaken still more when he came home, his eyes wide, mad, and darkly dilated. Marty, it seemed, had found a new door into the parallel world that he craved.

25

I do not want to chronicle Marty's decline in any detail.
Drugs and their addicts may be fashionable topics now, and
indeed they were pretty fashionable then, although not in
their more sordid and inevitable manifestations. We had not
reached the life-denying heights of heroin-chic which blossomed as the century drew to a close, but by 1975 we all
lived under the spell of Timothy Leary and had copies of
Huxley's *Doors of Perception* on our brick-and-plank bookshelves. And the music industry, though we did not know it
so clearly because there were fewer celebrity magazines,
already embraced excess with practised ease.

So in some ways this part of our story would be easier
to tell if I could weave a legend of romantic doom around
Marty. I would like to give you a gaunt rock 'n' roll hero,
hammering out the eternal rage of youth on a bass guitar as
he hurtled towards oblivion. It would even be easier if I were
to spell out, in squalid clinical detail, the details of everything he smoked, snorted and finally injected in his last grim
year. I might gain a bit of credibility with the Trainspotting
generation by flashing my familiarity with horse and skunk,
THCs, poppers, uppers and crystal meth. I could theorize
about addictive personalities and chemical imbalances. But
no, to hell with it. The most important truth to tell you is
that after his disastrous outburst at Max's wedding, Marty
had perhaps a dozen days of happy normality left in his short
life.

One of those days stands out in my memory, though: an infinitely pathetic exemplar of the hope and the disappointment of trying to live with him as he crumbled from within. It was a shining day in early summer after a long difficult spring of tears, ranting, broken promises, whining paranoia and all-too-easily-explained absences, some of them lasting a week or more. I tried to reclaim him after the wedding binge, but he had taken a lot of methamphetamine over the missing days and was distrait and sweating, scratching and slapping at invisible insects and straining as if to hear other voices beyond mine. I know now that I should have held on, stood firm, policed him and discovered the root of his distress. Or at least tried rather harder to do all of those things. But I gave up and turned my back on him, telling myself it was for Charlotte's sake. He slept after that binge for two days, so I did become worried about dehydration and forced cold water between his flaccid lips where he lay; then I rolled him over as he choked on it.

When he came round he said, 'Sorry about that,' but without conviction, as if I were a stranger whose foot he had trodden on. It was not like the morning after Marienka and I found him with Charlotte in the flat: whatever it was had taken a stronger grip on him, and muffled any remorse he might feel. Then he muttered, 'Got to see a guy,' and left the flat wearing only his underpants. I ran down the road after him with his trousers, remonstrating (though not, I fear, nearly violently enough) and he pulled them on and kept walking, barefoot. Hours later he came back happy and excited, but bleeding from a bad gash on his face. I took his hand and his pulse was racing; stupidly, preoccupied with my own fear, I veered off the subject of where he had been and what he had taken, and accused him of having pinched the last of the housekeeping money – a roll of five-pound notes – from the jar hidden in the kitchen cupboard.

He had, of course. But he became furious with me, talked a lot of gibberish about 'undeterminated infiltrationism' and Satan, and after roaming round the flat knocking things over with unco-ordinated movements, he went out again for two more days. I had suspicions about where: a dark silent friend of Friggy's called Charles was almost certainly his source. But I did not know where Charles lived, and held back from ringing the others in the band. Oh, I should have raged and interfered and shouted at them all and punched my way through the infuriating fog of his addictions. I should have tried. I did not.

And so it went on, week after week; I took the baby into work with me, where Sylvie played with her and left all the typing for me to finish. Mr Brignell said nothing. Business was good, and he must have been afraid of losing me. The back room where the files lived was now more or less a day-nursery. I grew very fond of my boss during those months: his acceptance of an irregular situation was greatly soothing and his stocky, workaday normality eased my sense of panic, enabling me to detach myself from the uncertainties of home. One day Marty came in to the office in a state of confused self-righteousness and talked disjointed nonsense, accusing Mr Brignell of stealing his wife; but Sylvie and I got him out before our boss got back. Sylvie was subsequently a lot less respectful of my rock-chick status than she had been before, and became engaged to her dull solid boyfriend. I like to think that our example saved her from certain dangerous illusions about glamorous men.

I came to dread the nights when Marty came home, though God knows he was harmless enough: he never raised a hand to me or the baby and could usually be reduced to whimpering self-pity by a sharp word. But somehow, on one particular lovely June Saturday, for no reason that I could discern he woke up almost normal. He was miserably thin, needle-marked, intensely tired and with teeth which were starting to look truly horrible; but he was able to sit on the carpet and play with the baby when she woke in the dawn. From the bathroom I heard him singing to her, one of our old songs about sailing away on a clean wind and bidding the dark waves goodbye. Tears came to my eyes. On an impulse, I called through the door: 'Mart, shall we go out? Right out of London? There's that free festival, we could get the train from Paddington and make a day of it?'

Big Gordy Wise from the squat had given me a flyer for the festival a few days earlier, when I ran into him and Jake shopping down the King's Road. I was inordinately pleased to see them, and welcomed the bear-hugs in which they enfolded me and their extravagant admiration of Charlotte. She had learned to wave, and Gordy thought this a most extraordinary achievement. So I kept the flyer tucked behind the bathroom mirror, and at this moment my eye fell on it and I suddenly thought that given Marty's temporary equilibrium, an outing might set us all back on track. He had had an outbreak of whimpering remorse the night before, and for once I almost believed that it was more than a mere symptom of his latest crash. He had smoked a joint afterwards, and seemed quite like his old mellow self, even glancing towards the long-neglected Spanish guitar in the corner. He had sold the other instruments weeks ago for drug money.

So we took Charlotte and her push-chair, and rode the underground to Paddington and the 9.30 train out into the freshness of Berkshire. By happy chance, Gordy and Jake and Damien were still hanging around at the little station when we arrived, waiting for a minibus. It arrived, painted with hideous and improbable flowers, with one mudguard hanging off and no tax disc. With some trepidation I crammed the folded push-chair in beside us and sat clutching the baby, myself perched on Gordy's knee, as we bumped down cart-tracks towards the free, and doubtless illegal, festival of noise. Amplifiers thudded ahead of us and a crowd of several hundred gaudy ragamuffins milled around. Marty looked around him and took an interest, swaying slightly as he stood as close as possible to the sounds. I had packed a hasty picnic, but Jake led us ceremoniously to a makeshift tent beneath which presided Natalia, Sukey and Anna – the Southwark friends I had nearly forgotten but who greeted me as calmly as if we had met yesterday. They were cooking some sort of bean patties over a pair of gas bottles, and we sat on the dry grass and ate with them; or at least Charlotte and I did, for Marty had no appetite that day. He just sat quietly looking towards the music, lost in thought. For a while he rested his tangled head on my knee; I can feel it there still when I think of that day.

When he finally got up and moved closer to the amplifiers, Gordy leaned carefully towards me and said: 'Your guy doesn't look too good.'

'He's not. He's taking a lot of drugs.'

'Yeah, well, but – he doesn't look good on it.'

'No. I have no idea at all what to do. It's gone beyond anything I really understand.' The big man's matter-of-fact kindness made me tearful. 'Gord, it's been a nightmare, half a year of it, I'm desperate!'

He leaned towards me and was about to say something, but Marty wandered back. 'OK, Sal?' he asked, almost normally.

'OK. You OK?'

''Course I am.' He wandered off again, and at that moment I realized with a shock that I was more upset and afraid when he seemed normal than when he was asleep, or gibbering, or paranoid. I had got to the stage when reminders of the old Marty were too painful to bear. It was actually easier to accept him as an infantilized, whimpering, hopeless lunatic who had to be ignored, managed, or controlled with sharp words, like a dog. I had taken his door keys away from him as long ago as March, after he brought one of his dealers home, a gap-toothed and whey-faced lad who said he needed 'to keep outa sight, like'. My response was to take Marty's keys and threaten to call the police unless the dealer left instantly. So these days, if my husband got home and I was out he just had to sit or sleep on the concrete stairway until I got back.

But now this smile, this 'OK, Sal?', this harmless social gathering all around us made the whole thing unbearable again. I saw Gordy looking at me with gentle understanding and could stand it no longer. The floral shuttle-bus was not far off; I scrambled to my feet and said that we must go. Marty said vaguely, 'Yeah, see you around. Lend me a tenner?' and ambled back with his note in his hand towards the music. And, no doubt, the nearest dealer. Certainly he did not reappear for two days.

Gordy did, though; the next day he knocked on our door, having got the flat's address from me, and sat solidly on the sofa for an hour, peering kindly through his dense ginger whiskers, trying to persuade me to take some action.

'He ought to go into rehab. He was well out of it after you left yesterday.'

'I can't make him,' I said flatly.

'Guys often get clean because they love their women and their kids,' he said with dignity. 'My brother did. He was on smack. He's clean now. Won't even smoke.'

'I don't know how to start.'

He gave me a card with an address on, a charity called Street Aid. 'They'll help.' But when I rang Street Aid they said they couldn't do anything unless he turned up in person. Marty got home that night earlier than usual, and I offered to go down with him in the morning; he vaguely agreed but then slept, unwakeable, for the next eighteen hours by which time I was back at work, with Sylvie reading board-books to Charlotte while I answered the phones and typed out maisonette particulars with my free hand.

I never did get him to the Street Aid centre. My resolve crumbled, and I shrugged and let things slide.

That was our life, or the last part of it. Other things happened, of course: Mr Brignell tried to persuade me to go on a professional estate agency course, but it lasted a fortnight and I could not leave Marty and the baby. Marienka wrote and asked all three of us to come for a short break in Paris, promising airily that Peter would pick us up off the Dover ferry. Again, Marty's unpredictability made me turn it down. The royalty cheque came at last, translated from dollars into sterling just two weeks before the pound abruptly sank in value by a quarter and inflation reached 22 per cent. The lump of royalty money helped, but suddenly as prices rocketed the baby's food and nappies came to represent a frightening cost. The landlord said the rent would have to go up. My focus, for some weeks, was entirely on money: how to stretch it and how to hide our savings from Marty. He and I ate mainly rice, courgettes and fried chicken, to save using the oven and provide mushable leftovers for the baby. Sylvie got pregnant and married – in that order, just like me.

The other thing which happened during that time is that against all probability I got to know Annette. I had been surprised, in late March, to receive a note from her in flowingly beautiful italic writing, on very expensive paper headed with the address of the neat little mews house in Kensington which David and Helena had given the young couple as a wedding present. If I close my eyes I can see it now, so much concentration did I afford it thirty years ago.

Dear Sally,

I'm so sorry we didn't get a chance to speak much at the wedding, but I did admire that beautiful baby. Now that we

are sisters-in-law, I thought it might be fun if we got
together one day for lunch or coffee. I've got some sort of
blood-pressure thing so I'm not supposed to travel far, but I
would love an excuse to buy you lunch in the Harrods
restaurant one day! I gather from David that you work
pretty hard, so I suppose a Saturday might be best. It would
be lovely if you brought the baby, I need to learn about
babies now . . .

Over the pale-blue expensive page were some dates and a
dignified sign-off. My first reaction was of revulsion, but as
I carried the letter round with me and re-read it at work
throughout the day, I was surprised and seduced by the
apparently open, cosy, girly tone of it. She was making it
clear that she would treat me to lunch, but did not crow at
her good fortune nor mention Max (I assumed, with a stab
of humiliation, that Max had told her all about my greensickness. I doubted, though, that he had told her about
Charlotte's paternity). But the more I read the letter, the
more inclined I was to go and meet Annette. She was trying
to be family, and I have always believed in family. Marty, at
the time, was going through one of his two- or three-day
phases of relative docility, and I even wondered about leaving
the baby with him; but in the end I did not dare. Instead I
rang Annette and made a date for a Tuesday – my half-day
off that week – and arranged to leave Charlotte with Sylvie
at the agency. Tuesdays were always quiet.

In the Harrods restaurant I looked around in a moment's
panic that I would not know her; I had only met her that
one weekend in Oxford and then seen her looking fragile in
a bunchy wedding-dress. I stood for a moment, feeling
horribly shabby. On either side of me complacent middle-
aged women shoppers sighed and dumped their green bags
by their tables and began to order in commanding county

voices. Then at my elbow a high hesitant voice said: 'Sally? It is, isn't it? But no baby?'

I turned to her in relief, a little shocked at her pallor, and said, 'Yes, but I left Charlotte with a friend – I thought maybe this wasn't quite the place – I don't see any baby stuff . . . you know, highchairs.'

Annette glanced round, and indeed there was not a high-chair in sight. She gave a nervous little laugh and said: 'Yes, well . . . you see I don't know about babies at all. That's partly why—'

She broke off; a waitress was motioning us to a table at the edge of the big room. Following her, I kept glancing at Annette. Her old balletic grace had not entirely deserted her; the blue-black hair was swept up as smooth and shining as ever. Even her six-month bump was discreet beneath a navy linen jacket. I remembered her hauteur in the Oxford house and wondered what she wanted with me now: what could this smart lady get from the lumpen, broke, undistinguished wife of the family black sheep? For it was clear that she did want something, and the emanation of that need kept me interested and willing. In that spring of 1975 I was used to having the infant Charlotte depend on me, not to mention the increasingly chaotic Marty; yet to be summoned in aid by this elegant creature was intriguing and flattering.

When we had sat at the table and gone through the polite rigmarole of ordering prawn cocktails and cutlets and green salad, a silence fell and after a moment I felt I should break it.

'Annette,' I said, 'it's nice of you to ask me, but I'm a bit puzzled –' I stopped, wretched in the conviction that Max's wife would give me a cold upper-class stare and say that it was mere family politeness, with the implication that even a low-bred hick like myself should have known that. To my astonishment, however, she gasped and blinked and an unmistakable tear rolled down her pale cheek.

'Oh, please no,' she said, in her breathy little-girl voice. 'Yah, I know it's a terrible cheek, with you working so hard and everything, but I don't know anyone else I can talk to about – about –' Her terrified downward glance resolved the puzzle.

'About being pregnant and having the baby?' I said, quite gently. 'Girl talk. Well, I'm your man.'

This attempt at levity failed to stop the tears which, sobless, ran down her face until she dabbed at them with the Harrods' napkin. Looking up at me then, her great eyes candid, she said, 'Thanks. The thing is, I'm terrified. Just so scared –'

'Oh, it's OK! Once the baby comes you forget all the uncomfortable stuff.' I had learned to say 'uncomfortable' from the brisk nurses in the hospital. Talking about 'pain' was prohibited there. 'You'll be fine.'

'My mother,' said Annette, 'isn't someone who talks about these things. But I know she had a bad time with me, because Daddy once said that was why I'm an only child.'

'Well,' I said, 'I can tell you some stuff, but the hospitals have classes, and there's gas and air and things for the pains, and really, it's not rocket science you know – babies – we all have them!'

'I'm narrow,' said Annette. 'Like my mother. And I've got high blood pressure already. And my heart bangs, it bangs!'

She had her hand clasped, rather theatrically, over the banging heart and I wondered uneasily whether this was perhaps a real problem. Certainly she did not look robust enough for childbirth, but plenty of narrow fragile women have babies. I was at sea in this strange conversation, and mercifully our food arrived and we both began to eat; me heartily enjoying the treat of restaurant food, Annette picking miserably at the shreds of lettuce which surrounded her fat, foetal prawns. Eventually she began again:

'I shouldn't unload it on you really, but my husband – he's

a bit squeamish about all this, it upsets him. We've agreed he needn't be there for the birth, and I am more and more scared, and suddenly I thought of you, at the wedding you looked so – *solid* and happy with your baby. Oh, I'm sorry, I didn't mean solid that way –' she almost giggled.

I smiled. 'I know. I looked like someone who's got to the other side of the river and set out the picnic. You thought that while you're worrying about the current and the piranha fish, it might be good luck to talk to me over the water.'

'Oh, yes, brilliant, Max said you were brilliant with words, that's exactly it.'

I found that I could hear her speak of Max without too much pain. It was like probing a sore tooth with your tongue: cautiously, you discover what is bearable. Real pain, however, stabbed me when she asked after her brother-in-law.

'How's Marty? *So* talented. Daddy thought he was a hoot at the wedding, you mustn't think he minded about all the fat-cat stuff, he said it was a tonic to meet a young man with opinions who said his piece.'

I evaded the question as best I could. I had left Marty in a drugged sleep, twitching and dribbling, sprawled across the bed. I was by now sleeping on a camp bed I had bought from Milletts on the Fulham Road for £3, so erratic were my husband's nights.

'He's fine. Changing direction a bit, artistically.' I crossed my fingers under the table in superstitious horror at my own facility with lies. 'And Charlotte's tremendous, you must see her, she's learnt a couple of words, we think –' The mention of the baby steered us into safer waters, and by and large the lunch went well. We talked about her new house, its decorations, and the difficulty of stopping Helena from doing it all herself; she admitted to being shy of David Jakobowitz and gave a little scream of admiration when I said I had had lunch alone with him once.

When I dropped back into the office and picked up Charlotte, Sylvie said enviously:

'Well, *you* look like the cat that had the cream,' and I realized that I did. For a short while I had not been a harassed working mother with a chaotic no-hoper of a husband, but a guru of womanhood, looked up to for my wisdom by rich young women in mews houses.

The relationship continued; several times I went to her pretty little house behind its veil of summer clematis, and ate thin biscuits with my continental coffee, or a plateful of olives and cheese if it was lunchtime. Charlotte took to her, and performed all her tricks and smiles to order. Marty, on the rare occasions when he was interested in where I went, sniggered with coarse incredulity. 'Off to see Frigid Freda again, are you?' When I was at Annette's the conversations always followed the same pattern: obstetrical reassurance, me dismissing her symptoms as quite normal, then general light gossip and admiration of the baby. Only once did we come near quarrelling, when the subject of Marienka arose.

'So *awful*,' said Annette. 'Such a double *betrayal*, considering that Marienka was Susie's friend, and had come to the wedding!'

I demurred. 'Well, no – she was a friend of Max's really, not Sue's—'

'I don't *think* so,' said Annette with icy sweetness. 'Max hardly knew her.'

I gaped and began, 'We were all housemates – you came—!' but Annette had pulled herself to her feet and gone to the little kitchen to fetch more coffee – I never knew a pregnant woman with such an appetite for coffee, for my part I could never touch it.

So she did not take in what I was saying, and my voice faltered and I realized that I did not want to contradict or quarrel with her. These chats – in which I was so much the more powerful partner, with my unrivalled experience of childbed – had come to mean a lot to me. They were civil-ized little oases in my increasingly squalid and perilous life, and I suspected that they would end once her child was safely delivered and in the hands of a smart nanny. Meanwhile her house, immaculate and elegant with its ruched old-rose blinds, good rugs and smooth little bronzes, was restful and calming after the studentish makeshift of our flat. The heavy panelled door leading to Max's study was sometimes ajar, and I could see the familiar purple folders and heavy art books. He was never there, preferring to work in the Courtauld Institute library according to Annette. She rarely mentioned him, perhaps out of delicacy but more, I suspect, because her chief preoccupation was the ordeal awaiting her sometime in July.

It should, I thought, have been a dreadful pain to me to be in Max's house with Max's wedded wife, but somehow it was not. It calmed me and I did not want to give it up. So, as Annette turned back from the coffee-pot, I faltered and stopped in mid-sentence.

'Sorry, what were you saying? Marienka?' she said.

'Oh, nothing. Just that I knew her quite well at college.'

'Little tart!' said Annette, and I had no courage to defend my old friend. Anyway, I thought, Marienka *was* a bit that way inclined. She would not have grudged me my tolerance of her being called a tart, since it got me some nice biscuits and domestic peace.

When I got home that afternoon Marty had passed out on the concrete stairway to the flat, his head lolling against the wall, his arms flung loosely between his sprawling knees. There were new needle-marks and crusted blood on his thin left arm. I heaved him indoors once the baby was settled, put a pillow under his head and wondered whether to call a doctor. But he groaned and stirred and I decided he was fine.

He wasn't, though. He never woke up. In the morning I became alarmed at his stillness and called an ambulance; at three o'clock that afternoon, in St Stephen's Hospital, he died.

I had had no idea at all that disaster was so close. Death was not on my horizon, and I had not known it was on his. There were two doctors, one young and black and one older and silver-haired; they argued a little, *sotto voce*, about the cause of death but grudgingly put it on the certificate as 'heart failure'. Although the drugs had compromised his resistance, said the older of them kindly, he must have had a weak heart to start with. Perhaps it stemmed from a childhood fever. 'No need to put the drug use down, I think. Heart failure.'

I knew better. Marty Bellinger died because I didn't love him enough to keep him alive.

26

It may seem that I have recounted Marty's death abruptly, unkindly even. But that is how it was. Abrupt, unkind, shocking. On the day I came back from Annette's immaculate little house I had no conception of his possible death. I knew plenty of people who took drugs, and quite a few who lived chaotic lives and slept a lot by day. I knew nobody who had died. It seems, at this distance of time and maturity, a culpable and reckless naiveté, but when you are very young and grow up in peacetime, I suppose dying seems remote and irrelevant. It is one of those tiresome grown-up things you need not think about for years – like arthritis and mortgages and pensions. Certainly in the days and hours after Marty died I kept feeling – beneath the shock and misery and shame – another sense, a sense of incongruity. He would be back, surely, with a shambling apology and explanation? He would say, 'Sorry, babe,' and pick up his guitar? I realized that I had seen his last six months' decline as little more than an exaggerated sulk brought on by the band's separation. I had expected him to snap out of it. I had patronized him, ignored him, belittled his decay while I turned to my own affairs: work and babycare and smug mentoring of the pregnant Annette.

And now he was dead. For ever. I would never write a song with him again, never see him laugh at Charlotte's gummy grins. Nor would I ever – this began to prey on me very much – formally thank him for rescuing me from loneliness and embarrassment and fear.

These feelings took days and weeks to develop their full misery. At first, in the bleak bland hospital room, I was merely stunned. I had left the baby with Sylvie when the ambulance came – she was staunch, said, 'I'll square it with Mr B, you go, 'slong as you need, love, I'll take her to my mum's if you're not back.' In the ambulance Marty was still and pale, his pulse fluttering; they gave him oxygen and every attention, but the faces of the ambulance crew frightened me. In the hospital I was sent to a 'relatives' room' rather than the main waiting area, and given a cup of tea, which scared me still more. My only experience of hospital was the cavalier brusqueness of the maternity ward, in itself a kind of reassurance that all was well and there was nothing to fuss about. The solicitous kindness of these nurses terrified me. When the news was brought by the older doctor, his colleague a few paces behind, I had difficulty understanding it at first.

'You mean he'll be in hospital for a while?' I said stupidly. 'That might be for the best, the drugs – I mean, he was going to go to Street Aid to get help –'

They told me again, more carefully and slowly. My legs became weak, my knees soft; I sank onto a plastic chair and stared up at the men in their white coats. Marty's thin hawk face swam before me and almost instantly turned into his father's.

'David,' I said. 'David Jakobowitz. His father. I've got the number. And, oh!' I had remembered Helena. Marty's mother. I was a mother now, for all my immaturity, and I felt the tearing of her heart as if it were my own. 'Oh, the parents. They must be told.'

The doctors melted away; a nurse came, brought me more tea which I could not touch, asked gentle and seemingly irrelevant questions. I was taken through to see him, or a strange wax model of him; I did not believe it. Somebody called the Almoner appeared in ordinary civilian clothes among the medical uniforms, and said that the Jakobowitzes were on their way. There were formalities I cannot remember, nightmarish signings and decisions, an undertaker's business card, cool information about autopsy. Then there was Helena, hair unprecedentedly dishevelled as she screamed about her 'baby boy', and David, white as chalk beside her, trying to hold her as she flailed and sobbed.

Helena demanded to be taken to see her son's body, alone. David hesitated, wanting to insist on being with her, but eventually stayed with me instead. For all Helena's grief it was his stricken face that I found hardest to look at. She, at least, had had her son's casual affection all his life. So David and I sat side by side, looking ahead, and after a few moments he spoke, in an almost normal voice but without taking his eyes off the far wall: 'We saw this coming, you and I.'

'I didn't. I honestly didn't understand how dangerous—' I was choking on guilt and terror.

'The danger,' said Jakobowitz coolly, 'is that once the mind starts to go askew, an individual loses all sense of self-preservation. He wouldn't have thought it was dangerous, either. I assume he was taking a mixture of drugs?'

'Yes.' Guilt sat so heavy on me that I could not say more.

'Well,' said Jakobowitz heavily. 'Too late for Marty. But we shall need to put the finger on his dealers. This talk of heart attacks will help nobody. My wife will not be happy about the risk of publicity, but I see that as a duty.'

I started. In the presence of death, the idea of illegality had not crossed my mind.

'You will be able to help,' he said, a flat statement of fact. 'I have asked the Almoner to call the police so we can begin the process.'

I shivered. 'I don't really know the drug people. One did come to the flat – but with the baby there, I made Marty take him away – you might get more help from the others in the band, perhaps . . .'

I wanted to scream at him to stop, to shut up about police and dealers and think about Marty who was dead. It seemed a callous conversation to be having in this dark moment.

'The police have photographs of suspects,' said David flatly. 'You will be very helpful. Every confirmation is of value. We will make sure that you and the child are in no danger.'

I turned to look at him now, expecting his face to be as efficient, cold and bankerly as his voice. It was not. It scared me very much: for all my grief and guilt I still had a child, and I had my youth and an instinct towards hopefulness. David Jakobowitz' face offered a premonition of what happens when all these things are gone.

Helena came back, quiet now. 'Poor baby,' she said. 'He looks so young. David, do you want to go?'

David went through without another word. I was glad that he was able to do this thing alone, as I had done. I sat with Helena in silence, until, just as he returned, the policeman came and made arrangements for a formal interview. It was evening before I got away. David, with heavy courtesy, called a second chauffeured car from his bank so that I could collect Charlotte from Sylvie's mother and take her home. There was a brief, half-hearted movement from Helena to take me to Knightsbridge – 'You shouldn't be alone' – but I could not bear that. I had farewells to say and forgiveness to ask, in private.

Max, I thought, would at least be a comfort and support to his parents. Long afterwards I heard otherwise. He came when summoned, but not for long, and remained uneasy and restless until he left again. David took charge of the funeral arrangements – having politely asked my leave to do so – and broke his normal reserve during one of our funeral meetings by saying to me with startling sharpness that Max was 'a cold fish' and that if studying fine art couldn't teach a man to support his mother in her grief, he didn't think much of it. I was too numb at the time to think much about this remark, but it came back to me often in later years. Max came to the funeral itself – a quiet heartbreaking affair in the same church he had married in that spring – but Annette was not at his side. She was, he explained stiffly to David, 'in a very nervous state, with the baby coming'.

I knew that, and could imagine the fastidious terrors and *timor mortis* tremblings of Annette; to go near a coffin in her particular state of mind would clearly be hard. But it did occur to me that I had been a friend to her these past weeks and that it would have been graceful, to say the least, for her to turn up to support me in turn. She was just gripped by an irrational fear of the perfectly normal process of childbirth. Marty was actually dead. Dead, at twenty-one years old.

I gave these unkind thoughts free rein at the funeral, perhaps because they dulled the rising misery of the occasion. A fortnight later, I was truly sorry to have done so. On a sultry, sweaty day Annette was taken into hospital with soaring blood pressure. Alexander Devereaux Bellinger, a healthy child of 8 lb 3 oz, was born at 3 a.m. by emergency Caesarian section. His mother never came round from the anaesthetic.

27

In August, Paris is no place to be. Sensible Parisiens head for the country or the coast, leaving the sweltering city to tourists and their exploiters, and to a few penurious students leading self-consciously bohemian lives along the Rive Gauche. Marienka's little flat was in the Marais, and the noise from the building of the weird new Pompidou Centre penetrated our lives from breakfast to teatime, accompanied by clouds of thin gritty dust that swirled in if you dared to open the peeling old double windows. Charlotte and I slept together in a single bed in the hot, narrow slit that was the second bedroom, and the baby kicked merrily all night and forced me to cling to the edge of the mattress. But for all that I was deeply grateful. Paris was another world, and I needed one.

Marienka had phoned me two days after Marty's funeral: Peter had spotted the announcement in the overseas edition of *The Times*. 'It is fucking typical,' said my old friend force-fully, 'that it didn't occur to Max to ring me. And come to think of it –' she added after a moment when the phone line crackled and hummed against silence '– nor did Sue think to tell Peter. They all know where we are, even if we are *outcasts*. Christ, that family!'

I said nothing; I was standing in the middle of the messy flat, hair hanging in unwashed rats' tails, ambushed by the latest wave of grief. The funeral was very hard: I had not really understood that the coffin would be lying in the church, two feet from my shoulder. I had not expected Helena to cry, nor to collapse in her husband's arms at the graveside saying it was her fault and going on about how he must have had a weak heart from a fever he had when he was little and she hadn't got the doctor in time. Nor had I bargained with the guilt and difficulty of having my parents there, kind and emollient and entirely ignorant of the way our marriage was. I was in a poor state after that funeral, only just able to get the baby through her day. There were more police interviews as well; Friggy was questioned and dark Charles arrested, but I could take no satisfaction from that.

So after a moment, Marienka sensed my petrified grief and confusion and modified her observation.

'Well, I say that family . . . all except Marty, he was the pick of the bunch. I am so sorry.'

'Perhaps he was. I don't know.' I twisted the curling plastic cord around my finger, trying not to cry.

'Look, Sal,' said the phone, 'I think you should get away. Come over here, like you were going to. We've got a spare room. Peter and I are both working through August, you'd have the run of the place all day and in the evenings we might get the concierge's daughter to babysit, and show you Paris.' She paused again, then said, 'Look, I know you. You're not going to go home to Suffolk, are you? You're going to sit in that flat on your own staring at the wall, or go back to work. No. You mustn't. Come for a few days, anyway.'

I went, with no expectation of pleasure, but Paris even at that season gradually seduced and distracted me. I walked the streets with my push-chair, soothed by the statues and the sheer grace of the place, loving the way the iron balconies stretched like dark lace borders along the apartment blocks. I shopped for baby clothes at the Samaritaine and sat out with coffee and *pains au chocolat* on the hot pavements, a book lying unread before me and Charlotte by my side contentedly gnawing crusts in her buggy. When Marienka and Peter got back from work they would shower in the clanking bathroom, change and take a glass of Kir with me. Several times they persuaded me out to dinner, choosing quiet places so that I would not be offended by exuberant tourist gaieties. I came to like Peter: he was quiet, self possessed, slightly lisping, deliberate and shy. The last man, in fact, I could ever have imagined Marienka falling for. Yet they seemed utterly at ease together, fond and kind, and I often saw her eyes following him with proud satisfaction as he moved around a room. I sometimes wondered about Sue, the only member of the Bellinger family I had never properly met. Odd remarks in the past from Marienka, Max, Annette and Marty had given me the idea of a stolid, rather bossy young woman of the Sloane-Ranger type, and glimpses of her at Max's wedding and at the funeral reinforced the impression. She had come up to me at the funeral, though, and awkwardly expressed a dutiful regret. But there was no charm there, no spark: it was hard to see why gentle Peter had married her at all, if his taste was for a louche and larky firebrand like Marienka.

She and I had little time to talk at first, with Peter there, but on the fifth day of my stay, a Saturday morning, she suggested that we climb the Eiffel Tower.

'Peter will babysit. He's getting on rather well with that fat little sprog of yours.' She was always flippant about the baby; I suspected, rightly as it later turned out, that Marienka wanted one of her own and was having trouble conceiving. 'It'll do him good.'

I objected. 'Surely he should come?'

'Scaredy cat. Afraid of heights. Go on, ask him!'

Peter had come in to the sitting room, towelling his hair dry. 'It's true,' he said. 'I can't go up that thing for anyone. Marienka bloody loves it, so you'd be doing us both a favour.'

So she and I took the curving lift up the leg of the tower, and then the straighter one, and wound round an iron staircase until we were as high as we could get and Marienka flung her arms wide and breathed in deeply. 'Hoorah! God, I needed this!'

She was next to the grille; I joined her, my calves pricking with apprehension at the height, and looked out over the heat-haze of the city towards the dome of the Sacre-Coeur.

'You find it therapeutic?'

'I do. I hope you will too. Up above the world so high, like a tea-tray in the sky.' Her hair was dishevelled from the windy climb, and she had undone another button of her silk blouse; she was the student Marienka I loved. I smiled at her, and she moved closer.

'Sal. Tell me really. How was it? The funeral, all that stuff you had to go through. You don't talk about it.'

I hesitated. She was right: I had brushed off kind enquiries all week, yet there were things I longed to express. I looked around; a knot of tourists giggled and pointed in the far corner by the souvenir stall, but the northern corner where we stood felt private and confidential, with our language casting another veil of secrecy around us.

'It was bloody awful,' I said. 'I'd had a sort of hope, I dunno, that the band might play, that they might do one of his songs as a sort of memorial, that someone might stand up and say what he was like before all the last bit, the bad bit . . . I should have arranged all that. Some funerals are like that, celebrating.' My eyes were filling. Marienka's steady regard did not falter, nor did she reach out to touch me in sympathy. I was grateful; I found I could go on.

'But David and Helena took it all over and it was very Anglican, very formal, they sang The Lord's My Shepherd, not to Brother James' Air even, but the gloomy one. And that was it. The readings were standard Bible stuff, and the vicar did a short sermon about how you never know when you'll be Called so you'd better be good all the time, just in case.'

'Jeez,' said Marienka. 'So, the full repressed Knightsbridge bit.'

'Yup. I did think David might have wanted some Jewish prayers.'

'But Helena's not Jewish, is she, or her first husband?'

What harm could it do now? Why should I not tell her? 'No. But Marty's actually David's natural son. They must have been having the affair for years while the first husband was alive.'

Marienka stared. 'God almighty.' Then she thought for a moment and nodded. 'Actually, they do look alike. Did, I mean.'

'I saw it the first time I ever met David.'

'I suppose I wasn't looking. God, though! Did Marty know?'

'Yes. He didn't talk about it, except obliquely, and I think it's why he hated David.'

She was quiet. Then, 'Poor bloody Marty. Poor old David, tough for him too.'

'Yes,' I said. 'And I didn't help Marty, or anyone.'

'You did. He adored you. Even back in Oxford any fool could see that.'

'That's what didn't help.'

Marienka, softened by her own discovery of love, pulled at a loose thread in her jacket for a moment, eyes downcast, then looked me full in the face. 'Did you know? That Marty loved you? I mean, did you know it wasn't just because of the baby and the jam you were in?'

'No. Yes. No. Oh, shit!' I began to cry, with noisy gasps; but up there high above Paris it didn't seem to matter.

After a few moments Marienka very gently put her arm around my shoulder and shushed me like a baby. 'Not your fault. Don't think for a minute it was your fault. Poor bloody Marty, he always was a catastrophe in the making, you know!'

We went back early to the flat, and had a quiet friendly

evening with Peter. He told me, for the first time, how frustrated and bored he was with his financial job, and how he thought he might take up his uncle's offer of a lower-paid but more interesting job in a small theatrical agency in London.

Marienka laughed at the idea of Peter tangling with show-business and said, 'London could be too hot to hold us for a bit . . . poor old Jakobowitzes. But we'll see. The money's handy in this job. We've got to save up if we're going to work for that old bugger one day. I reckon his agency's on its last legs.'

'It could be good,' insisted Peter. 'Once this government gets thrown out, I reckon we're in for a boom. Showbiz does well in booms.'

I had been in Paris for a fortnight and was beginning to plan what to do next, when the bombshell news of birth and death came in a letter from Max. It had been sent to the London flat and forwarded by the faithful Sylvie, who had appointed herself guardian of the place in my absence. I had asked for letters to be sent on because I had not dared tell the Jakobowitzes who I was going to stay with. If they phoned the flat, I hoped they would think I was in Suffolk. Max's letter was brief.

> *Dear Sally,*
>
> *I know you were a good friend to Annette during her pregnancy. She spoke of you very appreciatively. It seems hard to burden you with another tragedy so soon, but because of your care for her you should be among the first to know. Annette died in childbirth. Our son, Alexander, is alive and healthy. We would of course love to see you, when you feel able. I hardly know what to think about it all.*
>
> *Yours ever*
> *Max*

In the same post came a letter forwarded from David Jakobowitz.

> *My dear Sally,*
>
> *I have tried to telephone but I assume you are with your parents. I hope you are resting and recovering from our common tragedy. You may have heard by now about the second tragedy to strike our family, the death of my daughter-in-law Annette. She did not suffer, it seems, but the stress of bearing our grandchild Alexander Devereaux Bellinger was too great for her frail body. God be with her.*
>
> *Maximilian is distraught. He needs his friends now, though he does not know it and has retreated into silence and will not communicate much even with his mother. I hope you will be one of those who can comfort him, if only for the sake of Helena and her grandchild.*
>
> *Yours ever*
>
> *David*

I showed the letters to Marienka and Peter, who were sitting together on the landlord's chipped gilt sofa drinking their morning bowls of milky coffee. Reading the first, Marienka let out a little sigh of sadness and a murmur of 'Poor cow!' The second one she read with beady attention, several times by all appearances, then looked straight at me and said, 'No. Sally, no!'

'What do you mean?'

She glanced sideways at Peter, who was still reading and shaking his head in disbelieving pity.

'I mean, no. Don't get tangled up – in all this. With Max. Don't think it's your job to help. He's got plenty of support without you falling over that cliff again.'

'I have to. Family—' The protest died on my lips. I knew she was right. Another part of me knew, equally clearly, that she was wrong.

'They're not your family, not really,' she insisted. 'You know that. Marty was semi-detached. You and he and the baby, you were a new family. It's up to you, honeybun, but before you go anywhere near Max, think about your own survival. Cut and run.'

Peter looked up, puzzled. 'Marienka, what on earth are you on about? If Sally wants to stay in touch with her brother-in-law and his parents that's perfectly civilized! If Sue and I had had children, we wouldn't just feel we could cut ourselves off through divorce, whatever happened.'

'Keep out of it, darling boy,' said Marienka. 'You know nothing. Sally has reasons to steer clear. Believe me.'

I knew she was right, and I knew she was wrong. And right, and wrong again. But two days later, with thanks and embraces I left the sane gentle world of these irregular lovers and returned to the dangerous waters of home. In a scruffy post office by the Gare du Nord I cabled Max: RETURNING LONDON TUESDAY RING ME.

28

He rang me. Charlotte and I got off the boat train late on Monday night, sweaty and exhausted, and at eight o'clock next morning the phone was shrilling in the kitchen. I had found the flat in beautiful order. Sylvie and her mother, unasked, had put fresh sheets on the bed and cleaned everything to hotel standards; Marty's guitar, I noticed, was apologetically but visibly stashed on top of the wardrobe. I was about to ring and thank her when the phone burst into life and I knew, before picking it up, that it would be Max.

'Sally. Sorry to ring early. Oh God – Sally—' I had never heard him so tremulous and distraught; my heart turned over. 'Is there any chance, any chance at all you could come round?'

'I'll have to bring the baby. We're just getting up.'

'That's fine, more than fine, I've got a nanny person living here – oh, Sally, where have you been? I rang and rang!'

For two years now Max had made no attempt to contact me directly. I had borne his child, married and buried his brother, befriended his frightened wife. He had been to Paris and confronted our wayward former housemate who had stolen a husband from his sister, my sister-in-law. Our child had learned her first words and pulled herself doughtily to her own small feet. Yet all that time Max, who had made me pregnant and whose shirts and underpants I had ironed for a whole academic year, had not tried even to hold a conversation with me.

Even at Marty's funeral he did not really speak, merely offered an embarrassed duck of the head, a nod of British sympathy as if we were distant acquaintances. He had no right at all to ask me now where I had been, or to reproach me with not being there when he rang. Yet now, within a heartbeat, his power over me reasserted itself. I could not resist the tremor in his once-beloved voice, the naked expression of need for me and for no other. There was another dangerous sensation rising in me, too: I felt suddenly strong. I had lost Marty yet I had not fallen to pieces or pleaded like this. Not with anyone. I had gone to Marienka and Peter as an equal, not a petitioner. My baby was with me, content and confident. He, on the other hand, had lost a wife and could not even look after his own baby without a nanny at his elbow, or contain his confused grief without calling on an old flame to hold his hand. I was strong, Max was weak. I could, so I informed myself briskly, reach out and help him now, without the slightest risk of following will-o'-the-wisps and being lost in the swampland of old unrequited love.

'I'll be with you in an hour,' I said. 'I'll get the bus.'

'A taxi? It'd be quicker.'

'I can't afford taxis, Max. The bus is fine.'

'You know the house?'

'Yes. Of course. I'll be there. Hang on.'

Invincible, calm and maternal, I packed the baby's spare clothes, nappies and drinks and set off to rescue Max, humping the push-chair down the concrete stairs where Marty used to sprawl dopey, keyless and unrescued when I worked late at the agency. I did not even think of him. If you despise me for that, be assured you are not alone. I can hardly bear to write it down.

Max opened the elegant bottle-green Georgian door before I could knock. His arms were wide, and I went straight to

them murmuring, 'You poor love!' When he let me go it was
to reach down and help me indoors with Charlotte's buggy,
as a father would. She smiled up at him, and I forgot in that
treacherous instant that she smiled at everybody.

Indoors, the emotional moment past, we stood for a moment
awkwardly and then Max said: 'Tea? Coffee?' Thinking that he
would turn away to make it, and give me a chance to recover
and get my bearings, I asked for tea; but he only turned his
head and called imperiously: 'Doreen! A tea and a coffee, if
you would!' I had forgotten the 'nanny-person'.

'Oh – of course – you've got someone living in for the
ba— I mean for Alexander,' I began. 'That's good. It must
be hard.'

'David's paying,' he said, perhaps misunderstanding what
I thought was hard. 'He very kindly offered. He was going
to give Annette one of those maternity-nurse people as a
baby-present, so he says it's the same thing. They seem to
cost an awful lot, these women, for what they are.' He paused,
and I trembled lest the invisible Doreen should hear him.
'But it certainly helps. I have no idea about what to do with
a baby and Mother can't do much.'

'How *is* Helena?'

Max was pacing now, distracted, his hair flopping over his
face like the Lord Byron of my teenage imagination. He
turned and shrugged.

'Mother's in an awful state. She's convinced herself that
she didn't take Marty's baby fevers seriously enough.
Apparently he had dozens of them, and convulsions and
stuff weaken your heart. The doctors said that the drugs
or the heart attack would have been survivable on their
own, but together they weren't.' He seemed to have
forgotten, in his distress or confusion, that Marty's death
was a blow to me, too: his wife. He scowled at a misty
Lenare portrait of his mother in her youth, which stood on

a side table. 'I think she's just in denial about having a son who was a junkie.'

I did not like the word, but did not know how to protest against it. 'Marty was fine, mainly,' I said weakly. 'The drugs sort of took over, but only for the last bit.'

'You're so sweet. So loyal,' said Max, and came over to put his hands on my shoulders. 'Dear Sally. And you've done so well with little Charmaine –'

'Charlotte.' I wriggled free of his hands, but subtly, so as not to offend him.

'I'm so sorry. I'm not myself,' he said miserably, and began to pace again. Now I wanted to reach out and touch him, but did not dare.

A staid, stout young woman, a couple of years older than us by the look of her, came in with tea and coffee, and Max glanced at her and said, without thanks: 'Bring the baby in, would you? For a moment?'

She nodded, and disappeared into the little hallway. Beyond the kitchen, as Annette had once shown me, lay a second bedroom, 'the baby's room'. It was dark and elegantly furnished and, I thought, rather airless. Presumably the nanny slept there too. I felt a rush of pity for Max, grappling with his new baby and a stranger in this smart unsuitable un-homely little house. We looked at one another for a moment, and then big Doreen returned holding a tiny bundle wrapped in a white cellular blanket.

'Here's little Lexy-poo,' she said. 'Boofuls boy! Isn't 'oo?'

Max shuddered slightly. I hoped it was merely at her language, not at his child. He motioned abruptly to her to bring the bundle over to me. I peered in the wrappings and saw a clenched and wrinkled little red creature in a Babygro, eyes and fists tight shut. The eyes began to open, lizard-like. I had got used to thinking of my own daughter, round-faced and robust at seventeen months old, as the norm for a baby:

this little scrap with its toy hands and screwed-up face seemed ludicrous.

Charlotte was tugging at my skirt, and I reached down to pick her up.

'Look! A baby!' I said. 'He's your—'

My hesitation, mercifully, was covered by Nanny Doreen crashing in with, 'Alex-poopy, this is your big cousin come to see you! Isn't that lovely!'

Faces of various sizes stared at one another for a few moments, then Max motioned Doreen away to the back room with a distracted, 'Perhaps he should go to sleep or something.' When she had gone he muttered to me: 'I don't know why she talks to him all the time as if he knew what she was on about. And the nicknames! Lexy-poo! It's driving me mad.'

'It's natural,' I said. 'You wait, you'll be calling him nicknames and talking stupid, any minute now. Babies need talking to, and they seem to like silly repetitive language.' But I doubted, somehow, that Lexy-poo would ever get that from his father.

'His name is Alexander, no more no less,' he said stiffly. 'I look forward to when he can talk and listen intelligently.' He glanced at Charlotte, who had returned to a placid private game on the floor with the silk tassels of Annette's Turkish rug.

'Does *she* talk?'

'Few words. Seems to know "mama" and "doggy" and "baby" and "milk", but she says "mloke".'

'Extraordinary,' said Max again, running his hand through his hair. 'Oh God, Sally, you're a breath of sanity. So grounded in the *ordinaire*. Me, I don't know what's hit me.'

He flopped on the sofa and was once again the endearing, the irresistible, the magical Max of two years earlier. He patted the cushion and after a moment I surrendered and went to sit by him. He began to talk about practicalities, about the difficulty and embarrassment of having the nanny and the impossibility of not having her. He did not speak about Annette, yet I felt her absence so powerfully and sorrowfully in that elegant feminine room that after a few minutes I blurted out: 'Poor Annette. Was the funeral awful?'

Max shivered, and put his warm hand on my arm. 'I can't think about it. Mother didn't come, she couldn't, not so soon after Marty. David was wonderful. Her parents, the Devereaux – I can't describe how awful it was. The funeral was very small, only a dozen of us in the church, she didn't have many friends. In a way that makes it harder, you all keep catching one another's eyes. I did ask David to see if you wanted to come.'

'I was away.'

'Suffolk?'

'Not exactly.' I could not bring myself to admit to Paris. 'Anyway, as you say, after Marty, too soon for all of us for another funeral. But poor Annette. She was so nervous about the birth, too.'

Max was silent. I ascribed this to husbandly grief, but I think I knew even then that it was something far closer to husbandly guilt. Annette, without crude complaint, had made it clear enough to me that Max was not prepared to listen to her terrors about childbirth, which was why she needed me.

After a while he resumed, with a question I had no idea how to answer. 'What do you think I should do?'

I gaped. 'Max, I don't know – do what you have to do, I suppose. Raise your child.'

'How? Sally, I can't!'

I took charge. 'Of course you can. How much money have you got? What can you afford?'

'David,' said Max, 'has been supporting me through my doctorate. I've got another year, maybe a year and a half, some travelling –' He waved his long fingers agitatedly.

'Annette's parents were going to help by funding a nanny, but now they've got other ideas.'

I was silent. There was an incongruity that even I could not miss in this situation. Here was this elegant, well-subsidized, affluently connected householder asking *me* how to cope: me, a widow with a baby living on baked potatoes and stale cheese in a shabby flat the wrong end of the King's Road.

But he went on: 'You're so well organized – I thought I ought to ask your advice. About Alexander.'

'What about him?'

'Do you think I ought to – give him up?'

I stared. This conversation was getting beyond anything I had expected. I saw myself giving Max little hints on babies, dropping in to see him and the nanny, acting like a dignified and friendly sister-in-law. Such a question was way off my radar.

'Give him *up*? For adoption, you mean?'

'Not *public* adoption,' he said hastily, as if I had suggested the child should be sent down the pit. 'But Annette's parents have offered to bring him up. It would be formalized, he'd be as if he was their own. They say it would be too confusing for him otherwise.'

I was silent, shocked but playing for time. 'How old are they?'

It seemed to me that if they were young grandparents – in their early forties, say – this might not be such a dreadful idea as it at first sounded.

Max was a little shifty in his reply. 'Well – they married quite late. He did, anyway. I know he's just retired but I think it was an early retirement, he can't be more than sixty or so. She's a couple of years younger I'd say, but terribly active. She was a dancer, you know.' His eyes slid to a photograph I had not noticed, on the far side of the sofa where the other polished mahogany side-table stood. Mine followed. 'That's why Annette nearly joined the ballet.'

I could not speak. I had seen the child, unconscious of its future, in the capably mercenary arms of big Doreen. I gazed at the elegant old couple in the photograph – he silver-haired and senatorial, she with a permed blue rinse and the drawn, lined face of the lifelong dieter. I thought of a boy of ten wanting to run and play, with anxious septuagenarians clipping his wings; I thought of a student setting out for university and a new life, fretting about a frail 'mother' approaching her eighties, perhaps widowed. I know that many children have lived with, and dearly loved, their grandparents in time of war and tragedy. I know that in this brisk 21st century it is thought by many to be desirable for old women to raise babies, having borne them from donated eggs. But I was twenty-three years old, with a robust big baby I could roll on the floor and play with. Charlotte climbed over me daily, shrieking with amusement, crawled away at speed and would soon be running towards water, cliff edges, fire, every kind of danger. I was keenly aware of my own protective agile strength, the surviving streak of childishness that enjoyed playing with her, and the absolute fitness of my body to keep hers safe.

But Max was alone and fit for nothing much just now.

I temporized. 'I don't think you ought to make any quick decisions. He is your son.'

'I don't feel as if he was,' said Max. He was looking down. I thought for a marvellous moment that he was admiring Charlotte, who was still unconscionably interested in the rug's bright fringe. But his eyes were glazed: he was staring through her. She might as well have been a dog on the floor. 'I can't feel anything for him. It may be that I never will. The shock, you know. It might be best to let his grandparents deal with it all.'

'Wait,' I said. 'Things will get clearer. Honestly, they will.'

'Dear Sally,' he said. 'I couldn't do without you.' He

hesitated, just long enough, then diffidently said: 'Will you have some lunch? We could go to a little Italian round the corner, your baby could stay here with Doreen.'

Charlotte did not seem very pleased about this arrangement, and squawked irritably when Doreen picked her up and called her Charleykins. But I went, hardening my heart against my child's cry of indignation. I told myself I was going for Max's sake, out of kindness. I thought he would want to talk more about Annette, and about the baby's future, but he did not. He led the conversation to general things, mainly his research on some mosaics newly uncovered near Assisi. Once, in a pause, while I chased a portion of fish round my plate he looked at me hard and said: 'You've changed, haven't you? Really grown up.'

I swallowed the fish. 'Well, a lot of stuff's happened. The baby. Things do change you.'

'I really admire you, you know. For the way you dealt with Marty.'

There was a tightness in my throat; I did not want to feel so pleased at Max's approbation, and I did not want to consider how well or badly I had 'dealt' with his brother. But Max went on: 'I felt a bit guilty, you know.'

I stared. This was unexpected. For a moment I thought he was going to acknowledge his daughter, but then he qualified it. 'About introducing you to Marty. I mean, he always was a magnet to girls, but I wondered how much you knew about his dark side. I'd dealt with it for years, of course . . . he depended on me very much for a steady example. David always said so.'

My memory of Marty wavered for a moment, then returned to solid reality. He did not have a dark side, only a weak side. He despised his elder brother, or half-brother, and always had. He regarded him as an effete bookworm and a sponger. Some of his funniest gibes, when he forgot to consider my feelings, were at the expense of Max. But there was something about Max's claim to have been his little brother's role-model that was to me so touching, so vulnerable, that my heart melted and I did not demur.

Casting around for another subject I said: 'Did Annette have any brothers or sisters?'

'No,' said Max. 'Just the parents. That's why they made their offer. There is a logic in it. I really think it might be the best thing. I'm not fit to look after a baby, my heart is too heavy.'

'Max,' I said seriously 'Promise me one thing. You won't decide about Alexander straight away. Two or three weeks, at least.'

'OK.' He smiled across the table, his dark brows high. In his tone was something that, had he not been a widower of two weeks' standing with an avowedly heavy heart, I would have interpreted as flirtatiousness. 'For you, Sal, anything.'

I slept badly that night, the prey of nightmares. Marty and Annette were constant figures in a string of images: Marty in the worst of them sitting up in his coffin, dishevelled and swearing, then laughing at me and falling back to dissolve into a dead horror. I half woke, sweating, but was tired enough to fall asleep again straight away. The dream changed: although Marty was still there on the edge, this time he was confused with my father who was taking a service on the edge of a sandy sea-cliff like the ones I played on at Dunwich as a child. 'You'll go over the cliff,' said Marienka's voice. 'Right over.' But it was Annette who was wandering near the edge, disrupting the sermon by calling in a high piping voice to an invisible child; suddenly she vanished, sliding down the sand, and I saw a tight-curled baby fist in the rumpled sand and grass at the cliff-edge. But I could not run to grab it, my legs would not move, and all the time I was saying, pleading: 'It can't be there, it can't crawl yet, it's safe.'

I sat up, damp and afraid. It was only four o'clock and still dark. The London air of late August was suddenly unbearable to me, thick and dank. I went to the window and slid the sash open wider, but there was no relief to be had. For a while, huddled in my nightdress, I sat on the bed and thought through the day's events. They made no sense. I thought about work in the morning, Mr Brignell and Sylvie and the makeshift care which Charlotte got at the agency. Despite her tractable, sleepy nature it was never quite as easy an arrangement as it seemed, and could only get harder as she grew more mobile and demanding. I looked round at the shabby flat, now my sole domain, and at the shadow of Marty's guitar on top of the wardrobe. I thought of Max and his new neediness and his extraordinary willingness to hand over his baby to a pair of posh geriatrics.

A great revulsion for it all came over me. It was too complicated. I was too sad and guilty and confused to cope. I was a new widow, after all, a single mother; there should be someone looking after me; not just me fretting about Max and his child. I would go home to airy Suffolk for a week or two, walk along the muddy creek paths and let my own mother fuss over me. The Bellingers could all go hang.

At half-past eight, not long enough after I finally got back to sleep, the phone rang again and it was Max, with a problem. So I didn't go to Suffolk after all.

29

Max's early-morning problem was with Doreen, who had left a stiff note saying that her accommodation in the tiny baby-room was 'not what she was accustomed to', and that she could not commit to staying more than another fortnight at most. At Max's earnest request I went round to talk to her, 'woman to woman', about the vulnerable and difficult status of a young widower and how important she was to him.

As I arrived the nanny was just back from a walk with the large black pram she had insisted on; mercifully, the thing could be stowed in a low shed in the mews rather than taking up the whole of the hallway. Despite my weariness I had a momentary stab of amusement, remembering how Cyril Connolly's self-exculpating list of 'Enemies of Promise' included 'The Pram in the Hall'. Clearly the man just needed a shed. Doreen stowed it, and fixed a neat tarpaulin over it with a lot of tutting while I held the baby. Charlotte was in her push-chair, suitably restrained. Indoors, the nanny put the uncomplaining infant in his cot with the air of a woman who takes no nonsense from babies where bed is concerned, and took me into the shiningly neat little kitchen, while Max retired to his study and Charlotte sat safe within my eye-line on the sitting-room floor, winding the carpet fringes round a rubber Noddy she loved extravagantly.

'I wouldn't mind the room so much,' said Doreen formally, when I explained my mission, 'if there was a little more general consideration from Daddy.'

I took a moment to unscramble the code, and correctly surmised that Daddy in this case was not Doreen's father, nor David Jakobowitz, but Alexander's father.

'Mr Bellinger is quite reserved,' I said defensively. 'Finds it hard to show how grateful he is, sometimes.'

'I'll say!' The stout young woman spoke vehemently, showing in her exasperation the first sign of unadorned humanity I had seen in her. 'Never a thank you nor a please. Leaves his shirts out to be washed and ironed, which I do *not* do and never have. I have a professional training, you know; from Norland'.

I rather liked her for standing up for herself. Still, I was there to plead the cause of Max and the baby.

'Yes, perhaps – I'm sure you can explain about the shirts, or else I will – but he *is* grateful and he *does* need you, and the baby needs a mother-figure right now. And cut him some slack, he is in shock, he's newly widowed.'

Doreen was immovable. 'Two weeks' notice,' she said. 'Widowed or not, there's such a thing as manners. And there's no shortage of jobs with politer employers for the same money. I'm telling you,' she added, with a note of scorn for my weak advocacy of Max, 'if I wasn't so professional the notice would be a damn sight shorter.'

I murmured my appreciation on the family's behalf, and went – by way of a salute to Charlotte and Rubber Noddy – to knock on the door of the master's study. Max was immersed in a book; he half turned as I came in, with a flash of irritability and a sharp 'Yes?'

'She's going,' I said. 'Definitely. She's adamant.'

'Unbelievable,' said Max, on a sharp frustrated exhalation. 'What is the *matter* with these people?'

'I don't think she feels appreciated,' I said cautiously.

'How could she be? The baby's too young to appreciate people.'

'Not by the baby –' I found it hard to go on. Max, at that

moment, looked to my eyes so pale and vulnerable that I could no more scold him than I could a hurt child. Looking back now, typing out his actual words and remembering his impatient, wilful detachment from domestiticity, I am baffled at my own tolerance. I was, after all, as much widowed as he was, and a lot poorer. I find it hard to understand why I was mentally programmed to see only the problems Max suffered, and not the ones he caused.

He made as if to turn back to his books, and after a moment I said, 'Look. It's not a disaster. There are all these nanny agencies springing up. If she goes, you can get someone else in and start afresh.'

'Another stranger? As if it isn't bad enough, having Annette gone?'

It was almost the first time he had willingly mentioned his wife. With a huge effort, for I hated to do battle with him, I said gently: 'Max, Annette would want the baby to be properly looked after.'

'Yes,' said the father bitterly. 'Which is exactly why I am writing to the Devereaux, to say I agree to the adoption.'

He tapped the paper in front of him. I could not quite see it, but it did not look in fact very much like a letter, more like a sheet of notes on his art book. 'I don't have a choice. I'm a poor scholar and I can't look after a baby on my own. QED.'

'But try one more nanny? Just one? It might be brilliant, and things could all work out fine, and David said he'd help with the money, I thought.'

My heart was pounding in distress, my dream of the small hand and the cliff haunting me. I felt that a great wrong was being threatened to the sleeping scrap of humanity in the next room, Charlotte's half-brother and Max's first-born son.

'How can I?' asked Max rhetorically. 'No, there's no other way!'

A wail of indignation rose from the sitting room. Turning,

I saw Doreen assisting Charlotte to untangle Noddy's bell from the fringe of Annette's Turkish rug. When I looked back at Max, I saw that the papers under his hand were crumpled beneath his tense, white hands. After a moment, he began to cry.

So that is how, as August mellowed into September, I gave my notice to Mr Brignell and came to live at the Mews on a strictly temporary basis, to look after Annette's Alexander alongside my Charlotte. Max, in the days following my interview with the relentless Doreen, had more or less collapsed. I left him weeping that morning, and rang Helena. The maid Serafina took the message; for a moment I wondered whether the best option would not simply be for the Jakobowitzes to lend her, faithful creature, to Max for the next six months. At least he would be used to her. The next call I had, however, was a day later and came from David Jakobowitz. It was seven in the morning and Charlotte was not even awake; blearily I hauled myself out of bed to the phone and was jolted awake by the susurration of panic in that strong suave City voice.

'Sally. It's a lot to ask, but you've been such a tower of strength to poor Marty and to Annette. Our family owes you a great deal.'

'What's a lot to ask? David, what do you want?'

'That you should help Max, now. Having your tragedies in common, we thought . . . well, Helena and I hoped . . . that you would be able to support one another. You told me you were close friends, at Oxford?'

'Yes. We were. We shared a house.'

'Could you, do you think, do that again?'

I stared at the black telephone, numb and confused, suddenly envisaging a move back to the damp little house by the canal to turn back time. Charlotte was waking, grumbling in her cot in the other room.

'What do you mean?'

'He's in a terrible state. Helena can't help, she raves and cries, she's by no means getting over losing Marty. He was the favourite, you know. Susan has her own problems just now, and I feel she should be free to find herself happiness after her unfortunate marriage. And now it seems that this nanny we hired for Alexander has said she won't even work her full fortnight's notice. She says that Max was offensive.'

'He's not himself,' I said. 'Surely she sees that?'

'It's her right to make her own decision,' said David's voice, with some of its old edge. 'She's an employee. But it creates a family crisis. I believe you know that Annette's parents want to take over the baby?'

'It might,' I said, tired and full of an unformed dread, 'be the best thing. I was horrified when Max mentioned it, they look so old, but if he really can't handle things—'

'Did he tell you they're emigrating?'

'No.' Behind me, Charlotte's morning plaint intensified.

'Mrs Devereaux has a much younger stepsister in Australia, who's keen for them to come and live near her, and she's offered help with the child. Sally, Max is risking the loss of his son for good! My wife's grandson!'

'But what can I do to stop it? If he's determined?'

'Move in. Take over. Look after the baby – we'll see you don't lose financially, I want to talk about that anyway – and you would have your own child with you without any need to go out to work.' A brief artful pause while that temptation took root in me, then he continued, 'Just for a while, a few months, while Max recovers himself. He says he can't bear anyone near him except an old friend, so we suggested you and he jumped at it. If he's to keep little Alexander, it'll have to be all in the family. If he has a series of nannies who leave, the Devereaux are quite capable in their grief of seeking custody. You see the problem?'

I tried one last throw. 'Couldn't Helena . . . ? Couldn't Max and the baby come home, perhaps, to Knightsbridge?' I remembered that vast house, its luxury, its soft-footed Filipina maid. 'I mean, why should he stay in the Mews?'

'Please think about it,' said David. 'I can tell you in family confidence that things are very tense here. Helena is not well, not well at all. But she sent her love and adds her appeal to mine. Please think about it. We need you very much.'

When I had put down the phone I went through, picked up Charlotte and buried my face in her damp warm solidity. I had known, two days earlier, what Max was driving at. I had seen enough to believe David's assertion that he was genuinely falling to pieces. Without even articulating the situation to myself, I had resolved not to become a substitute for the put-upon Doreen, even if Max himself asked me.

Yet here I was, wavering. David's reiteration of family solidity and identity moved me very much. I had my own family, of course – parents living gently in Suffolk, Ben at sea – but in that moment they seemed less real and certainly less important than the glamorous, stricken clan headed by David Jakobowitz.

I thought again about work, and my heart plummeted: for all Mr Brignell's enthusiasm and support, for all that I had become fond of Sylvie, I did not want to spend my life as an estate agent and quailed at even the thought of whiling away four more years in that office until Charlotte could go to school. I had been vaguely entertaining another idea, of abandoning polite society completely and throwing myself on the mercy of my friends in the squat. Gordy Wise had been in touch after Marty died – there was a tiny paragraph in the *London Evening News* headed 'Rock singer death mystery' – and had said that if 'life gets heavy, man' I could stay there for a while. Natalia and Sukey had moved out to live on the city-farm they ran, but Damien and Anna were

there and Gordy was happy to move out of the second room
into the attic. I was deeply touched by this, and briefly imagined a hippyish life south of the river, braiding weeds and
beads into Charlotte's hair and sharing bowls of rice and
peanuts. In that sort of life, I thought, my intermittent income
from song royalties might keep us going, though I would
have to use my parents' address due to the illegality of the
squat.

So I had three likely paths to consider, though in truth I
was still too shocked to consider them reasonably. I could
live in a smart mews house in Kensington and look after two
infants on a good income, seeing Max every day and earning
his undying gratitude. Or I could stay in the dreary flat with
the dreary brown furniture and work at Brignell's for just
enough money to keep me going, until the inevitable moment
when Charlotte got rumbustious, Sylvie left to get married
and the babysitting nonsense became impossible. Or else I
could live in a squat, boil up water for washing in a kettle
over a gas bottle, and be surrounded by gentle undemanding
half-stoned vegetarians with guitars and pan-pipes. Or – it
suddenly occurred to me as a fourth option – I could just
go home to Suffolk, get an evening job in the pub to
contribute to the housekeeping and live with my parents until
Charlotte was at school.

I gave that no more than three seconds' consideration. I
was, after all, an independent adult, an Oxford graduate. In
those days there was still a certain stigma in being what today
is known as a Kipper: an adult kid in its parents' pockets.
Inevitably, I took the first option, of living in Max's pocket.
I rang David Jakobowitz, arranged to lunch with him, begged
Sylvie's mother to look after Charlotte for two hours, and
wrote to the landlord saying I would be leaving the flat.

I had come on a little way, though, from my doormat
status. I told David, firmly, that I was not trekking across to

any of his city haunts, but that he could meet me in the little Italian restaurant round the corner where I had been with Marienka. Then I began to gather together and organize my clothes and the baby's.

I knew I was doing the right thing.

30

It was nearly a year before Max and I slept together, and even longer before the shattering day when he proposed. I suppose I had always known, or hoped, that both these things might happen, but never admitted it to myself when I first moved to Onslow Court Mews. I arrived that September in as businesslike a frame of mind as I could manage and laid down my conditions. I informed Max first of all that if I was to sleep with the two babies we would have to move his large bed into the tiny bedroom – it fitted, but used up nearly all the floor space – and that the single bed and the two cots must be in the master bedroom.

'Otherwise,' I said firmly, 'the three of us won't have enough air, or space. Doreen was right.'

'Do what you need to,' he said vaguely. 'We're grateful. David thinks it's the best thing. I can't face another stranger.' He looked so tired and sad that my heart fluttered; it was only on the far side of some more mundane details about moving that I could carry on saying the things I had promised myself to tell him plainly from the start. The main one was that a house with small children in it was always going to be messier and less formal than one without, and that while his study could remain sacrosanct he would have to get used to the clutter and jangle of Charlotte's plastic toybox in the corner of the living room. Indeed, I added, daringly warming to my theme, it might be better if the polished drum tables either side of the sofa were stored in his parents' home and replaced by roomy Habitat cubes which the babies could use as handholds and where we could store their board-books and other impedimenta.

'I think they belonged to Annette's family,' he said, in a faintly protesting tone. 'They *could* go back to the Devereaux. But they're very good pieces, French, I'd miss them.'

'Babies change things,' I said, with a firmness I had never suspected in myself, not where Max was concerned anyway. 'This is a freaky experiment, and we'll just have to see how it works out. The other thing is that when you're feeling a bit stronger, eventually there will be things *you* have to do to help with the children. Both of them.'

'What sort of things?' he asked nervously.

'The sort of things modern fathers do,' I said with my new ruthlessness. 'Give them their tea, or get them up in the morning if I've been up all night.'

Max said nothing, but looked at me in an odd way. I think he had considered, until that moment, that the family was doing me a favour by taking me in, as if I were a Victorian waif governess starving in the storm. He did not see himself as a modern co-operative dad, rather more perhaps as Mr Rochester.

'You'll have to give me time,' he said eventually. 'This has all been a shock. I'm not ready for baby things.'

Given that he had had nine months for Annette's growing girth to accustom him to the idea of fatherhood, I did not think it wise to answer that. But he had calmed down considerably since he knew I was coming; I felt comfortably powerful when I saw how his panic attacks had yielded to a firm promise from me. I had felt helpless and humble around this man for so long that there was a sneaky pleasure in this. 'He needs me!' had been the cry of my deluded heart for too long: now that it was palpably true, how could I resist it?

I was, I admit, also morally fortified by a lunch with David

Jakobowitz. Its purpose, to my surprise, was chiefly to inform
me that the trust fund he had accumulated for Marty would
now pass unconditionally to me, whether or not I agreed to
help Max with the baby.

'Marty,' said David heavily, 'would have had this money
under his control once he either established himself as a musician or else got a proper job. Or when he turned thirty. I am
afraid I had to put that condition in, as when he was a teenager
it became clear that giving him a lot of money would be a
mistake. I felt very keenly that I did you an injustice by not
transferring it on his marriage, since you have such good
sense. But I feared he might reject it. It isn't from Helena's
first husband, it is from my own resources.'

'As it should be,' I murmured, and he nodded gravely,
acknowledging our sharing of that secret knowledge.

He continued, with calm bankerly precision: 'He would
only rarely accept interim help from myself and Helena, as
you know. But I made certain investments on his behalf a
long time ago, which have borne fruit. I realize that having
these funds may make you think again about taking up our
offer or request to assist Maximilian, but it seems right to
play fair with you.'

When he mentioned the sum my eyes widened. It was not
vast wealth, not the sort of money that means a person need
never work again. But it would produce a modest, steady
income, and for a while at least I would not be paying rent
or utility bills. It would buy a home one day, or simply make
me able to save while I was living at the Mews.

'Are you sure?' I asked stupidly. 'I mean, it's a lot of money
and –' the additional words stuck in my throat, but I forced
myself to say it '– I wasn't much of a wife to Marty, and I
blame myself that he died.'

The words hung in silence. David put down his knife and
fork and stared past me for a moment, his keen dark eyes

– so very like Marty's – misted with tears. His profile, I saw
with a pang of compassion, was sharper than it used to be,
the skin stretched tight over the fine bones. Finally he spoke,
stiffly and with difficulty.

'He loved you, and the child, I think. He would want you
cared for and safe from trouble or from any compulsion by
others. That is more than enough. To carry out his presumed
wishes is for me a duty . . .'

Now it was he who could not continue. Neither of us could
say much more; he paid the bill, took a few details from me,
and thanked me again for confirming my decision to help
Max. 'Take care,' he said, without saying what might threaten
me. 'Look after yourself.'

I went home after that lunch and wept a little: for Marty
and for the father he would not accept, and because the baby
he had so happily cuddled was not even his own. Then I
looked at the guitar and wept some more, because he was
dead and would never write another tune. Yet that hour of
weeping was for me a turning point. I said goodbye to Marty,
asked Gordy to look after the guitar carefully because I did
not want to take it with me, and embarked on the task of
helping his brother. For the first time in all my dealings with
Max Bellinger, I convinced myself that I was keeping a level
head.

Alexander proved to be a model baby: calm, quick to smile,
intelligent and sociable. He woke only twice during each
night and I found him easy to settle back. I had been afraid
that Charlotte would resent him, but she was mostly gentle
and would stroke his small hands murmuring 'babybaby-
baby' and plant ostentatious smacking kisses on his brow.
Our days together were reasonably harmonious. I got up
first, made tea for myself and left some in the pot for Max.
He would appear in the little kitchen halfway through the

children's noisy breakfast routine – Alexander sucking furiously on his bottle on my lap, Charlotte throwing cereal
around – grab his tea and take it to the sitting room to read
the paper. Charlotte would usually follow him as soon as she
had finished, and crawl or eventually stagger round him,
burbling contentedly. I had blocked off all the electric sockets,
banished the standard lamps and put all ornaments up high;
the room was nowhere near as elegant as before, and the
Turkish carpets had been rolled up in a plastic bag in the
shed and replaced by bright, washable wool rugs from Inca.
From time to time Charlotte got at the newspaper before
Max did, or decided it was fun to hit it violently as he held
it up; on those days he would leave the house breakfastless,
fleeing to the sanctuary of his favoured coffee shop near the
Courtauld Institute library.

If Charlotte found some less aggressive outlet for her
morning high spirits he would go to the kitchen and make
himself toast while I tidied up and played with the babies in
the sitting room – Alexander had a newfangled bouncing cradle-
chair which Charlotte loved to rock, and she only occasionally
up-ended it. During that time we adults exchanged few words;
parents in any ordinary ménage with small children will recognize how easy it is to suspend all adult communication for days
on end. I would spend the rest of the day as all young mothers
do: seeing to baby needs or taking slow walks with the big
pram to see the ducks in Kensington Gardens. Eventually as
Alexander grew more robust I took the pair of them farther
afield, even by Tube, in a folding double-buggy. We went to
the Almost Free Theatre to see a children's show once, and I
showed the babies off to Damien and the others without making
it too clear that they weren't both mine. Max would get home
around five at first, but when he discovered that this was bath-
time he found it easier to stay in the library until six. When he
got back, the chaos of bath and supper would be abating slightly,

and he could sometimes be prevailed upon to supervise them while I got their cots ready.

'Is there any chance,' I said one December day, about three months in to this regime, 'that you could read Charlotte her bedtime story? She likes the Goodnight Moon book.'

I was holding Alexander, who was grizzling with a cold, and I was tired after a long wet day indoors.

'I wouldn't know how,' said Max a little stiffly. But he took the book, and sat gingerly on the chair beside her cot and began to read in his deep, beautiful voice.

Charlotte stared up at him, interested but wary. When he reached the end she sighed, snuggled down, looked up at him and said: 'Goonight moon. Goonight Max.' I had not realized until that moment that she knew his name. I was 'mumuh', Alexander was 'babybaby', Helena and David were collectively 'Gannos' and the ducks, milk and moon all had their fairly recognizable names. But I suppose she heard me speak to Max often enough, even at 21 months old, to pick up his name. Max looked at her in astonishment, as if he had just woken up.

'Did you hear that?' he asked. 'She called me Max!' His hand went out and touched the hump of her small shoulder under the bedclothes. 'Goodnight, Charlotte.'

After that, he took over the bedtime story, bringing home expensive and beautiful baby books from the bookshop near his library, until I became almost jealous of my daughter. He still showed little interest, though, in his son. When I handed the baby to him for a minute in those early-evening moments he would handle him gingerly, with more fear than interest, and be glad to give him back. There was, I see now, no mirroring adoration in the baby's clear eyes. Max liked females best, and females who worshipped him he liked best of all.

As for other domestic chores, we had a cleaner two days

a week paid for by David, and Max did routine jobs like washing-up and taking out the rubbish, always fastidiously slipping on rubber gloves before he did so. I had nothing to complain about on that score. After the children were settled he either ate a quick basic supper with me and retired to his study, or more often went out to meetings with other post-graduates or with his supervisor – so he said, though I never quite believed that academic supervisors worked quite so many evenings. When he got back I would be asleep.

But a change came over me after we had got through our first low-key Christmas (we agreed, as an extended family, not to do anything festive this year as we were all too raw. My parents were under the impression that I was staying with a friend; I had not had the nerve to tell them I was virtually working as a live-in nanny in Kensington).

One January evening I said: 'Max, the babies sleep through the evening now. I need some time off babysitting. I haven't been out without a pram or a push-chair for four months. Suppose you babysit?'

'But if they woke up?' he demurred. 'It really isn't my thing. I wouldn't know what to do.'

'I'd be back by ten,' I said. 'Look, Max, I need time out.'

'My mother might babysit,' he said hopefully. 'I could ask.'

Helena was a fairly frequent visitor, usually by day; she had aged thirty years in appearance since Marty died and lost most of her old haughtiness where I was concerned. The babies were a delight to her, but she looked too frail and too elegant to be left in charge of them. Charlotte, a large and positive child, looked strong enough to push her grandmother over.

'Max,' I said, 'we did a deal. I'm doing this for you, I'm not an agency nanny and I'm not a charity case. I want two nights off a week. And if you won't babysit I will ring a nursing agency, and you can pay.' Money was a delicate area between us: although he – or more likely David – paid the rates and electricity, it seemed to me that I was paying rather more of the food bills than the master of the house, although he expected bread and milk and real coffee, the makings of a quick supper to be always to hand. I did not yet have the energy to tackle him about this; in any case, with the income from Marty's fund I was saving substantially, and a new royalty payment was due later in January. All the same, it rankled a little that I was effectively subsidizing Max as well as raising his baby.

It was, I think, the mention of money which made him acquiesce over the babysitting. 'OK. But please be back by ten-thirty. In case they wake.'

They never did; and two nights a week I went out, down to Southwark usually, or to one of the eccentric theatrical performances put on by Damien and company. I found I could laugh; I found I could help out with words for songs that Jake and Gordy were trying to write for a folk-and-protest festival they were helping to set up in a field in Norfolk. Anna and the other girls were, as ever, mild and accepting of my company and utterly incurious about my circumstances; when we first met again after Marty's death Anna merely murmured, 'Sorry about Mart, what a bummer,' and Natalia offered to do a healing karmic chant over me. I usually left about ten, getting home by half-past; Max would be pacing up and down, muttering 'You said ten,' and I would say 'ten-thirty,' and rejoice a little at my ability to resist apologizing to him.

Did I, through this strange time, still love Max? Was I in love, in that golden transforming way I had been in Oxford, or even in the tormented miserable way that had ruined my life with Marty? It was certainly not the latter. I saw him, after all, at breakfast and at dusk every day. I knew he had no other girlfriends, or at least I assumed not. I shared the raising of the child he acknowledged, as well as the one he did not (Charlotte's parentage was a taboo between us). I had a degree of power over him. I was coming to understand his weaknesses and pettinesses as well as his charms. Those things made yearning torment impossible.

On the other hand, there is a power in familiarity, in daily contact; he became as much a part of my life as bread or tea or the wails and gurgles of the babies. And as Marty's accusing image faded and strength and optimism returned with the spring weather, I found my eye falling in the old way on the turn of his shoulder, the flop of his hair, on his bare chest as he emerged from the bathroom with a blue towel tight around his narrow hips. His smile was the same as it ever had been, and was seen more often now, especially when he looked at the increasingly appealing Charlotte, who adored him. Thus it was that, one evening, it happened. I had returned breathless and still laughing after walking home from an absurd kabuki-themed performance of *King Lear* by Damien's group, in which Cordelia toured the auditorium after her death handing out tiny paper cups of sake. Max had almost finished a bottle of wine and he shifted to make room for me on the sofa. I started to tell him about the play, and he twisted round suddenly and took me by the shoulders.

'Don't leave me, ever,' he said. 'Promise.'

I could not promise, for he was kissing me. Emotion, too long dammed-up and channelled into daylight commonsense, returned with all its ancient midnight power.

31

Things changed. We kept the double bed in the small room and moved Charlotte, with great ceremony, into the single one with a new continental quilt and Mickey Mouse pillow.

'Baby Zander gotta cot,' she said. 'Lottie gotta big bed. Lottie big girl.' Max and I, like man and wife, shared the bed he had slept in with Annette, and there seemed no harm in it but only healing. For the first few weeks we were avid, hungry for the comfort of one another's arms as soon as the children were asleep. His evening appointments with the phantom supervisor vanished. He was, I thought, passionate; sometimes I had a fleeting sense of triumph when I thought of Marienka's assertion that he was cold. Occasionally I was troubled that he did not talk to me in bed, nor laugh; I could not identify what I now see was a lack of intimacy. One night, unable to sleep, I lay effectively alone and reflected that for years in my teens I had been puzzled by historic or arranged marriages, or by those Victorian or romantic novels in which husband and wife produce children while appearing to have no close personal connection or love. How on earth, I would think, could you share the entanglements of bed with a man without utter intimacy and trust; or, at the very least, a frankness about physical need? Now I thought I knew. I understood those acquiescent royal brides in their chilly beds, that mouselike heroine of *Rebecca* who hardly knew the man who swept her off to Cornwall. But then, I thought, Max had always had depths I could not plumb. I was still humble enough to accept that.

Mere tiredness set in eventually, in any case, as the novelty wore off. By summer we were probably in the same state of attenuated, increasingly rare passion as plenty of young parents. Charlotte had become a Terrible Two and alternated bouts of charm with bouts of fiendishness which startled me, though not as much as they startled Max. Just as he seemed, to my joy, to be growing close to his unacknowledged daughter he withdrew again as if he was surprised and hurt by her small defiances.

'She adores you,' I would say encouragingly, when her scowling little visage was out of sight, but he would either grunt and withdraw, or say 'Could have fooled me.' His evening academic appointments returned as suddenly as they had ceased.

'He only likes being adored when it's undiluted,' said Marienka with a crooked smile. 'You should know that, Sal. Of all people.' As it happens Max and I had our first real argument on the subject of Marienka and Peter: they had returned to London to join Peter's uncle's agency, and in the near future to take it over completely. I was overjoyed at the thought of seeing them regularly, and rashly suggested we all eat out together.

Max was scandalized. 'Completely out of the question. You know what happened, and how badly that man treated poor Sue.'

'Sue's got another bloke now. She's virtually engaged, Helena said, off to live in Sussex or somewhere with horses. Water under the bridge. Poor old Peter, he wouldn't hurt a fly. Come on, Max.'

'Marienka behaved disgracefully,' he said coldly. 'A complete slut. Frankly, I'd be happier if you didn't have any contact with her.'

Even then, I let him win, and told Marienka that the pair of us would have a quiet drink together from time to time. I dreaded it a little, as I thought she would rant at me for living with Max, but she only sighed and smiled affectionately, and wished me luck. Her hand was on her belly: she was at last pregnant, and the cowlike serenity of the state suited her very well.

Alexander's first birthday was celebrated in great style at the Jakobowitz home, with champagne, a huge pointless cake which Charlotte sabotaged, a candle which she put out by banging it with her shoe, and smoked salmon canapés for the adult guests which she stole and then sicked up in David's company car as it brought us home. When I had put her to bed, resisting all the way, and settled the still amiable Alexander, I went to the sofa where Max was sitting with a book and flopped next to him, my head on his shoulder. We did not often cuddle outside the bedroom, something I put down to his natural dignified reserve. But I had never actually been repulsed before. He moved away quite sharply, saying: 'That was a disaster. I don't know what David and Mother thought.'

'She's two and a half, for God's sake. Kids are like that.'

'I don't like that word.'

'Which word?'

'Kids. I prefer to say, children. If you talk of them as animals, they'll act like animals.'

'Oh, for God's sake!' I was a little tipsy from the champagne, and tried again to snuggle up to him. 'Every family goes through this stuff.'

He moved away once more, seeming to flinch a little on the word 'family', and I gave up and flung myself to the far end of the sofa. After a moment he said: 'My mother isn't too keen on the way we're living. She noticed the bedroom

arrangements when she came the other day, and she
mentioned it to me today.'

'Oh God. What *is* her problem?'

'She says she never thought I'd do anything like this when
the arrangement was first mooted. Otherwise she wouldn't
have supported it. She says she thinks of you as my sister-
in-law. She says, and apparently Sue agrees, that your coming
to my bed is bordering on the indecent.'

I was stunned for a moment, then found the nerve to say,
'Christ. The old witch *has* got over her grieving process,
hasn't she?'

'I don't think you should talk about my mother like that.'
He did not smile. Hearing an echo of the way he phrased it
– *your coming to my bed* – I became suddenly, unexpectedly
angry.

'Well, what does David think? He wears the trousers, as
far as I can see. You've all kowtowed to what he thinks, all
your lives. Except Marty.'

Max looked at me with positive dislike, and in that giddy
moment I realized that I did not very much care. There was
a sense deep within me of huge things moving, perspectives
shifting, old worlds shrivelling like party balloons.

'David,' he said, 'thinks rather the opposite. He says it's
very biblical. There is a concept called Levirate Marriage, in
the Old Testament.'

'Wha-aat?' I bleated, almost forgetting my anger in embarrassed astonishment. I pulled a cushion to my chest.

'Moses, apparently,' said Max coolly, 'said that if a man's
brother dies and leaves a wife but no son, that man must
marry his brother's widow and have children for his brother.
It was a trick question, or something. The Sadducees. A widow
must not remarry outside the family, while there is a brother
available to do the duty.'

I jumped up. 'Look, Max!'

'You asked. I'm telling you. There's quite a family confer-ence going on about it. David thinks I should marry you, my mother thinks I should keep my hands off you.'

'And they all think I should carry on keeping house for you and bringing up your baby, do they? Is that what they all think?'

'It makes sense,' said Max. 'I thought it suited you. Gives you a proper home so you don't need to work.'

'I have a *perfectly good home* with my parents when I want it, and enough money to live on anyway, thank you. With *my* daughter.'

'Enough money because our family gave it to you,' said Max coldly.

'Enough money,' I said, 'because my *husband*, who is dead, inherited it from his natural father. Who is, as you bloody well know, your stepfather.'

Max glared; I was glad of the confirmation that he had known the family secret all along. I wondered why I had never raised it with him, and marked it down as more evidence of our lack of real intimacy. A kind of shame was burning in me now, for reasons I dared not inspect. But I went on, reckless:

'Another reason I have enough money to keep all four of us in food and three of us in clothes, Max, is because, unlike you, Marty and I happen to have earned money of our own, by our own creative work.'

I had just had a good royalty cheque; some of our songs had been horribly bastardized by American balladeers and my building society account was looking healthy. It may be a repre-hensible thing, but I have noticed through my life that a healthy bank account sometimes has this effect of buoying up an indi-vidual's spirits and confidence, so that hitherto unthinkable emotional revolutions are enabled to take place. Certainly I was having one, and the hot exhilaration of it took my breath away.

Max went white. 'Your songs – pap for the popular market – are not something I envy you the credit of,' he said. He always became a bit convoluted when he was angry, as I remembered from his rows with Marienka in the house by the canal.

I jeered like a schoolboy. '*Envy you the credit of*? Christ, since when do learned PhDs finish a sentence on a preposition?'

'Jesus! You bitch!' He was on his feet now, facing me across the room that once had been so elegant and calm, home of poor Annette's ladylike terrors. 'You cheeky little bitch!'

An odd detachment took me; over his shoulder I noticed that the gilt eight-day 19th-century French clock on the mantel had stopped; it was terribly hard to remember to wind it, especially once we had silenced its chimes for the babies' sake. Eight days is an awkward cycle to get into, I reflected. Monday one week, Tuesday the next – why couldn't clockmakers have thought of that and stuck to seven days?

Max continued to rant against me and I stood firm, arms folded, staring at the stopped clock. I was almost frightened by how little I loved him, or cared about his feelings. Only months ago I had felt a new spring of adoration for this man, rising from old girlhood passion and idealism and made tenderer by his closeness to my daughter, and by the daily familiarity of our lives with the babies. Only weeks ago all had seemed well, and I had secretly entertained thoughts of permanency, even of marriage (Levirate marriage, as I now was informed).

Yet now I felt nothing, except a vague curiosity as to how Charlotte and I were going to extricate ourselves from this humiliating mess. Only the thought of Alexander troubled me, for I had grown to love him almost as if he was my own. Almost, but not quite. There was a cool, classical cast of feature in the baby which reminded me too often of Annette, and kept me a fractional distance from him. All the same, he was a worry. I could not stay in contact with him easily if my domestic partnership with Max was going to explode as nastily as it seemed about to.

Max was asking me something. 'What?' I said stupidly. 'Sorry, what was that?'

'I asked,' he said coldly, 'if you would now please stop these histrionics, marry me and regularize this ridiculous situation, for all of our sakes. As you don't appear willing even to listen—'

'Max, don't be stupid! You don't want to marry me. You don't even like me, right now.'

He did not deny it. 'The children,' he said heavily, 'come first. And if we were married we could at least provide them with a conventionally decent home. We could sell this house, put our resources together and get somewhere with a garden and room for both of us to get some privacy.'

'Separate bedrooms, you mean? You want to annex *my* money to buy yourself a room you wouldn't have to share with me, huh?'

'It would appear,' said Max primly, 'to be the best option. Feel assured that I would not interfere with any other affairs you might have, as long as you were discreet, and I would expect the same. The arrangement would offer you the protection of a proper home and enable me to carry on with my work. You used to be glad to do that.'

I had, from time to time in the hazy delight of our first sharing a bed, possibly gushed a bit about his damned research into the Assisi mosaics. I may have given him the impression that I regarded his PhD more highly than the songs Marty and I wrote. Yes, I may. At that moment, though, his pomposity and assumption of my gratitude filled me with the kind of horror and revulsion that I suppose one only feels for a former object of obsessional love. I could hardly breathe.

'Max,' I said carefully, 'stop talking about me needing the protection of a proper home. This is *nineteen seventy-six*, not eighteen thirty. Anyway, if you were the last man in the universe I wouldn't marry you. Not with a *long pole*.'

'I suppose you have to be flippant and childish about it,' said Max stiffly. 'But I did think that given our long friendship, you would at least civilly consider the offer.'

I had no answer. I shook my head dumbly, went into the children's room and slept that night very uncomfortably indeed, wedged in the single bed with Charlotte kicking and flailing and the baby snuffling noisily in the cot.

32

'What 'oo doing in my *bed*?' demanded my daughter, loudly, an inch from my face. 'Mummy, what 'oo doing in *dis* bed?'

'Story of my life, that question,' I said. 'One wrong bed after another, really. Sorry, lambkin. It's a funny sort of day.'

Stiff and dazed, I eased my feet onto the floor and pushed myself up. I was fuzzy with sleep and hunger. I had not gone out of the bedroom last night until I heard Max's door close on the far side of a bout of angry bathroom sounds, and had only dared have a quick wash, slip down the stairs and grab the heel of a loaf with lemon curd slapped on it as a makeshift supper. I did not want to meet him on a similar errand. It would have been too comically embarrassing.

'Is it de-cause of Lexy's birfday?' persisted the child. 'We went-a party an' I was sickup.'

'Indeed. That's more or less it, darling. All over now, all happy. Now just stay quiet a minute while I see . . .'

I was peering round the door and down the stairs. The hallway was deserted and there was no sound; I crept down and saw the bedroom and study doors both open – which was unusual for Max, who guarded his work fiercely. His briefcase was missing; he had gone out. I went back to Charlotte and hastily dressed her, then while she bumped efficiently downstairs on her bottom I stood for a moment looking at Alexander, still asleep in the pretty pine cot unaware that his little ship of life had hit the rocks. I had no idea what to do. Max had vanished for the day and I had

no desire to be waiting for him whenever he got home. That
our cohabitation was at an end I was quite certain; yet there
remained so much to organize that I felt quite faint. Since
the original arrangement had been made with David and
Helena while Max was overcome, I felt that I should ring
and tell them straight away, like any domestic who resigns
for personal reasons. Indeed I had an awful premonition that
Helena would screech, 'You can't leave without giving proper
notice,' as if I were a tweeny, and that David would be sad
and disappointed.

If Alexander were my own baby, I thought, it would be
simple: just an old-fashioned flitting, a note pinned to the
kitchen table with a sharp knife saying 'Don't try to find us,
jerk.' But I could not take Alexander, who was no relation of
mine, and nor could I leave him alone.

Fury mounted in me that Max had not considered any
of this before flouncing out in the dawn. Then the wave of
surprise came back: sheer amazement that I could feel
anything like fury towards Max, my distant star and dream
lover these four years. Looking back, I began to see that the
obsessive love had lost its extreme power during the months
of living together, and been rekindled artificially by our sexual
relationship. Even so, on that summer morning I felt as if the
world had tilted on its axis. At some level I also knew that
when matters settled down there would be a reckoning to
be paid. I had behaved like a fool, and there would surely be
damage to contemplate as well as triumphant relief. Also, I
missed something already: I had come out of an impenetrable
fog, but while I knew it for a poison cloud, at other times it
would seem an illimitable, beautifully scented rainbow, full of
sweet airs; a dream from which it was sorrow to awake. Now,
in the light of common day, I was just a harassed and dishevelled young mother facing a life without support and
considering the moral responsibility of walking away from a

one-year-old baby who had known nothing but the warmth of my arms.

Alexander woke, placidly sliding his calm blue eyes open and smiling; I picked him up and took him through the morning routines mechanically, still puzzling over what to do next. Charlotte was no trouble that morning, for once, and when they were clean and dressed and fed I left them together on the living-room floor and went up to make myself presentable. We were, I decided, off to call on Granny in Knightsbridge. She could screech all she liked. It had to be faced.

Helena was home, and surprised to see us so soon after the party. Charlotte smiled radiantly at her (her little head emerging from several square feet of pink smocking, put on expressly for her chic grandmother's benefit). She continued to be charming, and duly expiated her awful behaviour of the day before. Charlotte has always had this gift of knowing just how far to push her luck, and pushing it no further. Alexander demonstrated his precocious sense of balance, inherited no doubt from his Granny the dancer, by pulling himself up at the side of the sofa and then letting go and waving his hands about. We made small-talk. We ate a light lunch. Nobody would ever have guessed that Helena thought my recent behaviour 'bordering on the indecent'. The occasion was all very sweet and emollient and upper-class English. I was just about to spoil it by loosing off my devastating announcement after lunch when in the distance the front door opened, a voice called 'Darling?' and I realized with a stab of relief that I would be able to tell Helena and David together, and get it over with. David would be fair. David was always fair. At that moment I really loved David.

He came in, pale and composed, his step a little heavier and his hair greyer than when we first met and Marty was alive and defiant.

'Sally, my dear. What a nice surprise. And the children. I came home early, by good chance.'

He glanced at me and – in the eerie way that we always seemed to divine one another – I knew that he knew. Max must have phoned him at work. I raised an eyebrow, inclining my head towards Helena, and he gave a tiny, almost imperceptible shake of his. When he had greeted Charlotte gravely and put a grandfatherly hand on the baby's head, he asked Helena if he could have a cup of tea and some cake 'to settle my stomach' as he sat with us. She got up to look for the Filipina maid, and as soon as she was out of the room he said quickly: 'Max tells me that you want to end the arrangement.'

'Yes. I do. It's not healthy.'

'No. I see that. Helena and I were perhaps naïve to think it would remain on a sisterly basis – or progress to something better.'

I blushed, and hated myself for it. 'No, you weren't naïve. It might well have worked. But it hasn't. Really, really hasn't. I have to move on. Now.'

'Of course.' He nodded gravely and I saw Marty's eyes looking at me; my own filled with tears and as ever old Jakobowitz knew why. He put a hand on my shoulder. 'We are grateful, Sally. Alexander has had a good year, safe and loved and well cared for. Maximilian has had time to recover from his loss. We are grateful, always.'

'It's Alexander—' I began, but a sob rose and choked me. Alexander had just fallen asleep on the end of the sofa, bum in the air, his fist gripping Charlotte's dress as she sat turning the pages of a rag book with frowning concentration. They looked wonderful together, a page from a sentimental Victorian novel.

'Yes. That must be considered. His father, of course –'

'– can't cope. Really, he has no talent for babies.'

'Few men do. We must advertise. For a nanny.'

'Well, it's Max's business really – it's just that it's a bit awkward for me to stay even a few days in the same house – I was thinking of going to my parents with Charlotte – but I can't take the baby away.'

'The solution is obvious,' said David drily. 'Max can move out while you organize and brief a professional nanny. Helena and I will pay. Max can stay at my Club. I took the precaution of getting my secretary to book him in to a guestroom for a couple of weeks, as soon as he rang. I told him to go home and get his things. He must be there by now.'

Not for the first time I marvelled at the ease with which money and secretaries oiled the wheels of difficult domestic situations, and at the unquestioning obedience that a rich stepfather can command.

'Already? He's packing up now?'

'Yes. I suggest you stay here for tea, to give him time to move his necessary chattels.'

I could hear Helena outside, talking to the maid. Quickly I looked up at him – we were standing together by the mantelpiece, his elbow resting on it – and muttered, 'David, we're friends, aren't we?'

'Indeed. Near or far, I think we always will be. You are a good woman. Almost a daughter. Remember that in the time to come.'

I did not quite understand what he meant. I persisted. 'So answer me one question honestly. When Max rang up, what did he actually tell you had happened?'

David's face split into a rare grin, and again I saw Marty in him.

'He said that you had become hysterical and possessive and were making too many demands, and that he wasn't ready for a new commitment of the kind you insisted on, given your –' he hesitated, but in a sly glance judged that I could take anything he could throw at me '– given your mental instability.'

I took a deep outraged breath. 'And you believed that?'

'No. Of course not. Youthful male pride is something I am professionally familiar with, at work, and I know how to discount it and by what percentage. In Max's case, ninety-eight per cent as a rule. I assumed that you had – ah – seen the light at last.'

'And you weren't disappointed about the Sadducee Levirate marriage idea thing?'

'No,' said David, still smiling. 'I am sorry that was reported to you. I had rather hoped it might force the issue, but I trust you will believe that I am not in the habit of using the Old Testament as a guide to modern living.'

'How *dare* he say those things about me!' I began again, and paused. 'I certainly did see through him!'

'See-through?' said Helena, coming back in. 'I hate that fashion. Girls today are so obvious, don't you think? David, there's soup and bread coming.'

'Sally's staying to tea. The children need a sleep,' said her husband.

'Lovely,' said Helena without conviction. 'Do you think it's time Charlotte had her hair cut properly?'

So that was that, for me and the Bellinger family. Helena never spoke to me again. I spent a week interviewing nannies with ferocity and fussiness, engaged a kind Scottish girl to whom I explained the entire situation, and after a week caring for Alexander alongside her and preparing Charlotte for the break, I packed up my few clothes and books and went home to Suffolk, where the last of the harvest was being brought in and the same old river ran smooth and quiet and unchanged through the same old reeds.

PART THREE

Charlotte

33

'My dad was a rock star,' said Charlotte complacently. 'Back in the sixties.' She flicked away a curtain of blue-black hair and examined her jet-black fingernails. 'He was wild. He got into a big fight in America and got banned and wrote a lot of songs that *still* get covered.'

'Cool,' said her friend, another Goth whose rejection of all things wholesome did not extend to turning down a lift home from school in a nice safe people-carrier. 'Did your dad, like, die?'

'Yerr,' said my daughter. 'When I was a baby. He died young because that's what rock stars are supposed to do. Like Sid and Nancy. And John Lennon. I mean, the Stones, *please*, they're so wrinkly – going on and on! It's like, embarrassing.'

A torrent of giggles rose from the back seat, and the word 'gross!' Eventually the friend asked respectfully: 'What songs did he write, your real dad?'

'Oh – *Silken Julia*, and *Love is the wind*.'

'The one Madonna did? Cool!'

'And some cheesy country and western stuff like *Round and around goes my old heart*.'

'Yeah, but the Barrack Boyz did that too and it was OK.'

'S'pose so. Anyway, my mum saw him at a concert and she was like, a groupie—'

I rarely bothered to intervene in exchanges of wild misinformation in the back of my car, but could not let this one pass. 'I was *not* a groupie. I was the lyricist. I wrote the words

to those songs for your bloody boy bands and American trol-
lops to sing. Every word, I wrote it. And I was Marty's wife,
not his groupie.'

The sixteen-year-olds subsided into amiably contemptuous
giggling as I negotiated the broad brick gateway to Don's
school. Most of the mothers had to try to park and then find
their boys in the maelstrom; Donny, as usual, was right on the
edge of the pack and looking out for me keenly enough to
spot the car and run towards it with his bag hanging off his
shoulder by one strap. He dived for the front seat.

'Hey, Mum, guess what?'

'She can't guess *what*, dumbo. Just tell her and let's have
some peace.'

'We got our library tickets today! It was the day for Year
Seven to sign the book there. I found the way with my friend
Chaz; can Chaz come round on Saturday and do SuperMario?'

'Sure. Was the library good?'

'Ace. I got a Willard Price and a Dickens, Miss Archer in
the library says it's a cool one, there's this graveyard and a
man that creeps up on a boy, he's an escaped prisoner; I
read a bit at lunchtime. When Chaz comes, can we have
chips? He only eats chips.'

'No wonder he's so *spotty*,' said Don's big sister, not yet
too ladylike and grown-up to mix it with childish abuse.

'You've never even *seen* him, he's not spotty!' Poor Don
rose rapidly to the bait, as ever.

'What books did he get out?' Stopped at the traffic lights,
I felt able to exert my powers of soothing troubled waters.

'Oh, Chaz doesn't like reading. He only came to keep me
company. He likes computer games and *fighting*.'

The girls snorted, knowing full well the effect this
information would have on me.

'Don's new friend is clearly a *yob*,' said Charlotte sweetly.
'Spotty yob.'

Older and wiser than my son, I managed not to rise to the
bait but drove the last half-mile home in a state of voluntary
deafness which I had become very good at assuming during
these childrearing years. I liked to think that I was still alert
for key words, particularly the street names of drugs, but could
not guarantee even that. I did not think Charlotte was especially vulnerable to the drug culture anyway, although God
knows her Camden school was rife with it. She had begun
very early to ask questions about her invisible father, so she
had heard the story of Marty's death from the first days in
terms she could understand. I believed she had taken it in.
Beneath the Goth silliness, the vamping and the posing and
sighing, I discerned a core of hard commonsense and a keen
instinct for self-preservation.

Don was another matter: soft, compliant, loving and almost
too sensitive for his own good. My baby boy: every inch his
father's son. I glanced at his round face in the mirror and
blew him a secret kiss. A faint pursing of his lips rewarded
me: still Mummy's boy, for all his big-school airs. The girls
had got back on to the subject of Marty the romantic rock
hero, Charlotte larding on the glamour all she could; as we got
near the house I heard my son trying to compete: 'Mum, tell
about *my* dad when you first met him.'

This demanded an old ritual answer, which never failed
to give the boy pleasure even at the grand age of nearly
eleven.

'It was in a city with golden towers called Oxford. He lent
me his big umbrella because it was raining, and took me to
hear singing in a Cathedral because I was sad.'

'Was he the best singer?' Another ritual question, to be
answered mechanically but with conviction.

'He was always the best singer. He still is, isn't he?'

'*Opera* stuff,' said Donald's stepdaughter contemptuously.

Don considered for a moment then asked a new one: 'When

you heard him singing, did you ask him to marry you straight away?'

Gales of rude laughter from the girls. I kept my eye on the road.

'No. He asked me, about three years later. After Charlotte was born and Charlotte's dad died.'

'Most families,' said Charlotte's Goth friend enviously, 'don't have all this dying and stuff. They have divorce.'

As I swung into the little driveway which mercifully preserved us from needing to park on the London street, I saw the motorbike and realized with a rush of pleasure that Donald was home. One never quite knew what his rehearsal schedule would permit, but I cherished these family hours of late afternoon, especially when he was going out again to perform in the evening. He was Sparafucile at the moment, and a sinister one too; I had only been able to watch my husband do the terrible assassin once, whereas I happily went again and again to see all his Egyptian kings, Commendatores, Dukes, elders and Landgraves. The heavy solemnity of bass-baritone parts never failed to bring me great satisfaction, even when I had heard them practised, discussed and cursed at around the house. There was a golden, kingly lion quality about Donald on stage which I found irresistible. I knew now the technicalities of a singer's life: the hours of work, the care of the throat, the focused creative anxiety, the difficulty of singing expressively in a foreign language. Soon after he made the decision to go professional, when little Don was two, Donald had locked himself away for hours every evening with Linguaphone tapes so that he could learn Italian and German to his own satisfaction, not wanting to trust the répétiteurs' interpretations of the parts.

I smiled as I locked the car and shooed the children indoors, remembering the heady excitement of that time, the financial terrors that Donald went through on resigning from the bank and how proud I was to be able to say OK, he must try, he must go for it or regret it all his life. I told him that even with the mortgage we could survive on my trust income plus my earnings from the agency and the song royalties that still trickled in.

'But it seems so unfair,' he would say, over and over again. 'Three years ago you married a merchant banker with prospects. Now you're going to be stuck with a struggling singer.'

'I'm used to struggling singers,' I said lightly. One of the joys of Donald was that from the first day when he found me crying in the back of St Paul's at Covent Garden after the lunchtime concert, I had always been able to talk to him about Marty. It gave him not the slightest embarrassment or offence.

'I liked the guy's stuff,' he would protest. 'I love the songs. They're musically very subtle, you know. Just because I sing Bach doesn't mean I don't like pop songs when they're good ones.'

I even liked to think, sometimes, that it was marrying a musician's widow which gave him the resolution to throw up the City career he disliked and train to sing professionally. Perhaps my background, my familiarity with life's uncertainties, drew him unconsciously to me and saved him from wooing some nice fresh upper-crust girl who would expect affluence and an Aga. I had said this to him once.

'You married me because I had a track record with artistes, didn't you?'

'Could be,' he said, teasingly. 'Or perhaps it was that you were working for a theatrical agent.'

'Well, Marienka and Peter did try to help you out . . .'

'Nearly got me chucked out of college, you mean.' He made a face. 'Near thing.'

'You didn't have to do it. I told you we didn't need the money that much.'

For, just after Donald made his big change of life, I had had an excited call from Marienka at the office. I was on a short leave, and thought she was after me to come back and sort out one of her administrative tangles, but it was something quite different.

'Hey,' she said without preamble, 'Donald's a bass, isn't he?'

'Bass-baritone, is what they seem to say.'

'Well, there's a great commercial job. Really high-class sausages: Plummers Magnificos. They're doing an animation and it's brilliant, it's a sausage opera. We've cast it, and we've got Maria diFaranda doing a soprano chipolata –'

'She's retired, isn't she?'

'Not from the world of singing sausages, she's not. And there's some tenor guy who teaches at Guildhall doing his bit with the pork-and-leek sausage, but there's this big Cumberland sausage that comes in at the end and sings *Magnifico*, to the tune of that bit from *Turandot*, he's the punch-line, it's a very important—'

'Marienka,' I had said, jigging the fretful baby on my arm, 'you have no idea. This opera training, it's a bit like priests studying in a seminary. They are not supposed to do any commercial work during the year. They could throw him out for it.'

'Sal, they're offering four thousand quid for two days' recording. At least tell him. I've had a devil of a time getting opera-type singers, snotty bastards, and we could really swank a bit if I pull a bass out of a hat, all within twenty-four hours. The ad agency would be dead impressed.'

'Oh, if it's a favour to *you* . . .' I said sarcastically but without rancour. I knew that she knew of our financial in-security. I did not think she could be that desperate for a bass.

'Go on, tell him.'

Donald had jumped at it, since it alleviated his guilt over not earning anything during his training. He came home from the recording rather pleased with himself, saying that he had found a new *basso buffo* comic voice when he had always thought of himself as *profundo*, or as he put it, 'terminally dignified, doomed to be the Duke. But I can do sausages too, I find. I could even express the gravy'. But his sharp-eared senior tutor saw the advert six weeks later, recognized the timbre of the singing Cumberland sausage in the big finale, and challenged him. Donald could not lie. He risked losing his scholarship, but after a solemn lecture his teacher finally smiled and observed that it was quite something at his stage of life to have a voice that could be recognized even when emerging from an animated latex sausage. He was forgiven.

When I told Marienka about this fright, she laughed; but Peter sent round a case of very good port and a note of apology for the trouble.

Donald, I thought as I pulled the shopping out of the boot and followed the children in, was worth every misery I had gone through in the years before him. In the weeks after I left the Mews forever and fled to Suffolk, rags of the poisoned rainbow cloud still hung around me. I missed baby Alexander very much indeed, and worried about him endlessly, waking in the night with the thought that perhaps he craned his little head around for me, missed the particular curve of my breast and crook of my neck where his face had rested so often and so snugly. When I thought of Max, the main feeling was of rage, regret and embarrassment at having been so badly taken in for so very long. The loss of the wider Jakobowitz family, even Helena, felt like another bereavement. I understood what David had meant about remembering him in 'the time to come'; no doubt at Helena's behest he made no contact with me after the day I left. It felt like another step away from Marty, and it hurt. I thought endlessly of Marty in those weeks, and wondered whether if I had listened to Marienka back in the house by the canal and learned to love him properly, he would still be alive and happy and singing. With another baby perhaps, a child truly his own.

A darker cloud enveloped me then, as if the vanished rainbow of obsessive love had taken all the world's colours with it. I would sometimes wake in the morning weeping. I spent two months in my childhood bedroom growing ever sadder, before Marienka rang on a crisp autumn morning and offered me a job.

'Peter's uncle finally retired. We've taken over the agency – Addison's – and it is such fun, I don't know why I wasted all that time in Paris. We do comedians and some pop singers and voiceover people – you would not believe the weird sub-world they live in, praising biscuits in dark cubicles in Soho. I'm getting the client list sorted out, and Peter's brilliant at looking for business, but the admin is in complete chaos. Now! You're what we need. You've been in an agency—'

'An estate agency!'

'Same difference. Flats, biscuit-praisers, maisonettes, after-dinner speeches to Rotary Clubs – all the same thing. Got to be booked, chased, reminded, billed . . . I just thought it might be fun, all of us together.'

It was fun, or as close to fun as I was capable of in that dark time. I found a high, tiny flat in Soho near the agency and a raffish little religiously run nursery which would take Charlotte from ten till four. She came home chanting, 'Dess, Jesus love me, the bagel makes it so,' and enjoyed herself with tambourines. It seemed to suit her very well, and she was, I told myself, a vicar's granddaughter after all. I worked a short day at the agency, with occasional bouts of taking work home. The neighbourhood was filthy: restaurant bin-bags heaved by night with prowling rats and were rarely collected on time, and the glow of strip club neon reflected in Charlotte's bedroom window at night. Marienka and Peter, kindness itself, urged me to find somewhere airy close to them in Primrose Hill and to stay in their spare room while I looked; but my flat had a tiny roof-terrace, and I was still so fragile and angry and abased that it suited me to look out at sinfulness and chaos and excess. The peace of Suffolk and my mother's kind uncomprehending solicitude had driven me half crazy.

Once Marienka's own child was born, though – over Christmas, conveniently, so she only missed one day at her desk – Marienka suggested that on Saturdays her cheerful Australian nanny could look after Charlotte all day as well as the new baby. 'You need a break. Go out, walk about, go and see your hippie friends or whatever.' I demurred at first, but the nanny – Claire – was so encouraging and so much more fun than I was for my daughter that I took up the offer.

And so it was that one spring day, finding the old Almost Free Theatre shuttered and locked, I heard music from St Paul's church in Covent Garden and wandered in to get out of the rain.

I had been avoiding poetry and music quite deliberately in the months after leaving the Mews; they were too much entangled with the mad old cloud of longing, and I feared them. I was right. Only a few minutes into the Fauré Requiem I felt tears running down my face; I wept all through it, silent in a dim corner under the gallery, and knew with grey certainty that the colour and hope had gone from my life for ever now because I had thrown away honest love and chased a chimera. Into this misery, hesitant and polite, stepped Donald. He spotted me when the concert ended, and came into my corner unaffectedly delighted to see me, remembering my name, brandishing another umbrella.

Our courtship was slow and on my part unflatteringly

wary. I told him most of the mess I had made of my life, and he nodded and murmured sympathetically and never once looked shocked or disgusted. He proposed very soon, and was rejected more than once. But one evening, when we had taken Charlotte to the zoo together and fed her in a burger bar, he turned to me as I pushed the buggy home-ward up Berwick Street and said, 'I won't marry any girl, you know, if it isn't you. Not ever.'

'Don't say not ever. That's terrible. Promise me that if I walk out you'll find someone else. Nobody should *ever* say never. It's an illusion, the soulmate thing. I should bloody well know.'

'I didn't say you were my only soulmate, I'm not an idiot. But I want to marry you, I do. And that line just sounded really convincing.' He stopped, forcing me to stop and turn to him. 'You do quite love me, you know.'

And I did know. It was a slow-burning affectionate love that had grown up, unlike anything I had ever known. It was, I thought a little guiltily, more like having a new best friend at school: comradely, kindly, a reassuring love rather than a tormenting one. It was the love I should have let grow for Marty, long ago. It was easiest to define by absences: there was no self-abasement in it on either side, no racking doubt, no space for jealousy. We were, and are, good mates. With Donald I was the best of myself, and with me he was at his happiest and most relaxed. It was obvious what to do.

So we did it: married quietly at St Paul's church, with my parents and his staying in a hotel on the Strand and becoming very convivial, we are told, late that night in their shared happiness about us. The only other guests were Donald's five best friends and his sister, and for me my brother Ben and his Wren, Peter and Marienka, and Gordy Wise. I could not track down Damien and the others, though I wanted to: they had left the squat, fed up with pressure from the local council who, sensing the approach of the sterner Thatcher years, had finally stopped turning a blind eye to the inhabitants of the old house. Gordy was shortly off to Scotland to work for a prison drug charity, but in a gesture that brought tears to my eyes he brought with him to the church Marty's old guitar with a white ribbon around its neck, 'because it's time it came home'. It hangs on the wall to this day, a family relic.

Charlotte – who mercifully had stopped asking for Max every day – made an early decision to call my new husband Daddy and have done with it. All around us that summer were the celebrations of the Queen's Silver Jubilee, with fluttering flags and street parties. It was a time of rejoicing. The oily deceptive rainbow cloud was gone, replaced by the golden light of a long quiet afternoon. A year later young Donald was born.

34

I suppose it was at that point in 1978, when Charlotte decided
for herself that Donald equalled Daddy, that I hardened my
resolve never to tell her the truth about her parentage. It
would be one father too many, and after all, the knowledge
that she was Max's was not widely spread. I knew; Marienka
knew, so presumably Peter did too. David Jakobowitz knew,
though I had never explicitly told him so; and Max himself
obviously had known ever since my original letter, although
the subject had never been directly broached between us. In
our months together I was made very much aware, from
hints and frowns, that he did not want the matter mentioning.

As for Charlotte herself, after Marty's death it seemed
natural, respectful to his memory and a balm to my guilt and
grief, to tell the baby he had loved that Daddy had gone to
heaven and would watch over her. Hell, who wants to tell a
baby that Daddy doesn't give a damn, that he left Mummy in
the lurch and is now too embarrassed even to mention her?
During the brief period when Max took an interest in Charlotte,
before she became too unruly for his refined tastes, I did for
a while hope to make him acknowledge her, at least to me. But
he never did. If he didn't want her, why should she want him
or know about him or be bothered in any way by him? We
were, perhaps, less neurotically conscious of genetic affiliation
in those days. Today, with home DNA test kits offered for sale
on the back of every service station lavatory door, such lies are
a little harder to countenance. For me, this one was easy.

Babies are persistent in their early affections, and she still asked for 'Max read Goonight Moon' after we left, but it did not go on for long. Only in the first year of my marriage to Donald did she become old enough to ask questions and want proper answers; in the atmosphere of easy family love and thrilling pregnancy it was instinctive to me to tell her more about Marty, because Marty had loved her. So the illusion grew into a solid statement, albeit a false one. Once or twice Marienka frowned when the child said something that made it clear she believed herself to be genetically Marty's child; but motherhood had softened my friend's decisive and scornful ways, and she said nothing. The subject generally came up in the context of music, because I had told Donald the sad tale of Marty's father and he used to express puzzlement that the daughter of a rock singer and granddaughter of a Russian-Jewish violinist had absolutely no aptitude for music. She refused or hideously disrupted any lessons he arranged, even on the recorder.

'Skips a generation, maybe,' he said resignedly. 'So wow, I look forward to my stepgrandchildren!' He did not have to wait so long: to his father's delight Donny was a songbird from the start, and could carry a tune before he was two.

So the question faded and was forgotten. For my own peace of mind I took to cutting a thick fringe in Charlotte's dark-brown hair once her brow developed into Max's square handsomeness, and mercifully during her teens she kept to a shaggy style which hid it. I also came down very heavily indeed on any sign of Maxish arrogance or coldness. It troubled me a little how cavalierly my daughter discarded friends she was bored with, but I told myself that this was typical small-girl behaviour, then typical teen behaviour, and that I must not expect my daughter to be as sentimental and marshmallow-hearted a young woman as I was. By now, you will note, I was looking back at Max through a very dark distorting prism indeed, the reverse of my old infatuation. Every sign of him in his daughter rattled me, and in turn I rattled crossly at her.

In the early days after I left the Mews I wrote to Helena a couple of times, saying that of course she was welcome to keep in touch with her granddaughter, but received no reply. In any case, once Donny was born, we became a solid little nuclear family in our own right and such considerations faded. Donald loved Charlotte in a typically easygoing, affectionate, warm and teasing way; she loved him as an infant and child and in her teens treated him to friendly familiar mockery. She went through brief fierce interludes of citing her 'real' father, the rocker and rebel, and Marty's image came in very useful to her in her own rebellious years.

So everything balanced out. By the time she reached her sixteenth year I felt that no service at all would be done to my daughter by informing her that her biological father was neither rocker nor rebel, but a rather cold-hearted Professor of Fine Arts believed to be at Harvard. It would have been, I felt, a terrible comedown.

And so the years passed, and life changed all around us. Addison's Agency prospered mightily through the eighties: Marienka had a fiendish instinct for silly money and dull timid corporate clients desperate for a bit of showbiz glitter. She was among the first agents to dare charge ten thousand pounds for an after-dinner speech by a comedian: others flocked to her, and after a while we stopped doing theatrical work, which was fiddly and depressing (too many desperate actors) and thereafter stuck to conferences and speeches, voiceovers and a bit of TV hosting. We moved out of the tiny Soho office into the one next door, spread over two floors, and Peter insisted that I should be made a partner. We had two secretaries to do the administration now, and I had moved on to a more central role. I enjoyed dealing with the companies and agencies that used us, soothing their anxieties and meeting their fairly vacuous needs. I was rather less at home massaging the insecurities of our showbusiness clients. The TV presenters I found particularly poisonous, vain as monkeys and greedy as gannets; I got on rather better with the old-school comedians, minor radio voices and jobbing actors. But where outrageous flattery and flirtation were needed, Marienka took over. She also wielded the knife with more brio than I did, telling clients in pitiless terms when they were asking for more than the market would stand for an after-dinner speech.

So we prospered, as much of Britain did in the eighties (unless you were a miner or a steelworker, or just unlucky). There were two Royal weddings, a sea war in the South Atlantic and a general smartening-up of society; quite normal people could be seen reading the *Tatler* without having to give little ironic shrugs if anyone noticed them. Our corporate clients gave parties of extraordinary and rather nasty extravagance, with novelty canapés like miniature fish-and-chips, giant croquembouche pyramids of diminutive profiteroles which nobody ate, champagne fountains and bands flown in from Cuba as a kitsch 'statement'. Our performing clients started to command mad sums of money for a couple of hours' work: we once got £25,000 for a horribly dim and conceited TV game-show host merely to mingle with guests of an international bank at their Christmas party and draw the tombola tickets. Around us, the London of InterAction and vague, unpoliced squats and floppy idealism in floppy Indian cotton clothes vanished. We employed a smart nanny for Donny and could afford to buy her a little car. Marienka and I took to wearing jackets with wide shoulder-pads and pinched waists when we wanted to look like power women in the office, though my shoulder-pads tended to slip off-centre and give me a vestigial hunchback.

Donald's career flourished, and he could more or less choose his parts. Sometimes I went abroad with him when Donny was too young for school, leaving Charlotte to stay with a schoolfriend. By the time Donald and I had been together for ten years, our world seemed aeons away from the years of Marty and Max, the seventies just a faint embarrassing memory like loon pants and military jackets. I had no contact with the Jakobowitz family except once, in Harvey Nichols, when I came face to face with Sue Bellinger and she cut me dead. I think and hope she didn't recognize me.

In the stock-market crash of the late 'eighties I did wonder whether David and his bank were all right, and tried to read the business pages but got no information I could understand. Once or twice later on I walked past the Knightsbridge house on the way to visit a client, and saw a strange family, Arabs, going into it with dark beautiful children. David and Helena must have moved out, I thought: retired to some elegant pile in the Royal Triangle or deep in Devon. The only way I knew Max was at Harvard was when Marienka, without comment, dropped a copy of the *Art Newspaper* on my desk with a ring round a small piece about his Professorship. He was, said the piece, a surprise appointment made over the head of the more likely candidate, an American woman. She withdrew herself from the competition at the last minute and went abroad suddenly. I wondered a great deal about that. But I was glad to know he was three thousand miles away and unlikely to return in a hurry.

So it was all gone, water under the bridge: the seventies, Marty, Max, the Jakobowitzes, old friends like Gordy (who emerged later, as it happened, in another smudged newspaper photo as Scottish Prison Officer of the Year 1998, with a citation for his work with addict inmates. I was pleased to read that he was by then a father of five. His beard, in the black-and-white photo, looked as if it was still mostly ginger).

Amid all this change and progress and bustle, Charlotte grew into a mouthy teenager and it seemed not to matter at all who her father was.

Yet I did, in the end, tell Donald. The reason I was especially pleased to see his motorbike outside on that school afternoon, thirteen happy years into our marriage, was that the previous evening we had had the nearest thing ever to a serious marital row. We had been talking, casually at bedtime, about the first time we met in London when I was pregnant.

'I had a dream about that the other night,' he said, wiping off a stray wisp of Sparafucile's grey beard which had stuck to his ear in his haste to get home from the Royal Opera House. 'It was odd, like an instant replay thing in the football. Sort of real but slow.'

'What was it?' I was taking off my make-up, yawning a little, relaxed.

'Well, it was about the day we first met in London. You were prattling on in the street and I was looking at you and thinking how pretty you looked. I'd never seen a pregnant girl up close before, and there was the glow – now that *is* a real memory.' He paused. 'And while I was staring at you and mainly thinking "wow!", you said something about the baby being "not associated" with the marriage. And then I woke up.'

'Uh,' I said. My back was to him at the dressing table, and I was glad of it.

'Thing is,' he said, 'when I woke up, I realized that it wasn't a dream, it was a memory.' He paused again, waiting for a response.

I turned round. One does not lie to Donald, not directly.

'You're right. It was a memory,' I said. 'I was pregnant before I ever slept with Marty. Actually, he married me out of kindness.'

His first reaction was altogether typical. 'Poor Sal. Oh,

poor duck. You must have been terrified, it's not like today with film stars sprogging babies everywhere. What a nice chap Marty must have been.'

'I was scared. Stupid, but I was. The father didn't want to know. Look, Donald –' The look on his face was scaring me, it was too thoughtful for comfort. 'I've never told Charlotte. I really don't want to. You won't, will you?'

'Who was it? I mean, whose is she?' He frowned as I stayed silent. 'I mean, God – you weren't *raped* or something awful were you, Sal, I'm so sorry, I shouldn't –'

He was being so kind, so focused on my suffering rather than any possible guilt, that I had to tell him the whole truth. After I had finished he sat on the bed in his pyjama trousers and bare chest, fiddling with the collar of the jacket and grimacing, as was his habit when thinking hard. After a few moments he said: 'But you lived with him – with Max – for a while after Marty died?'

'Yes. I didn't mean to, I don't think. I mean, his parents asked me to help with the baby because he was half off his head with shock and stuff. I didn't think we'd have an affair. Another affair, I mean.'

'But you must have hoped,' said Donald. 'He was the love of your life.'

'I didn't say that!'

'It's clear enough. He was the guy you were crying about that day you came to Evensong. Look, Sally, I'm not *jealous*.'

'I should think not! Donald, this is history, you asked me so I'm telling you, but it's years since I even gave a thought to the frigid old bastard, I was an idiot then, a twisted romantic berk!'

'I said,' he repeated with ominous patience, 'I'm not jealous. I love you. We love each other and the kids. We're a family. But I know how I feel about Donny, and I know that it's different from the way I feel about Charlotte. I'd die for her, you know that, she's a sweetie and I've watched her grow up. But she's not mine. There isn't that sense of – of wonder that I get round Donny. It's different. It's basic. It matters.'

'You've been wonderful to Charlotte,' I said, weakly. 'Wonderful.'

'But she's not mine. And she's not Marty's, is she? She's his brother's. He was just her uncle. A really good uncle, but that's all.'

'If she's Max Bellinger's,' I said coldly, 'it's only technical.'

Donald put his pyjama jacket on and slowly buttoned it up. I watched him, my stomach sinking.

'Please . . .' I began weakly, and stopped.

'Sally,' he said, 'I can't say technical. I'm sorry, but it's wrong, what you're doing. Charlotte's got a father alive. It's her right to know.'

A knot was tightening in my chest. I had not panicked like this for years, and needed to lash out at someone to make myself feel better.

'You're just doing this to *torment* me because I never told you everything about Max, who doesn't bloody matter anyway – why are you doing this? You just want to ruin everything, her life, my life, everything – you want to punish me!'

'No, I don't,' he said simply, and climbed into bed. 'And it won't be me who tells her. It's not my story. But I've been in an awful lot of operas where people find out secrets when it's too late . . .'

He lay flat on his back, looking at the ceiling, not reaching for his usual bedside book. 'I'm tired now. Let me sleep.'

'We have to talk about it!' I said wildly, furious that he should throw this net of guilt and memory over me and then think himself entitled to escape into peaceful slumber.

'No,' he said. 'I've said my piece. I just feel very sorry for Charlotte. And for Max, actually, even if he was a bastard. It's wrong.'

'You're saying I'm wrong! You're saying I'm bad!' Through all the vicissitudes of our lives together Donald had seen me sad, and happy, and worried, and angry, and overwrought. I do not think he had ever seen me shrill and defensive. From the pillow he looked at me in astonishment for a moment, then closed his eyes. 'I have to sleep.'

The big Verdi roles always left him drained and needing ten hours in bed.

I left well before he was awake in the morning, got through a morning's work like a robot and left early, because it was Thursday and my day for picking up the children. I was afraid he would stay up West for the afternoon before his performance and avoid me, but there he was: his motorbike like a talisman of normality and love in the corner of the driveway. He always thoughtfully left space for my car, and had left even more than usual today, pushing the front wheel carefully into the shrubs. I discerned love in that, and apology, and conciliation. I chased Charlotte and her friend upstairs to do their homework together, and Donny bounded gladly up to the attic room to practise his violin.

Then I went to find my husband in his study. I felt as if something very precious was in unprecedented danger and must be saved.

35

I went straight to him, put my arms round his neck as he sat in his chair reading a score, and said, 'I'm sorry.'

He twisted round immediately, put his head on my breast and said, 'So am I.' We stayed like that for a moment, then he said, muffled by my jacket, 'I love you, whatever. You know that, don't you? You come first.'

'I love you too. I wish I could do what you think is right, but I can't.'

'I know. Let's forget it. Charlotte's doing fine. I had reasons for getting a bit over the top last night, actually, which do me no credit.'

'What?'

'I was a sperm donor back at college. Medic friend talked me into it, and they paid enough for a good night in the pub. I used not to think about it, but since Donny I keep looking at twenty-year-old men in the street and wondering. It's all this gene DNA stuff in the papers, it frets me a bit.'

'Me too. But mostly I worry,' I said, relieved at being able to say the unsayable after all these years. 'I worry that some awful gene will spring up and make her grow up as cold and nasty as him.' Tears sprang to my eyes. I had never said this before, not to anybody; Marienka and I never spoke of that part of the past. 'I see her when she's on her high horse, or going "uh, whatever", or not ringing back some boy who's taken her out. I worry.'

'Nature and nurture,' said Donald. 'She had you, she had

me, she had Marty when she was tiny. She's never been treated badly or neglected. Didn't you say that the Bellinger boys lost their father when they were teenagers? And their mother seems to have been a bit preoccupied elsewhere, even before that?'

'Mm.' I agreed doubtfully.

'Perhaps you're too hard on the poor old Art Prof.' He hauled himself out of his chair and drooped affectionately, leaning on me as if I were a walking-stick. 'Perhaps he's a victim of upbringing. We Are All Guilty. Maybe he's had therapy.'

'He lives in America now. Marienka saw a cutting. He's at Harvard.'

'Well, there you are! He'll have had heaps and heaps of therapy and be touchy-feely and kind and lovely.' He straightened up, planted a kiss on the top of my head, and yawned. 'If he decided to seek out Charlotte, now, that'd be different.'

'He won't. If there's one thing I know for sure, Max won't change his spots in that regard. He was always tight with money, and he'd be terrified of another dependant.'

'God, you're hard on him. Oh Jesus, look at the time. I've got a long night of murdering ahead of me, in tickly whiskers. Must get some food. Are you doing children's tea?' On performance nights ever since the children were small he had dearly loved the comforting stodge of six o'clock, the fish fingers and macaroni cheese and turkeyburgers. He said they made him feel safe when he was nervous.

'Yep,' I said. 'Cauli cheese and bacon and grilled tomatoes, OK?'

'Very OK,' he said. 'And as for Charlotte, it's up to you. I'm going to forget the whole thing.'

'Me too.' I did my best to do so, and let the happy healing months roll by.

★   ★   ★

It was two years later, on Charlotte's eighteenth birthday in fact, that my father rang me from Suffolk. It was unusual for him to ring, as he and my mother preferred to send chatty notes every month or so, concluding with a wish that we would all come down very soon for a weekend. Quite often we did; Donald loved my father and would talk aesthetics and philosophy with him by the hour.

But this time Dad rang with news, and I had to hear it while fending off plaints from the birthday girl in the other ear. She was in the throes of A levels and highly temperamental, so we had planned nothing beyond a family supper, the usual array of sweet and silly minor presents, and a cheque. 'I might go out with some mates,' she said evasively when I asked her about further arrangements. 'Don't question me!' Charlotte had picked up the latter expression from a television comedy show, and used it relentlessly. When Dad rang at half-past five that day she was just home from school, rolling her eyes in exasperation because the family supper now clashed with her planned excursion.

'Mu-um! What *time* can we eat? I'm meeting Joey and Caz—'

'Shush, I've got your grandad on the phone, it's not a good line –'

'Oh, Mu-um!'

'Sally darling,' said my father, 'I'm sorry to interrupt but I've had a message for you, from your former father-in-law.'

'From David? How on earth did he know – oh, I suppose he came to Suffolk for the wedding, didn't he? And you haven't moved so he'd look you up – Charlotte sweetie, don't eat that now, you'll spoil your supper –'

'He wants to see you,' crackled the telephone. 'It seems that he lost his wife.'

'Mu-um! Where's my pink socks? If Donny's nicked them –'

'Don't be ridiculous, what would he want with pink socks? Boys of thirteen don't wear pink socks, who do you think he is, Boy George? Dad, sorry, I'm still here – where is he? Where does he live now?'

'Chipping Norton or thereabouts. But he said he's coming to London this week. Stays at his club. Pall Mall. He gave me a phone number. Do you have a pencil?'

'Yes. Right. Gimme the number. Charlotte, I've told you – I'll find your *bloody* socks –'

I wrote down the number, thanked my father, and was rewarded with a distant chuckle and some facetiously Biblical remark about children being a blessing like olive plants around the table, only noisier. Then I turned back to Charlotte and Donny, who were arguing loudly about the missing socks, and heard with relief my husband's key in the front door. I put down the envelope with the scribbled number, found the socks in the clean-clothes basket in the hallway – ours was always that kind of house – and proceeded with the hasty birthday supper. It was when Charlotte had stamped out of the house and into her friend Caz's frightening new car that I remembered the paper, and found it smeared with mayonnaise on the draining board.

I took it, as I took all worries, to Donald. He was about to play a game of chess with his son, and Donny was carefully setting out the pieces on the board. I did not want to disrupt this ritual, but said hurriedly to him, 'Don, you won't believe this, but my long-lost ex-stepfather-in-law wants to see me. David Jakobowitz.'

'You liked him, didn't you?'

'Yes, very much. I was always a bit scared of him, but he was a good man and amazingly generous to me over Marty's money.'

'Where do they live, now?'

'Seems that Helena died not long ago. She must have been

in her seventies, not much older. He's a good bit older than her. He's going to be in London. He rang Dad.'

'Well,' said Donald. 'You'd better see him. Ask him for supper.'

But when I got through to the St James' gentleman's club, via a ludicrously old-fashioned Ealing Films sort of porter and a telephone that I swore made winding noises, David's voice asked me to go there instead.

'I don't get around much. Not in the evenings, anyway. But they do a good lunch here. Might you? I have no right to call on you like this, of course – after all this time.'

'David, I'd love to see you. I've no quarrel with you, never have had.'

'Nor I with you. But we have unfinished business, perhaps.'

I lay awake that night, waiting for Charlotte to come banging and crashing through the house at the appointed curfew hour of half-past midnight, and thinking about old times. So Helena was dead, her querulous elegance no more than a memory: poor David. For all his self-possession and affluent seniority he had been wrecked on the shores of passion every bit as much as I had. He must have loved Helena for years to have begotten Marty while she was still married to her first husband. He had been married to her for a quarter of a century, and a blurred conflation of memory and maturer intuition made me reflect that perhaps it had not been as happy a time as he hoped for. It must have been hard for him living with Marty's contempt; I had never wholly realized that until now, perhaps because these days Charlotte doled out occasional toxic lumps of something not unlike contempt for me.

At the time, Marty's rejection of David had seemed quite violent but all of a piece with the legacy of the sixties: the protest generation who hummed Bob Dylan and insisted that fathers and mothers should give up the habit of command.

Now, a parent of teenagers myself, I tried to imagine how it would be if one of them rejected my love and help so completely, and how bitter it would be if the one who accepted every favour and subsidy was the one who was not my own at all. How David must have cringed at Max's glib dependence! How ironic must have seemed his acceptance of the smart little Mews house and the nannies, while Marty and I lived in rented shabbiness and parked our baby daughter by day in the back room of an estate agency! I remembered too the moment when his eyes rested in hope on the newborn Charlotte and saw instantly that she was no blood of his. I recalled how gentle he had been to me all the same.

None of these things troubled me in the old days. Now they did. I was aware that I had never made any effort to reconcile Marty with his father, even when I had most influence on him. Not for the first time, a wave of shame at my former self overcame me.

Charlotte came back, noisy in the hall and bathroom, and at last I turned over and tried to sleep. Beside me lay Donald, broad and warm and kind, and I breathed a prayer of gratitude for him. I had come out of the débâcle far better than poor old David. Far better than I deserved, really. I would go to see him, and offer at least my friendship. A small flicker of pure self-interest surfaced too: I hoped for news of Alexander, my first beloved boy-baby. I had thought of him often during Donny's babyhood, and wished him well in his chilly orphanhood.

I had no wish for news of Max.

36

David's club porter proved to be as much of a period-piece as he sounded, a pleasing cross between Jeeves, Stanley Holloway and a Galapagos giant tortoise. He directed me to sit in a curious overarched leather chair, designed in some bygone age of freezing draughts to shelter the waiting visitor in a cave of mouldering quilted brown leather. I sat here for a while in my smartest suit, remembering the first lunch I had with David eighteen years earlier, heavily pregnant and shy, dressed in my terrible cheap brown smock with the Peter Pan collar. He had warned me quite explicitly about Marty and his vulnerability to drugs. He had been right. Perhaps he had been too late; perhaps it was I who did not do enough.

I shivered in spite of the enveloping chair, for it was a raw spring day with cold fog swirling off the river. The porter seemed to have lost interest in me, and the few members who wandered up the steps and nodded to him walked straight by, their footsteps echoing on the ornate chequered tiles. After a few minutes, though, one set of footsteps stopped alongside the chair, and David Jakobowitz peered round the side and smiled at me.

My first reaction was almost of horror: this was an old man, shrunken and wrinkled and balding and bent, his strong brows no longer dark, his stride muted into a shuffle. When he smiled, though, recognition came flooding and with it a leaping of affection. I jumped up and hugged him without ceremony, then looked again: the keen dark eyes were the same and the hawk profile was sharpened, if anything, by age. His voice was unaltered too.

'Sally. Little Sally. It's wonderful of you to come.'

'How could I not?'

'After the way our family kept away from you so long? Despite all you did for Marty and for Max? Oh, I would not have blamed you if you hadn't come. You could have told me to clear off.' He smiled. 'I believe the more modern expression is, fuck off.'

'David! That isn't like you!'

'I am not much like myself, these days.' He sighed. 'Much has changed. But we did treat you badly. Admit it. And I was too much wedded to keeping the peace at home to do the right thing.'

I could not believe how frank, how comfortable, we already were as we stood together in that forbidding hallway.

'Look, I do understand,' I said, squeezing his hand. 'Things were terrible when Marty and Annette died, all of us were floundering all over the place. You do what you have to do to survive, when things are like that.'

'Yes,' he said. 'Absolutely. You understand, then? About doing what you need to do, to survive?'

I nodded, and he offered his arm with old-fashioned courtesy to lead me to a gloomy apartment titled, in dull gold leaf, *Ladies' Dining Room*, where a waiter even more tortoise-like than the porter took our order and plodded off to some inner region leaving us alone.

'Oh dear,' he said, looking around, 'we are alone, as if walled up in the tomb. The Members' Dining Room is actually quite convivial in tone, and I have never been in this one before. Would you rather go to a restaurant?'

'No. It's quiet here, and I bet the whitebait and steak-and-kidney pudding will be amazing.'

'Yes. Nursery food, Helena called it. The staple of the London clubs. Even more so now, my old friends in the City tell me, because the wives have taken to serving up Nouvelle Cuisine, which is paltry and sits in puddles of cold gravy. Helena at least had the maid cook real roast beef.'

'I heard about Helena. I am so very sorry.'

He inclined his head. 'Yes. But in a sense, better for her to go first. She was, you see, a woman who needed looking after.'

The notion of looking after people made me glance at his shirt-cuff: it was of the best Jermyn Street quality still, but noticeably frayed.

'Are you living alone?'

'Yes. I am selling the country house now. It was Helena's place and Helena's garden, and far too much for me. I am taking rooms close to here.'

In that gloomy dining hall the archaic idea of 'rooms' seemed quite in place. I supposed some serviced flat would suit him, within reach of club and library; suddenly a wave of pity and sadness came over me for all old men alone.

'Will you come and have dinner with us sometimes? Please? We quite often eat early.'

'It would be a pleasure. You are married, then? Your good father told me so. I have often wondered about your life, but Helena was very unhappy at the idea of further contact. She became, you may have realized, rather unreasonable, and there were issues surrounding Maximilian's attitude. I took the coward's way, and went along with their wishes.'

He flinched a little as he said it, so I told him in a rush about Donald, and how happy I was, and little Donny, and how we had hoped for more children but somehow not had them, but were, again, honestly very happy.

'And Charlotte? She must be of age, now?'

I told him about Charlotte's eighteenth birthday, and how

difficult she could be at times, wilful and contemptuous, but how she would revert without warning to her sweet childhood self so that I never knew where I was. 'I suppose I begin to understand now how it must have been for you and Helena, with the two teenage boys and Sue. It doesn't get easier, as they grow up, does it?'

'Marty –' he began, but stopped. 'Better not to talk about Marty, maybe. He was my boy and he did not want to be. Enough. I think it would distress us both, too soon in our reunion.'

'One day we'll talk about Marty,' I said. 'Promise. But remember how young he was. He would have been reconciled to you, you know. I have learnt that people change.' He inclined his head gravely once more, but said nothing, so I carried on.

'Talking of teenagers, did you get on well with Sue, when you married Helena? Donald has always been wonderful with Charlotte.'

'Susan was already at university. I think she was grateful for the way of life I was able to support her in, but I cannot claim we had a close relationship. She has married a second time now, and we rarely meet. Maximilian, now – *he* was an easy stepchild.'

'I bet.' He glanced at me, amused at the way my eager prattle had shrunk to monosyllables.

'Yes. I thought at first he would be a bridge to Martin, but my son seemed to have little respect for his half-brother.'

'Max was happy to be supported, though.'

'Yes. But to be fair, after his thesis was complete, he did manage eventually to get a salaried position in America.'

'After how long?'

'Eight years.'

'And you kept him till then?'

'He did some teaching. I believe so. But we kept the

allowance going. Helena would not have it any other way. There was the child to consider.'

I took a deep breath. 'David, it's the baby, Alexander, that I'm really curious about. I was virtually his mother for the first year, after all, and I haven't heard a word about him from anyone since the day I handed him over to the nanny.'

'Unforgivable,' said David. 'Partly Maximilian, I fear, but partly my late wife. He did, I think, traduce you to her.'

'I bet,' I said again. The whitebait had come now and we were both eating, absorbed in our confessional memories but happy to be sharing food. 'What did he say?'

'Enough. Come now, Sally, we have not come here to wound each other.'

'Fair enough. I bet he said I was a nympho psychopath. But Alexander?'

'He is now coming up for seventeen, you know. A fine boy. I hope the American system of education does him well; his father wanted him to go from his boarding prep school to Eton, but he became very upset at the idea of staying alone in England. Even with myself and Helena to visit him.'

'So Max gave in?'

'No, Maximilian in fact insisted he go to Eton. But I explained that – ah – given the child's reluctance I could not in conscience pay the fees.' David smiled, but his eyes were hard. Sometimes I got a glimpse of the qualities which had made him his money.

'Ah,' I said. 'So you pulled the financial plug. Max wouldn't have liked that.'

'He didn't. He has little communication with me now. He did see his mother a couple of times, but apparently it was too difficult to fly home for Helena's funeral. He had a lecture to deliver.'

I wanted to move on hastily from this; his eyes were frightening me now.

'And the Devereaux? Could they have helped with the fees or anything?'

'They went abroad soon after Annette died; as you know, they failed to get custody of the boy. They write to him on Christmas and birthdays, with a cheque. Mrs Devereaux became quite ill in the aftermath of it all.'

I was silent for a minute, subdued by the unrolling catalogue of cold horridness in this family which I had once, and nearly twice, belonged to. I was fond of David and grateful to him, but an edge of blame came into my feelings. He was a strong clever man, head of a family, and must bear some blame for its shortcomings.

'I did hope you and Helena might have stayed in contact with Charlotte,' I said baldly. 'As grandparents.'

'So did I,' he said simply. 'Sometimes we disappoint ourselves. Ah, your steak-and-kidney pudding.'

When I had duly admired its sculptural form and the smooth flow of gravy from my knife's incision, I reverted to the subject of the former baby Alexander.

'If Alexander didn't want to be separated from Max,' I said, 'At least that means they've had a close relationship. I'm glad of that. You did the right thing making sure they stayed together.'

'I hope so. Maximilian was quite angry at the time. I hope they are still getting on well.'

'Did Max re-marry?'

He stared at me in astonishment. 'Of course! You don't know, do you? How would you?'

I put down my knife and fork and stared at him. But I suddenly knew what he was going to say.

'Maximilian,' he said, 'performed five years ago the manoeuvre known these days as Coming Out. He lives with a fellow academic, an older man called Adam Stephanopoulos.'

I gaped. He went on, smoothly enough. 'Helena never

knew. She was never well enough to travel to America. I had some small concern for Alexander when I found out, but it seems from my contacts in Harvard Business School, who keep me pretty well posted, that the ménage is all it should be. Mr Stephanopoulos is fond of Alex but in a perfectly acceptable and kindly way. They go to American football matches together.'

'But Max—!' I could go no further.

'Oh, he doesn't like American football. He stays at home.' David's smile was warm again now, laughing at my discomfiture. It was the one thing I had never thought of until today.

It was also, I reflected as I went out into the bleary light of St James' Street, one more reason Charlotte must never know whose child she was.

37

Charlotte left school that summer with a straight row of A grades, confirming her place at Cambridge for the autumn. She promptly displayed the independence of thought which had won her such grades by refusing point-blank to go there.

'I only applied to show I could,' she said contemptuously. 'Stuffy old mausoleum. Halitosis Hall.'

I handled it badly, scolding and threatening and advancing ridiculously snobbish arguments about the likelihood of her ruining her whole life. I do not know what came over me. I, after all, had all but ruined mine as a direct result of going to Oxford, so I had no right to berate my adult daughter. Charlotte ignored me, and it was Donald who saved the day by proposing a gap year and a fresh application to any university she chose.

'I could get you some work in the admin office at the Opera,' he said mildly. 'They don't pay much, but living here and eating free you could save enough by Christmas to do some travelling.' Charlotte listened, reflected, and a week later mentioned casually at supper that she had told Cambridge she was deferring her place a year and that they had agreed.

'So it's not a mausoleum,' I said a little sourly.

'I just needed some space, Mum. S'obvious. I should have had a gap year anyway. I don't know why you were against it.'

'I wasn't!'

'You were. You said they were a waste of time.'

'I may have said something in *general*.'

'Well, it's what I'm doing. So.'

'Fine. I'm glad. You'll enjoy Cambridge.'

'Praps.' She relapsed into silence, picking at her food. She was a pretty girl now, not a classic beauty but handsome and healthy, with an effortless style of her own in clothes and hair. We were not close, though: I reflected in dismay that with every passing year it was growing harder, not easier, to deal with my daughter harmoniously. All my friends, her schoolfriends' parents, talked humorously about the tantrums and rows of the teenage years but expressed general relief that by eighteen or nineteen their daughters held quite reasonable conversations and treated them as equals. 'I do love students,' said one. 'A joy, after schoolgirls.'

I, on the other hand, had dealt with Charlotte's underage turbulence without too much pain – she was, for instance, unusually tidy and pernickety about her room and her clothes – but now it was her poised, chilly young adult personality which filled me with dismay. I tried very hard not to think of Max, but when she shot me disapproving glances or frozen stares, or conversely when she turned on the charm with push-button efficiency to bend Donald to her whims, it was hard not to. David Jakobowitz had been to dinner on one of the rare nights that Charlotte deigned to eat with us, and I could see by the way his gaze rested on Charlotte that he was thinking exactly the same. The broad brow, the sullen mouth curving suddenly into an irresistible smile, the veiled contempt expressed for classmates, smitten boyfriends and indeed anyone of no use to her – it was all there, and I trembled to see it. I had asked him not to tell her that he was her grandfather, not yet; he agreed, not least as he pointed out 'since I am not'. I shrank from the sheer complication of it all, and above all from the idea of sharing such ambiguities with a creature as confident and clear-cut and scornful as my daughter.

She had a series of boyfriends, in the way that modern schoolgirls do. Nearly all of them, it seemed to my heated imagination, had something concrete to offer at the time and were disposed of when it became irrelevant. Kenny had a car at seventeen, and was chauffeur for the whole group until Charlotte annexed him as her personal transport. As soon as she passed her test and spent her birthday money on a runabout, Kenny was on the scrapheap. Henry, whose parents were unbearably trendy concert promoters from Stoke Newington, got her tickets for desirable gigs. Kemal helped with her History coursework; Jonathan did a weekend job at John Lewis and got staff discount, so his responsibility was keeping her stocked up with cheap tights and cashmere sweaters. As each boy was discarded it was I who answered the phone and promised, vainly, that I was sure Charlotte would ring back when she got the message.

'She *uses* them,' I said to Marienka once in the office. She was perched on the edge of my desk, her hair a tousled golden cloud around the small, piquant face. 'She just uses them and chucks them aside.'

'Oh, rubbish!' said Marienka. 'She's a normal girl of her age, she's experimenting with friendships and lovers and her own power. We all did. Well –' she paused and peered over the rim of her mug at me. 'Perhaps not all. You were a romantic mooncalf with your nose in a poetry book, yearning for the impossible dream. But most of us played the field a bit for fun.'

'Nobody quite as energetically as you. But you didn't drop boys so cruelly, did you?'

'Not when you knew me. But at school I probably did. I'd probably got a bit of finesse by the time I got to university. I could usually get them to drop *me* by doing something appalling.'

'I wish she'd get some finesse. That poor Henry came

round the other day to see if she wanted tickets to some gig
or other, and she said "yeah, sure" on the doorstep and took
them off him and didn't even ask him in for a coffee.'

'Well, he knows where he stands, then. Honestly, Sal, don't
fret about it. She's not unusual. It's just that she hasn't fallen
for anyone yet, she's brittle. She'll soften up when she falls
in love, like I did. If you're bothered, talk to her.'

'That's the thing, I *can't*, she won't tell me anything.
Donny chats away and comes for a hug in the evening and
tells me all about school, but Charlotte never even told me
she was getting Cambridge to defer her entry till after it
was all signed and sealed. She talks more to Donald than
she does to me. She seems to hate me, or think I'm a fool
anyway.'

'Sturdy independence. Petra tells me every damn thing
that happens all day at school – drives me nuts!'

We veered off onto the subject of her own highly satis-
factory daughter, still an only child and extravagantly doted
over by Marienka and Peter. It was still astonishing to me
how contentedly domestic my wild old friend had grown.
Petra looked freakishly like her father, and the three of them
had a cottage in Norfolk for the weekends and the long
summer break. They competed between themselves in the
Flower and Produce Show for best jams and sweet-peas.
Sometimes, seeing the trio together, the terrible thought came
into my mind that it would be like that in our house, if it
was only me and Donald and Donny. Charlotte's cool scorn
had a subduing effect on family outings.

When she had saved up a couple of thousand pounds – with
remarkable ease, I must say – Charlotte set off on a prolonged
holiday in India and the Far East, phoning home once every
week or two with news. Donald got more of the news than
I did, if he happened to pick up the phone. When it was

me I seemed to say something wrong or tactless, and get a
snappish reply to the effect that she knew perfectly well what
she was doing, thank you very much, she wasn't a baby.
Certainly she and her two friends, one boy and one girl, were
intrepid travellers and went long distances on local slow
trains. I heard years later that she had been ill with dysentery
and lain up in Delhi for a whole week alone. She never told
us at the time.

When she got back it was August, and she took some wait-
ressing work to save up for the start of term. I hardly saw her;
she got up late, worked lunchtime, met friends in the afternoon and worked again in the evening, taking her meals at
the bistro. In September I suggested we all sit down together
and discuss her finances for the coming three years. The
agency was still doing well, though not as well as during the
peachy Thatcher years; I was still banking song royalties from
time to time, and Donald was getting all the work he could
comfortably handle. It was in our minds to offer her a very
good allowance, so that as he put it, 'She can really get the
most out of her university years, and not be worrying about
holiday jobs and student loans.'

'That's right,' I said. 'We didn't, much, did we? I remember
always being broke, and working in the pub kitchen in the
summer, but no bank would ever lend us a bean, let alone
these huge overdrafts and loans they have now.'

Charlotte, however, was surprisingly non-committal about
our offer. 'That's cool,' she said, 'but I'm not a school kid.
I've looked into the student loans thing, and I'm going for
the maximum.'

'But, darling, why?' asked Donald. 'We want to help out
all we can.'

'And luckily, we can,' I added.

'I don't want you controlling me,' said Charlotte suddenly.
'Might as well say it. If you pay the bottom line, you'll want

to interfere. Like you did before, Mum, when I wanted a gap year.'

'I wouldn't want to control you –' I began angrily, but she shrugged her slim shoulders and turned away.

Donald persisted. 'Look, honeybun, all we're saying is that we'll make you an allowance, just as our parents did for us, it's quite normal, it doesn't mean a spy in the wardrobe.'

'You had full grants,' said my daughter flatly. 'I read about it. The country wanted students, so it paid for them.'

'Our parents still had to put in a bit,' said Donald. 'Come on, don't be a mule about this. Let us slip you five hundred a term, anyway.'

'OK,' said Charlotte. 'If you must. Is that it, because I'm going to see Zoë?'

It speaks volumes for my attitude that it never occurred to me that one thing she had not inherited from Max was a willingness to take any money that was offered. When she had gone I said angrily to Donald, 'She's impossible. Arrogant, ungrateful – I don't know what I've done wrong. I'm sorry.'

'Oh, she's fine,' he said easily. 'She's got a point, you know, about not wanting to be controlled. My parents virtually thought that I was still at school; they were quite depressed not to get reports on headed college paper every term.'

'I give up,' I said. 'Let's hope Donny's going to be easier.'

And he was, of course. Four years later he got A levels almost as stellar as his half-sister's and hugged me in glee and without self-consciousness in front of all his friends and teachers gathered round the school noticeboard. He further rejoiced his father's heart by getting a music scholarship to his old college.

That same summer Charlotte left Cambridge – from where she had barely returned, spending vacations with friends whenever she could. She had a good enough History degree to get a year's postgraduate bursary in America. Friends said,

'Aren't you lucky! Such clever children, doing so well!' All I could think of, with a sinking heart, was that her bursary was to Harvard, and that Bellinger was a very unusual name. It would jump out at her from any faculty list, as one's own name tends to do. I wished I had changed it when I married Donald, but he had been chivalrously against the idea, feeling it dishonoured poor dead Marty.

'Hm,' said Marienka when I told her. 'You'll have to tell her a few things now. I bet she doesn't even know she's *got* an Uncle Max, does she?'

'I didn't want to talk about him when she was small. It was all too messy. I always thought we might when she grew up. But since she's been grown up, which happened at about fourteen, she hasn't wanted to listen to a word I say. She seems to hate me.'

'Oh, for God's sake, of course she doesn't. Anyway, Sal, I think you ought to mark her card. Who knows what the new, caring sharing gay-style Max might say to her? Three thousand miles from home?'

'He may be gay,' I said with an attempt at coolness, because Marienka had mocked me so much ever since I told her what I learned from David, 'but I doubt he's very caring and sharing.'

She looked at me seriously now. 'Sally, tell her. If she hates you anyway it won't make much difference. If you don't and she finds out some other way, God help you all. What does Donald say?'

Donald had said the same, adding that it was not his secret and not his business but reiterating that the rules of opera plots decreed that openness was the only safe policy – 'Look at *Trovatore*, all that trouble, then the wrong baby!'

But I was not going to tell Marienka that. I felt increasing anxiety that she might take it upon herself to tell Charlotte everything, in her role as unofficial godmother. But as the time grew near for my daughter's departure to America and she had to come home to pack and organize a visa, it happened to be the summer month which Marienka and Peter devoted to their Norfolk cottage garden. So I successfully kept them apart until the day when Donald drove her to Heathrow. I wanted to go, but Donny needed driving in the opposite direction to a youth orchestra rehearsal. When I had dropped him I drove all the way home in tears. I thought I had grown up, left the follies of youth behind, paid my dues and cast away stupidity and obsession and misjudgement. That day, with a premonitory squeeze of fright, I knew that I had not.

38

Marienka came back from Norfolk invigorated, full of September zeal. I had been keeping the office ticking over with our two secretaries and the latest pair of keen young interns; we had a crowded autumn of bookings and few headaches. Apart, that is, from one comedian famous for his womanizing and bouts of depression, who was refusing to turn up for a big, and long-planned, event the following Saturday. When Marienka clacked into the office in her killer office heels I was on the phone to him, and with my spare hand made the particular rude gesture which – ever since a *News of the World* exposé by a girlfriend – had always been our office code to identify him. My senior partner grimaced and gestured towards the phone with a grabbing movement. We had worked together long enough to have an impressive repertoire of mime communication.

'I'll put you straight through to Ms Tilton,' I said, emolliently. 'I'm sure she can sort things out. One moment.' I handed Marienka the phone.

She mimed two beats and then barked: 'What's this? One more no-show and this agency cannot handle you. We have a name for reliability.' She listened, not for long, then said, 'Darling, who cares? If you can stand upright and read cards, you're fit to work. If you can't, then bloody well retire. OK? Got it? No, sweetie, simply not impressed. No tantrums. Naughty naughty. Ring me back when you're coherent.' She slammed the phone down with a tight-lipped smile, then turned to me with a real one.

'Hey!' I said, half admiring and half horrified. 'He'll go straight to Premium Performers if you talk to him like that!'

'Good riddance,' she said. 'He's on the turn anyway, silly old fart. I feel a new era dawning, free from spoilt old luvvies with only six jokes. What else is brewing? Peter's gone to see some education ministers about the conference in October, I think we can get Woodhead. So I'm here to catch up.'

I riffled through my papers. 'Lovely jobs for Denis D and the new girl from Breakfast. Half a dozen enquiries for Poncey Paul, and a fabulous, fabulous commercial for Trudi – if we can get her to do it, without compromising her artistic in-te-gri-tee . . . look!'

I went into her office with my papers and we buzzed over the intriguing amusements of our strange job. We pushed square pegs into hexagonal holes, made wild suggestions to timorous conference managers, argued about expensive autocue and giggled about the endearing insecurities of our showbusiness clients. When we had caught up she clicked her fingers at the secretary for coffee – something I had never been able to bring myself to do, but which Marienka did on purpose – 'It helps to psych me into a proper old-fashioned kickass agent'. I usually explained this to new secretaries so they knew it was not personal. Then she perched on her favourite spot on my desk, legs dangling, one expensive red shoe hanging off her toe.

'Guess who I saw in Norfolk?' she began.

'Dunno. Prince Charles?'

'Nope. Kate!'

'No! Really? What's become of her?'

'Divorced Ted years ago. Remarried to a shrink. She's a headmistress, big comp near Norwich. Took it from rubbish to quite high up the league table, she's got an OBE, even. Government-approved superhead, all that stuff.'

'Golly. How was she?'

'Lovely. Bit taken aback at first, I could see her looking me up and down. But she gave me the whole life story sitting near the ice-cream shed on Blakeney beach, while Petra and Peter were swimming. I thought it was sad about Ted and said so, and she insisted on telling me in fluent therapy-speak what went wrong.'

'Eow. What?'

'She wouldn't sleep with him for over a year, after the wedding, so he had an affair – but the *reason* she couldn't was just awful –'

So it was there, in an office coffee-break, that I heard the story of the sorrowful night when Kate walked out on David Jakobowitz' right-wing views, and Max stayed at his commanding stepfather's feet and did not bother to see her safe across the park.

'She said that the irony is that these days, her own views are more or less where David's were then. Only in nineteen seventy-two, or whenever it was, he sounded like a right fascist.'

'Ah, the dear dead seventies . . . funny thing is, I reckon David's moved left just as she's moved right. He's very mellow about a lot of things these days. He comes to supper occasionally and broods over Thatcher's Britain. God, though, poor Kate.'

'Yeah. I felt awful that we didn't get it out of her after it happened. We all just sort of drifted, right? Selfish little cows really,' she added reflectively. 'I certainly was.'

'But she's OK now?'

'Fine. Nice husband. He was her therapist after the divorce. Sweet, eh?'

'Sweet.'

All the same, this startling news took me back again, farther than I would wish to go into the muddled and miserable years. The story of Kate's vulnerability as a girl alone made me think of Charlotte in America and the different perils that could beset her. I had tried once or twice in her teens to warn her about street danger, but she was already blocking me out, rolling her eyes and shrugging herself into deafness. Marienka must have noticed that I was quiet the rest of the morning, because at lunchtime, instead of ordering up her normal sandwich, she insisted I come down the road for a cheese omelette at the corner café. When we had ordered she said, without preamble: 'You could write to Charlotte, you know. Tell her that way. It might be easier.'

I shook my head. 'I tried a while ago. Sat down, wrote, kept tearing it up. Doesn't work.'

'Written words are what you do best. Try again.'

'Can't.' I was almost crying, and she always hated that; she desisted, and we ate our lunch and went back to work.

Charlotte had gone out to America early, before Harvard's term: she travelled a little, looking up friends of friends from university in New England and Florida. We got postcards, three of them; the last one showed the campus and bore the words: 'Got here. Got into room OK. Meetings tomorrow. Spookily friendly. People keep giving me muffins.'

After that I waited, trying to distract myself with work. Donny's departure for Oxford hit me harder than I thought it would; I let Donald drive him there alone. The fact was that I had never visited the town since the day I left the house by the canal, and was not sure how I would react. I did not want any mood of mine to overshadow my son's enthusiasm for his new start. Donald protested a little, saying we should both go and commemorate our first meeting at Christ Church, but I felt too uneasy and unsure of myself; depressed, even. The feeling intensified; with both children gone the house seemed empty and tidy.

Through that autumn Donald was rehearsing intensively

for a new *Parsifal* and thought day and night about little but
the Grail Knight Gurnemanz; I knew better by now than to
prattle and demand constant company when he was deep
into a new part.

I could not watch television or settle to a book; to fill my
evenings I began to make new curtains, something I am not
good at. Stained with sweat and occasional tears, they failed
to progress. Their patterns did not match and their hems
drooped. I could have afforded to throw them away and
order new ones from John Lewis, but I was in a penitential
mood and suffered on. Sleep was fragmented, and the night
hours lonely as I stared at the dim ceiling and replayed old,
difficult times. The autumn was heavy, hot and humid with
little wind and occasional violent thunderstorms. I sweated
and waited, and at last came the news I had been dreading.
Another postcard from Charlotte, this time a trendy monochrome number showing a horror-film monster with staring
eyes.

'There is a Professor Bellinger here, same name as me!
Not met him but must be distant colonial-type relative.
Doesn't seem to teach v. much but might sneak to dead-art
lecture to have a look. Still warm here. Went upstate to see
famous leaves, just looked like leaves to me.'

Donald passed it across the breakfast table to me and said
mildly, 'That'll be him, won't it?'

'Could be. But it isn't *such* a rare name.'

'Bet you there aren't two Professors Bellinger teaching art
history at Harvard.'

'Oh, I don't know!' I stared at the card and began to shake
violently. 'Donald, help me.'

'Write to her,' said Donald, just as Marienka had done. 'At the
very least warn her he's an uncle. It's not like a second cousin
once removed or something. She might want to sheer off if
she thinks she's embarrassing him by being a long-lost niece.'

'I'll think about it.' But I was paralyzed, terrified by something I could not put a name to.

I could sense Donald growing worried in the days that followed. One weekend, just before *Parsifal* opened, he announced that we were going for a drive into the country, and before I realized it we were on the M40, heading purposefully towards Oxford.

'We're taking Donny out to lunch,' he said. I smiled and shivered, but was glad to be forced.

As it happened, there was no Proustian moment to face at all. Oxford was prosperous, buzzing with shoppers and expensive-looking coffee bars; the golden towers and spires were one-quarter memory but three-quarters postcard, too much of a cliché to affect me. Nothing took us in the direction of the canal house, and the little restaurant in Jericho which Donny had chosen was new to me. Not that my own time, as I told him, had involved many restaurants of any kind. Our son's delight in his life, friends, studies and college overwhelmed any self-centred mawkishness I might have felt. As we drove away I felt more relaxed than I had for months. I was once again safely centred in the happy present, with my beloved husband and my joy of a son.

When we got home Donald hugged me close, nuzzled my neck and said: 'See? No problem.' Then after a moment, 'They were good days, weren't they? Student days. I wish you and I had had more of them together.'

'I couldn't have done. I was too stupid to see the point of you, then.'

'Probably just as well. You'd never have written the songs, would you? If you'd been happy?'

'So maybe it's worth being an unhappy deluded idiot for a while, then?'

'Maybe. Breeds art, doesn't it?'

'But I love seeing Donny so happy – is that wrong, then?'

Donald laughed. 'I shouldn't worry. Some girl will break his heart soon. And some chap will break Charlotte's. And so the world rolls on, singing its sad old song.'

A week or two later, just as we were looking at diaries to work out Christmas arrangements, a letter came from Charlotte in America. This was a rarity because her preferred mode of communication was the telephone or the postcard. Donald opened it, frowned, hesitated, then pushed it across the table to me.

Hi folks,

   Don't go ape on me, but I reckon it's best I stay here over Christmas and come back in the spring recess. There's a lot going on here and I've been invited for the holidays to stay with some cool people. Saves on flights, too. By the way, I ran into the namesake Bellinger guy at a social, he's really nice but a bit pompous. Said he knew you and Marienka at Oxford, and weirdly he had a brother who died who was a rock singer like my real dad, only he wasn't at Oxford, so you probably didn't know him or anything. He's gay, with a really nice old guy he lives with, Adam, who has fluffy Einstein hair and is crazy about American football and the Knicks who I think is basketball. Anyway must dash. C.

'What's Max *playing* at?' I said when I had recovered my breath. 'Telling her he knew me, but not letting on that Marty was his brother? He must know who she is – well, obviously.'

Donald frowned. 'It is weird. I don't much like it either. You have to tell her, or the whole thing's too odd.'

So I wrote.

Darling Charlotte,

   Of course we understand about Christmas. We're just pleased that you're making friends and getting on so well in a new country. We'll keep your stocking for when you come home in spring! Donny will miss you but he's loving University too.

I'm glad (I bit my lip at the perjury) *that you've met Max Bellinger. Obviously it was a quick meeting and perhaps things were a bit muddled, but you ought to know that his brother who died was, in fact, my first husband Marty – your dad. I knew them both, though Marty wasn't at Oxford, he was a year younger than me actually. Perhaps Professor Bellinger didn't want to upset you. So he is your uncle. I've never told you about him because he was so far away and I wasn't sure where, I just knew it was America.*

Anyway, have a great Christmas, we'll be thinking of you. All my love,
Mum

A week later a postcard came: *Thanks for note, bit of a surprise but hey, that's life. Unk Max sends his best, says he didn't want to presume or come all uncly on me, which is sweet. I told fluffy-head Adam that this formally makes him my auntie! He took me and cousin Lexy to the football, God it's violent, they wear helmets like Hannibal Lecter. Jude and Harry and me are going to ski-lodge. Merry Crimble. C.*

At least, I reflected, she was more cheerful and more communicative in this long-distance exchange of written words than she had been for the past few years when we lived on the same landmass. If Max was being pleasant to her that, surely, was good? If she was getting to know her young cousin 'Lexy' that too was good. She seemed more amused and attracted by this Einstein-haired gay lover than by Max himself, anyway, and her cards were peppered with other names of friends. Perhaps she would come home from America a changed girl, relaxed and communicative and forgiving of her mother's neuroses.

David Jakobowitz, after much persuading, agreed to come

to us on Boxing Day, and when the others had wandered off after lunch and we were sitting by the fire I told him how Charlotte had quite fortuitously hooked up with Max and his partner at Harvard.

He looked grave. 'I have been told not to fly, not ever again,' he said, tapping his heart. 'Otherwise I would call on them all myself. See what's going on.'

'Nothing's going on,' I said indignantly. 'She met up with them, went to a ball game, met her long-lost uncle.'

'Her *father*,' said David, his hard dark eyes on me. 'She met her *father*.'

I flinched. 'Don't. David, don't say it out loud, even here – Donny might hear.'

He stood up, and although his old shoulders were bent now he towered over me, authoritative and dominant as he once must have been in the boardroom.

'Sally, you have to tell her the truth. If you don't, I will get on an aeroplane even if it kills me, and seek her out and tell her.'

'I can't.' Even to me, my voice sounded hateful, cowardly and childish.

'If you don't, *he* might. Have you thought of that? Three thousand miles from home, and she hears that from a middle-aged homosexual Professor? Do you *want* to estrange her forever? Do you know how much it will hurt when she feels stupid for not knowing and comes to despise you? Sally, I can tell you a long tale of that, I can tell you how one foolish deception will eat your hearts hollow!'

I was silent. David stood, rocking slightly, then fell forward, silently, almost into my arms. I was supporting him, slumped across the sofa, when Donald and my son burst in to answer my screaming call. The ambulance came quickly, but he was gone.

'You really loved that old man, didn't you?' said Donald gently, as we left the hospital.

39

Neutral, silent and dim, the great plane seemed to hang still over the Atlantic. The air sussurrated over the muffled hum of engines; the cabin staff, their supper service long over, retired behind their curtain to ease their aching feet. Most passengers snuggled under blankets and wriggled on their paper-sheathed pillows, though a few stared and yawned at the little screens set into the seat-backs.

I kept mine set on the route map, our tiny plane a clumsy symbol in mid-ocean. Inexorably it moved on, the miles reeling off towards Boston. It was early February, and I was flying to America to tell my daughter the truth. I had promised it, silently, in a pew beside the coffin of David Jakobowitz. After the shock of Boxing Day it took me a full week and all Marienka's ingenuity to track down Susan, his stepdaughter and the only relative I knew of apart from Max. Sue turned out to be breeding horses in Sussex, and was surprisingly pleasant to me; it was apparent that she had not deliberately cut me dead that day in Harvey Nichols. We met at her sugges-tion in the tearoom of Brown's Hotel.

'How time does pass!' she said in her brisk county tones. 'I never saw much of him really, after he and Mother moved out of London. But he was a model stepfather, when you come to think about it. Paid for two weddings for me, poor old David, and never a word of complaint. Nice that you kept in touch. And sweet of you to do the arrangements, *do* let us know the cost.'

'You'll tell your brother?' I ventured, and she gave the nearest thing to a pout that a county lady can manage.

'Oh, Maxie won't come. He didn't come over for Mother's funeral, you know.'

'David told me. But he had a lecture, something special he couldn't pull out of.'

'Rubbish. He's detached, that's what it is. He doesn't want to be reminded that he ever had a family. You know he's become a poof?' She spoke of it as if it was an ill-advised career change, then sighed and went on: 'Well, I'll send cards out to quite a few people, him included. But don't hold your breath.' She gave me a sharp look. 'Aren't you still in touch? I thought you were thick as thieves. Mother used to sniff about it.'

'No.' I passed on to the most difficult thing I had to ask her: Marienka had delegated the job to me, and I did not relish it. 'Susan, I have to ask you this, and you seem a sensible person to me . . .'

'We're all middle-aged,' said Sue Hampton, née Bellinger. 'Sense comes with the territory. I know what you're going to ask, and of course the answer's yes. I'm not *silly*.'

'It's whether it might be all right for Peter to come to the funeral. He hadn't seen David for years, but he liked him a lot. And I think it's good when a lot of people come to funerals.'

'Of course. Yes, wasn't Annette's just awful? Ugh.' She shivered. 'I was thinking about it the other day when our MFH was buried, church packed, everyone roaring out hymns to the rafters, and they played John Peel as the coffin went out. If these Labour yobboes get in we'll not be told we can't hunt! What was I saying? Oh yes, Peter. More the merrier. And he'll bring his floozie, too, I suppose?'

'Marienka would like to come. Yes.' I could not be offended on Marienka's behalf: I could hear her hooting with laughter at Sue's vocabulary.

'Well, it's no skin off my nose,' said Sue pleasantly.

'Honestly, Sally, you mustn't get so tender and wincey about things that happened twenty-whatsit years ago. I was well rid of Peter, to be honest. Imagine if he'd wanted me to go and work in that awful theatre agency!'

I was momentarily diverted by the idea of Sue Hampton at my desk, dealing with neurotic TV presenters and alcoholic comedians past their prime; but then I reflected that it might possibly pay off if we started handling them as if they were difficult horses and pregnant mares. Perhaps a curbchain on the bit and a slap across the nose was exactly what some of our performers needed.

'Well, thanks,' I said. 'And you're quite happy for us to carry on with the funeral details? And do the newspaper announcement, in case anyone else wants to come?'

'Absolutely. David was never *orthodox*, you know, so you don't need to do the Jewish stuff, whatever that might be. Stamping on glasses or something, or is that weddings? Can he be buried with Mother?'

'Probably. Give me the details.'

At the funeral itself, though, she softened. The undertakers had driven the coffin off to the rural cemetery where Helena lay, and we were a subdued little party of twenty-five or so in a hotel function room near the church. I was glad to see that his club had sent a wreath and two committee members, and his old bank produced half-a-dozen colleagues who made a point of coming up to Sue and praising him as an honest man, one of the old school. Other mourners, to my surprise, turned up from nowhere; quiet conversations revealed that they had been recipients of considerable financial help and moral support from David in difficult times. When at the end she came over to thank me for doing the arrangements, Sue Hampton said, rather less briskly than usual:

'Awful family, aren't we? Totally out of touch, spread to the four winds, nothing cosy about us. It was terrifically sad about Marty, silly boy, but honestly, you were well out of the tribe. Your Donald seems lovely.'

'He is. And I don't think you were so bad. Families are all different.'

'Oh, for heaven's sake, we were ghastly,' said Sue, with a return of her crisp manner. 'Nothing was ever the same after my father died. And it didn't help everybody knowing about Marty and David, and not saying a word.'

'You all knew?'

''Course we did. Stood out a mile. They were like mirrors of each other. Father knew too, when he was alive, and never let on. He was extra nice to Marty because of it, so Marty adored him, then when Mother married David he was the most upset – and nobody ever let on that they knew, or that they knew that everyone else did . . .' She shrugged in her bravely unfashionable fur coat. 'Dear, oh dear, water under the bridge. As I say, you're well out of it.'

I thought of all this on the plane: safe at thirty-five thousand feet, safe in the breathing silence of midnight. I knew my duty now more clearly than ever before. I had to talk to Charlotte whether she liked it or not, and give her the full truth about all of us. She might rage at me, but it was better than having our family drift apart in cold mutual incomprehension. Yet I dreaded landing, dreaded ringing her, dreaded whatever hotel room or restaurant I would choose to break the news in. Donald had offered to come too, breaking his contract to sing Gurnemanz in Paris, but I was too much of an agent these days to countenance any such treachery. Besides, this was my mess and I should deal with it. David Jakobowitz, in his last minute of life, had finally shaken me into sense.

By the time I had got through the immigration line it was nearly midnight, East Coast time, and I took a cab to the hotel I had chosen close to the halls where Charlotte lodged. When I landed I left a message on her phone claiming that business had brought me to Boston for a few days and that it would be good to have lunch with her. Then, in the bland hotel bedroom, I slept until mid-morning. When I came round the bedside phone was ringing. My daughter's voice was different from the tight, contemptuous North London bleat I remembered: she sounded blithe, open, almost American.

'Mum. Hi. Fancy you turning up. Smallio worldio.'

'Can we meet?'

'Thing is, I'm actually off out to Adam and Max's cabin upstate for a couple of days. We've got a reading week. But they say they'd love it if you came too. There's lots of rooms and a spare sledge.'

'Sledge?'

'It's in the mountains. It's cool. I spent Christmas there with a couple of mates. They like filling it up with students, it makes them forget how old they are.'

'Well, I don't know –'

'We're off now, but Adam's got to stay and do something, so he's picking you up at the hotel at half-past three. You'll get there for late supper. OK? Make sure you get a warm jacket, there's a good shop two blocks east of your hotel called Snowbird. Very cheap. Remember American sizes read one smaller than ours. So, seeya.'

I sank back on the pillow, baffled and a little scared. But after a moment a new feeling asserted itself. It was a good sensation, I thought, to be ordered about by my daughter. She sounded happy, and she had grown up enough to make masterful arrangements for her slow-witted mother. Clearly she was on friendly terms with her newfound relatives. Perhaps it would all be far easier than I had thought. On this comforting reflection I drifted back to sleep, to wake with a start realizing I had just enough time to check out, run along to Snowbird,

buy an anorak and meet this Adam. I rang Donald to tell him
where I was off to but he was out. I was on my own in a new
country and a new situation. It was strangely stimulating.
Perhaps everything would be all right.

When Adam breezed in to the hotel lobby I saw straight
away what Charlotte had meant by her reference to Einstein.
He had a corona of fuzzy white hair round a high, high forehead; but he was tall, tanned, thin, broadly smiling and
unnervingly agile for his age, which I put in the mid-sixties.
He picked up my bag as if it was no weight at all, and led
me out to a big square vehicle, tough as a truck, which stood
by the pavement opposite. As he threw the case in the boot
I saw a tangle of snow-chains and a shovel.

'Gosh,' I said, sounding ridiculously English. 'Where *are*
we heading? Alaska?'

'White mountains,' he said. 'New Hampshire. Should be
fine, but we do get dumps of snow. You'll love it. I'm coming
back down on Monday early, so don't worry, we'll get you
to your meetings.' He opened the door and half bowed to
me. 'Climb aboard, ma'am. We'll show you the back
country.'

There was something so easy and frank about this man
that as I settled in my seat belt I blurted out, 'Actually, there
are no meetings. I wanted to see Charlotte and I thought it
was more diplomatic not to let her know I was flying all this
way to talk to her.'

'Very wise, very wise,' he said. 'Independent young lady,
is Charlotte. You know we think very highly of her, in the
department?'

'You're a historian?'

'So-so. I specialize in education, and right now I teach
history teachers. She's taking an option in case she decides
to be one of those critters later on.'

'Oh. I didn't know. She doesn't tell me much about her plans.'

'She's gonna do just fine. We love that little lady. Max is tickled pink with his niece. Christmas was a blast.'

I told him, friendly as he was, a bit about our Christmas and how Max's stepfather had died in our house on Boxing Day. He nodded but made no response to this, seeming to concentrate on the road. After a while we cleared the city traffic and sped north along the freeway; Adam talked lightly about university matters and the American education system and a rumour about President Clinton and one of the girl interns. I dozed for half an hour, still jet-lagged, and when I woke up we were among tall trees on a country road and he had stopped at a gas station and was walking towards me with two paper cups of coffee.

'Gotta stay awake a bit,' he said. 'Or you won't get into American time till you're back home.' I drank gratefully, and before he pulled away he broke a Hershey bar in half and gave me some. 'Do you know the United States well?'

'No – I've only been here twice, when my husband was singing with the San Francisco opera. Never here in the East.'

He nodded, negotiated a junction, then abruptly said,

'Ma'am, are you planning to give Max a hard time about not going to the funerals?'

'Well – no – not my business really. I did bring him an Order of Service card for his stepfather's.'

'If you knew the old guy, then you know that Max didn't go home for his ma's funeral?'

'Yes. Busy, I gather.' My voice rang in the subsequent silence, prissily English even to me.

Adam sighed, and glanced sideways. 'Wasn't that. Come on. You know that.'

'Well, I thought – I don't know what I thought. Not my business.'

'It was, a bit. You were married to his brother, yeah?'

'Yeah.'

'The thing you gotta know is that Max is not a very strong person and there's a lot of family damage there. He wrote his ma really often, they talked on the phone, he was an OK son as far as I could see. But when she died, he gets this call from old Jakobowitz ordering him to drop everything – and there was some other stuff going on there, too.'

'About you?' I hazarded.

'Yeah. Old Jacko said as how he wasn't to bring his boyfriend, because it would be a "breach of taste". Like I'd have gone and muscled in wearing pink pants! Old guy probably thought I was a chorus boy. Max was really upset. Said his stepdad had always wanted to arrange his life for him and thought he was owed, and he was damned if he jumped through hoops for him any more. Well, I told him not to be *stoopid*, and to go home for his ma's sake, but by the time he'd calmed down and come round it was too late to get a flight. He ate himself up over it, he really did.'

'And David's own funeral?'

'What do you think? Postcard from his sister Sue, with "best to come on your own" written across the bottom. Groundhog Day!'

I had seen the film with Donny, and smiled at the reference.

'So you think he's sorry he didn't come?'

'Yeah, I do. But like I say, he's not the strongest. Soft guy. Don't you give him a hard time.'

I was silent for a few miles, but so comfortable a companion was this blithe old man that eventually I said: 'You know, I knew Max very well when we were young. And I don't really recognize this picture of a soft guy who gets hurt by people.'

He looked sideways at me, and in the dusk I saw a grin spreading across his face. 'He told me about you, too.'

'Ah. Nothing good, I bet.'

'No, he's got a few regrets. Says you were really good to him when Alex was a baby, but it went kinda sour. He hasn't talked to Lexy or Charlotte about all that, by the way. It's a problem for him, too. His ma didn't like you much, it seems, though I do hope that's not news to you?'

'Certainly isn't.'

'Between the lines, all things taken into account, ma'am, where it comes to you and him I'd say he was admitting he was an asshole.'

'Well, that's a change. He was a very cold person, Adam – I'm glad he isn't cold with you, of course I am, but I can't pretend that he was very nice at all. I thought he was. I wasted some good years of my life on Max Bellinger.'

'Oh Jeez. Yeah, I can see that. But come on, you know kids, I know kids, I taught Grade School for twenty years. What is it we say about the class bully? He's the one who feels small and pushed-about. Passes it on.'

'I can't see David Jakobowitz as a bully. He was a lovely man.'

'There you go!' he said lightly, and I saw we would get no further on that track.

'When did *you* meet Max?'

'When he was in the pits. He came to Harvard to give some junior classes, and six months in he could hardly look them in the eye. He was terrified of the students, terrified of the Professors, and his son wasn't eating anything and sawing at his arms with a razor blade. So one day I'm wanting a muffin and a latte and a leak, and I come in from my class and find him crying in the staff rest-room.'

'And you – helped him?'

'Helped Alex first. Found him a school he could handle. Then Max and I – well, I didn't think he was gay, I got terrible gaydar, me. It was more of a shock to me than to him. He came out of therapy and there it was. And here we are. Growin' old together like Ma and Pa Kettle.'

'I didn't think he was gay, either,' I said feelingly. 'He never used to be.'

His reaction was a giggle, the only moment of effeteness I had encountered in him. We were, in any case, drawing closer to our destination. The road grew narrower, forked off into a mountain track and climbed, our headlights dazzling against banks of snow, our roof brushing powdery whiteness which slid down the rear window. Looking out I could see lights of a settlement now way below us, and felt for the first time a twinge of nervousness. I have never been good in wildernesses.

'How far?'

'Ten minutes. Hold on.' We snaked on upwards, until just below a snowy arête the lights of a little house illuminated a plume of smoke rising from a chimney. It was like driving into a Christmas card, and I said as much to Adam.

'Yeah, we love it,' he said. 'Swimming in the lake in the summer, sledging in the winter – it's not a ski place, but there's a great run down through the trees there for a sledge. Gets us out of town. And we love having the young folks around.'

Minutes later a door was flung open, a slanting rectangle of warm light fell on the snowy track, and my daughter skipped out in a furry jacket and swishing red woollen skirt, her hair cropped short and tousled.

'Christ!' I said, before I could stop myself. 'You look like Heidi!'

40

Max had a beard. I don't know why this detail surprised me so much, after twenty years, but it did. It was brown, spade-shaped, oddly soft looking and streaked with grey. It made his eyes look bigger and balanced his square brow, which shone more noticeable than ever with the recession of his hair. He was sitting at a rough-hewn rustic table, a book open before him, and he stood up as I came in and said: 'Sally. Welcome.' He looked wary; I remembered Adam's idea that I might berate him about the funerals. I shook his hand a little formally, then shyly sought something else to look at rather than his anxious bearded face.

The room was lovely, its warm wooden walls and floor free from cute rustic pretensions but adorned with small splashes of colour: an old plate, a couple of modern abstracts, a reproduction icon of St Michael the Archangel. A wonderful rug covered the middle of the floor, Native American work by the look of it; the fire was piled high with logs held in place by an incongruous but wonderfully intricate wrought-iron grate with roses enamelled red-and-green at its edges. It looked Victorian, or rather – I corrected myself – Early American. I thought back to the arid elegance of the Mews and wondered whether all this generous warmth was Adam's taste.

A slim, beautiful boy – so like Annette that I caught my breath – emerged from the shadows of the inner room. Charlotte seized his hand and dragged him forward.

'This is Lexy,' she said. 'My long-lost half-cousin. This is my only-slightly lost mother, come all the way to Boston to make more lovely money from the international speaking circuit. Who're you booking out here, Mum? Michael Barrymore? The Dalai Lama? A double act of both on a trampoline? She could, you know, Adam. She and Marienka are the killer agents from hell.'

She was showing off, exuberant; I had not seen her like this since she was fourteen and I rejoiced in it. America clearly suited her.

'How d'you do, ma'am,' said the boy politely, his voice almost wholly American but with a faint distant undernote of upper-crust English. He held out his hand, as if taught his manners by a nanny, which I suppose he had been. Looking closer I saw that he was more than a boy: he must, I realized, be twenty-one now. I saw no trace at all of the baby I had looked after from his first weeks to his first birthday. 'Pleased to meet you,' he went on. 'Charlie and I have sorted out your room, we're the maids round here. Would you like to see it?'

I acquiesced, as much to get away from the extraordinary new Max as anything else, and wondered as I sat on the creaking, folksy wooden bed how on earth I was going to break into this domestic idyll with the news I had come to transmit. Max clearly had dropped no such hint, though the 'half-cousin' in Charlotte's version suggested that he had given her enough family history to know that Marty was not his full brother. It was all very confusing and unnerving, and I was growing sleepy again. In England, I thought, it must be four in the morning by now.

I washed my hands and went back; supper was on the rustic table now, bowls of soup with frankfurters, hot fresh bread, a jug of red wine and a huge blueberry baked cheesecake made, Adam assured me, by 'the kids'.

'So Adam taught you to cook, Charlotte?' I said. Through all her teens I had never managed to persuade her to do anything beyond heating beans.

'Nah. Lexy did. He's a cool cook.'

'I've had to be. Dad doesn't cook *anything*, he'd rather starve.'

'He used to cook,' I said, for I had loosened up a great deal under the influence of red wine and sleepiness. 'When we all shared a house in Oxford, he cooked rather well.'

'Then it wore off,' said Alexander, with a grin. Charlotte twinkled at him; their comradeship was pleasant to see. She had never been so sisterly with Donny, but I supposed sadly that this could be put down to sibling jealousy.

'I gave up cooking when I came to America,' said Max gently. 'So much is ready-made here.'

'And I started cooking for you anyway. Why keep a dog and bark yourself?' said Adam, shooting a fond glance at his partner. Max answered it with a smile, half smothered in his beard, and a quizzical raising of the eyebrows.

Warm and muzzy with firelight and wine, I let myself relax into gentle wonderment, as if it were a dream. I thought of the chilly, edgy clan from which Max came back in England and contrasted it with this easy familial warmth in the cosy cabin, old and young joshing contentedly together, and marvelled. For the moment I was content to listen, to watch my daughter sparkling and the men laughing. Gradually my head drooped, and suddenly Adam's voice was saying, 'Hey, bedtime! C'mon, kids – give the lady a hand.' I was hauled to my feet and given a hot-water bottle; cuddling it I fell asleep immediately, lulled by the cold wind blowing through the pine trees.

I woke early, still haunted by UK time, and dressed quietly, pulling on my new padded jacket and red fleece hat. Creeping out into the main room in the fragrance of last night's woodsmoke, I identified the heavy door that led to the track outside, raised the latch and went outside in the dimness where the last stars were fading. I trudged up the track, wishing I had thought to buy gloves, my hands deep in my pockets; in a minute or two I realized that the cabin lay very close to the treeline, and that I was coming on to an open slope. All around me, still dark, lay the white peaks falling away into distance; after a few minutes more the light began to change and soon I was rewarded by a pink-and-orange dawn gilding the western slopes. Eventually a sliver of sun too bright to look at was swelling beyond the eastern peaks.

The beauty of it calmed and elated me; I slithered back down the track and was pleased to see that Max was first out, alone, heading for the woodpile.

'Can I help?'

He nodded, and said, 'Got to get the back boiler stoked up, it keeps the cabin warm all day.' When he had piled my arms with logs we went in together and stacked them round a wood-burner in the kitchen which I had not seen before.

'Nice house,' I said.

'We're lucky to have it. It was Adam's father's, he built it before the restrictions came in. Not many private lodges up this high.'

The mention of a father gave me my cue.

'Max,' I began, 'Charlotte seems really at home here.'

'Oh, she's a jewel,' he said, enthusiastically. 'Full of life, very bright, gets on with everyone. It was a bit boring for Alex, I think, always coming up here with the old guys, so it was tremendous having her and her friends for Christmas.'

'You were,' I said daringly, 'pretty good friends with her when she was tiny. For a while.'

There was a heartbeat's silence, then he finished stacking the logs and turned to me. 'Sally, I don't like to go there. Things were pretty bad for us both, back then in the

Mews, and I find it's a negative energy to think about it too much.'

'It's part of our history,' I said. I was on edge now, wrong-footed; there was something annoyingly priestlike and serene about Max, I thought; yet I felt guilty too.

'Perhaps I should say,' he said with forceful gentleness, 'that I do know I behaved badly, but I was in a very bad place. You know I had therapy, over here? I know I shouldn't have married Annette, I know that. Or gotten involved with you either. The whole gender, woman thing was a disaster waiting to happen. When Annette began to swell up, and was full of these physical fears, it was psychically necessary for me to close down, to defend myself with gender-terror denial – Dr Reece said that, and I believe it.'

'Max,' I said as firmly as I could, 'I really can't do with this therapy-speak. What happened, happened, and we have to deal with it as a piece of true history.'

'I know it was hard on you,' he began, but at that moment Adam appeared with a tray of croissant dough shaped into new-moon curves.

'It rises overnight in the hot linen cupboard! Neat, eh? Unless Miss Charlotte pulls a towel out and pitches the dough into the bath!'

Then Charlotte herself appeared, clad only in a Hawaiian shirt which barely covered her pubes, saying,

'Hey, has dat Adamov done de croissant-dough ting? Wick-*ed*!'

'Why're you talking like Roberta Marley, minx?' asked Alex, appearing from the bathroom in a towel.

'Dis shirt ob Adam's does enforce da ji-ive speak,' said Charlotte, whirling round and displaying more buttock than was seemly. I realized that I would not be able to carry on a serious conversation; Max, in any case, had shimmered off to claim the empty bathroom.

The whole day was like that. No sooner did I get Max alone – for I had decided to tell him first that I intended to tell Charlotte – than Adam appeared, or one of the young, or more likely both of them together. Then I was dragged out to try the sledge track, and surrounded by shouts and larking; then we were all eating lunch together in a shouty holiday atmosphere, and then Max had gone for a walk and the young had vanished for three hours up the mountain with snow-shoes, returning to speak enthusiastically about a moose, and a snowman they had built with sinister pine-cone eyes ('truly psychedelic, like the guy in *The Fly*'). Then we were all together again, tired with fresh air, eating supper and listening to music, and I despaired of ever speaking intimately to either of them.

By the fire, though, when the men made their final excursion of the day to the woodpile I managed to say quietly to Charlotte: 'You're really happy here, sweetheart, aren't you?'

'Yup. I love America. Harvard's cool, and I like getting out into the mountains, and Adam and Max are great.' I had noticed that she always put Adam first – sometimes flippantly as 'Auntie Adam', which still disconcerted me. She spoke as if he were the real friend and Max the mere appendage. I was obscurely glad of this. I went on: 'And you seem to get on well with Alexander. Lexy.'

'Oh, yup.' Suddenly she had the shutters down in a way I was all too familiar with. It was not hostile now, nor contemptuous: just shuttered, private, impregnable. *Oh, yup.* A terrible thought came to me, and I shivered so visibly that Adam, snow-flecked with an armful of logs, apologized and shut the main door. When Alexander came back in I watched his eyes very carefully. When they fell on Charlotte sitting tousled by the fire, they did not seem to change, and I was momentarily reassured.

But then I glanced towards my daughter as she answered

him, and her eyes were very different: dark, soft, the pupils wide.

I shivered again. Not this, anything but this. I had not foreseen this. He was, after all, over a year younger. Didn't that matter, these days? I must be wrong. After a minute, Charlotte stood up and stretched her beautiful self so that her sweater rode up and showed a flat firm midriff. I looked again at Alexander, and this time his head was turned towards her, and a faint unmistakable glazing of his eye filled me with new terror.

41

I knew what to do the next morning; after a troubled night I got up before dawn again and instead of going up the hill I walked around near the house until Max appeared by the woodpile.

This time I began my campaign straight away, out there in the nose-prickling cold of the mountainside. He was mildly surprised to see me and stood by the neatly stacked logs in his heavy jacket, flakes of snow in his beard like some benign mountain man in a film, head inclined to hear what I might say. I jammed my hat down over my cold ears and began firmly: 'Max. I have to talk to you. I don't want to contradict your therapy, or go over stuff about you and me, or anything like that. But we have to talk about Charlotte and Alexander.'

He looked at me in mild astonishment. 'They're fine. They get on really well. It's nice.'

'Max, they get on *more* than well, it's a disaster! We have to stop it, fast!'

Had his therapy, I wondered, involved the excision of parts of his brain? Or did the laissez-faire approach of the East Coast gay community extend to not worrying about incest? He was looking at me incredulously, as if I had suggested sending both children to bed with hot milk at six o'clock.

'Sally, I'm sorry if you don't think Alexander's good enough to run around with your daughter, but I'm rather pleased. I'd have thought you would be. He's a good lad, got

through a lot of teenage problems, he's doing well with his
Master's. They're young adults. They know their own mind.'

'Max! Can't you see what's under your nose? They're
falling for each other, they *fancy* each other!'

He put down the logs and sighed. 'Sally –' I thought for
a moment he was going to say that they clearly didn't, that
it was all my imagination because Lexy had another girlfriend, and my heart rose a little. I might find I could believe
him. Last night's hot glances might have been the product
of my own frightened imagination, my own guilt at half a
lifetime's dissimulation. But Max went on, with an air of
patient superiority: 'Sally, so what if they do? I think it's nice.'

I gasped. He went on with that infuriating therapized calm:
'They're not even full first cousins – and even that would
be fine by law. But I suppose you know that Marty and I
had different fathers? It wasn't something the family talked
about, but he knew and I suppose you know? So see – they're
only half-cousins. One shared grandmother. Not a big deal.'

'Max!' The word was torn from my mouth, as if by the
chilly dawn wind. 'Charlotte isn't Marty's child!'

His face hardened; beneath the soft beard I saw once more
the old, cold, disapproving Max I remembered from the last
days at the Mews.

'Well,' he said. 'You *are* full of surprises. Poor old Marty.
Did he know?'

I was gaping now, gaping and gasping. 'Max. Get a
bloody grip! You know perfectly well Marty married me
because I was pregnant. By *you*! Have you forgotten? Have
you been brainwashed? She's your daughter! For Christ's
sake!'

As our wide eyes met in horror, from the kitchen doorway
came the sound of Adam, banging down baking-trays and
singing to himself. *Gimme a home, where the buffalo roam . . .*
He was too close. Max, with commendable presence of mind

under the circumstances, hissed: 'Up the track! Quick!' I saw what he meant; we needed private space now, and urgently. I scuttled up the hill with him close behind until we both got well out of earshot, round the corner to the place where the trees ended and the wide views opened. Snow was falling in heavy flakes now, whirling on the rising wind. We faced one another, panting slightly, and a small, cynical observant part of me murmured, 'Cathy and Heathcliff!'

Max was beyond any detachment. 'Say that again,' he said hoarsely.

'She's yours. I got pregnant during those days when you were on your own in your parents' house, after Oxford. You remember? For God's sake!'

'Of course I remember. But why the *hell* did you never tell me?'

'I did! I wrote to you! I wasn't trying to make you marry me or anything, just telling you! And you completely ignored the letter and ducked away from the subject for two years afterwards!'

'I did *not!* I never had any letter! What on earth do you bloody well take me for?'

'But you—' I stopped. His shocked disbelief was all too convincing; in those seconds my mind raced over the bare facts, stripping them of both infatuation and anger.

I had sent a letter. One letter. He had not responded. He had come to my wedding to his brother, coolly showing no sign of embarrassment. He had never afterwards referred openly to Charlotte's parentage. I had assumed a great many things: that he was detached and cold enough not to answer the letter, that he was brazen enough to come to the wedding and keep up the pretence that Charlotte was Marty's. Forgiving him for this had been part of my toxic mooncalf love: sick with humility, I had let myself believe that even while we shared a house for a year and a bed for months he could not be expected to refer to the situation. I had never forcibly broached the subject.

This was the poison at the heart of worship: in my callow years I built him up into an impossible ideal, St Michael and all his angels, the sunrise and sunset, the Platonic Good, the lifeblood of a million poems. The same dazzled blindness, once it turned to hatred, had been able to accept without questioning in later years that he was a cold, unfeeling, consummately selfish creep who could not be bothered even to acknowledge his own daughter or to offer a kind word to her frightened mother.

The Max who was staring at me now, wild-eyed, was neither saint nor monster. He was a fallible human being, a bearded gay Art History professor with round shoulders and a reddening nose, standing very upset indeed on a freezing mountain track. Suddenly, softly, I said: 'Oh poor Max. I didn't do you any favours, did I?'

He did not understand but pressed on urgently, desperate to untangle the past before moving on to the unfolding horror of the present.

'This letter. Where did you send it?'

'To Knightsbridge. With "please forward" written on the envelope. I always imagined you getting it in Assisi or some-where. With –' I hesitated, 'lots of mosaics of the Madonna and Child all round you.'

He frowned. 'They did forward a lot of poste restante –' then more quietly, 'Ah. Mother.'

'Helena.' My chest heaved with something like a sigh. 'She didn't like me, did she?'

'No,' said Max. 'Said I could do a lot better than a bumpkin vicar's daughter. She went on and on about your clothes. Later on, when someone had to look after Alexander, she said that you were better than nothing, a good solid lump of a girl. Then she was angry when we tried to be together.

When you left me, she said terrible things.' He exhaled hard, and looked at me with a species of shocked kindness. 'Sorry. But we ought to get this clear. My mother will have seen the Suffolk postmark, opened the letter and binned it. She may not even have read it, just looked at the signature and decided enough was enough from your direction. She did things like that.'

'So you'd gone to Assisi because she wanted you well clear of me.'

'No – well, they paid. So yes, perhaps. I didn't know. But I knew that I had to get away. You must have felt something wrong. You've seen how things have turned out for me. I am not a woman's man. I was an idiot ever to try and make myself straight.'

'But you knew I was devoted to you, you should have guessed it was yours.'

'I found you naked in the sauna with Marty,' he said flatly. 'If I'm honest, that's perhaps why . . .' he stopped. 'Look, never mind. I just assumed you and he were lovers. Of course I didn't know it was my baby. I just thought you'd gone back to Marty and I was glad, it solved a lot of things.'

'I never even slept with Marty till Charlotte was months and months old.'

'Oh God. But, Sal, you have to understand – it was awful, like hell, all those years for me, pretending. I'm glad I had Alexander, he's a dear boy, but living the lie nearly drove me to the edge. I felt as if I'd somehow killed Annette, by being so disgusted about her swelling up – and then I tried again with you – it was denial – Dr Reece says—'

'Oh, never mind Dr Reece,' I broke in hastily. 'We're dealing with hard historical facts here. Charlotte is yours. I came out here to tell her. I've always bottled out of telling her before, which is unforgivable. And now we both have to tell her, pretty damn quick.'

Jolted back to the present, Max looked at me with frightened eyes. 'Oh yeah, that's horrible. Oh God. If I'd known two months ago, the kids would've known they couldn't think about each other that way.'

'It's my fault,' I said. 'Now, let's clear up the mess. Max –' I felt there was still an apology to be made. 'I thought you were God Almighty, then later I thought you were Satan. Like I said, I did you no favours.'

He smiled, and put out a hand to touch my shoulder. I saw with a start of compassion that it was a middle-aged hand now, starting to wrinkle, and that the nails were bitten short. I was about to speak again when a cold, dry voice at my elbow said: 'Well, well. Lovers' reunion. I shoulda guessed you'd want to re-run old times, Max.'

Adam, shorn of his easygoing bonhomie, looked smaller, pinched and old. 'Don't let me innerupt'. He turned, and stumped back down the track. Then he turned, his face a mask of hurt and malice. 'Guess it's somethin' in the mountain air. I just caught Alex sneaking out of Charlotte's room. You can have a double wedding.'

42

We ran down the track, all three of us, all shouting confused messages, half off our heads with shock. 'It's not what—'

'Adam, come *back*—'

'What did you—'

'Max, don't!'

Our wild career was brought to an end just above the log house when Adam slipped on a patch of ice and fell hard and painfully on his backside; Max threw himself down, slithering on his knees alongside him, taking him in his arms, frantic, saying, 'Love you! Adam, listen!' Even in that moment of confused terrors I registered that I had never seen Max passionately in love before; not at his wedding, not with Kate or Annette, certainly not with me. He leaned over Adam, babbling apologies and explanations which his lover, winded and clearly in some pain, could hardly assimilate.

'Sally told me something – from long ago – it's been a shock – we've both been wrong about something. Adam, it's too important to tell you out here on the hill but we have to get in – what did you say about the kids?'

'Kids,' croaked Adam, trying to sit up. 'What about the damn kids? Couple of kids. Doing what kids do. 'Bout time they did, been coming for a while – young love—'

'But they mustn't!' I was on my knees beside them both now. 'We've got to stop it! He's—'

'What are you, ma'am? Born again? What *is* your problem?

I told you not to upset Max with your funeral talk – if you've come here as the morality police –'

'What funerals?' said Max wildly. 'Oh, Adam, do get up – is your leg all right? Come on, lean on my arm.'

Alexander was standing beside us now in pyjama trousers and an anorak, looking puzzled. 'What the hell is going on?' he asked, quite reasonably. 'Whose funeral?'

Charlotte joined him, in some sort of tracksuit trousers and a huge pair of sheepskin boots which must have belonged to one of the men. She was still in a sleeveless vest, though, and the huge snowflakes fell on bare goosepimpled shoulders.

'God, what *is* going on, wrinklies?' she asked kindly. 'Have you been trampled by the moose? Has the abominable snowman turned nasty?'

The young people's nonchalant normality steadied us a bit, and with Max and Alexander supporting a limping Adam and me fussily throwing my jacket over my daughter's naked shoulders, we made our way back into the cabin. The snow was now so heavy that we could hardly see the angle of the log store from the door, and it was a relief to be contained once more in the dry warmth from the back boiler. Alex had put his tray of pastries in, and their fragrance hung on the air, sweetly domestic.

By tacit consent we laid the table and settled to a communal breakfast without broaching the matter of the day. Max and I seemed able, now, to communicate instantly by glances and nods; together we reassured the shaky Adam until his old bonhomie resurfaced and he said, 'Well. I always say a good ole magic-lantern melodrama before breakfast is the thing to raise an appetite.'

'You believe me, then?' said Max quietly.

'I do. I just lost it. Insecurity, Dr Reece would say –'

'You did fine. We're fine,' I said hastily. 'Look, I think the time has come for some plain speaking between me and Max and Charlotte. Adam, it would be really helpful if you and Lexy sat this one out. You'll know everything later on, but it would just be easier.'

'OK,' said Adam. He ran his hands through wild white hair and grinned. His flare of suspicion seemed to have faded quite away; I had a sense that the scene we had just witnessed between him and Max was not unique, but part of the normal texture of their relationship. They were now darting one another hot loving glances one could hardly ignore. 'Lex, c'mon, we never did get the logs in.'

'Is your leg all right, dear one?' asked Max solicitously.

'Yeah. I'll not lift, I'll supervise the boy. "Why keep a donkey idle?"' Alexander aimed a punch at him, which the tall man dodged, and they passed beyond the heavy door and closed it.

Max and I looked at each other, but Charlotte spoke first. 'Shit, I know what this is. Are you two going to come the heavy about Lex and me?'

'No,' said Max, and, 'Yes,' said I, at the same time. Max looked helplessly at me and I took a deep breath, laid my hands flat on the table to steady myself, and began.

'Charlotte, Max and I knew each other years and years ago. We shared a house, at University. We had a short affair.' She stared, uncomprehending and embarrassed as any child faced with a mother's old sins. 'But I married his brother.'

'My dad, yeah.'

'No. Not your dad. I'm sorry. I was pregnant before I married Marty. He took you on, he loved you, he adored you –' my voice broke, because suddenly I was remembering Marty very clearly, and feeling the weight of his horror at what I was doing to the baby he cherished. 'He loved you, but he wasn't your biological father.'

She stared at me. 'Are you saying . . . ?'

'Max is your father.' I could have sworn I heard all three of our hearts beating, syncopated, out of time.

Max broke the silence. 'I didn't know. Charlie, I swear it. There was a mistake with a letter, I didn't get it. Your grandmother, my mother . . . I think she threw it away to stop me knowing. I honestly thought I was your half-uncle, no more.'

'Oh come *on!*' said my daughter explosively. 'Mum, you're telling me that all these years you never told Max? That's sick!'

'Yes,' I said. 'It is. Worse still, I never told you.'

'Why not?' She was shrill now, holding down hysteria.

'I didn't want to hurt you.'

The lame line hung on the air, then Charlotte in one violent movement pushed the table away, knocking her plate onto the floor, and stood up, towering over us like a Fury. One hand clutched her dark hair, the other curled into a fist. But her face, screwed up with shock and rage, looked so like her angry toddler self that I could have wept and taken her in my arms.

'Oh, fine. Oh, brilliant. So I've got a new-found long-lost father, and a—' Her eyes widened with shock, and the next words came as a quiet croak. 'Oh God.'

'Lexy is your brother. Half-brother,' said Max quietly. 'I'm so sorry.'

Charlotte looked at us with wide mad eyes, and a deep flush spread across her face and down her beautiful neck. Unaware that she spoke aloud she whispered, 'So my first –' then, coming to herself, she dropped her head, trembled, then jerked it back again and said quietly: 'You two are *disgusting*. Perverts. I wish you were both dead. But specially you, *Mother.*' Then she turned, banged out of the door and left us in silence.

'Go after her,' I said to Max in a moment. 'She's gone outside with that stupid vest on; it's snowing.'

He went to the door and looked out down the track, then called to Adam, who limped across at the sight of his face.

'Did you see Charlotte?'

'Nope.'

Alexander came up behind him with the logs. 'Yeah, where's she going? She ran down the track like the dogs were on her. Is it the moose? Has she gone to take a picture? She's not dressed.'

'Get the SUV out,' said Max. 'It's cold. We've got to catch her. Adam, she's beyond upset. Something we told her. She'll come with you. No, Lexy, stay here.'

We were all huddled in the doorway now; Adam reached for the keys on the hook and went over to the big square vehicle; its wheels were half buried in snow and he hauled out the spade and began quickly to dig around them.

'What *is* it?' demanded the young man, pale as a sheet. 'Is it because we—Jesus, is this some sort of church camp? Have you upset her?'

'Alex, I think you ought to know as well,' I said, ignoring warning frowns from Max. 'Right now. Charlotte is your half-sister. She's Max's child. Not his niece.'

'Aw, c'mon!' protested the young man. 'It has to be a mistake, that. I'd have known.'

'No. Nobody knew,' said Max, 'except Sally, and she thought I knew, so she assumed that was fine. She didn't expect to find us all together here, and she had no idea you two were such close friends.'

'Friends!' said Alexander, with a furious exhalation, sounding now one hundred per cent American. 'Jeez, you are disgusting! You've made us – for Chrissake, I don't know what.'

Max and I looked at one another as he strode away from us, dumping the logs on an armchair and slamming his bedroom door behind him.

'Incest,' I half whispered the ugly word. 'Oh God forgive us!'

'I'll stay with him,' said Max. 'Go help Adam.'

In the car, craning out of the windscreen and side windows, I rapidly filled Adam in on the situation. He was concentrating hard on seeing the track through the blizzard and controlling the big vehicle's intermittent skids, but found time and sense to say: 'It's not unheard of, ma'am. It's not the end of the world. The important thing is that children shouldn't be born of it, it's mainly a genetic taboo. And one that protects kids under the same roof. Otherwise, genetic attraction, it's not unknown. It's one of the pitfalls of sperm donation and broken families and all the shit we go in for these days. You get fathers and daughters falling for each other, even. Doctor Reece—'

Before he could start quoting Dr Reece I broke in, 'Yes. I know. But it's the effect on the kids right now, on how they feel, it's a devastating thing, that's why I'm worried—' I broke off, seeing a glimmer of pink through the trees ahead. 'There she is.'

Adam braked, and the car skidded onwards then sideways, almost tipping into a deep drainage gully filled with snow. 'Je-eeez!' I jumped out.

Charlotte, shuddering and limping a little, walked towards the car. I was glad to see that her instinct for self-preservation made her head for its light and the blasting warmth of its heater. She did not want to die in the grey snowscape. I was reassured. When she got into the car, though, she climbed in the front with Adam, keeping her back turned on me where I stood in the snow.

'I'm not coming back in the car if she gets in it,' she said in a small flat voice. Adam looked at me, and I nodded; I had boots and a jacket and could walk up the track. I closed the heavy door. He turned the vehicle uphill with some difficulty, backing and advancing with whirling wheels on the slippery track, and Charlotte sat rigid at his side until they vanished in the whiteness.

I followed the path up; we had come further than I thought and it was a good twenty minutes' walk. Pity and horror and fear for the future fought within me against a new and un-expected sense, which I identified after a while as relief. No, not quite relief: but a sense of completeness. I had long deserved to be punished for my various idiocies. I had known at some level that disaster was coming and now it had come. For all my shame and fear for Charlotte and Alexander, at a deep and puzzling level I was glad. Nemesis can be a curiously welcome visitor. I had lost a daughter, might well lose a husband when he learned what my intransigence had achieved. I deserved both punishments. The only comfort lay within the warm lights of the wooden cabin on the hillside as I trudged up towards it. She had two kind men to comfort her. Kind men, blameless for her disaster.

It was when I reached the house and approached the back door that I saw her outlined against the golden light, a dark forbidding little figure flecked with white. She was standing in the doorway, barring it. She said icily as I slithered towards her: 'OK, Mum. You've had your fun. You've always hated me and thought I was a selfish cow, you've always been down on me. Now your little trick has put the lid on it. Fuck off home.'

Adam came up behind her and put a hand on her trem-bling shoulder. He glanced at me and said quietly: 'Shall I get your bags? I can run you down to the station. I'm sorry, but I think Charlotte might be right for the moment.'

With head low I accepted it.

'Will you be all right, sweetheart?' I said feebly to my daughter, who was already turning back into the warmth. I might as well have asked the snow for an answer.

'We'll look after her,' said Adam. 'It'll work out. Hang on there, I won't be long.'

So Adam and I drove back towards the city, in silence at first but eventually finding words.

'They'll be OK,' he said. 'It's important that people round them don't act like it's the last ten minutes of a suicide opera. It's not quite such a big deal to them these days, you know, sex. Not like it was for us. A bit of wrong sex isn't as scary. I don't think it happened more than once. The real sad thing is I guess it'll spoil that friendship.'

'I can't believe I've caused this,' I said wearily. 'I don't deserve to live.'

'Aw, c'mon!' said Adam, and there was comfort in his deep old voice. 'Divorce, donor eggs, sperm banks, there must be heaps of parents who don't tell the whole truth, and usually it don't matter squat. This time you had bad luck.'

'I knew Alexander was here. I knew she'd met him. But he was a baby and she was a great stamping two year old, I hardly thought of them as the same generation. I mean, we always went for older guys. I never possibly thought a girl and a younger boy –'

'That's our generation,' said Adam. 'We think they're like us, same conventions, same ideas about life, the universe an' everything. But they aren't. The world moves on.'

'What will you do?'

'Play cards. Act normal. I'll talk to her. Max'll have to convince Alexander he wasn't left out of the loop on purpose. We all go back to the city, day after tomorrow. I guess I'll move out of Max's back to my own apartment for a week or two, so she's got somewhere to come and rant and chill out if she can't stand being round them.'

I looked at him: his profile now was steady and grave, utterly different from the jealous freak on the hillside earlier.

'You've really made friends with her, haven't you, Adam?'

'Yeah,' he said. 'I've got no kids, so I like looking after them.'

He dropped me at the station, and I headed for Boston

and Logan airport. Mercifully there was a standby ticket to Heathrow. I bought it, left a message for Donald and one for Donny, and once again put an ocean between myself and my betrayed daughter.

43

Marienka didn't say, 'I told you so.' She folded me in her arms and just said, 'Oh, Sally!' I had come in ready to work but could not carry on. She sent me home for a few days. In the house I roamed anxiously, unable to do anything; I tried to numb the pain by drinking whisky on an empty stomach one day, but it made me sick. Donny rang, full of enthusiasm for his university life, and I listened and tried to sound normal till he said, 'You've got this flu, haven't you? Vitamin C, my tutor says.' Finally Donald, back from Paris and sated with Wagnerian thunderings, had to be told the whole story.

He was shocked and quiet at first, and for a terrible minute I thought that I had indeed lost him. Then he said: 'Greek tragedy. Classic. Except that I don't think it will be a tragedy. It's not the American Way, is it?'

I knew what he meant. 'It's a terrible thing to accept, but I think Max and Adam are probably the best people to look after her, right now. Therapy-speak. Also, maybe, being gay . . .'

'Mm,' said Donald. 'Sexually transgressive, in traditional terms. But poor baby! Her first love!'

I winced. 'I can't bear her knowing that we know. I'm going to write and tell her that you and Donny won't ever know. It's another lie, where you're concerned, but hell!'

'I think that lie might be allowable,' said Donald with a shudder.

'Yes, when I think of all the emotional stuff I had at her age, and how my parents knew absolutely nothing about any of it . . .'

'It's another era,' said Donald. 'And the therapy stuff's another era, too. I know you hated Max going on about his Dr Reece, but it might well be that Dr Reece is the best hope for Charlotte right now.'

'I feel I'm abdicating. Handing her over.'

'Well,' he said mildly, 'you've had her for nearly twenty-three years. Perhaps it's Max's turn.'

'Well, and poor Alexander.'

'I suspect he's more embarrassed than hurt,' said Donald surprisingly. 'I'm a bloke. I know these things. He'll put a lot of effort into forgetting all about it, and it'll work.'

Another time I said: 'The funny thing is that David knew all along. I mean, I absolutely know that he knew, because of things he said to me on Boxing Day. He had antennae for this stuff, because of him and Marty.'

'You mean it's odd that he never mentioned it to Max?'

'Perhaps he believed Max knew. Well, he did believe it.'

'So he thought as little of Max's character as you did? He assumed he was just ignoring the fact it was his baby, and letting you struggle?'

'David didn't have much respect for Max. I don't suppose this business helped. Having met Max now, I can see that the way David treated him, over school fees and all that, must have been intolerable. He knew that David despised him.'

'But he didn't know the whole reason why . . . Oh Sal, I told you, family secrets are poison.'

'I know. I'm sorry.'

'You thought you were doing the right thing,' said my husband comfortingly, and took my hand.

'How did I end up with someone as good as you? I love you.'

'Love you too.'

Thus, consoling one another, we limped through the rest of the winter months, and when the spring came and a break in his work, I mooted the idea of us both going to America to see them all.

Donald was unexpectedly firm. 'No. Absolutely not. Under no circumstances. Let Charlotte decide when she wants to see us.'

I had written, one long exculpatory letter and a number of bland friendly ones. There had been no postcards or calls from my daughter, only two brief cards from Adam. One said: 'Things not going badly. C. on level, mostly. A. took a transfer to USC.' California, I thought. A good distance. Good.

The other card, a month later, said: 'Still OK. Boyfriend in offing. Destroy this, C. has vetoed communication/reports.' In smaller writing, an afterthought, along the bottom it said: 'M. sends his best.' It was the most I deserved.

I was longing, itching to see her though. I told Marienka of this longing and she was typically brutal in her smiling flippant way. 'You only want to see her because you want to unload your whole bloody history of mad feelings into her lap so she bleeds for you and forgives you everything.'

'I do not!'

'Yes you do. Don't think about it. The time for you and Charlotte to get together is when you've lost the urge to tell the story, and she's got enough attitude to prevent you. Mothers' emotional memories are fifty degrees below awful. I mean, do *you* want to know about your ma's torrid early sex life with the vicar?'

'Marienka!'

'See? So button it.'

Donald, less unkindly, said much the same. Spring took us to Prague, where he had two nights singing Zaccaria the

high priest in *Nabucco* and we spent four nights afterwards
wandering around the liberated city, drinking in small cafés
off Wenceslas Square. I was immensely moved by the opera,
more deeply than I had been touched by story and music
in years. Being married to Donald I had over the last two
decades heard a great deal of music and enjoyed it; but not
until now did I experience again the inward loosening and
exaltation which in my youth was common, that incoherent
sense of limitless possibilities and numinous certainty that
all shall be well, and all manner of thing shall be well. In the
English bookshop I bought a limp leather volume of Shelley
and found myself reading poetry in bed for the first time in
decades.

'This country had a revolution of artists,' said Donald. 'A
writer as its first free President. They used to meet secretly
in flats, making carbon copies of uncensored writing.'

I did not say anything to him, but knew, giddily, that I was
having a kind of revolution too. One night, walking across
Charles Bridge, we came on a busker singing 'Your love is the
wind', the song Marty wrote to my lyrics, with images ripped
off from *Troilus and Criseyde*.

'Listen!' I said to Donald. 'There goes my youth!'

Outta these dark waves, O babe, I'm gonna sail ya—

He tightened his arm around my shoulder. 'Good songs,'
he said. 'They'll come back into fashion every five years
forever. I wish I'd known Marty.'

'A diamond,' I said sentimentally, forgetting the darkness
and the ending. 'I can see why Charlotte would be furious
that he wasn't her father after all.'

'Half-uncle, though,' said Donald. He stopped and turned
to me, his face serious. 'Now, tell me, honeychild, on a scale
of one to ten, how's it going with you?'

'Seven,' I said without thinking, then with a rush of remorse,
'oh, but it can't be, not until I know Charlotte's all right.'

'Get to nine,' said my husband, 'and you'll be fit to see her.'

'Give me till Christmas.'

But it was not as long as that. When we got back from Prague there was a telemessage, read to us in a robotic voice down the phone.

'In London Wednesday eighth. Not for long, got job interviews but could do lunch. Charlotte.'

'It shouldn't be her!' I wailed. 'It shouldn't be her who makes the first move!'

'Well, it is,' said Donald. 'Good thing. Bet you Dr Reece told her to do it. Come on. Message her back, bland and friendly.'

So we met in a restaurant on the river, chosen with agonizing care to be chic and new as a tribute to her adult status, but relaxed and discreet. She had changed again: was not a Goth teenager, nor a sneering denim student, nor the romping Heidi of the White Mountains. She was sleek now, groomed to a hair, wearing a very expensive suit and an air of masterful assurance. We talked of general things: the new Labour government, the Lewinsky scandal brewing at the White House. She told us that she had an Australian-American boyfriend, some distant connection of Rupert Murdoch, 'only in finance, not media,' and that if she got the job with the people she was seeing today, she would be one of a team starting up a Boston branch of a holistic health and therapy practice. 'As administrator, obviously. It's unusual for a British company to be trying to break into that market, but it's a particular niche . . . and we're lucky we've got Dr Reece as clinical director. It's because I brokered that meeting that I've got a chance of this job. He's fixed that I can get a green card as an essential worker, isn't that a hoot?'

We let her chatter on about her burgeoning career, and I

marvelled quietly at how much she had changed since February. Reinvention, they called it. It had never occurred to me, back in the doldrum years of the seventies, that I could one day disown my daftnesses, and simply draw a line under my old self and reinvent a personality from scratch. Maybe it was impossible, just a modish chimera; maybe she was bluffing. But it was a good show if so. I was convinced.

At last I could not hold off asking and said timidly, 'How's Adam? And Max?'

'Oh, fine.' Only the slightest tensing prefaced her next line. 'Lexy went to LA for his Master's, so Max's flat is a lot tidier. Adam's moved back in, they're decorating.' She said it all in one breath, and then looked hard at me to check that I had noticed how calmly she mentioned Alexander.

I said the only thing I could, which was: 'Well, you look fantastic, and the job sounds amazing. We're proud of you. And Max must be bloody proud.'

'Oh,' she said. 'He is. Soft old bugger.' I gasped inwardly to hear Max so described, and she grinned. 'But I've told him my heart belongs to Donald –' her stepfather blew her a kiss, accepting the compliment '– and that keeps him on his toes. He and Auntie Adam bought me this suit; I do like shopping with poofs. I'd have settled for the first or second one I tried, but this was the eighteenth.'

It was not intimate, but it was enough: an unsought, un-deserved blessing. She went off sharp at two o'clock for her interview, phoned later to say it was 'in the bag', and as far as we knew flew straight back across the Atlantic to start this new career peddling holistic nostrums.

'Therapy!' I said to Donald disparagingly, unable to help myself.

'Enough of that,' he said, yawning, for we had both drunk a lot more wine than usual at lunch to calm our nerves. 'Don't diss therapy, man. You sound just too nineteen fifties for words, and soon it will be a new century and we'll be the dinosaurs. This is the bright new age of letting your feelings hang out and healing the old wounds. Think of Princess Diana.'

'What hurts,' I said, trying a joke about it all for the first time, 'is that it should be Max who leads us all to the broad sunlit uplands of letting it all hang out and sharing our pain. Max!'

'I quite like growing older,' observed Donald. 'People changing, it's half the fun. Look at Marienka. When I first saw her dancing in her knickers at Christchurch, I'd never have had her down for a champion knitter of the future.' Petra was pregnant, and Marienka was indeed developing a craze for knitting wacky multicoloured baby-hats.

If you leave scars alone and keep them clean, they heal. Slowly. We were all invited out for Christmas. Not the first Christmas, but the one after; and not in the old mountain cabin but in a much larger, closer, rented one with a ski-lift nearby. Donald and Max talked gravely about art and music, Adam took Donny off snow-shoeing, and Charlotte introduced her very sharp-looking boyfriend, whom I instantly disliked but gradually accepted. He was a brash, talkative, highly confident young man five years her senior, but he appeared to be more devoted to her than she was to him, which helped. Alexander turned up on Christmas Eve with his girlfriend from California, an athletic blonde who ski-ed like a demon and called him 'Ally'.

He and Charlotte were amiable enough together, she introducing him as 'my other brother'. They did not lark or mock one another any more, though, and there was an edge of reserve between them which I thought with a pang of sadness would now be permanent.

Alex, to my joy, took me aside on Boxing Day afternoon

and shyly asked about his babyhood, and his mother. 'Dad says you were her main friend when she was expecting me.' I told him how graceful and courteous Annette was, and how beautiful and good natured he himself was as a baby, and the Californian girlfriend joined in and said. 'He still is, oh yeah.'

I had my first ski-ing lesson from him and sprained my knee so badly that I had to lie up for three days, waited on with varying degrees of ironic devotion by the assembled company. Charlotte patronizingly offered to put me in touch with a holistic knee woman who used Native American Indian prayers to improve the joints. By and large everybody was well mannered – perhaps a little unnaturally so – cordial and moderately high spirited.

'Family!' said Adam one evening as the Scrabble and chess games convened. 'I do like family gatherings, don't you? We could be the Waltons.'

44

All through Donny's time at Oxford I visited him a couple of times a term; I was never the kind of mother who could easily be kept away from a son. We had lunches on the High Street in a restaurant which I remembered as a bank, and in Jericho at a café I remembered as a church. We drove out of town to the Perch and the Trout, and picnicked by the river in the summer term. But we never happened to walk along the section of the towpath where, in a vanished summer long ago, I first swore secret fealty to Max Bellinger. Nor did we go near the house itself. I will not admit to having deliberately avoided it, yet some inner radar kept me always on the other side of the road, always taking the longer way round, following the opposite towpath to the one with the willows that Annette so daintily identified as being of the Babylonica variety.

I knew the house was still there, because once or twice Marienka took it upon herself to go across to Oxford and take my son out to lunch. 'I am his godmother,' she said sententiously. 'And since dear Petra is clearly opting for the University of Life, I feel entitled to share the Oxonian parental privileges. You wait till he graduates, I will be there, drying my tears on his fur-trimmed gown and clutching a copy of *Gaudy Night*.' Donny liked her and was quite proud to be seen escorting her dashing, slightly Bohemian London smartness; she bought him extravagant meals and occasional cashmere sweaters. One day, it seemed, she decided to show him the house by the canal and regale him with ornate stories of our ménage there.

He rang me that Saturday evening, happily tipsy, saying: 'Mu-um! Had lunch with Marienka, and she showed me your old gaff!'

'The college? I thought you'd been there for seminars?'

'Naow! The house – my *God*, it's millionaire's *row*, it must be worth half a million, the prices Oxford houses are now – right on the water, madly posh.'

'Well, believe me, it wasn't posh then.'

'Marienka told me. She said there was no heating, and rats, and water under the floorboards that you could chug a clockwork boat in. And she told me how you all sat round gnawing a single potato with a candle stuck in it, only once the potato was gnawed away the candle toppled over and you sat shivering in the dark –'

'She may have embroidered it a bit,' I said, and laughed with him because he was such a blithe spirit. But I was filled with vague dismay at the idea that Marienka had been cavalierly relating the history of that part of our lives. I had always thought of it, irrationally, as essentially mine. 'She was never in much, as I remember, always at parties or off with men.'

'Oh, I know,' said my son. 'As for parties, she *told* me about your hot pants. Butterfly on the crotch. The night you met Dad. Woo-arrr!'

I laughed again for a moment, but when I got into work on Monday I challenged Marienka.

'You've been taking Donny to the old house. Telling him about our student days. You have, haven't you?'

'Yup,' said Marienka, looking vaguely round in the hope of coffee. 'Lauren! Oi! Coffee! Yeah, we went right down memory lane.'

'What did you tell him?'

'Well, most things. He rather sweetly said, "Uncle Max

wasn't gay then, was he"? and I told him about his fling with
Kate and we had a solemn little conversation about how
people experiment when they're young. Don't worry, it
wasn't himself he was thinking of apropos being gay. He's
got a friend in college who's just been playing the bisexual
game.'

'What did you tell him about me and Max?' I asked. Donny
had been given the bald facts about his sister's paternity, and
boy-like, ducked away from the subject as fast as possible.

'Nothing. Nitch. He does not want to know, I told you not
to bother the poor young things with wrinkly erotic memories. Petra puts her fingers in her ears and goes LA LA LA
LA when I start reminiscing. But you should see the house,
Sal! Oh my goodness, Oxford's got so *posh!*'

Coming from Marienka, that was a startling verdict. For
all her life's work in the democratic showbiz world she was
still at heart rather posh herself. I took a grip, and told myself
not to mind about her showing my son the house.

'I suppose,' I said philosophically as we drank our coffee,
'that we all have our own darker memories of the place. Kate
had her troubles, I had mine, you probably had yours.'

'I did not, so!' said Marienka. 'Happy as a grig. Never jollier.
Not a dark cloud on the horizon, except Professor Green and
the bank manager. And if you think back carefully, you were
quite jolly yourself a lot of the time.'

'Was I?'

'Yup. Blankets over the windows, Monty Python at the
pub, bloody good laughs with Marty. You weren't a basket
case *every* day. C'mon, back to work.'

I still did not visit the house. My trips to see Donny
remained firmly in the present tense; when Donald came
with me he went to his old college with delight, but I stayed
safely anchored in the latter days of the twentieth century.
In the millennium year, though, visiting Donny before his

Finals, I left him in the early evening because he wanted to go back to his books, but felt suddenly unwilling to leave the green-and-golden summer city for the spreading grey of London.

I was close to the Folly Bridge, and on an impulse began to walk along the towpath, past the line of tired rowers tramping back to college or to digs. I noticed that droopy unstructured Indian cottons had come back into student fashion, and as the girls flowed past chattering and flirting with the oarsmen I thought I recognized old faces, or at least old types. There was sporty Maureen, slinky Marienka, healthy Kate. Far more women were rowing than in our day; women, of course, had invaded the male colleges. I supposed that my own college in turn was beset with young men, their feet clumping on the shiny old parquet, their voices dominating the Junior Common Room.

I walked on, lost in thoughts of change and advance and loss, wondering what Donny would feel when he walked here again in 2030. I wondered a little about my son's emotional life: was it as hotly coloured as mine? Did he too walk through rainbow clouds of deceptive glory? Or did some girl some-where dream hopelessly of him, elevate him to the high notes of evensong and the colours of the sunset, and ratchet up her devotion to compete with the tragic unrequited heroines of all the ages? Were there willow cabins built unheeded at my son's gate?

I thought I found the spot where we met Max to share our stolen peaches and champagne. There was a new boathouse there now, full of sleek shells, being locked up by an offi-cious man in a blazer who eyed me suspiciously as I walked the wrong way at this evening hour. I ducked my head in greeting, walked on a few paces then turned back, following his brisk duck-footed walk up the towpath.

I was retracing old steps now, and in a few minutes found myself outside the house where it began, half unconsciously looking for a coalshed to step over and a pantry window that could be forced to get in for a giggly picnic.

It was all gone, of course: coalshed and larder were subsumed into a smart extension with a conservatory at the end, the front garden was immaculate and adorned with an expensive-looking modern sculpture, and when I peered through the window my eye met an array of German kitchen appliances in polished steel. The old chipped cream-coloured Rayburn must lie in some landfill or scrapyard now; I found myself hoping it had been recycled and burned on bravely at the heart of some humbler home. There was a light in the living room, and for a mad moment I thought I would knock on the door.

I stood irresolute, then turned away and noticed the willows opposite: dusty green, drooping towards their rising reflections in the brown water. They were far smaller than they had been, probably a new generation of willows entirely. I thought of Annette and hoped, with all the remnants of my childhood faith, that somewhere out there she knew she had a fine son.

Alone by the canal as the sun sank I was swept by a wave of pity: for her, for Marty, for David who was despised by his son and who, thanks to me, despised his stepson in turn. There was pity, too, for Max and his long years of awkward haughty defensiveness, and for his mother who, whatever her misdeeds, had lost her favourite son and cut off her first grandchild.

Tears sprang to my eyes. Life! You loved, you deluded yourself, you clung obstinately to rainbows, and even when you moved on you let the last wisps of those rainbow clouds obscure your judgement. You blundered along wrapped in illusion, looking the wrong way for disaster while it crept up behind you. I had spent years watching Charlotte in fear that she would be as chilly and uncaring as the Max of my imagination. I had pushed her away with my disapproval and dread, and aspired to give her my own characteristics, for all the world as if I were a fit model to live by. But the one thing I really owed her, the truth, I had withheld. I had plunged her into a humiliating disaster, and her recovery from it was no credit of mine.

I looked at the house again, shook my head, and walked away. Back on St Aldate's the sunset gilded the stone and the swirling June dust. I knew where I was going now, and minutes later slipped into Christ Church Cathedral in time for Evensong.

Te Deum Laudamus . . . *keep us without sin, let us not be confounded, have mercy on us.*

I have had great mercies, more than I deserved.